To Hank Davis

Fellow writer, fellow Nam vet,

fellow lover of pulp SF

TO HELL—AND BACK

Daniel Leary grinned and said, "All right, Woetjans. Lead on—and remember that we're the stern but just forces of law and order, not the Shore Patrol breaking up a drunken brawl."

The bosun, waiting farther back in the hold with a detachment of armed spacers, grinned and said, "What would I know about the Shore Patrol, Six? Except being on the other side, I mean."

"Let's go, then," Daniel said. Though Woetjans was treating the warning as a joke, he knew she and her unit had understood him. Spacers didn't have the formal discipline of Marines, but neither were they out of control.

Led by Woetjans herself, half the detachment double-timed around Senator Forbes and Daniel. Some were shouting, "Hup! Hup!" or similar things, and the clatter of their equipment added to the drumming of their boots on the steel ramp.

Each carried a sub-machine gun or stocked impeller, but almost all had a club, knife, knuckleduster, or similar personal weapon as well. Daniel didn't see any pistols, for which he was thankful. Despite training, most spacers were more enthusiastic than skilled with projectile weapons. Pistols greatly increased the risk of accident that was inevitable even with long-arms.

"Great Gods," Forbes muttered in amazed horror.

"They'd follow Captain Leary to Hell, Senator," said Adele primly. "In fact, they've done so a number of times in the past and come back from it."

BAEN BOOKS by DAVID DRAKE

The RCN Series

With the Lightnings • *Lt. Leary, Commanding* • *The Far Side of the Stars* • *The Way to Glory* • *Some Golden Harbor* • *When the Tide Rises* • *In the Stormy Red Sky* • *What Distant Deeps* (forthcoming)

Hammer's Slammers

The Tank Lords • *Caught in the Crossfire* • *The Butcher's Bill* • *The Sharp End* • *Paying the Piper* • *The Complete Hammer's Slammers, Vol. 1* (omnibus) • *The Complete Hammer's Slammers, Vol. 2* (omnibus) • *The Complete Hammer's Slammers, Vol. 3* (omnibus, forthcoming)

Independent Novels and Collections

The Reaches Trilogy • *Seas of Venus* • *Foreign Legions* edited by David Drake • *Ranks of Bronze* • *The Dragon Lord* • *Birds of Prey* • *Northworld Trilogy* • *Redliners* • *Starliner* • *All the Way to the Gallows* • *Grimmer Than Hell* • *Other Times Than Peace* • *Patriots*

The General Series

Warlord with S.M. Stirling (omnibus) • *Conqueror* with S.M. Stirling (omnibus) • *The Chosen* with S.M. Stirling

The Belisarius Series with Eric Flint

An Oblique Approach • *In the Heart of Darkness* • *Belisarius I: Thunder Before Dawn* (omnibus) • *Destiny's Shield* • *Fortune's Stroke* • *Belisarius II: Storm at Noontide* (omnibus) • *The Tide of Victory* • *The Dance of Time* • *Belisarius III: The Flames of Sunset* (omnibus)

Edited by David Drake

The World Turned Upside Down (with Jim Baen & Eric Flint)

IN THE STORMY RED SKY

DAVID DRAKE

IN THE STORMY RED SKY

This is a work of fiction. All the characters and events portrayed in this book are fictional, and any resemblance to real people or incidents is purely coincidental.

A Baen Books Original

Baen Publishing Enterprises
P.O. Box 1403
Riverdale, NY 10471
www.baen.com

ISBN: 978-1-4391-3364-4

Cover art by Stephen Hickman

First Baen paperback printing, August 2010

Library of Congress Control Number: 2008051055

Distributed by Simon & Schuster
1230 Avenue of the Americas
New York, NY 10020

Pages by Joy Freeman (www.pagesbyjoy.com)
Printed in the United States of America

ACKNOWLEDGMENTS

Dan Breen is back on the job as my first reader, thank goodness. The remaining mistakes are my fault, but there are significantly fewer of them than there would be without Dan's help.

Dorothy Day and my webmaster, Karen Zimmerman, archived my texts. I started to write, "I didn't blow up any computers this time," and then realized that I haven't run off the final yet. I hope I don't have to change this line when I read the proofs.

Incidentally, at least one of the reasons I haven't blown up a computer (yet) is that I went back to composing longhand when the temperatures got into the Nineties, then typed up the day's work in the evenings when it was cooler. Another alternative would be air conditioning, but I prefer to avoid that for a number of reasons. I repeatedly had respiratory problems when I worked in a climate-controlled building. Nowadays they recur only when I'm at conventions in climate-controlled hotels.

Dorothy and Evan Ladouceur were (as generally on this series) my continuity checkers. Again, the mistakes are mine; but because of my friends, I fall on my face less often than I otherwise would.

I owe a particular debt to Rana Van Name, who replaced a piece of my own very early childhood. It appears in this novel, but my debt to her goes much deeper than that.

My wife Jo continues to keep the house and yard in shape, and to feed me superbly. I'm not easy to live with, and my focus is generally on the current book. The fact that I live in a clean house is not my own doing, and I appreciate it.

My books would be different and much less good without my friends and family; so would my life. Thank you all.

AUTHOR'S NOTE

I learned with the first book of the RCN series, *With the Lightnings*, that I have to explain that I use English and Metric weights and measures as a convenience to readers, not because I think the same systems will be in use three millennia hence. To me, that went without saying. Here as often, I was wrong.

There are many snatches of song in this novel, as generally in my work. They're all my paraphrases of real music ranging from *The Handsome Cabin Boy* to the *Carmen Saeculare* of Horace. I do this for my own amusement—but people *do* sing, and I think it gives the work resonance to use pieces that people have sung instead of pieces that I've invented.

My fantasies are generally based on folk tales. My science fiction (and this is true of both Military SF and Space Opera) almost always grows from historical events, more often than not from ancient history.

That's certainly true of *In the Stormy Red Sky*, where I weave together three separate incidents which took place in the Mediterranean Basin during a five-year period (216 BC to 211 BC):

1) The death of Dionysius II, whose grandson Hieronymos succeeded to the throne of Syracuse.

2) The successful revolt (or coup, if you prefer) of a group of young aristocrats in Tarentum, aided by Hannibal.

3) The successful assault by Scipio (later Scipio Africanus) on the fortress city of Cartagena.

On the face of it these events had nothing in common, but in another sense they're woven about one another like strands in a sweater. They were aspects of the war which decided who would rule the Mediterranean Basin for the next thousand years.

The unseen impetus of all three situations was the Battle of Cannae, Hannibal's crushing defeat of a large Roman army in 216 BC. Cannae was the epitome of the decisive battle except in one crucial aspect: it decided *nothing*, beyond the fact that certain individuals would die that day instead of dying later.

Cannae affected the attitude of the teenaged boy who suddenly became the Tyrant of Syracuse. It affected political calculations within the Greek cities of Southern Italy. It affected the choice of an initial field of operations made by perhaps the best Roman strategist of all time.

What Cannae didn't do was determine the outcome of the Second Punic War, any more than the Battle of Chancellorsville determined the outcome of the American Civil War.

In history as in life, big events aren't as important as the way people react to those events. Rome couldn't go back and undo the mistakes that led to the disaster at Cannae, but the Republic could and did buckle down and deal with the consequences, both good and bad.

I write about people who deal with consequences. I try to *be* one of those people as well. I don't hold myself out as a role model generally, but I think the world might be better off if more people accepted responsibility and dealt with consequences.

— Dave Drake
david-drake.com

And we came to the Isle of Witches
and heard their musical cry—
"Come to us, O come, come!"
in the stormy red of a sky. . . .

— *The Voyage of Maeldune*
Alfred, Lord Tennyson

CHAPTER 1

**Bergen and Associates Shipyard,
near Xenos on Cinnabar**

"Heart of Steel are our ships!" played the band on the quay. The Bergen and Associates shipyard was decked with bunting and packed with temporary bleachers for this unique occasion. *"Heart of Steel are our crews!"*

Like Adele Mundy, the twenty-four bandsmen wore the white 1st class uniforms of the Republic of Cinnabar Navy. Unlike Adele, they were used to Dress Whites. She almost never wore them.

"We always are ready!" played the band.

Ordinarily Adele had nothing against great public gatherings in which everybody put on their best clothes and stood around wasting time. She simply found an out-of-the-way corner and amused herself by using her personal data unit to hack into whatever nearby database seemed the most interesting.

She couldn't do that here, because the ceremony was in honor of her friend Daniel Leary; soon to be Captain Daniel Leary.

"Steady crew, steady!"

The band had been playing marches for twenty minutes, filling time while frantic officials took care of the final details of the ceremony. Adele didn't pretend to be knowledgeable about music, but she could tell when everybody kept the same time and the notes followed one another in a proper pattern. Both were true here. She frowned, wondering where the musicians came from.

"We'll fight and we'll conquer for we never lose!"

Adele carried her PDU in a thigh pocket which she'd insisted on in complete disregard for the uniform regulations. Her fingers twitched toward it, but she restrained them with conscious effort.

Though Daniel wouldn't mind, others would think that Lady Mundy didn't respect him. She'd rather die than allow that false notion to spread.

"That's the *Lao-tse*'s band, mistress," said Sun, her longtime shipmate and Daniel's as well. He was now a senior warrant officer, gunner of a heavy cruiser, as a reward for his loyal service—and because he'd survived. "They was with us in the Jewel System, you remember."

"Yes, Sun, I do," Adele said dryly. She wondered how the crew of the battleship *Lao-tse* would react to the implication that they had accompanied the corvette *Princess Cecile* during the Battle of the Jewel System.

Though in truth, the *Sissie*—or at least her captain, Daniel Leary—probably did have more to do with that RCN victory than any other ship present.

A private shipyard like Bergen and Associates ordinarily worked on ships of 1,500 tons or less. RCS *Milton*, a heavy cruiser of 12,000 tons, filled the pool and dwarfed the yard's equipment. She'd been repaired here not only because of the demands put on RCN facilities by all-out war with the Alliance but also because the "Associates" in the yard's name was Corder Leary, no longer Speaker but still one of the most powerful members of the Cinnabar Senate.

"We ne'er see our foes but we wish them to stay," boasted the *Lao-tse*'s band musically. *"They never see us but they wish us away!"*

The *Milton* would lift with a crew of more than three hundred, a hundred short of establishment but remarkably good when the RCN needed crews worse than it did ships. The spacers were here, packed into corners and angles; standing on the gantries and lining the cruiser's extended antennas.

"There's never been anything like this before!" said Woetjans, the *Milton*'s bosun. She was six and a half feet tall and would've been abnormally strong even for a man of her size. Like Sun, she'd risen by following Daniel Leary, but it'd been at Adele's side that she'd taken three slugs through the chest. Woetjans claimed to have made a complete recovery, but her face, always craggy, now was cadaverous. Sometimes a gray flash seemed to cross her eyes.

"If they run, why we follow them," played the band, *"down to their bases."*

Woetjans was looking at the shipyard offices above the shops. There, sheltered from direct sunlight though the sashes were swung up from the windows, Daniel's elder sister Deirdre sat with four Senators who were allied with her father. "And nobody bloody deserved it like Six does, neither!"

"For we can't do more if the cowards won't face us!" played the band, climaxing the stanza with a flourish before swinging into the chorus again.

Adele's lips quirked in a tiny, bitter smile. Perhaps she was only projecting her own heart when she thought she saw bleakness in the bosun's. Adele's ribs occasionally twinged from a wound in the further past, but if physical injuries had been the worst damage she'd taken in RCN service, she'd have slept better.

"I never dreamed of this," said Borries, the Chief Missileer. He was a Pellegrinian by birth, but he'd decided not to return to his home world after he survived a battle which took the life of the eldest son of Pellegrino's dictator. "We're great men because we're with Captain Leary. *Great* men."

"Woetjans and I might disagree with you," Adele said with a straight face. The society of outworlds like Pellegrino was more sexist than the norm of the civilized regions ruled by Cinnabar and the Alliance. "About being men, that is."

"Sorry, ma'am," Borries muttered, flushing. "I didn't mean that, truly."

RCN signals personnel were quite junior. According to the Table of Organization, Adele should have been out on the fringes of the crowd with the common spacers instead of standing beside the dais with the senior warrants.

The crew, however, had insisted she take a higher place than her rank justified. She was Mistress Mundy, Captain Leary's friend and a real lady. Adele knew that it wasn't her title, Mundy of Chatsworth, that impressed the spacers but rather herself—or at any rate, her legend.

To hear the crewmen's stories, Mistress Mundy could learn all a databank's secrets by looking sideways at it and she could shoot her way through a regiment of

Alliance soldiers. Those were gross exaggerations—but there was a core of truth to both statements.

The band swung into a cheerful ditty called "The Rocketeers Have Hairy Ears." Spacers in the *Milton's* rigging cheered wildly, and both Daniel and Admiral Anston on the low dais grinned.

It struck Adele that Captain Stickel of the *Lao-tse* had a robust sense of humor. She'd found a number of different versions of the piece involving Engineers, Cannoneers, and Mountaineers. The various lyrics ranged from obscene to absurdly obscene.

Adele looked toward the dignitaries in the office. Daniel's father wasn't present. Corder Leary and his teenaged son had broken violently on the day Daniel joined the RCN. The elder Leary had made a great number of enemies in a career focused on gaining wealth and power. In particular, he'd crushed the Three Circles Conspiracy in a series of proscriptions that took the lives of many of Cinnabar's political elite, their families, and their associates.

No one—no survivor—was willing to deny that the bloody response to treason had been necessary, but afterward even Corder Leary's closest associates—he had no friends—looked at him askance. He'd had to give up the speakership, though most people still referred to him by the title as a mark of honor and of fear.

Adele had escaped the Proscriptions by the chance of having just left Cinnabar to study in the Academic Collections on Blythe, the intellectual heart of the Alliance of Free Stars. Her parents and ten-year-old sister Agatha had provided three of the heads nailed to Speaker's Rock in the center of Xenos, however.

Adele's left hand twitched. The tunic of RCN

Whites didn't have pockets, and she hadn't added a concealed one for the small pistol she normally carried. Senator Mundy had seen to it that his children became dead shots to prevent the sort of challenges which his political radicalism might otherwise have drawn. The ability to shoot accurately with either hand had benefited Adele in the slums she'd frequented when the Mundy fortune was expropriated during the Proscriptions.

Since she'd met Daniel her pistol had helped him, the RCN, and the Republic of Cinnabar. It had kept Adele alive in difficult circumstances; but when the faces of the dead visited her in the hours before dawn, she wasn't sure that survival had been a benefit.

She wasn't wearing the pistol today; and besides, Corder Leary wasn't present at the ceremony.

She forced herself to relax, smiling faintly. Many people thought that Adele Mundy was emotionless. She worked to conceal her emotions and she certainly didn't let them rule her actions, but they existed. Until she'd met Daniel and become a part of the RCN family, the main emotion she'd felt was red fury. Courtesy alone would've made her conceal that to the degree she could.

Daniel caught Adele's eye and grinned more widely. She thought it was the first time she'd seen him looking comfortable in the closely tailored Dress Whites. Daniel was fit, but he tended to put on a few pounds if he didn't watch himself. The rounds of dinners and parties which Xenos offered to a naval hero on leave would've made temperance difficult for even someone less sociable than the dashing young Commander Leary.

His 1st class uniform fit now because Miranda

Dorst, standing with her mother in the front of the crowd facing the dais, was an accomplished seamstress among her other talents. Daniel had never lacked for female company, though he'd had high standards: his companions had to be very young, very pretty, and very intellectually challenged. They'd generally lasted a day—more often a night—and Daniel never even pretended he was going to remember their names.

Miranda was young enough. Her brother Timothy had been one of Daniel's midshipmen before his duties put him in the way of a 20-cm plasma bolt from the cruiser *Scheer*, before its capture and commissioning into the RCN. It was now the *Milton*, towering above the ceremony.

Miranda wasn't strikingly attractive, though Adele had noticed that she became oddly beautiful when she was in Daniel's company. It was as if she were a silvered reflector behind Daniel's brilliant flame.

And unlike the bimbos who'd preceded her, Miranda Dorst appeared to be very clever indeed. Her brother had been a fine officer: brave, well-liked, and equipped with an instinct that took him to the throat of an enemy. He'd have risen high in the RCN, had he survived.

Intellectually, though . . . Well, the best that could be said was that Midshipman Dorst studied very hard and that his personality encouraged others to give him all the help they could. It was unscientific, but anyone who'd met both siblings had to wonder if the sister had gotten a double share of intelligence.

Adele let her eyes return to the crowd facing the dais, though her mind was still on her friend Daniel. She was smiling as widely as she ever did. He was a reasonably good-looking fellow of average height. He was young for a full commander, and soon he'd be the youngest captain on the Navy House list. You'd see nothing special in an image of him, not even a three-dimensional hologram.

In person, Daniel gave the impression of being twice his real size. His engaging smile lighted a room, and if he'd chosen to make women a business rather than a hobby, he'd have lived very well.

Adele had always been alone before she'd met Daniel Leary. Since then she had gained Daniel as a friend, and through him the companionship of not only the ship's company he commanded but also the whole RCN. She had a *real* family, in a fashion that the politically focused Mundys had never been to a studious girl like Adele.

The *Lao-tse*'s band was trooping off the quay, playing "What Do You Do With a Drunken Spacer." Replacing them were young men and women, ten of each in parallel files, wearing white shirts and black trousers. They wore shoes as well, but from their awkwardness Adele suspected that for some it was the first time they'd put on any footgear but shapeless farm boots.

It was a cool day, but the newcomers were sweating profusely. Adele smiled in rare sympathy. She'd felt lost and out of place many times in her life, so she could easily identify with these poor folk.

She wasn't lost any more: she was a member of the RCN.

Adele looked up at the yard offices where Corder Leary would have been had he attended the ceremony. If that cold, brutal man hadn't had her parents and sister murdered, Adele Mundy would never have found the RCN and the place in the universe where she fit.

She didn't believe in Gods or fate or even purpose in any real sense. But sometimes it puzzled Adele to see how very unpredictable the consequences of an event could be.

Daniel Leary had spent much of his youth in this shipyard, listening to Stacey Bergen and other old spacers tell stories. Uncle Stacey was a legendary explorer who'd opened more routes through the Matrix than any other officer in the RCN. He'd showed his young nephew how to conn a ship from the masthead, *feeling* a path through the infinite bubble universes instead of simply calculating one. More important, Daniel had learned to love the romance of star travel because Uncle Stacey and his friends did.

Though now Daniel owned Stacey's half of the shipyard, he was still a boy full of wonder and delight every time he walked through its gates. Like the swirling majesty of the Matrix, Bergen and Associates was a magical thing which hinted at infinite secrets.

Daniel instinctively glanced at the sky, though he knew better than most that if there really was a heaven, it wouldn't be found by going upward. "Thank you, Uncle Stacey," he whispered, his lips barely moving. "This wouldn't be happening except for you."

He stood in the middle of the dais. To his right were the *Milton's* three lieutenants, while to the left stood six retired officers who'd served under Stacey Bergen at some point in their distinguished careers. They were honoring Commander Bergen by attending the promotion of the nephew who'd been like a son to him.

When young Daniel hadn't been spending time in the shipyard, he'd been on the family's Bantry estate learning to hunt, fish, and generally appreciate the natural world. His teacher had been a retainer named Hogg who looked—then as now, standing behind Miranda and her mother—like a simpleminded rustic who'd dressed in a random collection of old clothes.

Hogg was rustic, all right, but a variety of concealed pockets were sewn into his baggy garments. On Bantry the pockets were for poached game; now they hid a variety of weapons, in case somebody on a distant world thought he'd make trouble for the young master. The man who'd regularly snapped the necks of cute furry animals for his dinner had even less compunction about dealing with wogs who got in the way of a Leary.

And though Hogg was likely to be direct, there was nothing simple about his mind. Sharpers who thought they'd clean the rube out in a poker game learned that very quickly.

Mistress Heather Kolb, the wife of Bantry's overseer, marshalled her paired choruses so that they faced the dais rather than the crowd. She'd told Daniel that the estate's youths and maidens—if they *were* maidens, then things had changed since Daniel was a youth at Bantry—had begged to appear at the young master's promotion ceremony.

Daniel had been disinherited when he broke with his father. He wasn't any kind of master now, but he was still a Leary, and he knew the tenants of Bantry would've been crushed had he snubbed them. He'd granted their wish, but from the terrified faces they raised to him, they'd have been much happier cleaning offal from the estate's fish-processing plant.

Admiral Anston, who'd been Chief of the Navy

Board until his heart attack, shuffled toward Daniel from the group of retired officers at the end of the dais. Daniel felt a twinge to see with what difficulty the old man moved.

Everyone in the RCN respected Anston, perhaps the finest chief who'd ever blessed the service. Daniel had met him a few times one-on-one. He didn't claim to know the admiral well, but he'd known him well enough to feel personal as well as professional regret at Anston's ill health.

"Any notion of what's holding up the show, Leary?" Anston said. "I told them I didn't want a bloody chair here on the stage, but I'm half regretting that now."

"Sir, I'll get you a chair at once!" said Daniel in horror.

"You bloody won't," said Anston forcefully. "But I'll put a hand on your shoulder if I may. Old shipmates together, you know."

"Sir, I'm honored," Daniel said. He didn't add flourishes to the words; the truth didn't need embellishment.

The older man let himself sag against Daniel's arm; he was as light as a bird. Illness had melted away his flesh and turned his ruddy complexion sallow. Daniel thought of repeating his offer of a chair, then swallowed the unintended insult and said, "I believe they're waiting for two more senators to arrive, sir. Ah, I believe this was some of my sister's doing."

Anston laughed with unexpected good humor. "Bloody politicians, eh, lad?" he said. "But maybe it'll do us some good in the Navy Appropriation. I know the Learys too well to ignore their judgment when it comes to politics."

He coughed. "No offense meant."

"None taken, sir," said Daniel. "But that isn't me, you know."

"Pull the other one, Leary!" Anston said, glaring at Daniel like a sickly hawk. "Yes, you're a fighting spacer, but you're a bloody politician too or you wouldn't be here. And don't you think *I'm* the one to know a man can be both?"

Daniel found himself grinning. "Well," he said. "Thank you, sir."

Mistress Kolb slashed her baton down and up three times with as much determination as if she were beating a rat to death in her pantry. The last stroke was toward the male chorus, which dutifully responded, *"Mighty Cosmos, all enclosing, filled with worlds and peoples bold...."*

Anston bent close to Daniel's ear. "Who're the liberty suits on the gantry? They're not your crew, are they?"

"As You wax and wane eternal, one stands out of all You hold—"

"No sir," said Daniel. "They're the shipyard staff. My uncle Stacey believed in hiring old spacers where he could, saying that they knew their way around a ship better than any landsman and knew the cost of bad workmanship to the folks who'd have to repair it in the Matrix. We've just followed his lead."

"Cinnabar, the crown of all worlds," sang the youths. *"Cinnabar, Your chosen world."*

"And it's not charity!" Daniel said, with perhaps a touch more vehemence than was helpful to being believed. "An experienced spacer is often more use in a shipyard than a landsman who has all his limbs still."

"I never heard complaints about the work we contracted out to the Bergen yard, boy," said Anston softly.

Liberty suits were RCN utilities decorated with embroidered patches and, along the seams, colored ribbons bearing the names of the various ports the spacer had called on. A senior warrant officer like Woetjans went on liberty in gorgeous motley, an object of admiration to all who saw her.

The *Milton's* crew were in unadorned utilities for this ceremony, but the yard personnel could wear what they pleased. If that was liberty suits, then they'd earned the right. The peg legs, pinned-up sleeves, and eye patches were proof of that.

And they *were* bloody good workmen!

Mistress Kolb poised her baton. It was a sturdy thing, suitable for battering an opponent into the floor; Daniel wondered fleetingly just how she'd rehearsed her choristers. She cut it down, toward the girls. They caroled, *"Fate, Thou Who worlds rules, never bending..."*

Admiral Anston swayed. Daniel put his hand on the older man's waist, taking more of his weight. Anston muttered a curse, but he got his strength back and straightened.

"I never let the bloody politicians stop me before," he said. "That isn't going to change now."

"Fixed Your course, to triumph tending...," sang the girls. The brunette on the left end had a remarkable pair of lungs in a remarkable chest; Daniel remembered her elder sister well.

Daniel smiled. He supposed he and Anston looked odd, gripping one another in the middle of a crowd waiting for something to happen, but the two of them were the only folk here who could do as they pleased without people looking askance. Daniel wore only his Cinnabar decorations, not the gaudy trinkets he'd been given by foreign governments. Even so, Anston alone of the officers present had a more impressive chestful of medals.

"Cinnabar, the crown of all worlds," sang the girls. *"Cinnabar, Your chosen world."*

Anston turned slightly to look at the spacers lining the *Milton's* hull and yards. "You've got a full crew, or the next thing to it," he said approvingly. "Volunteers, I shouldn't wonder."

The joined choruses were praying that Fate and the Cosmos would continue to bless the youth of Cinnabar with purity and their elders with wisdom and peace. It was all silly if you thought about it. Daniel had been a youth recently and a senator's son all his life; he had no high expectations of purity, of wisdom, or certainly—he was also an RCN officer, after all—of peace.

But the "Festival Hymn" struck him much the way each fresh sight of the Matrix did: it rang a chord echoing deep in his heart. Call it childish superstition or patriotism or just the urgent wonder of the not-yet-known—it was there, and Daniel was glad for its presence.

"Yes sir, volunteers," Daniel said, grinning with rightful pride. Spacers *wanted* to serve with Captain Leary. "The change in regulations permitting spacers to follow the officer of their choice had a good effect on the *Milton's* recruitment."

Anston shuddered in what after a bad moment Daniel realized was laughter, not a coughing fit. "Vocaine didn't have much choice," Anston said, swallowing the last of a chuckle. "Every successful officer in the RCN was on him to stop locking their crews up between commissions and parceling them out to whichever ship was short; which all ships are, we don't have enough spacers. He may dislike you, Leary, but not even the Chief of the Navy Board can ignore what school chums like James of Kithran are telling him."

"It worked out well for me," Daniel said mildly. He wouldn't brag to Anston, and anyway he didn't have to.

He cleared his throat and added, "I was a little surprised, because, well, we both know that the *Milton*'s an oddball ship. We know it and every spacer on Cinnabar knows it. And I couldn't promise them loot, not on this commission. But they still came in to volunteer."

The male chorus boomed out the names of the many worlds frightened by Cinnabar's armed might. The women answered with a similar catalogue of worlds which had embraced Cinnabar's mercy and protection and thus were being guided to peace and prosperity.

Daniel had seen a good deal of how Residents from the central bureaucracy in Xenos governed planets which had fallen under Cinnabar's control; the reality was less idyllic than the "Hymn" would have it. Nonetheless, Cinnabar's rule was greatly preferable to the system of organized rapine by which Guarantor Porra's minions administered members of the Alliance of Free Stars. Politics and life are the art of the possible.

"Oddball?" repeated Anston. "A bloody *stupid* design, I'd call it. Four eight-inch guns instead of eight six-inch on the same hull means you don't have either the coverage or the rate of fire to deal with incoming missiles. Sure, an eight-inch packs a wallop when it hits, but three or four six-inch bolts do more good anywhere but at long range. And you shouldn't be burning out your tubes at long range anyway."

"Yes sir, as far as defensive use goes," said Daniel, being very careful not to let his tongue get away with him. *The* Milton's *my ship, or next thing to it!* He coughed. "But eight-inch bolts are *very* effective against other ships. As I know well, having been on the receiving end of them."

The admiral laughed again. "Sorry, Leary," he said, "sorry. I guess you'd make a garbage scow look like a useful warship if you took her up against the Alliance. And we have our share of peacetime designs, too. But as for spacers joining you—"

He glanced up at the cruiser's yards, then met Daniel's eyes again.

"I know you didn't promise them loot, but they're certain that Captain Leary knows what he's doing and knows how to take care of his crews. And besides, boy, they know how lucky you are and probably figure you'll find them loot besides. Which is what I think too, by the Gods!"

"Sir . . . ," said Daniel. He paused to organize his thoughts. "Sir, I appreciate your confidence, but we'll be shepherding a senator to the Veil as an ambassador. As I'm sure you know. We won't see action, let alone gather up prizes, if we do our job correctly. Which I certainly intend to do."

There was a bustle beyond the raised windows of the shipyard office. Looking into the shadowed darkness from this low angle, Daniel could only guess that the missing senators might at last have arrived.

The workmen on the gantry had a better view of the interior, however. In the center of the trestle stood the man who'd been Lieutenant Mon when he served under Daniel on the *Princess Cecile*. Mon was a skilled and methodical officer, but a run of bad luck had gained him the reputation of being a jinx. That doomed his chance of success as a ship's captain, whether in the RCN or the merchant service, but he'd proven an ideal manager for Bergen and Associates while Daniel pursued his naval career.

Mon's reserve commission gave him the right to the Dress Whites he wore today, though they bulged at every seam; nobody had let out his set with the skill Miranda had lavished on Daniel's. He'd chosen to wear his uniform for the same reason his workmen were in liberty suits: this was the RCN's day.

Three serving officers came down the outside stairs from the yard offices. The last was Captain Britten, the deputy head of the RCN's Personnel Bureau; Daniel assumed the male lieutenant commander and the female lieutenant preceding him were aides from the bureau. They made their way toward the dais as briskly as the crowd could part before the aides' crisp orders.

Mon raised his arms and snapped, "Ready!" in a carrying tone. Then he dropped his arms and shouted, "Hurrah for Mister Leary!"

"*Hurrah for Mister Leary!*" the yard staff bellowed in answer. Obviously they'd rehearsed this.

The cheer silenced the crowd like a trumpet call. For a moment the chorus of girls sang piercingly of fruitful lands and fecund seas; then Mistress Kolb chopped her baton down. The assembled flower of

Bantry bowed low to Daniel, their faces flushed and beaming. Turning, they bounded off the quay with a cheerful enthusiasm that made a striking contrast with their stiff, terrified approach.

The delegation from Navy House passed between the two choruses. The lieutenant commander handed a ribbon-tied scroll to Britten; then both aides halted, leaving the captain to take the single step onto the dais alone.

Britten transferred the scroll to his left hand, then came to attention facing Admiral Anston. He threw a much sharper salute than Daniel would ever have been able to do. It was unexpected and completely appropriate.

Anston no longer had an active commission, but he was largely responsible for the RCN's present strength. Britten, who'd spent much of his career as a Navy House bureaucrat, was well aware of his former chief's importance.

"A pleasure to see you again, Admiral," Britten said. "Ah . . . would you care to say a few words? There's a directional microphone upstairs—"

He gestured with his chin toward the yard office.

"—feeding the loudspeakers. I'll just signal them to aim it at you."

"Well, to tell the truth, Darwin," Anston said, "I talked to my friend Vocaine last night and he's authorized me to deputize for him. I hope you don't feel that I'm stepping on your toes."

"By the Gods, sir!" Britten said, holding out the scroll. "You certainly are not."

Anston untied the document. He was standing unsupported, which made Daniel's eyes narrow with concern. For the moment at least he seemed as solid as a bollard. Taking a broad-nibbed stylus from his sleeve—Dress Whites didn't have pockets—he said, "Give me your back as a table, Darwin."

Britten obediently turned and hunched slightly to provide a slanted writing surface. Anston crossed out the signature of Klemsch, Secretary to the Navy Board, and wrote his own above it.

"All right," he muttered, putting the stylus away as Britten scuttled to the side.

Anston looked at the yards of the *Milton*, solid with spacers, then faced the crowd. Britten pointed toward the office and swung his finger toward Anston before dropping his hand to the side.

"Fellow spacers!" Anston said. The new speakers on both sides of the office boomed back his words, but his unaided voice was stronger and steadier than it'd been when he was talking to Daniel. "Fellow spacers, senators, and citizens of Cinnabar!"

Daniel grinned without intending to. It was typical of Anston that he'd give spacers pride of place over members of the Senate. He probably would've been more politic if he were still in office, but as a private citizen he could make his personal preferences known.

Anston waved the crackling document to the crowd. It was real parchment, impressed with two red wax seals from which fluttered a blue ribbon and a white ribbon.

"This is no longer my duty," Anston said, "but I'm glad to say that I find it a great pleasure."

Spreading the document with both hands and moving it slightly outward to where his eyes could focus comfortably, he read, "By the powers vested in me by the Senate, I hereby appoint Daniel Oliver Leary to the rank and authority of Captain in the Navy of the Republic of Cinnabar—"

Hogg cheered like a boar challenging the world. The Bantry contingent joined with enthusiasm, followed by almost all the other civilians at ground level. Madame Dorst started to cheer also, but Miranda laid her fingertips over her mother's mouth to shush her.

Daniel held himself at attention, blushing with embarrassment for what his friends had done. Anston looked nonplussed for a moment; he'd probably never attended a promotion ceremony at which many of the spectators were civilians who didn't know the drill.

When the noise died down, he resumed, "The rank of captain, as I say, his duties to commence with the reading of this order. This is signed by Darwin Britten, Captain, Deputy Chief of the Bureau of Personnel, and countersigned by Admiral Eldridge Vocaine, President of the Navy Board, by George Anston, his deputy for this purpose."

Anston let the parchment roll itself up and handed the scroll to Daniel. "Captain," he said, "allow me to be the first to give you the salute in your new rank."

He shot his right hand to his brow, wincing as his arm rose above shoulder level. Nonetheless, he completed the salute.

Daniel returned it, his eyes blurring with tears. This was all quite improper: admirals don't initiate an exchange of salutes with junior officers. It was the greatest honor anyone had ever paid him.

People were babbling and cheering. Captain Britten helped to support Anston, moving him back from the crush of folk mounting the dais to congratulate Daniel.

Hogg bumped Daniel from the side. "Hold your bloody arms still, young master!" he said. "Else I'm likely to put one of these pins through your wrist while I give you your new stripes. And won't you look silly then, all blood over your white uniform?"

"What?" said Daniel. "Oh, sorry, Hogg."

He held both forearms out from his body while his servant pinned a narrow gold stripe around the right sleeve above the two broad stripes of a commander. The *Milton*'s crew cheered from the yards like a choir of hoarse, profane angels.

Hogg moved around to Daniel's left arm. "And if they look a bit worn...," he said. "That's because they're the pair off Admiral James' old captain's uniform that he told me to fetch for you when I got back to Xenos. I guess it's not much of a comedown for them to go on a Leary's sleeve, is it, young master?"

"I'd like to think it wasn't," Daniel said, his eyes glittering again. He was no longer sure that Anston's salute was the greatest honor he'd ever receive.

CHAPTER 2

Bergen and Associates Shipyard, Cinnabar

"Captain Leary?" said the lieutenant who'd accompanied Britten. She was slender but obviously wiry: she'd fought her way through the crush to reach Daniel.

She extended a sealed document, this time a functional plastic bifold rather than a parchment to be hung in a place of honor. "I've brought your orders from Navy House."

"Thank you, McCoy," Daniel said, reading the nametag on her left breast. He reached out, trying to hold his left sleeve in place for Hogg but tilting his torso sideways to take the document. "Lieutenant Vesey?"

He frowned. He should've called for Robinson, his First Lieutenant; he'd named Vesey instead by reflex, because of the number of cruises they'd made together. Vesey had risen from midshipman to lieutenant under him, and she was an important part of the team which had catapulted Daniel to captain.

"Call the crew to stations," Daniel continued, raising

his voice over the babble. "I'll read my orders to the company, as soon as I reach the bridge."

Vesey was in Whites like the rest of the officers, but a quartermaster holding a commo helmet stood just behind her. She put the helmet on in place of her saucer hat, technically a violation of regs. The helmet's active sound cancelling was much more practical than a hand communicator in a crowd chattering like surf on the rocks.

"*All crew to liftoff stations!*" ordered the *Milton's* external loudspeakers. Distortion robbed Vesey's voice of character, but in truth that voice was in keeping with the plain woman it belonged to. She was a good officer with a real flair for astrogation, though. "*All crew to liftoff stations!*"

Daniel frowned to see the confusion on the upper hull. The cruiser had eight airlocks, but only the four on her dorsal spine were usable while she floated in harbor as now.

Even so the business would've gone smoothly if the riggers who handled the antennas and sails were the only ones trying to use those locks. The Power Room crew had been mustered on the hull also, since there wasn't room for them to watch from the shipyard proper. Some of the technicians were very nearly as clumsy out on the hull as Adele, which—Daniel grinned—was saying something.

The thought made him turn to find her. No one was more important to his promotion than Adele. Not Signals Officer Mundy or Lady Mundy, though she was those things too: my friend Adele.

To Daniel's surprise, Adele was already going up the ramp into the main hold. She was a little apart from the *Milton*'s other officers but walking in close company with Britten's male aide, Lieutenant Commander Huxford.

"Officer Mundy?" Daniel called, raising his voice to be heard twenty yards away. He'd nearly said, "Adele."

Adele turned, her expression calm and mildly inquisitive. She rarely smiled and almost never frowned. Daniel didn't make the mistake of thinking that she was emotionless because she didn't show emotion.

He mimed shoving a path through the crowd of well-wishers. "Wait a moment, Officer Mundy," Daniel said, stepping into the ruck. Because he kept his eyes focused on Adele, he could bump through the people around him without being obviously offensive. "I'll come up to the bridge with you."

"If you wouldn't mind, Captain Leary...," said Huxford. He was a *very* polished young man, a scion of the nobility who'd learned refinement and *politesse* in the years that Speaker Leary's boy had spent hunting and fishing on a rural estate. "Officer Mundy and I have some troublesome business to transact in the Battle Direction Center. I'm sure it won't take long, though."

"Ah," said Daniel. He forced a smile, though he didn't work very hard at making it believable. Apparently Huxford wasn't part of the Navy House bureaucracy after all.

Daniel was aware of Adele's duties for Mistress Sand, the Republic's spymaster, but the less he knew about the details, the happier he was. The less unhappy he was, rather. "Yes, of course. A very good day to you, Huxford. Officer Mundy, please join me when you can."

Now that he had time to take in the situation, Daniel saw that two husky men accompanied Huxford. They wore RCN utilities, but they probably knew as little about naval service as the lieutenant commander himself.

Daniel smiled tightly. Adele's servant Tovera was part of the entourage also. If push came to shove, Huxford's heavies wouldn't last a heartbeat. Tovera's bite probably wasn't poisonous, but the colorless little sociopath liked to kill and had gotten a great deal of practice.

The *Milton's* officers had paused when they heard their captain hail Adele. Daniel joined them, striding up the boarding ramp.

"Congratulations, sir," said Blantyre, newly promoted and the cruiser's Third Lieutenant. "We're off to burn the Alliance a new one with their own ship, eh?"

Robinson and Vesey murmured with similar politeness. The former, a slender lieutenant commander of Daniel's own twenty-six years, showed the degree of reserve to be expected of a stranger who knows that political pressure foisted him on a highly regarded officer.

Daniel laughed. "I hope and expect that we'll make a very sedate shakedown cruise," he said. "I want to learn the old girl's crotchets before we try conclusions with the Alliance. I'm sure that's what Navy House had in mind when they assigned us to take an embassy to a friendly place like the Angouleme Palace on Karst."

There were four companionways in the *Milton's* boarding hold. Armored tubes protected circular staircases wide enough to allow two spacers in hard suits to use them side by side, though whoever was on the outside covered twice the distance as the inner.

Robinson and the lieutenants paused so that Daniel could enter the forward Up shaft ahead of them, then got in behind him. Their soft boots set up a series of whispering echoes on the steel treads, joining those of the spacers already above them in the companionway.

Daniel kept his eyes turned up like a trained spacer rather than looking at his feet. This was more proper than that he should enter his new command at the side of a junior warrant officer, of course.

But he'd have liked his friend Adele to be with him. And if he'd ever cared much for propriety, he'd have been a less effective servant of the Republic of Cinnabar.

The Battle Direction Center was in the *Milton*'s stern, nearly two hundred yards from the bridge. It was unlikely that damage which destroyed both would leave anything of the rest of the cruiser. If the bow were blasted off, the team under the First Lieutenant in the BDC could fight what remained of the ship.

As Huxford closed the armored hatch behind them, Adele walked to the star of six control consoles in the center of the compartment. She sat on the couch of the nearest and rotated it outward, away from its holographic display. She didn't mind standing, but she had to be seated to take out her data unit and bring it live. The floor would've been satisfactory, but since the couch was available, she used it.

Huxford turned, beaming, from the hatch. "I thought this was a rather clever way to get privacy for our little chat," he said.

"Go on," said Adele. A smile lifted the right corner of her lips. Perhaps this Gordon Huxford thought that meant she was in a good mood. He appeared to be stupid and unobservant enough to think that.

She was actually smiling because by using his credentials from Navy House to send the usual BDC personnel to the bridge, Huxford had guaranteed that every officer on the *Milton* would wonder what was going on. The consoles were powered up and, though they were in resting mode, there were at least a dozen of the cruiser's personnel who could use them to eavesdrop on the BDC.

Even Daniel could do that, though he was probably too busy right now. Adele had a variety of regrets at this moment, but one of them was that she couldn't be on the bridge when her friend read his first orders aboard his powerful new command.

Huxford smiled again, this time triumphantly. "Well, not to dawdle, mistress," he said, "it's about the attempt to award you the RCN Star. Our department has had to quietly quash it, of course, and we'd thank you not to allow the matter to come up again."

"Pardon?" said Adele. She used a pair of electronic wands to control her personal data unit. They flickered now, calling up information on "the RCN Star," words which meant nothing to her. She found the wands quicker and more discriminating than a virtual keyboard, let alone trying to use a light pen in conjunction with a holographic display.

"I think you understand me," Huxford said, reinforcing Adele's contempt for his intelligence. "I assure you, mistress, that everyone appreciates the risks you've taken and which all of us in Mistress Sand's service take regularly. Nevertheless we give up hope of public honor when we accept the clandestine burdens of the Republic."

Adele read: *The RCN Star is the highest gallantry*

*award which can be granted to warrant officers and
enlisted personnel of the Republic of Cinnabar Navy.
A five-pointed star of red enamel, it differs from the
Cinnabar Star, granted to commissioned officers in
similar circumstances, by hanging from a blue-red-blue
ribbon and being mounted on a silver roundel rather
than a gold roundel.*

Daniel wore the Cinnabar Star, so she knew what
it looked like even without the image on her display.
It was a deliberately obscure medal, no bigger than
a man's thumbnail.

She still had no idea what Huxford was talking about.
"I'd never heard of the RCN Star until you mentioned
it," Adele said. "Have I been recommended for one?"

Huxford's expression suggested that he was considering expressing disbelief at what she'd said. Adele
smiled minusculely. It was just as well that her Whites
didn't have a pistol pocket; a pellet through the right
eye, her usual target, would spoil features so handsome that they counted as a work of art.

Perhaps her expression warned him, because Huxford
lost a little of his self-assurance. He said, "Of course
you wouldn't have been so foolish as to have involved
yourself in this, mistress. Navy House no longer has
any mention of the matter."

He coughed delicately into the back of his hand.
His manicure was as perfect as the rest of him. "You'll
please inform the uniformed friends who made this
blunder that they shouldn't repeat it. Though I'm sure
they acted with the best motives."

Before answering, Adele shut down her data unit and
slipped it into its pocket. She stood, facing Huxford.

"Lieutenant Commander Huxford," she said. Her

voice had no more emotion than a sword edge does. "Are you telling me that as my superior officer in the RCN? If so, I'll request you to put it in writing. If—"

"Mistress, I—" Huxford began.

"Hear me out, sirrah!" Adele said. "*If* you're a civilian speaking to Mundy of Chatsworth, I inform you that your tone has been remarked. You will apologize immediately, or I will treat it as an affair of honor."

Adele's eyes filmed with memories. She'd only killed one man in a duel, a fellow student at the Academic Collections when she was sixteen. She'd killed many, many more in the course of her duties as an RCN officer, but the bulging-eyed boy with the hole in his forehead returned with a particular vividness more nights than he didn't.

"I meant no . . . ," Huxford said. His mouth must've gone dry, because he kept trying to lick his lips. "Mistress, that is milady—"

"Did you not hear me, you miserable toad?" Adele said. She didn't shout, but even in her own ears the words cut like live steam.

"I apologize!" Huxford said, his posture rigid and his eyes on the blank consoles behind her. "Milady Mundy, I misspoke. My apologies if anything I said could be construed to be offensive."

"Then get out of here," Adele said, flicking the back of her right hand toward the hatch. "Captain Leary is a gentleman, and I don't want him embarrassed by the offal my other duties appear to have dragged aboard his ship."

Huxford turned and fumbled with the hatch controls for a moment before he managed to work them. The dogs disengaged and the hydraulic rams swung the armored panel outward. He stumbled through as soon as there was space for his slender, handsome figure.

Adele wondered if Huxford knew her reputation as a pistol shot. He'd given no indication of knowing *anything* about her background save her RCN rank. It might well be that he was just afraid that Mistress Sand would hear that he'd offended one of her top agents. He could lose the position that gave him such status among the members of his class.

Adele smiled again, tightly and without humor. As was generally true of her smiles.

Rene Cazelet, wearing a commo helmet, looked through the hatch without entering the BDC. "Mistress?" he said quietly.

Rene was the grandson of Mistress Boileau, the long-time Director of the Academic Collections on Blythe. Mistress Boileau had given Adele sanctuary when the Proscriptions slaughtered the members of the Mundy family on Cinnabar. In return, Adele had taken in her grandson when the Fifth Bureau, Guarantor Porra's personal security service, executed his parents.

"Yes, it's all right," said Adele, walking toward the hatchway. She felt tired and shaky from the adrenaline she hadn't burned off. "I'll go back to my quarters and change into civilian clothes. I have some business to transact before liftoff tomorrow."

"We thought of coming in, Tovera and I," Cazelet said. His family had been in shipping; it was to the RCN's benefit that Adele had asked Daniel to grant him a midshipman's slot aboard the *Milton*. Though Rene lacked formal training, he had more practical experience in starships than most Academy graduates. "But we didn't think you needed help."

"Not with that one," said Tovera contemptuously. "Though would you like...?"

She dipped one finger in the direction of her left side pocket; the bulge there was Adele's pistol. Tovera knew that she'd never be human, but she could learn to act the way humans did. She'd attached herself to Adele Mundy as a model of behavior whom a conscienceless sociopath could emulate.

"When I change," said Adele. She felt worn. Perhaps it was age, or it could be the fact that she didn't sleep well. She hadn't slept well for almost twenty years.

They started down the corridor. She and Cazelet were side by side, with Tovera a pace behind.

Riggers stood in the rotunda for the stern dorsal airlocks. That was their action station, though they weren't wearing hard suits while the *Milton* was in harbor.

The watch commander was Barnes; Adele had first met him on Kostroma before she joined—well, became a part of—the RCN. He and his friend Dasi didn't have the best minds in the RCN, but they knew their duties and were cheerfully willing to carry out any orders Captain Leary gave. They'd been promoted from leading riggers to bosun's mates when they followed Daniel from the corvette *Princess Cecile* to a cruiser with five times the complement.

"Good morning, ma'am," Barnes said cheerfully. As Adele and her companions walked on, she heard Barnes telling his riggers, "That's Lady Mundy in the Whites, you who don't know it. If she tells you to jump, you *jump*. You don't and I'll beat you to an inch of your life if she hasn't already shot you dead."

Adele didn't look around. She used to wince when

she heard her shipmates make that sort of comment, but now she took it as a mark of rough affection. She wouldn't shoot a spacer for being slow and stupid, of course; or even for dumb insolence. Probably not for dumb insolence.

"I was wondering, mistress...," Tovera said. "Whether Mistress Sand knows about the business."

Adele thought for a moment. "I doubt it," she said. "She'd have told me herself. But she's not going to hear about it from me or from either of you. It was a reasonable decision."

A party of officers was coming the other way, returning to the BDC now that it was clear. "Good morning, Officer Mundy," Lieutenant Commander Robinson said, dipping his head with a careful politeness which wasn't the due of a signals officer.

"Sir," said Adele, nodding in reply. Salutes weren't given aboard ships in commission, so she hadn't embarrassed herself by forgetting to offer one to the First Lieutenant.

She'd examined Dan Robinson's record—of course—and found nothing of concern in it. She was glad that the man seemed to be smart enough to understand that things weren't always done by the book when Daniel Leary was in command.

"According to my research...," Rene Cazelet said quietly when the BDC party had passed, "a warrant officer leading an assault similar to the one on Fort Douaumont would normally have been given an award. If there ever *were* an assault similar to that one, mistress. The RCN Star is almost required. Because there's nothing higher."

Bullets through the doorway taking Woetjans in the

chest. Stepping in, shooting the guard twice in the face. Into the inner office, the fat Alliance communications specialist reaching into her drawer and jerking as her face deformed above Adele's sight picture...

"To say so, Midshipman Cazelet," Adele said, her voice trembling despite her efforts to control it, "would imply that a Mundy was intriguing for vulgar honors, to the discredit of her house. We will hear no more of it."

She and Tovera were billeted forward, adjacent to the captain's space cabin and beyond that the bridge. As Adele entered the compartment, she turned to meet Cazelet's eyes.

"But thank you for your concern," she said.

CHAPTER 3

Bergen and Associates Shipyard, Cinnabar

"I've gathered you here, fellow spacers," Daniel said to the officers gathered with him on top of the *Milton*'s dorsal 8-inch gunhouse, "because there's more room and no consoles to get in the way as there would be on the bridge or in the BDC. Besides, we're going to see enough of *Millie*'s interior in a voyage to the Veil. That's twenty-eight days by the *Sailing Directions*, though I'm hoping we can do rather better if the lady's as handy as I hope she'll be with a full rig."

Also—which he wouldn't say to his officers, of course—he wanted to see how they'd react to being briefed out on the hull. Robinson and three of the five midshipmen hadn't served with him before: if their new captain's eccentricity disturbed them, Daniel needed to know about it.

"Sir?" said Robinson. "You say a full rig? Instead of what?"

"We..." Daniel said, smiling. "Woetjans, that is, largely, and it was indeed a large order—sailed her to Cinnabar from the Bromley System with a jury rig after she was captured."

"I had forty-two riggers," the bosun said gravely. "That's forty-three with Six there lending a hand on the hull as he did the whole run. It wasn't *half* a job, with most of the rig being yards raised in place of proper antennas that we'd skinned off her in the fight."

"You can do that?" said Nina Else, the only female midshipman since Blantyre had been promoted to lieutenant. "I mean—how long did it take?"

She was small and dark with only average scores at the Academy. Daniel had taken her as a favor to her cousin, Commander Fanshawe; a classmate and friend, and a valuable ally when he needed allies.

No one got ahead in the RCN without friends. Fanshawe *was* a friend; as well as being able, well-connected, and very wealthy.

"How long was did the voyage take, Lieutenant Vesey?" Daniel said. "About nineteen days, didn't it?"

"Seventeen days, six hours, and thirty-four minutes to Cinnabar orbit," said Vesey.

Daniel could've answered the question himself. Well, he could have said, "Something over seventeen days." He'd instead given his Second Lieutenant a chance to shine in front of the newcomers. Vesey was quiet and not physically impressive. It was important that everyone, particularly Mister Robinson, know that Vesey was the Captain's trusted shipmate.

Besides, it was more effective to be corrected downward from a "guesstimate" that would itself have been an amazingly good run on a jury rig. So much of life was salesmanship, at least if you hoped to succeed.

"Sir, that's, well...," Else said. Her eyes had widened as she stared at Daniel. "That's amazing."

"Don't expect to match it without Six conning your ship for you," said Blantyre, picking right up on Daniel's cue. "Isn't that right, Cory?"

"First you have to have Captain Leary capture the ship to begin with," Cory said. "And Mistress Mundy on signals, *I* think."

"We were lucky and our Alliance opponent was unlucky," Daniel said. He allowed himself a smile. "But yes, Officer Mundy was decoding Alliance signals more quickly than the intended recipients could, which was an enormous advantage to us."

Native seabirds wheeled above the yard, making *kek-kek-kek* sounds. Their long tails terminated with diamond-shaped rudders, and their beaks had saw edges to grip fish. On Bantry, some of them—the Furry Stripers especially; there were several glinting red and gold against the sky—were good eating, but not here. Harbor birds scavenged garbage and fish boiled in polluted water when plasma thrusters were run up for testing.

Cory had been an Academy classmate of Blantyre, but he hadn't been promoted yet. Initially Daniel hadn't thought Cory would even pass his boards, but in the past year he'd been making great strides. Adele said he had a flair for communications. That wasn't a commissioned officer's job, but at least it showed that the boy wasn't simply thick.

"As I say, we've a full rig, and we've been armed to RCN standards," Daniel continued. "We have full missile magazines, and our guns—"

He tap-tapped the roof of the gunhouse with the toe of his right boot.

"—are Cinnabar 8-inch tubes instead of the twenty-centimeter weapons the *Millie* mounted in Alliance service."

Plasma cannon were intended for defense, flash-heating incoming missiles so that the layers of matter which sublimed away thrust the remainder of the projectile out of a predicted collision with the target vessel. They could be useful against other ships at short range and were colossally effective against nearby ground targets even through an atmosphere. Daniel Leary was in the habit of closing to knife range with his opponents.

Daniel grinned engagingly. "Though she wasn't the *Milton*, of course, she was the *Scheer*. She lost her ventral turret when we took her, so rather than try to find two more Alliance weapons, the Bureau of Ordnance rearmed her completely. I suppose there's an RCN base being defended by a pair of twenty-centimeter guns somewhere. Somewhere in the sticks, I sincerely hope."

"Excuse me, sir," said Robinson, "but is this armament, well, practical? I would have thought two pair of slow-firing eights were less effective than the usual four pairs of sixes on a heavy cruiser."

"This isn't a design the RCN has copied, First," Daniel said, "or that the Alliance has proceeded with beyond the initial class of three. Having said that, the *Millie*'s a real fighting ship."

He grinned even more broadly than before, sweeping his gaze across the three commissioned officers and five midshipmen. Woetjans and Pasternak were the only warrant officers present, and they kept politely back from their betters.

"However," he continued, "we aren't going to fight

on this cruise unless something goes badly wrong. Half the worlds in the Veil Cluster are part of the Hegemony ruled by the Headman of Karst. Headman Terl ruled for thirty-two years—"

Daniel had looked up the background himself in the *Sailing Directions*. If he needed more detail, he'd ask Adele.

"—and Cinnabar couldn't have had a better ally."

"Once we'd slapped him down shortly after he took power, sir," said Vesey, proving that she too had checked the *Sailing Directions*. The *Milton*'s destination hadn't been a real secret, but that showed initiative on her part nonetheless.

"Quite right," agreed Daniel, beaming. "Unfortunately, Terl has died and his grandson Hieronymos has become Headman. Senator Forbes is going to Karst on behalf of the Republic to encourage the boy to follow his predecessor's good example. Right now wouldn't be a good time to spare enough ships to provide a personal lesson like the one we gave Terl."

"*Senator* Forbes?" said Midshipman Else. "Why, she's the Minister of Finance, isn't she? Surely they're not sending a cabinet minister off to the Veil?"

Fanshawe's cousin was by definition well connected, and it appeared in this case that the girl was more knowledgeable about affairs of state than most midshipmen were. Indeed, she was more knowledgeable than Captain Leary was, for all his father's connections.

I wonder where Adele is? In her absence, he looked at Robinson. All of them were looking at Robinson.

"Ah...," said Robinson, coughing into his hand. Speaking in a low voice directed at the armor on which he stood, he said, "I understand that Great

Aunt Bev came short in last week's vote to choose a new Speaker of the Senate. She'd given up the Finance portfolio in order to run, of course. Under the circumstances it seemed better to all concerned that instead of retiring to a back bench, she might carry out an important off-world embassy."

"Thank you, First," Daniel said appreciatively. Robinson had handled an awkward situation well. "As I said, the *Millie* is simply transporting an embassy to a friendly planet. We'll run in her rigging and power train, learn her quirks, and carry out weapons drills. Perhaps we'll even have a started seam or the like to give the damage-control parties practice ... but those of you who've served with me in the past should have a chance to relax."

He felt his face harden unintentionally. "You've earned it," he said.

"Look, Six ...," Woetjans said, using the captain's call sign as she generally did. "I hear what you're saying, but if it was that simple they'd be sending a communications ship like the old *Aggie*, right?"

"Ah," said Daniel, meeting the bosun's troubled frown. She didn't like to contradict him, but she wasn't the sort to back away from what she saw as her duty. His first voyage as lieutenant had been on the communications ship *Aglaia*, where Woetjans was a bosun's mate.

Communications ships had the hull and spars of light cruisers, but their armament was sharply reduced. Space that on a cruiser would've been given over to additional gun turrets and missile magazines was fitted out as luxurious staterooms. Communications ships were fast, comfortable, and designed to carry high officials on embassies to friendly powers. Just as Woetjans said.

"I'm not privy to the Navy Board's thinking, Chief...," Daniel said, speaking with a deliberate care that his listeners were intended to notice. "But I suspect a number of things could've gone into their decision. The Hegemony of the Veil is indeed a friendly power, but in a time of change it doesn't hurt to remind the new Headman of the power of the Republic, since he's too young to have experienced it himself."

The dorsal gunhouse was offset forward; Daniel stood at the back of it, facing his officers. Now he turned to look aft along the spine of the great ship.

Though Daniel was really making a gesture for emphasis, the view held his attention for a long moment. It wasn't the best way to see the *Milton*—only from a distance to port or starboard could you take in her full size and power—but she was an impressive sight nonetheless.

The cruiser was shaped like a steel cigar, 614 feet in length between perpendiculars. The thirty-two antennas and the spars which stretched the sails in the Matrix were telescoped and folded along the hull for liftoff at present: even so their size startled him every time he focused on them. The main yards were greater in diameter than the masts of the *Princess Cecile*, the corvette in which he'd served most of his career to date.

Indeed, each of the two outriggers which stabilized the *Milton* while she floated in harbor was greater in volume than a corvette. Battleships were much bigger yet, but even so the cruiser was ten times the *Sissie's* familiar size. She carried 312 missiles, and a bolt from her 8-inch plasma cannon was orders of magnitude more powerful than one from 4-inch tubes like a corvette's.

Am I going to be able to handle her?

Well, we brought her from the Bromley Stars to Cinnabar with a jury rig, didn't we?

Grinning to remember that past triumph, Daniel turned to face his officers again.

"The situation in the Veil might be part of the reason for the Board sending a cruiser instead of a communications ship," he resumed. "Also I imagine that quite a number of people in the RCN have reasonable doubts about *Millie*'s design, making her easier to spare on a junket than a cruiser of the Warrior class, for example."

He smiled and gave Robinson a friendly nod. It was good that somebody'd had the courage to voice the doubts about the *Milton* that they must all be feeling, though Daniel hoped that it wouldn't impair the First Lieutenant's performance.

"*I* believe," Daniel said, "that the *Millie*'s unusual features can prove a benefit, in the right circumstances and with the right crew. I've got the right crew—"

He felt a sudden rush of emotion. This crew was the cream of the RCN! Not only the spacers who'd followed him from the *Princess Cecile*, but nearly all those who'd volunteered.

"—which leaves it to me to arrange that the circumstances are right should we engage the enemy."

"Nobody here doubts that, Six," said Woetjans. She didn't make a boast of it, but the certainty in the bosun's harsh voice was obvious to anyone who heard her.

"Dismissed, then, fellow officers," Daniel said. It'd gone rather well, he thought. "Just remember that our *Millie* may be a bit of an oddball, but she's a real fighter nonetheless."

Cory turned to his fellow midshipmen. In a voice meant to be heard by all present, he said, "And you who weren't on the *Princess Cecile* with us? You remember the same's true of Captain Leary!"

Xenos on Cinnabar

The three-story brownstone a few blocks west of the Pentacrest was unmarked. It fit the imagery Adele had checked to prepare for the meeting, but so would half a dozen other buildings in this old-money section of the city.

"This is it," Tovera murmured from behind. Adele nonetheless reached for her data unit for a satellite position.

"Good afternoon, Lady Mundy!" the doorman said as he stepped forward. He was certainly sixty and perhaps older yet. "Bleeker's is pleased to welcome you at last."

Though the doorman's trousers and cutaway jacket were dove gray, his waistcoat was of incongruous red-and-white checks. Bleeker's was over three hundred years old. Quirks which would've been gauche in a more recent club were lovable eccentricities here.

The doorman pulled open the door. It was veneered in dark wood with a broad grain, but it moved with a sluggish inertia that indicated a steel core. Xenos had been largely peaceful since the suppression of the Three Circles Conspiracy and even for the fifty years before that, but the doors and heavily grated windows of buildings in the heart of the city were nonetheless built to keep out more than bad weather.

Adele stepped through. Another servant, younger but not young, waited in the anteroom; a girl in the same livery stood behind and to his left. Adele said, "I'm the guest of Captain Keeley, whom I'm—"

"Not at all, Lady Mundy," said the servant. "Your father entered you on the membership rolls the day you were born. And—"

His voice lowered with regret that Adele couldn't tell from the real thing.

"—may I say that all of us here at Bleeker's were saddened at the passing of Senator Mundy and his lady, your mother."

"Thank you," Adele said, dipping her head to acknowledge the condolences. Noncommittal politeness was her usual response when she received a complete surprise.

"If you'll follow me, Your Ladyship," the fellow said, "I'll take you to your guest. Destry, guide Tovera to the Servants' Lounge if you would."

At Adele's nod, Tovera followed the young woman through a doorway concealed beyond the impressive central staircase. Tovera hadn't expected to accompany Adele to this meeting, but she had to be told so specifically.

A pair of gentlemen were coming down the staircase, talking about either a marriage or a business merger. One was Senator Gripsholm, whose rumpled clothing must be the despair both of his valet and of the tailor who'd been paid the price of a modest aircar to create his suit.

"George," he said, acknowledging the servant. He nodded to Adele, who returned it coldly; his companion merely grunted. Neither had appeared to recognize her.

Adele followed her guide up the stairs, noticing

that the treads looked like polished wood but in fact had a surface that felt tacky to the soles of her shoes. Otherwise there'd have been a risk of members bouncing down the whole gleaming length after the port had passed too often after dinner.

In the case of Senator Gripsholm, that would've been a good result. He'd been a colleague of Lucius Mundy in the Popular Party. Back then, he might even have boasted that they were rivals for the leadership.

That Gripsholm had survived the Proscriptions implied that he'd had a hand in them. Adele wasn't going to check to be sure of that, because if the answer was what she expected it would be, she might choose to do something about it. That wouldn't help anyone, including the severed heads of her father, mother, and little sister. Far better to let the matter lie.

At the head of the stairs, George led Adele down a corridor to the right and tapped on the door at the end. "Lady Mundy is here."

"Enter," said a voice that had become familiar to Adele over the years since she'd first heard it as an exile on Kostroma. She stepped into a private sitting room as George closed the door behind her.

Bernis Sand was built like a fireplug in a suit of green shepherd's plaid. She had the features of an aging bulldog, but she couldn't have been much prettier as a girl of eighteen. For all that, she shone with an energy and determination that made her almost attractive when the light caught her at the right time.

Sand rose to greet Adele from across the leather-covered table in the center of the room. There was a

matching chair on each side, one of which could be
turned to face the information console folded into a
side wall. On the wall opposite was an open sideboard
with a selection of bottles.

"Sit down, if you will," Sand said, gesturing to the
chair facing hers. "Something to drink?"

"No thank you," said Adele. Mistress Sand had a
tumbler which, given her taste, would be a whiskey
and soda. Adele wasn't thirsty, and a meeting with the
Republic's spymaster would never have been a good
time to numb her intellect.

She seated herself primly and brought out her personal data unit, then glanced at the club's information
console. Did members really use it? She could only
assume that they did.

"Makes you wonder, doesn't it?" said Sand.

Adele felt the corner of her lips quirk in a smile.
"Actually, I was wondering whether Bleeker's has a
sideline in blackmailing its members," she said. "But
that's unworthy of me. Besides, you wouldn't have
asked me to meet you here if that were the case."

"Bleeker's is as safe as the Senate House," Sand
said. "And it gives me a chance to be *your* guest, Lady
Mundy. Someone in my position can't be a member
of a political club, of course."

She smiled, but her face looked tired. The war
was going well enough—the war was going *well*, in
fact—but the Alliance had half again the resources
of Cinnabar and her circle of client worlds. A single
misstep by the Republic could lead to a downward
spiral which nothing could arrest. Avoiding that misstep
was as much the business of the intelligence services
as it was of the RCN, and Mistress Sand didn't have

four colleagues to spread the burden as the President of the Navy Board did.

"Sure you won't . . . ?" Sand said, then spread her hands in apology when Adele lifted her chin curtly. "No, of course, you meant what you said. I'm—"

Her eyes drifted to the pair of portraits flanking the information console. Adele resisted the urge to pull out her data unit and learn who the couple—the man and woman, anyway—was. She could check the club's inventory list; there was bound to be one.

But it was more important to hear how Mistress Sand completed her sentence.

"I'm delighted that you'll be accompanying Senator Forbes to Karst," Sand said, which from the tone wasn't anything like the thought she'd almost offered. "The business is of critical importance to the Republic, so much so that I'd have gotten you assigned if my uniformed friends hadn't done just that without my interference."

"Gotten me assigned?" Adele said as her wands called up the folder titled *Ships on Active Service*; she'd downloaded it from a Navy House. Her voice was flat. Only the fact she'd made the repeated words a question lent emphasis to "me."

"Gotten Leary assigned!" Sand said. She reached for her glass, then instead took out a meerschaum snuffbox carved with mythological figures in high relief. "Dammit, Mundy, I don't need to fight about the obvious with you too, do I?"

I'm angry about Huxford, Adele realized. *But I've decided not to raise the matter directly, so it's dishonorable to let my anger out in petty ways.*

"No," she said, "you don't. Why is the Hegemony

so important? Their naval forces have been negligible since the Treaty of Karst, and they've never supplied us with ground troops."

Adele had been about to sort the Navy List for vessels with staterooms comparable to those on the *Milton*. That had been merely a task to occupy her fingers and the surface levels of her mind while her intellect worked on the greater problem of why Sand had summoned her. She now shifted her attention back to the Hegemony of the Veil, which of course she'd looked into as soon as she'd learned of the *Milton's* mission.

"What Headman Terl did and we're very anxious that his successor continue," said Sand, "is to supply food and naval stores to the Cinnabar forces in the Montserrat Stars. The Alliance was well on the way to completing the conquest of the entire cluster, which would give Guarantor Porra a large pool of spacers. We were forced to respond, so Admiral Ozawa took a large squadron there. We have no way of supplying him if the Hegemony withdraws its support."

Adele shifted her information fields once again. "Do you think it's likely that Headman Hieronymos will do that?" she said. "His grandfather died wealthy and in bed, because he remained a Cinnabar ally."

The Montserrat Stars had never united on their own, and none of the individual worlds had warships bigger than destroyers. There was a great deal of intersystem trade, however, and Adele knew that small freighters could provide trained spacers for the ships which Alliance yards were building.

Mistress Sand raised her left hand to her nose with a pinch of snuff in the cup of her thumb. She pressed the right nostril closed with an index finger and inhaled sharply. After sneezing violently into her palm, she drew a handkerchief from her sleeve and wiped her face.

Adele slid the data unit to the right so that its holographic display wasn't between them. She waited silently.

Sand finished her ritual and met Adele's eyes. "Jason Das on Paton is the governor of the thirty worlds of the Veil which are under Cinnabar authority," she said. "He's a career officer of the Ministry of Client Affairs, not a political appointee."

She smiled harshly. "The post isn't important enough to be political," she explained. "The significant worlds of the cluster are subject to the Hegemony. Regardless, Das as the nearest Cinnabar official sent his deputy to Karst to congratulate the new Headman on his elevation. Das reported that Hieronymos seemed uninterested in treating with local officials. As a result of this report, the Senate decided to send a high-level delegation."

"Yes," said Adele, to show that she was paying attention. Though there wasn't much reason she should: everything Mistress Sand had just said was so public that even news commentators were hinting at it. Whether they Viewed the Matter Darkly or considered it a Great Diplomatic Opportunity depended on whether they supported the opposition or the government.

"There are Alliance agents in the Headman's court," Sand said, turning the snuffbox over, then upright, between her fingers. "Their intercepted reports say that Hieronymos treated the deputy governor with utter contempt. The hall porter told him that the Headman would not recognize any subordinate as an envoy. The tone put a different complexion on Governor Das's description of the meeting."

Adele frowned. She started to call up another folder but paused when she realized it would be better to ask Mistress Sand instead. The file of officers, agents, and sources might give a more truthful answer, but she could check it when she was alone. It would be even more informative if she found discrepancies with what her superior told her.

"Mistress," Adele said. "We have agents on Karst also, do we not?"

"The Republic has agents, yes," Sand said. She chuckled and put the snuffbox away. "We may as well laugh, eh?"

Her expression focused, rather like Daniel's when he was working at the attack board. She continued, "For historical reasons, those agents report to the Ministry of Client Affairs. Which in its wisdom chose to route all information through the governor on Paton rather than setting up a parallel reporting network. I believe that Das's deputy, the man who acted as envoy to Hieronymos, has the Veil's intelligence portfolio also."

"Ah," said Adele.

"That's much milder than what I said when I learned of the situation," Sand said with a rueful smile. "Fortunately, I was keeping a closer eye on Alliance agents than I was on how Client Affairs ran their shop. Though for a time after I learned about this, I wondered if my priorities had been wrong."

Adele looked toward her holographic display—still showing economic data on the Hegemony—rather than appear to be staring at Mistress Sand while she considered options. After a moment, she met Sand's eyes and said, "How do you foresee my being able to help Senator Forbes?"

"I don't," said Sand. "What I want from you is a current, authoritative report on the situation in the Hegemony. With that in hand, I hope to be able to convince my colleagues in government—"

A smile brushed across her face as lightly as a cat's tail. Sand had no formal position whatever in the Republic's government.

"—to withdraw Admiral Ozawa from the Montserrat Stars to Karst immediately. That will mean giving the Alliance a free run in the cluster, but if we don't bring Hieronymos to a better sense of his place quickly, I'm afraid we'll lose the Hegemony also. And very possibly Ozawa's squadron to boot."

"I see," said Adele. After a moment's hesitation, she shut down her data unit and stood to put it away. Her gray civilian suit had hair-fine blue stripes on the bias; because it was cut fuller than the tailor had initially recommended, neither the data unit nor the little pistol attracted notice until she brought them out.

"Will you have a drink now, Mundy?" Sand said, still seated. "There's a good white wine in the sideboard."

"I have a great deal to prepare before liftoff," Adele said. "And frankly, I don't see that a drink will help."

Mistress Sand smiled like a crucified saint. "Nor do I," she said. "But at the moment I'm not confident that anything will help. I hope you'll prove me wrong, Mundy."

"Yes," said Adele. "So do I."

She paused and turned with her hand on the latch. Sand put down the whiskey decanter and raised a quizzical eyebrow.

"Mistress," Adele said, "Client Affairs has failed the Republic. I can see why you'd feel that the business is down to your organization . . . and I will try not to fail, of course."

"Thank you, Mundy," Sand said, waiting for the rest of the thought.

"But you're not considering the RCN as a factor," Adele said. "I think you should. Especially when Daniel Leary represents the RCN."

She heard Mistress Sand chuckling as the door shut between them.

CHAPTER 4

Xenos on Cinnabar

After the Battle of the Jewel System, Captain Stickel of the *Lao-tze* had invited Daniel to dinner at his club when they next were on Cinnabar together. Stickel was an able officer and far too senior to snub with impunity, so Daniel had sent in his card when the old battleship arrived on Xenos for refitting in Harbor Three.

Daniel had assumed "my club" meant Harbor House or the RCN Club; or just possibly the Land and Stars Institute, though that catered more to retired generals and admirals. In the event, Stickel's invitation turned out to be to the Sunset, a club for Western landowners.

As they relaxed over brandy, Daniel looked around the dark-paneled dining room. The fourteen occupied tables were each lighted by a wick floating in a saucer of stone-shark oil, the traditional source of illumination in the huts of West Coast fisherman.

That hadn't been true for hundreds of years, of course; the club must now have to render its own sharks to get the oil. That wasn't sufficient reason to drop the tradition, of course, and no other expense had been spared over the delicious dinner, either.

"Looking for your father, Leary?" said Stickel, a big, craggy man. "He's a member, but I haven't seen him here but the once. I'm not a regular myself, of course, between the RCN and preferring to spend my time at Three Piers when I'm on Xenos."

"No sir," said Daniel. "Though I do see one of the Tausigs; their holdings are on the Bantry Peninsula with ours. I was looking at the fishing gear above the paneling."

He gestured carefully with his snifter. "Back when I was ten, I put a pole gaff like that one into a sand sucker bigger than the boat I was in."

"Did you indeed?" said Stickel with interest. "Land him?"

Daniel laughed. "Bloody hell, *no!*" he said. "Hogg—my man—clouted me over the ear and kicked the gaff away from the boat before the sucker connected us with what was happening in his right gill slit. He told me the next time I did something so daft, I'd go into the water and he'd keep the gaff."

Stickel guffawed, then smothered further laughter in his napkin. The elderly gentleman at the next table glared, but no one else remarked on the outburst.

"Well, it really was stupid," Daniel said ruefully. "Sucker sprats roasted on a bed of ocean cress are delicious, at least if you're camping out, but an adult sucker, especially a big one, isn't good for anything but fertilizer."

Stickel took a sip of brandy; he eyed Daniel with the snifter still half raised. Another diner's knife clicked against his plate in the general silence.

"You haven't changed, though, Leary," he said. "Have you? I hear you took a corvette close enough to an Alliance battleship to dock with her."

Daniel grimaced. They hadn't discussed the RCN during dinner. Stickel's estate, Three Piers, was a hundred miles down the coast from Bantry. The similar culture allowed them to chat easily about home, which had appeared to be what the senior man wanted.

It now seemed that Stickel had waited for the brandy. Well, he was the host, so the subjects were his to choose.

"Let's say that I've learned to choose my occasions better," Daniel said. "There wasn't a great deal of choice during that action in the Strymon System, not if our squadron was to survive. I knew our rig would absorb the first salvo, and…"

He paused, wondering if he should explain that Adele was decrypting Alliance signals and providing him with their gist. He decided he wouldn't.

"And we were very lucky," he concluded.

"I'm generally luckiest after I've done the most planning," Stickel said, finishing his brandy and setting the goblet down. "I shouldn't wonder if it didn't work that way for you too, Leary."

Daniel noticed to his surprise that his own snifter was empty also. Stickel was friendly, but there was always the risk of putting a foot wrong when talking with a senior officer you didn't know very well.

"Yessir," he said, "it's generally that way. Off Strymon, though, there wasn't time to do more than act and pray. We were *bloody* lucky."

He grinned toward his hands on the bowl of the snifter. At least in a battle you *knew* that the other party was out to get you.

He cleared his throat. "I have five midshipmen," he went on. "Two I've sailed with in the past and am very satisfied with. Cory has already qualified for lieutenant; Cazelet, the other, comes from the merchant service but he's shaping up very well."

Cazelet came from the *Alliance* merchant service, which wasn't precisely a bar to his appointment in the RCN but wasn't something Daniel wanted to advertise either. He'd hedged a few facts in what he'd told the Personnel Bureau, just to avoid questions. If Adele trusted the boy, that was enough for him.

"Else, Fink, and Barr, the other middies, are new to me," he said, "but they come recommended by colleagues whom I trust. Fink was second in his class at the Academy, as a matter of fact."

"Five midshipmen?" Stickel said. "The establishment's eight for a heavy cruiser, isn't it?"

Daniel turned up his palms. "I'm carrying three early entrants for friends of the RCN," he explained. "Frankly, with a new ship to work up on the voyage, I'd rather limit the number of middies I have to train as well."

Stickel nodded approvingly. "Very wise," he said, "since you've got such solid warrant officers. As you say, you're not likely to need many trained astrogators for prize crews on a jaunt like this."

Anston, Admiral James, and Daniel's sister Deirdre had asked if Daniel could find room on the *Milton*'s books to list young persons—in Kithran's case, his ten-year-old niece—as midshipmen before the age of sixteen, when they could enter the Academy. If those recipients passed the midshipman's exam after graduation, their period of early enrollment would count as both time in grade and time in service. For the right officer, that could be a considerable benefit.

And favors done for people with interest could have considerable benefit to the young captain granting the favors. Occasionally an officer who was unable to raise interest would complain at the support luckier fellows were getting, but it was common sense to see that people like Anston didn't want to be associated with incompetents and failures. As Daniel saw it, everyone gained and very likely the RCN gained most of all.

"Which leaves my lieutenants," Daniel said, coming to the nub at last. "Blantyre, my Third, I've watched— I've trained—over several commissions. She's had more seasoning than many officers with far more seniority. Besides that, I know her."

Stickel nodded, but he pursed his lips. It was obvious that he'd heard discussions about young Leary's officers as well as about the *Milton's* crew. Daniel realized that he was speaking not just to Stickel but through him to the corps of senior captains who'd made the RCN a professional fighting force and the terror of Cinnabar's enemies.

He sipped brandy to wet his lips and went on, "Vesey, my Second, is more of the same—for good or ill, but I think good. She has a genius for astrogation. Now—there's nothing wrong with her courage, but she has a tendency to set up a battle as though she were playing both sides of the board."

He grinned, trying to take the edge off an analysis which others would read as criticism. Vesey wasn't a bad tactician, she simply wasn't as good at war as she was at astrogation. Almost *no* one was as good an astrogator as she was.

"I won't quarrel with another captain's choice in officers, not unless they've served with me...," said Stickel. That was probably a lie even with the limitation, but it was a polite lie. "But it seems to me that a fellow with your record could have found much more senior people. And ones who wouldn't challenge him, if you saw that as a problem."

"I wouldn't worry about that," said Daniel. He smiled, but he knew that his voice had roughened at the thought. He could follow orders when it was his duty to do so, but by the Gods! his subordinates would follow the orders *he* gave or they'd wish they had.

He cleared his throat and continued, "Yes, I'm sure I could find senior lieutenants who'd be glad to join the company of a heavy cruiser instead of commanding a replenishment ship or a base that you have to go to the *Sailing Directions* to identify. But sir—"

His smile was rueful and completely honest.

"—I'm not very senior myself. I was young for a commander and I'm bloody young for a captain. Picking officers whom I know and trust and who already know and trust me *isn't* just a whim or an affectation."

Stickel chuckled again. "I said I thought you were a planner," he said. "I didn't need the confirmation, but you just gave it to me."

He continued to grin over the rim of his snifter. "And your first, then? Another protégé?"

"Yes," said Daniel, letting the doubt show in his tone, "But not mine. Lieutenant Commander Robinson was strongly recommended by Senator Forbes. I—"

"Bloody hell, Leary!" said Stickel. "He's not one of that old bag's pretty boys, is he?"

"No sir, he's not," Daniel said, grinning at the

older man's vehemence. He'd had the same concern, though he'd kept his lips together until a look at the Navy List had reassured him. "She's bringing a, ah, supernumerary aide along on the voyage also, but Robinson is a real officer as well as the grandson of her first cousin. They'd been quite close as girls, and the cousin's side of the family is now in straitened circumstances."

Stickel nodded grimly. "I see," he said. "I can't say I like the thought of politicians forcing their pets on serving officers, Leary."

"Sir," Daniel said, "I've made inquiries."

And Adele had made inquiries, to the same result. Robinson sometimes drank more than he should—but less often than Daniel himself did. He made an effort to live within his pay, but he came from a good family and the effort wasn't always successful. Again, Daniel felt more sympathy than censure.

Robinson's record as an officer was exemplary, however. He would've been employed whether or not Daniel accepted him, but without interest he would've been less likely to stand out—which he needed to do for further promotion now that Senator Forbes was out of favor.

The request was flattering, when viewed in that light. Though it still rankled, for just the reason Stickel had given.

"I don't know how Senator Forbes viewed her advocacy, sir," Daniel said. "I will tell you—and any other RCN officer whom I respect—that if I hadn't been completely convinced of Mister Robinson's fitness for the post, I would have resigned rather than accept him."

He grinned in a fashion that another fighter like Stickel would understand. "I'd have *threatened* to resign, that is," he said, "though of course I wouldn't have been bluffing. I hope I don't overvalue myself, but I would expect my superiors at Navy House to support an RCN officer with a good record over a politician who's out of power for the foreseeable future."

Stickel snorted. "There'd have been more resignations than yours if Navy House didn't see it that way," he agreed.

Daniel made a hobby of natural history, and he found the language of animal behavior worked quite well even when the animals were human. He said, "It isn't simply dominance games, sir."

Bloody hell, I've polished off my brandy, and the bottles of Handler White we downed with dinner run fourteen percent alcohol! But drunk or sober, he'd tell Stickel the whole truth.

"I've got three hundred spacers who volunteered," he said aloud. "Who chose to put themselves in my hands. I won't have it on my conscience that I gave them into the power of a man I don't trust. But seeing that Mister Robinson *is* well fitted to be the *Milton's* First Lieutenant—"

Daniel shrugged, really stretching his muscles instead of making a rhetorical gesture. Feeling himself relaxing, he grinned.

"Quite frankly, sir," he said, "I'd rather avoid a fight if I can than win one. And this one I could honorably avoid."

"The Senate lost a bloody good politician when you joined the RCN, Leary," Stickel said. "I thought the same about Anston, too. But the real loser both

times was Porra and his bloody Alliance of Free
Stars. Now—"

He reached for the brandy bottle.

"—I don't mind being poured into bed either."

As before, the silent waiter forestalled him.

Adele started, realizing that the tapping was a footman trying to get her attention. Her study door stood
open, but the fellow quite properly had knocked on
the frame instead of entering.

Knocked repeatedly, in fact, which was embarrassing. Adele had been lost in *Thirty Years' Residency
in the Veil Stars*, a narrative by a Cinnabar merchant
of the past century. The events the anonymous writer
described were too trivial to be of even historical
interest, but Adele had learned that memoirs more
accurately gave her the feel of a culture than she
could glean from the factual precision of the *Sailing
Directions* and intelligence reports.

"Yes?" she said. From the way the servant winced,
she must have sounded as though she wanted to tear
his throat out. She didn't... though she would rather
not have been interrupted, now or generally ever.

Servants weren't allowed to touch anything in the
study, which was untidy but not disorganized: Adele
knew where to find each of the references she was using.
The footman's eyes were on either the parquet flooring
or the books and other documents in stacks on it.

"A Mistress Dorst is below, Your Ladyship," he said.

"Miranda Dorst?" Adele said in surprise. She closed
the memoir, using a volume of poetry by the late
Headman Terl to mark her place. "Daniel's dining
out tonight, I'm afraid."

"She's asking for you, Your Ladyship," the footman mumbled. "From her comments, I believe she knew that Captain Leary would be absent."

"Bring her—" Adele said, getting to her feet. "No, I'll go down. What time is it? Do you suppose she'd like dinner, or . . . no, never mind that."

Chatsworth Minor had been the Mundy townhouse when her father was a Senator. It had been confiscated during the Proscriptions, but the Edict of Reconciliation which was passed ten years later had made it possible for Adele to reclaim the property when she returned from exile.

The edict, *with* the machinations of Daniel's sister Deirdre, had allowed Adele to reclaim the house. Deirdre's interests were electoral politics and business, subjects which bored her brother to tears. The siblings shared sharp intelligence and cold ruthlessness in gaining their ends, however.

Adele occupied the second floor of Chatsworth Minor when she was on Cinnabar; Daniel rented the third floor. Her study opened onto the landing, so when she stepped out she could look straight down the staircase to the foyer where Miranda Dorst waited with the doorman.

"Mistress Dorst?" Adele said. "Ah, Miranda, that is. Please come up—"

To where? Certainly not the study. To the screened loggia at the back of the suite. The weather was on the cool side, but Miranda wore a short, fur-trimmed cloak and should be perfectly comfortable.

"Unless, ah, you'd like supper? I'm sure the staff can find something for, ah, us." *What in heaven is she doing here?*

Miranda quick-footed up the stairs, smiling pleasantly

toward Adele instead of staring at her feet. She held a package which was of a size to be a slim book or a manuscript.

"Please, no," she said. "This won't be a minute. I really didn't want to disturb you, but I wanted to give you this in person."

"We'll go onto the porch," Adele said firmly. Whatever was going on, she wasn't going to let Daniel's friend leave a parcel with her and flee into the night without an explanation. "You'll want to keep your cape. Ah—what would you like to drink?"

Adele reached behind the door and took the thigh-length jacket she kept on a hook there. Though she hadn't expected visitors, she was neatly dressed as always. Her tunic and trousers were cut like RCN utilities—loose, soft, and with many pockets—but they were light tan instead of the uniform's blotched gray.

"Well, a little sherry?" Miranda said.

The footman—Adele wasn't sure of his name—was hovering close. "Sherry, then, on the porch," she snapped. "And bring the decanter."

Tovera was off for the evening. Adele made a point of not learning what her servant did in her free time. There was almost no chance that she'd be happier to know; and if the recreations of a murderous sociopath turned out to involve something that Adele couldn't accept, the result would be bad all round. Tovera was useful to Adele, useful to Daniel (though he quite reasonably preferred to keep his eyes averted), and useful to the Republic of Cinnabar.

Which wouldn't prevent Adele from making an ethical though costly decision if she had to. Therefore she avoided the question.

Adele led down the hallway, past another sitting room—now a library—a second bedroom—now another library—and the master bedroom, which had room for a number of bookcases also. She had an urge to take out her data unit, though it couldn't possibly tell her anything that had bearing on Miranda's visit. It could only be a security blanket, and a proper effort of will would suffice in its place.

A thought made her smile as she opened the door to the loggia. She gestured her guest through.

"Ah, Adele?" Miranda said, pausing at Adele's expression.

"I was thinking that it's a good sign . . . ," Adele said. She was generally honest, and though she genuinely liked the girl, it was even more necessary that Miranda know how Officer Mundy's mind really worked. "That I want to take out my data unit—"

She tapped the thigh pocket.

"—instead of reaching into the other pocket."

Her left hand lifted the little pistol from her tunic, then let it slip back out of sight. It was light and very flat; you had to know it was there to notice it.

Miranda nodded, then smiled with what Adele thought was a touch of sadness. "Yes," she said. "I'm glad that you didn't think that was necessary too."

The loggia was shallow but the full width of the townhouse. It could be lighted to daylight brilliance, but at the moment a strip in the ceiling glowed just brightly enough to show color. The screens were anodized to matte black. They shadowed the vista beyond, but you could see through them even when the porch was illuminated.

Four wicker chairs with a small round table in the

middle stood in line. Adele gestured her guest to a middle chair, then settled herself in the one across the table from it.

Before either of them could speak, a different footman appeared with two glasses and a decanter. Adele gestured him to set his tray on the table, then waited till the door into the house had closed behind him.

The servants—all but Tovera—were employed by the Shippers' and Merchants' Treasury. The bank rented the townhouse for private meetings when Adele and Daniel were off-planet. Deirdre Leary was the bank's managing director, and her father was the majority owner.

Daniel didn't know that. Adele had long ago learned to live with unpleasant truths when it was necessary. She'd decided that this was necessary.

"What did you wish to see me about, then?" Adele said as she filled the glasses. She appeared to be giving her whole attention to the task.

"Adele," Miranda said. She held the packet in her left hand, not quite offering it but obviously intending to. "My uncle Toby—my mother's brother—was a district observer for the Beneficial Party. A ward heeler. He retired recently."

"I've met many officials of the sort," Adele said dryly. "Not, of course, members of the Beneficial Party. Before each election, my father would give a dinner for his leading supporters. The family was expected to attend these as a mark of honor to his guests. Even those of us—"

Adele smiled slightly, but it wasn't comfortable to force her mind back to those days. Even worse was remembering how she'd viewed the world then.

"—who weren't at all interested in politics."

Adele retained the smile despite the direction her mind was going, because it kept her next words from being too brutally a challenge. "I have a better appreciation of the importance of politics now than I did before the Proscriptions," she said. "But I only become involved in them as a part of my job."

"Yes, I assumed that was the case," said Miranda. She coughed; she was over five-foot eight inches tall and more athletic than willowy. Adele wondered if she played field sports.

"Don't mistake what I'm saying," Miranda resumed. "Daniel only refers to you as a friend and a trusted colleague. But other people are much more forthcoming about your work or what they imagine your work to be, Adele."

"Is that why you've come to see me?" Adele said in a deceptively quiet tone.

"No," said Miranda. "That's none of my business, and anyway I don't care about it."

She met Adele's eyes. Her face was too pleasant to go hard, but she was clearly determined. Neither of them had drunk any of the sherry.

"Because of my uncle Toby's position," Miranda said, "he could tell me the names of the people who would've organized the looting in the wake of the Proscriptions. I went to see them, the leaders, those who were still alive, and I got other names from them."

Her voice hadn't quavered, though she'd seen the pistol. If she'd talked to others about Adele Mundy, then she'd heard stories about the weapon and how Adele had used it.

"Go on," said Adele quietly.

Miranda held out the package in her left hand. "It's been many years," she said. "And these weren't... sophisticated people, Adele. Men, most of them, rough men."

"I know the type," Adele said. Her voice sounded harsh in her own ears, as though it hadn't been used in... eighteen years. "My father was in politics."

"Please," Miranda said. "Take this. I don't know, but I thought..."

Adele took the packet in both hands. The wrapping paper wasn't sealed or tied. She unwrapped the book inside.

THE CRYSTAL BOOK OF VERSE FOR CHILDREN, with no editor listed. On the pictorial boards a little girl sat primly under a tree, reading from a book to the boy who sprawled on his belly listening to her. He'd laid his straw hat on the grass beside him.

Adele felt her eyes tingling. She opened the book carefully. The end papers were decorated with anthropomorphized animals reading. Someone had scribbled on it with crayon, but very neatly printed in white on the upper outside corner was the number 0017.

"Adele, is it yours?" the other woman said.

"Yes," said Adele. She couldn't see anything, just the overhead glow scattered by her tears. "When I was eight, I catalogued my library. This was the accession number."

Miranda stood. "I wasn't sure," she said, "but...Well, I didn't know what the number meant, but I didn't think anyone living in Block G on Reed Street had put it there. I'll be going now."

"Wait," said Adele, standing also. She wiped her eyes with the back of her left wrist. She wasn't sure what she wanted to say, but she knew she couldn't let the other woman leave without having said *something* to her. "I... Thank you, Miranda. This is—"

She weighed the little book of poetry in her hand.

"I wasn't a boisterous child," she said, "but I was happy enough. I think I was happy. I had an innocence at that age which I suppose I would've lost regardless but which was appropriate to the time. And which I remember fondly."

Adele cleared her throat, her eyes meeting Miranda's. "Thank you for returning this," she said formally.

Miranda smiled broadly, but she was crying too. "Adele," she said, glancing aside. "You've done so much for Daniel. I know..."

She shook her head as if to clear debris from it. She looked up and said fiercely, "Daniel's strong and brave and very clever and I *know* that. He's smart enough to use you, Adele. He should, the Republic needs it, and you're willing—"

"I'm more than willing!" Adele said.

"Yes, of course you are!" Miranda said. "But that doesn't make the price you pay any less, does it? *Does* it?"

Her voice softened. "And I thought somebody ought to give you something back," she said. "I'm glad this little book was—"

She forced a smile.

"—something."

Adele consciously willed herself to relax. After a moment, she succeeded and took a deep breath. "Yes," she said, "it was a great deal. You're very perceptive, Miranda."

Miranda squeezed Adele's right hand briefly between

the fingers and thumb of her own. "I'm glad," she said. "But I have to be going now. Mother expects me."

"I'll walk you to the tram stop," Adele said, reaching for the loggia's door. To her surprise, Tovera opened it from the inside and nodded courteously.

"Oh, that won't be necessary," Miranda said. "I'm used to travelling alone. I'll be quite safe. We, ah, haven't kept servants since Dad died."

She reached into a pocket concealed in the cape's lining and brought out a stubby shock rod, holding it in her fist. A touch with either end on bare flesh would knock the victim into the middle of next week.

"And I was rather good at lacrosse in school," she added with pardonable pride. "So even without it I wouldn't be completely helpless."

"Yes, I see," Adele said, smiling faintly. "I'll walk you to the street door, then."

The doorman watched them coming down the stairs. He didn't swing the panel open until Tovera, leading with her attaché case in her left hand—though it was closed—nodded to him.

Miranda stepped outside, then turned and squeezed Adele's hand again. "Please take care of Daniel, Adele," she said.

"Yes," said Adele. "I'll try to."

She stood with Tovera on the doorstep, watching the young woman taking firm strides toward the tram stop at the head of the close. "Do you want me to go with her anyway?" Tovera said.

"No, that won't be necessary," Adele said. Rather than turning her head, she kept Tovera in her peripheral vision. "I didn't expect you back so soon."

Tovera shrugged. Her lips showed a smile of sorts.

"Castillo called me," she said. Seeing Adele's blank look, she added, "He's your butler. They were a little worried."

"Worried?" said Adele in surprise, now staring at her servant. "About Miranda?"

Tovera shrugged again. "They didn't know what was going to happen," she said. "Sometimes people like to have me around when they aren't sure what's happening."

Appearing to watch Miranda at the lighted stop, she added, "They like you, mistress, the staff does. They worry, and they're very proud of you."

"I don't understand," Adele said. "Proud of Daniel, you mean?"

"They think they're Mundys, mistress," Tovera said. "Whoever pays their wages, they think they're retainers of Mundy of Chatsworth. The cook's helper knows your biography backward and forward. Even if you don't know their names."

"I *will* know their names before I go to sleep," Adele said quietly. "I may need your help going over them."

A computer-guided tramcar pulled onto the siding and stopped; its magnetic levitators clacked against the overhead rail. Miranda got on and the car hissed off into the night again.

"Captain Leary has a clever one there, mistress," Tovera said.

"Yes," said Adele. She looked at the *Crystal Book of Verse for Children* until her vision blurred again. "And a very smart one."

CHAPTER 5

Bergen and Associates Shipyard, Cinnabar

Adele's kit was already aboard the *Milton*, but she carried what looked like a small toolbox as she arrived for liftoff. It contained specialist equipment and software from Mistress Sand.

The computers which guided starships through the Matrix were as powerful as human ingenuity could create. Adele's kit could harness that power to the work of decryption.

She smiled dismissively. For most of the problems she faced, the data unit along her thigh was more than adequate. Perfectly ordinary hardware was capable of doing more than one person in a thousand could imagine. The same was true of the pistol in her pocket.

"I wonder if some of the crew will get lost in the corridors?" Tovera said. "Being used to the *Sissie* and going to a ship this size."

Adele wasn't sure if Tovera was joking. Tovera *did* tell jokes, though again, Adele wasn't sure whether she understood them or if she was just working on her

self-appointed task of imitating a normal human being.
Tovera had gotten quite good at acting as though she
had a conscience, for example.

"Perhaps there's a sense imprinted at birth that
allows spacers to find their way around ships," Adele
said. "Like the instinct of migratory animals."

She wasn't very good at jokes either. There was
a reason Tovera had attached herself to Adele: the
personality gap wasn't as wide as it would have been
with someone like Daniel.

A black aircar overflew the harbor, then rotated
into the wind and lowered itself onto the pad on top
of the offices. It was a luxury vehicle, though from
this angle Adele hadn't been able to make out the
gilt coat of arms on the rear doors.

She wondered if Deirdre Leary had come to see
her brother off, though that hadn't happened in the
past. Admiral Anston doubtless had, or had access to,
a limousine also.

The quay of Bergen and Associates was as crowded
as it had been during Daniel's promotion ceremony,
but this time the human beings—largely the crew
going aboard, as Adele herself was doing—were less
of a concern than the trucks and lowboys carrying
the final stores for a long voyage.

The driver of a stake-bed carrying armored containers of main-gun ammunition was particularly noticeable. He kept edging up to the bumper of the laundry
truck just ahead, revving his diesel in blats of black
exhaust which subsided in the wild ringing of valves.

"I'll lead," said Tovera. "I think I'll ask that trucker—"
She was looking at the noisy stake-bed.

"—to shut down. Then we'll cross in front of him."

"Lady Mundy!" bellowed an unfamiliar male voice from behind them. "Wait for Senator Forbes, if you please!"

Adele turned, managing to halt her left hand's dive for her tunic pocket when she heard the senator's name. Twenty yards away, three servants—or aides—wearing green-yellow-green Forbes collar flashes were coming down the narrow outside staircase from the rooftop landing pad. Senator Forbes followed them, while last in line was the very muscular young man who'd called to Adele.

Tovera shifted so that no one on the staircase could read her lips. "Do you know Forbes?" she asked.

"No," said Adele without trying to conceal her face. She rarely said anything that she wouldn't repeat publicly in a loud voice if the occasion arose. "To the best of my knowledge, I've never seen her before."

She paused for thought, then added, "I believe Daniel met her socially. I looked into her background when I learned of our mission, of course, but she was a junior back-bencher at the time of the Proscriptions. She wasn't even part of the Beneficial Party, though she joined it not long after."

Adele touched her data unit. *Is Forbes still a member of the Beneficial Party, or did she resign when she lost the leadership fight?* Not that it mattered, of course, but Adele liked to have details right even when they didn't matter. Because in the long run, nothing mattered.

"Go on, make sure my quarters are prepared," Forbes said, brushing the servants toward the boarding ramp with the backs of her fingers. "I'll wait here with Lady Mundy till there's less congestion."

She grimaced, making her face look even more than usual like that of a marmoset. "I hate travel off Cinnabar, and this chaos on boarding—"

She repeated her brushing gesture.

"—makes it even worse."

The servants looked doubtful, but they joined a group of cheerfully drunken spacers on their way to the ramp. The traffic wasn't as bad as it appeared, because the heavy trucks were stopping under the big gantry. There the loads were transferred to grumbling lighters, to be ferried to the cruiser's C Level cargo holds. It was only when the trucks drove out from beneath the gantry that they crossed the line of pedestrians heading for the boarding bridge to the main hatch and they did that one at a time.

"Should I go, Bev?" the young man said. His expression was bovine but not unpleasant. His suit was tan with bronze highlights, hung on him as though he were a display mannequin. "Or stay with you?"

"Oh, go onto the ship, John," Forbes said. "I won't need you tonight. Lady Mundy and I will be all girls together for a time."

Tovera's eyes flicked from Forbes to Adele. Her look of mild amusement was perhaps a little more lively than usual.

"One of the things I dislike most about this business," Forbes said as the husky servant wandered off, "is that there'll be nobody aboard to talk to besides you, Leary, and of course Robinson. And it won't be much better any of the places we're going, though as I understand it we'll be landing on Paton. Isn't that right?"

"I can check whether Captain Leary has filed a

course with Cinnabar Control," Adele said carefully, taking the data unit from its pocket.

If Adele needed to, she could open every sector of the *Milton*'s astrogation computer even if the captain believed he'd locked it. She had no reason to do that. She and Daniel had discussed all aspects of the voyage, including planetfall on Paton to replenish and get the latest local intelligence on the situation in the Hegemony.

She didn't say that to the senator. Whatever Forbes thought, a politician wasn't in either of Adele's chains of command.

"Oh, no matter," said Forbes with a peeved gesture. "I'm sure we do. Beckford lives on Paton, in a palace, I gather. Do you know Prince Willie, Mundy?"

"I know of him," Adele said, even more carefully than before. "We've never met. He's a friend of yours?"

It was hard to say whether William Beckford was better known for his wealth or for his dissipation. His reputation had grown bad enough that he'd left—been encouraged to leave—Cinnabar. It was approaching the point that money wouldn't have been able to stave off official inquiries any longer.

There were stories about children being brought to Beckford's mansion and never being seen again. That might not be true, but it was quite certain that an investigation *would* uncover matters which would be extremely embarrassing to those who'd shared the entertainment. Some of those participants were rumored to be highly placed in the Senate.

Forbes snorted, though the reaction was good-humored. "Not in the way you mean," she said. "I've done a few favors for his business interests, and he's done some favors for me—and quite a few other people. But only in a *business* way, so far as I'm concerned."

She paused, looking at the great ship without affection. "Still, he'll have a chef," she continued. "He's famous for his table. And I'll be able to sleep in something other than a steel box for the nights that I'm on Paton."

She gave Adele a mocking grin. "That's worth smiling at the greasy little toad, don't you think? I wouldn't have done it before the Speakership election—but then, I wouldn't be traipsing off to the back end of nowhere if the election hadn't come out the way it did. Not so?"

"There's nothing in my family history, Senator . . . ," Adele said, smiling faintly. "To encourage anyone to take my advice on a political question. Perhaps Captain Leary could help you there."

Despite Adele's smile, Forbes looked dumbfounded as she took in the words. "By the *Gods*, Mundy," she muttered. "You *do* have brass balls, don't you? Well, I'd been told that."

Adele shrugged. "I've learned over the years that it's better to bring the past up myself," she said. "It's easier to confine the discussion to the facts than will be the case when others talk behind my back."

The truckload of 8-inch rounds roared into position under the gantry. The driver didn't shut down, but at least he kept his foot off the accelerator. The harbor was still very noisy, but the snarl of the diesel had been causing Adele to react at a subconscious level.

Forbes was saying something about travel. She broke off and in a sharper tone said, "You find it humorous, Mundy?"

"Not your discomfort," Adele said calmly. "Particularly since I share it myself. I find it useful to concentrate on something else during insertion and extraction, though I still feel as though—"

She shrugged. "Actually," she said, "it varies each time as to what unpleasant symptom I'll feel. I think the worst is when my whole body seems to have been turned inside out, but you may have a different particular dislike."

She repeated her slight smile. "Almost everyone does, you know," she said. "Even veteran spacers like Captain Leary and Woetjans. She's our bosun."

Adele had really been smiling at the concept of courtesy, which she'd been considering while the senator nattered about the few short voyages she'd made before now. People like the truck driver wouldn't ever learn courtesy—or rather, they'd never manage to control angry, discourteous outbursts when something frustrated them.

And it would probably be an overreaction to shoot them. They might try a little harder not to be offensive, though, if they realized there were people like Tovera and Tovera's mistress who considered *all* options for removing an irritation.

Forbes grimaced again. "Well, nothing to do about it," she said. "If I don't get off Cinnabar, I'll be snubbed by every back-bencher who thinks I should've treated him like the sun shone out of his butt. And don't think Speaker Bailey won't be egging them on, the little weasel!"

"Do you expect to be successful in your mission, Senator?" Adele said. She'd like to have brought her data unit up, but she'd have to sit down to use it.

She didn't want to do that here in the oil and dirt while wearing her 2nd class uniform, her Dress Grays.

She smiled again. She wouldn't sit down without a better reason than that she was bored by Forbes's chatter, which wouldn't be a politic thing to demonstrate anyway.

"Success?" snapped Forbes. "Yes, of course. This boy Hieronymos just wants to be told he's important. Fine, he's important—and I needed to get off-planet, as I said, so everyone gains. Why, I might've decided to take a junket like this regardless!"

And the grapes were probably sour anyway, thought Adele, remembering a very ancient fable. Human nature hadn't changed since long before humanity's development of interstellar travel.

Adele was sure her thought hadn't reached her facial muscles, but the senator looked sidelong at her anyway. "Perhaps," Forbes said, "I'll change my mind about having Johnnie DeNardo in tonight. He's not much brighter than a cucumber, but at least he's warmer."

Adele said nothing.

Forbes cackled in triumph. "I think I've shocked you, Mundy!" she said. "Haven't I? I'd heard that about you too."

Mundy of Chatsworth raised an eyebrow. She put the data unit back in its pocket, though she only needed her left hand free.

"Biology isn't one of my particular interests, Senator," she said in an upper-class drawl. "I wouldn't be shocked if a maggot crawled out of your eye socket, though I'd find it vaguely disgusting."

Forbes stared. Her mouth opened, then closed,

but she didn't speak. Her face settled into a stunned expression rather than anger.

"I think the crowd has thinned, Tovera," said Adele. "We'll board now, because I have work to do."

She glanced toward Forbes. "You're welcome to accompany us, Senator," she added. "We'll take care to keep you safe."

Daniel settled himself into the command console of the RCS *Milton* for his first liftoff as her captain. He listened for a moment to the sounds which filled the cruiser.

Starships were never quiet. The life-support system alone involved many hundreds of pumps, fans, and valves working through miles of ducts and piping. Add the electronics, the flows of reaction mass feeding plasma thrusters for use in an atmosphere and the High Drive which more efficiently combined matter and antimatter in vacuum, and the crew itself, there was a background that made it hard to talk across a compartment in a normal voice. Several hundred human beings breathing in a steel box stirred an echoing windstorm all by itself.

Daniel touched the virtual keyboard, sequencing the holographic screen from a systems schematic, through an astrogation display, the Plot-Position Indicator, and an attack board. Finally he returned to the schematic.

The keyboard was projected over a fascia plate which had a roughened surface; the *Sissie*'s console had been smooth when new and by now was worn to minute dips and rises by the touch of Daniel's fingers. He grinned. Adele had told him that he typed as though he thought his fingers were pummeling the ship into obedience.

Well, the technique had served him well thus far. If the fascia proved a real problem, one of Pasternak's technicians would either grind it smooth or fill the indentations with hull sealant. It wouldn't be a problem, though.

"Command Group, this is Six," Daniel said, verbally directing his commo helmet's AI to open a channel to the cruiser's commissioned and warrant officers. "We'll be lifting off shortly. Chief of Ship, do you have anomalies to report, over?"

A line of miniature heads, real-time images, appeared at the top of his display. If Daniel wanted, he could dispense with the images or have them float around the interstices of the schematics instead of squashing the main display down slightly. He liked having the faces in his peripheral vision, though he almost never looked directly at them.

There were many more faces than he was used to. As with the fascia plate, that would become normal soon.

"*Sir, the flows are normal and all the hatches say they're sealed,*" said Pasternak. "*I won't learn better till we're in vacuum and then I figure I'll learn, I've never taken a ship up first time after an overhaul that some bloody thing wasn't wrong. But not yet. Five out.*"

"Chief of Rig, anything to report, over?" Daniel said.

"*Squared away, Six,*" Woetjans said. She sounded like she had a mouthful of gravel. "*Rig out.*"

Daniel smiled at the contrast between the two chiefs. It was almost a given that on a ship the size of the *Milton*, some clamp or joint of the new rigging would fracture under the vibration and stresses of the first liftoff. The bosun felt that she could fix whatever happened, though she knew there'd be failures; whereas the Chief Engineer felt there'd be failures, though he knew he'd be able to fix them.

Daniel was convinced that they were both as good at their jobs as any other pair in the RCN. He had to admit that he preferred Woetjans' attitude, though.

He glanced toward his left side, where Adele sat at the signals console with her back to him. She and Pasternak had a good deal in common; but in her case, Daniel knew there was *nobody* who could claim to be her equal.

The bridge of the *Milton* was larger than that of the *Princess Cecile*, though the compartments were much closer in size than the ships were. The corvette needed the same consoles—command, astrogation, missiles, gunnery, and signals—as a heavy cruiser. Each of the *Milton*'s stations was back-to-back with a full display for a striker rather than the *Sissie*'s jumpseats with rudimentary controls, and there was more space between the cruiser's stations. Still, the volume was doubled rather than greater by an order of magnitude.

Daniel had rotated the command console to face the stern. Sun and Adele, gunnery and signals, were to starboard. Sun was backed by a technician named Ragi Sekaly, who'd held the rating of gunner's mate on a destroyer. Sekaly had technically been senior to Sun on the Navy House books, but a ship's captain had authority to promote any qualified spacer into an empty slot.

There were RCN officers—most officers, truth to tell—who expected a gift of the subordinate's first month's wages in exchange for the promotion, but Daniel didn't need the money. Indeed, he hadn't thought much about money even when he *had* needed it, a matter of some irritation to Hogg in past years.

Sun was skilled, trustworthy, and a companion from Daniel's first cruise in command of the *Princess Cecile*. The Learys expected loyalty from their tenants, but they gave loyalty in return. A good principle on the Bantry estate continued to be a good one when applied to the company of an RCN warship.

Nearest the command console on the port side was astrogation, where Lieutenant Vesey was working on a course projection. Daniel could've echoed it to see what course it was—or asked her, for that matter—but it didn't matter.

He doubted that Vesey was plotting their route to Paton and Karst, since she would've done that days ago when she'd learned the cruiser's mission. More likely she was preparing in case Captain Leary decided abruptly to raid some base in the heart of the Alliance, perhaps even the Castle System itself. It had happened before; and Vesey, while not a fighting officer with an instinct for the enemy's weakness, could be counted on to do anything that allowed her time for prediction.

Midshipman Cazelet sat on the mirror side of Vesey's station, observing her plot but not involved in it. He'd been Adele's, well, protégé, one would have to call him: a youth who'd fled to her from the Alliance because she owed a similar debt to his grandmother.

Daniel hadn't hesitated when Adele asked him to give Cazelet a midshipman's slot. Daniel had been impressed by Cazelet's skills when the fellow had travelled as Adele's assistant on the previous voyage; and anyway, he'd have backed Adele's judgment even if he'd disagreed with it. Adele was a Leary, now, for all she was Mundy of Chatsworth. The Learys took care of their own.

Vesey and Cazelet had spent some of their off-duty time together. Daniel didn't consider that any of his business—another way in which he differed from many RCN captains—unless it affected performance.

That had been a problem with Vesey in the past, and not simply involving her personal relationships. Though a crackerjack officer in most respects, Vesey had a tendency to hammer herself when things didn't go to plan. Most matters involving human beings and the cosmos generally went off the rails at some point, and when they did they were likely to take Vesey along with them.

Still, if Cazelet managed to avoid getting killed the way Vesey's fiancé had been, it ought to be all right. The trouble was, violent death was a common hazard of wearing an RCN uniform.

Borries, the Chief Missileer, was one of a dozen Pellegrinians aboard. They'd been captured on Dunbar's World and had decided service in the RCN was a better alternative than going home to learn exactly how angry their dictator was that they'd survived a battle which had claimed the life of his only son.

The missile station display showed a view of the dockyard, but Borries was looking past it toward the command console. He nodded when Daniel's eyes glanced onto him.

He was Daniel's most doubtful appointment: he'd been a good choice for the *Princess Cecile*, but many Cinnabar-born senior missileers had bid for transfer to the *Milton*. Captain Leary had the reputation of finding a battle, and battles were the only chance a missileer had to shine.

Daniel had nevertheless brought Borries with him. The Pellegrinian was skilled, but he was also willing to defer to a captain who liked to set up his own attacks. The last thing Daniel needed was a power struggle with a member of his own command group in the middle of combat.

The missileer's mate was Seth Chazanoff. He was new to Daniel's command, a Cinnabar native with a flair for the short-range computations that were in some ways more difficult than the long shots more typical of space battles. He'd been chief missileer on a destroyer at a higher base pay that he'd get as mate even on a heavy cruiser. The fact he'd been willing to take a pay cut to have a better chance of practicing his murderous specialty was enough to convince Daniel to take him aboard.

Across the compartment from the missileers sat Adele at the signals station, using her personal data unit as a controller for the console. Daniel assumed that there was some coupling loss incurred by slaving the larger unit to a small one, but when Adele was the operator, nobody would notice it.

She didn't look up, but Daniel was pretty sure that his was the face inset onto her display. Adele preferred imagery to a physical presence and preferred recorded data to the evidence of her own senses. It worked for her, and what Adele did worked very well for the Republic as well as for her friend Daniel Leary.

Midshipman Cory had the rear couch of the signals console. He had always struck Daniel as somewhat slow-witted—which wasn't, of course, a barrier to advancement in the RCN. The odd thing about Cory was that he kept learning—not quickly or easily, but consistently. He made mistakes that almost nobody else would've made, but he only made them once. There were successful admirals who couldn't say that much.

Adele would be listening to intercepted transmissions while Cory was handling the ship's normal flow of communications. Daniel didn't imagine that any useful information would appear in the chatter of a private shipyard on Cinnabar, but it was habit and practice for Adele.

She would do the same thing whenever her vessel was on a planetary surface. Several times her electronic eavesdropping had saved their mission and not coincidentally their lives.

"Lieutenant Robinson," said Daniel. "Any anomalies to report, over?"

"*Sir, the ship is ready to lift,*" Robinson replied from the BDC. "*Would you like me to initiate liftoff sequence, over?*"

No, I bloody well would not *like you to take my new command up the first time I'm aboard her,* Daniel thought. Aloud he said, "Negative, Three. Break. Mister Pasternak, you may light your thrusters in sequence, out."

"*Roger, Six,*" said Pasternak with gloomy enthusiasm. "*Lighting Group A . . . now! Lighting Group H.*"

The ship rang as though a pipe somewhere in her bowels were hammering. Steam roaring up from the pool smothered the hollow boom of the thrusters themselves. They were running at low output with their nozzles flared to minimize impulse. The *Milton* was coming alive, but she couldn't yet be said to be straining against gravity.

Thrusters ionized reaction mass, generally water, and expelled it as plasma, lifting ships through the troposphere to where they could safely switch to their High Drive motors. Ships could lift from—and land on—dry ground, but their exhausts scarred the surface and hurled chunks out like a fragmentation bomb.

If the thrusters hit a harmonic, they could set up a standing wave between the hull and an unyielding surface. A captain who reacted quickly could still land by changing the frequency or nozzle angle, but an inexperienced or ham-handed officer might flip his ship on its side in a heartbeat.

"*Lighting Group B*," Pasternak reported. The pattern of the cruiser's minute rocking changed, though not in a fashion that Daniel could've identified if he hadn't known what it was. "*Lighting Group G.*"

Most large warships grouped their thrusters. The *Milton*'s thirty-two nozzles were controlled in lettered quartets, starting from the starboard bow. Daniel knew that even with sufficient technicians in the Power Room to keep track of thirty-two separate thrusters, coordination would've been impossible. He missed the feeling of flexibility that the *Sissie*'s individual throttles had given him, though he supposed—

He grinned.

—if he pretended that the cruiser had eight thrusters instead of eight sets of thrusters, it was the same thing.

"*Lighting Group C, lighting group F,*" Pasternak said. The ship trembled again.

The band across the bottom of Daniel's display was set to a 360-degree real-time panorama of the

Milton's surroundings. Though the pickup lenses were on the upper hull, high above the surface of the pool, a blanket of steam and sparkling ions hid the view. Occasionally they gave a glimpse of the roof of the shop building.

Even at minimal thrust, the *Milton* was starting to feel greasy. The thunder of steam and plasma would've made it impossible to hold a conversation on the bridge without the intercom and the sound-canceling field of each console.

"*Lighting Group D, Lighting Group E,*" Pasternak said. "*All thrusters lighted. All numbers are within parameters. Six, we're green to go. Five out.*"

Daniel checked his schematic, not because he doubted the Chief Engineer but because he *always* checked his schematic. Each group was in the ninety-fifth percentile for flow, throttle response, and output. Furthermore, all four thrusters within each group were within two percent of their three fellows, which could be even more important.

The pool was a roiling hell-storm as the sea rushed through a canal to replace the steam vaporized by the thrusters. In the cruiser's stern, two pumps sucked water up 40-inch tubes, continuing to top off the tanks of reaction mass till the very instant she lifted from Cinnabar.

The *Milton* was bucking like a skiff in a riptide. It was time.

"Ship, this is Six," Daniel said, raising the flow to the thrusters with the collective throttle. "Prepare to lift. I say again, prepare to lift."

Often mass flow and nozzle aperture were handled by two officers on liftoff. At another time, Daniel might hand one or both tasks off to subordinates—but not now.

With the flow at eighty percent, he smoothly rotated the vernier which caused the petals of the thruster nozzles to iris down, focusing the plasma which until then had been dissipated as widely as possible. The cruiser throbbed with intention.

Thrust balanced gravity, then overcame it. The great ship surged upward on a pillow of steam and plasma.

"We have liftoff!" cried the speakers in the voice of Lieutenant Robinson.

The RCS *Milton* was headed to the stars on her first voyage under Cinnabar colors.

CHAPTER 6

En route to Paton

Midshipman Else, holding the brass rod to her helmet with one hand, pointed the other gauntlet toward the blur of iridescence just to port of the A Ring topmast yard. Daniel stooped slightly while following the line of her arm with his eyes so that he kept his helmet in contact with the rod's other end.

"C-6-7-9," Else said, using the four-digit terminator which the computer had assigned to that particular bubble universe. "C-6-7-3, then D-4-9-1 on this reach, sir. Is that right?"

Her voice sounded thin but remarkably clear through the communications baton. On the hull of a starship in the Matrix, the only competing sounds were your own breath and your heartbeat.

"I think you'll find that the computer solution will route us through 6-7-6, then 6-7-5 and into D Sector," Daniel said. He was amazed that Else—on her first real voyage out of the Academy—had correctly identified the visible stages of the *Millie*'s course. "Why did you choose the route you did?"

The batons were thirty-six-inch lengths of thin tubing, filled with a polymer gel that vibrated the way the column of air did in a stethoscope. An electronic signal, even a quarter-watt radio or the magnetic field generated by a charged wire, would distort the sail fabric. That in turn meant that the Casimir radiation which impinged on those sails would drive the ship in some uncertain—unguessable—direction through the Matrix.

No electrical communication device was allowed on the hull of an RCN vessel, except by permission of both the signals officer and the captain, and that only in sidereal space. The RCN operated on the principle that if you eliminated all possible risks of mistake, then you reduced—not eliminated—mistakes.

That didn't matter to the riggers who spent their watches on the hull and communicated with hand signals when they needed to. Experienced men didn't need to speak any more often than the elements of a gear train did. A rigger who needed regular instruction got it at the end of a bosun's starter of braided copper wire, heavy enough to sting even through the stiff fabric of a hard suit.

The ordinary way to carry on a spoken conversation was by touching helmets. On most ships the need to do that was so rare as not to be considered. The astrogation computer determined the course and the sail plan which would best achieve it, the hydromechanical winches adjusted the rig, and the riggers corrected the inevitable malfunctions in the automatic systems.

Daniel did quite a lot of talking on the hull. It was possible to read the Matrix and—if you knew what you were doing—to improve on the course that the computer chose based on calculated averages. Daniel could do it, thanks to his uncle Stacey's instruction, and he'd found that he could pass on the techniques to at least a few of the midshipmen under his tutelage. Vesey was his greatest success, but Blantyre was coming along nicely also.

The other reason for having a conversation on the hull was that it was the only place where you could be sure of not being overheard. Privacy wasn't possible in a warship with a crew so large that there were only enough bunks for the off-duty watch. For the most part that didn't matter; captains learned to keep their own counsel.

But a captain who had a resource like Signals Officer Mundy available would be a fool not to utilize her. Daniel had acted like a fool more times than he could've counted even if they'd all happened when he was sober enough to remember, but he wasn't so great a fool that he didn't mull his knottiest problems over with Adele.

Faced with a recurring problem, Daniel had designed the rods. He'd thought of going to Bergen and Associates, but instead he'd asked the maintenance overseer at Bantry to build them. A great estate was a self-sufficient community whose personnel were used to creating one-off solutions for particular tasks.

The chance to do something for the young master—though Daniel had been disinherited, and after nine years in the RCN he didn't feel especially young—brought out the best in the tenants. The four rods which a delegation from the shop had brought to Xenos were polished till they gleamed, and the Bantry crest—three leaping fishes—was embossed on each.

"Well, sir . . . ," Else said. She turned, shuffling her magnetic boots on the hull to face him. It was possible to do that while speaking through the rods, but Daniel was used to the older technique of standing shoulder-to-shoulder with the other party while touching helmets. He saw no reason to change, since you couldn't see much of another person's expression through the plates of a vacuum suit illuminated by the Matrix alone.

Besides, the splendor of the Matrix was the most wonderful thing in Daniel's life. He swam in its shifting magnificence whenever he found himself on the hull.

"Ah . . . ," the midshipman said, shuffling back in probable embarrassment when she realized Daniel wasn't going to face her. "6-7-9 is a high state, in the yellow-orange, and 6-7-3 has dropped into the deep blue, almost indigo."

She gestured again to the points of light, whole universes rather than individual stars, in the glowing swirl.

"It'll be some strain," she said, "but we have new rigging, and the gradients won't be excessive when the universes are in their current states."

She coughed and went on, "Mister Cory says we should always look to cut stages where that's possible. It reduces our duration in the Matrix, and *every* stage stresses the rig and hull more than the differences between gradients."

Daniel blinked; unseen, of course, by his companion. "Mister Cory told you that?" he said.

"Yessir," Else said nervously. "Ah—isn't it right, sir?"

Well, I will *be buggered*, Daniel thought. Aloud he said, "That's quite right, Else. If you take it to extremes, you'll jerk the sticks right out of her, of course . . . but that's certainly not the case here. You've proposed the course I've already loaded in the computer."

The hull transmitted a quick metallic staccato. Daniel turned to look behind him.

Hydraulic semaphores transmitted commands from the bridge to riggers on the hull. He stood with Else on the ship's spine, ten feet forward of one. The six arms clacked together at 180 degrees, then spread with the message. A moment later the port and starboard antennas began to rotate on their axes while winches shook out their topgallant sails.

Daniel cleared his throat. "Have you been talking a great deal with Cory, then?"

The port B Ring antenna turned about fifteen degrees and stopped; those to fore and aft—Daniel checked—continued to thirty. He couldn't see what was wrong; it was probably a kink which prevented a shroud from paying out properly. Three riggers, hidden among the tubes and cables while they were motionless, scrambled to clear the jam.

"Well, sir . . . ," Else said. She'd been watching the riggers also, perhaps to give herself time to refine her answer. "When we're studying in the midshipmen's berth, Mister Cory shows us things he learned from you. We'd heard about you—and Commander Bergen, of course—in our astrogation classes at the Academy. But, well, he's *served* with you."

"Yes, he has," Daniel said. "And I'm pleased that he's passing on what he learned. It makes my job much easier."

Daniel looked into the rippling, riotous beauty of the Matrix. If asked to bet last month, he would've given long odds that Cory hadn't retained—let alone understood—any of the instruction on reading the Matrix that Vesey as well as Daniel himself had provided. Had the boy become an astrogator when he had to teach astrogation to somebody else?

"Fink, Barr, and me're very lucky to have a senior midshipman like Mister Cory with us, sir," Else said. "I mean, the lieutenants are very good, and the instruction *you* have time to give us—this is wonderful. My classmates will be in awe when they hear. But Cory's with us all the time."

"Sometimes you get lucky, Else," Daniel said. "We'll go inside now and I'll watch you set up the course you just eyeballed."

Midshipman Cory appeared to have gotten lucky: he'd learned the trick that would allow him to become a successful RCN officer.

And Captain Daniel Leary had gotten lucky too. The officers of his new command were shaking down very well indeed.

Above Paton

The High Drive motors buzzed, holding a 1g acceleration to give the *Milton* the illusion of gravity while waiting for clearance to land in Hereward Harbor. The vibration sawed at Adele's skull.

She supposed her headache was a result of their strikingly unpleasant extraction from the Matrix. She'd felt as though ice water had replaced the marrow of every bone in her body. She didn't see an obvious connection between that and now feeling as though her head were splitting, but she doubted it was a coincidence.

"*Adele, are you feeling all right?*" someone asked.

Adele opened her eyes. She hadn't realized they'd been closed until the shock of light dizzied her. She blinked but put both palms on the console to steady herself.

Rene Cazelet had spoken over a two-way link from the astrogation station across the bridge. He must've been watching her through the camera in her own console.

"Tend to your own work, if you please," Adele said. She kept her tone neutral, but she cut power to her camera. Rene would take that as a sharp rebuke, which is exactly what she meant it for.

Oddly enough, Adele immediately began to feel better. The surge of adrenaline from her anger had apparently settled whatever biochemical imbalance was causing the headache.

She smiled faintly. Perhaps she owed Rene an apology. After the *Milton* had landed she'd give him one, but for now she had work to do.

Cory was handling ordinary communications with Paton Control on the ground in Hereward City, the regional capital. Paton didn't have either guardships in orbit or a planetary defense array, a constellation of nuclear mines whose focused blasts could destroy even a battleship. There was nothing either to protect or to steal here.

Das, the Resident of the Veil, had thirty worlds

under his authority, a larger number than most of Cinnabar's regional governors. That was only because none of the worlds was significant. The gross economic product of all thirty together was less than that of any of the five suburban boroughs of Xenos.

Normally Adele would've felt that her primary duty was to gather information from the ships in Hereward Harbor and from the Residency databases—particularly anything that Das and his cronies tried to keep secret. For now she left that to her equipment and, opening a shielded link to the command console, said, "Daniel, Senator Forbes has just entered the BDC. Lieutenant Robinson admitted her. So that you know."

"*Umm,*" said Daniel. They didn't bother with protocol when they used a two-way link. In fact, Adele had difficulty remembering to use protocol at any time. "*Well, I'd rather she were there than up here. I'll be interested to see if Robinson reports it, though.*"

After a pause he added, "*And make sure she can't speak to anyone on the ground, if you please. Ah—you can do that?*"

"Yes, Daniel," Adele said aloud. *And I can count to eleven without taking off my shoes*...but that she didn't say. She'd already snapped at one friend as a result of the headache which was fast fading to a memory.

She grimaced. Before turning her attention to the information which was flooding into her electronic nets, she repowered the camera and switched to the link with Cazelet. "I'm sorry, Rene," she said. "Extraction gave me a headache, but it seems to be gone now."

"*I thought for a moment I'd lost the use of my legs,*" Cazelet said. "*This was a bad one, all right.*"

After pausing again, he added, "*I've drafted landing*

plans for every berth in Hereward Harbor; none of which will be needed, of course. If there's some data stream that you won't have time to review till later, I could look at it."

There's nothing on Paton for which I require help, Adele thought. She said, "All right. The Veil Protective Service is the closest thing to a military here. I'm particularly interested in any contacts between them and the Hegemony."

She didn't bother to tell Cazelet how to find VPS databases or how to enter them, nor did she tell him that contact with the Alliance was even more important than contact with Headman Terl and his successor. Rene would ask for help if the information were unexpectedly well protected, but he was clever and had picked up specialist knowledge and tools from her in the past. There weren't likely to be any problems.

Cazelet's help wasn't necessary to her. That she apologize by permitting him *to* help was necessary.

Adele started with the ships in the harbor. There were two Protective Service gunboats. The *Cockchafer* had been deadlined for repairs: three of her High Drive motors had failed on her most recent cruise, and the remaining three could go the same way momentarily. She was likely to remain in dock for the foreseeable future because her log listed the replacements as OUT OF STOCK/ON ORDER FROM XENOS.

Presumably more was going on than the log showed, since High Drive motors were more or less interchangeable. Still, the situation didn't constitute a threat to the Republic or to the *Milton*'s mission.

The *Moth* had just completed a cruise touching seven of the worlds administered from Paton. She could lift again within a day or two if necessary, though it was hard to imagine any real need for that.

Local information confirmed the judgment of the *Sailing Directions* that there wasn't a problem with piracy in the Veil. The Cinnabar Residency didn't produce anything worth stealing, and the Hegemony had a small but very efficient anti-pirate squadron which enthusiastically exercised its treaty right of hot pursuit into Cinnabar territory. The *Moth* couldn't do more than show the flag, but that was all she would be required to do.

Most of the forty-odd vessels in Hereward Harbor were local traders: the largest was a little over 1,500 tons, and a number were well under a thousand. A hulk, formerly the 3,000-ton freighter *Jinyo Maru*, provided shops and accommodations for both ground and space elements of the Veil Protective Service. A slightly smaller freighter, the *Sallie Murchison*, had brought a semiannual shipment of merchandise to the Residency's only off-world trading house, Cone Transport. The Cone factor in Hereward would break up the cargo and transship the smaller packets to outlying worlds.

The only unexpected vessel below was the *Spezza*, a Hydriote transport of 5,000 tons. Adele dug into her particulars; the commercial code "protecting" them could be opened by any halfway competent signals officer in the merchant service. To Adele's surprise, she found that the *Spezza* was under charter to the Ministry of Defense on Xenos.

Adele echoed Daniel's display in a quadrant of her own to make sure that he wasn't in the middle of a critical operation, then cued her link to the command console. This might be something to report openly, but when in doubt she preferred to keep their conversations private. Daniel could open it up if he wished.

"Daniel?" she said. "The transport in harbor is here to pick up a regiment of Cinnabar troops. Well, allied troops. But the ship's from Hydra, not one of the Republic protectorates."

"*That* is *odd*," Daniel said. He'd been examining the degree of wear on the *Milton*'s thruster nozzles and the throats of her High Drive motors. He switched to real-time imagery of the transport with her specifications in a sidebar beneath. He didn't have to ask which of the ships below was the *Spezza*, nor did he fumble with the sensor controls: ships were to him what information generally was to Adele. "*What's their itinerary?*"

"The *Spezza* carried twelve hundred migrant laborers from Abraxis to Domedovo," Adele said. "It then proceeded empty here to Paton, that's three days, to pick up the troops. It hasn't logged a course as yet. That is, there isn't a course prepared on the *Spezza*'s computer, not just that they haven't reported one to Paton Control."

As she spoke, she called up the summary section on Hydra from the *Sailing Directions*. The Hydriotes had quite a lot of the carrying trade in this sector of human space.

War between Earth and her oldest colonies had created a thousand-year Hiatus in star travel. For the first seven hundred years following the Hiatus, the Hydriotes had been pirates. Bases on Hydra's two moons provided a defensive screen that none of the neighboring worlds could breach.

With the appearance of major powers, first the Kostromans and even more when Cinnabar and the

Alliance moved into the region, the Hydriotes had become traders with a reputation of rigid honesty. Hydra *might* have been absorbed by one or the other empires, but though the moon bases no longer conferred absolute safety, they did make the world an uneconomic mouthful to swallow.

Adele felt a flash of irritation at herself. She didn't have a list of all Ministry of Defense charters. She wasn't even sure that a list existed, but she probably could have compiled one back in Xenos. She hadn't thought to do so, and now she needed the information!

Well, she wanted the information. In what Adele Mundy regarded as a perfect world, *all* information would be immediately accessible.

Aloud she said, "I don't have record of any other instance of Defense chartering vessels from outside the protectorate for carrying troops. There have been cases of foreign ships being bought into service and given Cinnabar officers, that's all. But I have only a small sample available, a very small sample. I'm sorry, Daniel, I'm not prepared."

To her surprise, Daniel laughed. "*I don't know that you'll consider this to be real data,*" he said, "*but speaking as a politician's son, I can't imagine any contracting officer letting a lucrative transportation contract to a foreign carrier and keeping his job. There's quite a lot of money in those contracts, Adele, and they don't go to firms which don't have senatorial support in one way or another.*"

After a moment's pause, he added, "*How did the soldiers arrive here if the* Spezza *didn't bring them? They surely weren't recruited on Paton, were they?*"

"No," said Adele, switching files to answer the new

question. Data was pouring into her console from a score of sources, but she could access only one stream at a time. This answer came from Paton Control, not the log of the *Spezza*.

"The troops are from Thebes," she said. "They're the Brotherhood of Amorgos; some sort of religious order, apparently. Two small freighters registered on Sundog brought them to Paton from Horizon last month, then returned to Sundog with a cargo of dried fish. They, the regiment, lived in a Cone Transport warehouse until the *Spezza* arrived a week ago."

"*Gods above!*" Daniel said. "*The Brotherhood? Adele, they're crack troops. I know, most allied units aren't to the standards of the Land Forces of the Republic, but the Brotherhood's an exception. We must've stumbled into some sort of secret operation. Though I can't imagine what it could be around here.*"

Adele could very easily imagine an operation that required a first-class regiment: a swoop onto Karst, detaining Headman Hieronymos in his palace on Angouleme, and using him as a spokesman for directives framed by a senior RCN advisor. There was absolutely no evidence of that or other secret activities in the region, however, and there was no chance that Mistress Sand wouldn't have warned Adele about such matters even if her organization weren't involved in them.

Aloud Adele said, "That would explain why I'm not finding information about the regiment's past or intended route, certainly. I'm not sure it's the correct answer, however."

"*Six, this is Three,*" said Robinson over the command channel. "*We have clearance to land in Hereward Harbor. Will you be taking her down, sir, over?*"

The image of Daniel's face went professionally neutral. Then he said, *"Mister Robinson, I'd appreciate it if you landed our Millie today. I found her to run a few degrees nose-down when we lifted off, but she's not tender as I'd feared she might be. Six out."*

"Aye-aye, sir!" said Robinson. *"Ship, this is Three. Prepare for landing sequence in one, I repeat one, minute, over."*

To Adele, Daniel said, *"He should have a chance to shine in front of his aunt, don't you think? I'm very pleased with him as an officer, you know."*

Adele brought up an image of Hereward Harbor. It wasn't real-time because the *Milton's* orbit had her on the opposite side of the planet, but it was only ten minutes old.

"Daniel, why wouldn't he let the automatic systems bring us down?" she said. "There's nothing in a landing like this that requires human involvement, is there?"

Daniel's smiling image nodded. *"That's correct,"* he said. *"It's an open harbor. But it will give Robinson a chance to get the feel of the ship before he has to, say—"*

His face grinned. There was more than humor in the expression.

"—land her in the middle of an Alliance fortress, you see?"

"Yes, Daniel," Adele said. She thought of Fort Douaumont. *Woetjans' body flying backward with blood splashing the plastron of her rigging suit; the face of an Alliance soldier filling the sights of Adele's pistol. His mouth was open, shouting in blind terror, as her trigger released . . .*

"Ah, Adele?" Daniel added. *"I think we'd better*

leave the Brotherhood's course alone. We might call attention to matters that aren't our business and complicate another department's operations."

"*Beginning landing sequence—now!*" said Blantyre's voice from the BDC.

The thrusters' roar and vibration doubled in intensity as the *Milton* began braking to land. The real buffeting wouldn't start till the cruiser dropped into the lower levels of the atmosphere, but this was enough to draw a reasonable end to the conversation.

Adele settled back in her acceleration couch. She was glad to have an excuse not to reply to Daniel's statement. It hadn't been a real order, after all.

And she wouldn't have obeyed it regardless. She was going to learn what brought the Brotherhood of Amorgos to Paton, if it was humanly possible to do so.

CHAPTER 7

Hereward on Paton

"You can lower the ramp now, Woetjans," Daniel called. He straightened the sleeve of his best 2nd class uniform and mused aloud, "I wonder if I ought to have worn my Whites?"

Hogg snorted. "To meet the governor of *this* pisspot?" he said. "I don't bloody think so, master."

One side of Daniel's mouth twitched toward a grimace, but Senator Forbes and her aides didn't seem offended. The pair of burly males carried a trunk large enough to hold a body; they didn't bother to set it on the deck while they waited for the hatch to open. It would've been a problem to maneuver so bulky an item down the companionway of the *Princess Cecile*; Woetjans might've had to winch it out of an A Level access port.

The entrance hold echoed as the dogs locking the hatch withdrew in a quick series of clangs. Daniel grinned as it creaked down to become the boarding ramp. He wasn't sure he'd have been able to tell the sound from that of slugs from an automatic impeller raking the hull.

He'd been aboard ships taking ground fire a number of times in the past; he probably would be again, unless human beings suddenly adopted a philosophy of peace. That seemed slightly less probable than Governor Das and his aides opening fire on the *Milton*.

Hydraulic rams drove the ramp down with controlled determination. The opening sucked in whiffs of steam and the occasional sharp glitter of plasma, tendrils of exhaust which the atmosphere of Paton hadn't quite reduced to a resting state.

Hereward Harbor was an embayment that would've required artificial moles to be safe in a storm from the east. Presumably those were rare here. In any case, the sea's unhindered flow flushed away the residues of starship landings more quickly than an enclosure would've done.

Adele had put her little data unit on the attaché case which Tovera held out flat like a portable table. She turned her head toward Daniel and tapped her right wand twice. "The governor's waiting for us," she said.

The holographic display above the unit had been a blur to Daniel; it suddenly resolved into imagery of the harborfront. Adele had switched it to omnidirectional, giving everyone around her an opportunity to see what she was seeing.

An all-terrain truck with eight large tires waited at the land side of the quay. The crest on the driver's door meant it was as close to a limousine as the Cinnabar Resident in the Veil was authorized. Governor Das wore his diplomatic dress uniform of scarlet frock coat with black stovepipe trousers. His boots, waistbelt with shoulder strap, and transverse bicorne hat were all of gilt leather. He was a pudgy little fellow and looked as uncomfortable as he did silly.

Behind him were two aides, a middle-aged woman and a youth who couldn't be older than twenty. Both stood rigidly, but the woman kept shifting a flat datafile from her right hand to the left.

"Mistress, the hatch is opening," Tovera said. She wasn't exactly showing emotion—Daniel was pretty sure the little two-legged viper didn't feel emotion—but her tone hinted at stress. The reaction would have puzzled a stranger who didn't know that Tovera was as paranoid as she was lethal and that her sub-machine gun was in the case which she couldn't open while it was Adele's table.

Das looked over his shoulder and said something unheard to his aides. They started up the pier, marching in better time than Daniel's class at the Academy had generally been able to manage. Was that something the foreign service taught its recruits?

"In a moment," Adele said sharply, but even as she spoke she shut down the data unit. Tovera unlatched the case and turned, putting herself between her mistress and whatever waited beyond the lowering hatch.

Daniel smiled faintly. Because of his interest in natural history, he sometimes found himself thinking of human beings as though they were simply animals. They weren't, of course, not *simply*; but other species weren't simply animals either.

While Adele was unquestionably the dominant member of her small pack, there was a good deal of give-and-take between her and her servant. As there was—Daniel's grin grew broader—between him and Hogg.

The hatch was horizontal but continued to whirr slowly downward. The crews at Bergen and Associates had done an exceptional job in straightening the *Milton*'s frames, warped by her collision with another ship during her final battle under Alliance colors. Part of Daniel's duties as the vessel's first captain after a rebuild was to assess the quality of the work which had been done on her. He'd be able to give it an enthusiastic recommendation.

An honest recommendation, but that went without saying for those who really knew Daniel Leary. He was an RCN officer first, and he wouldn't have hesitated to shut down his own dockyard, no matter how profitable, if it hadn't been doing work he could be proud of.

"Well, they keep a cleaner harbor than some," said Hogg, eyeing the shore a hundred yards away. He stood with his hands in his pockets—probably gripping a pistol and his big folding knife—but managing to look sloppy rather than belligerent.

Daniel gave Hogg a sharp glance. He was trying to be nice. He was probably a little embarrassed to have spoken his mind in a fashion that could've caused his master difficulties with Senator Forbes, though that appeared to have gone unnoticed.

The outer edge of the boarding ramp was supported on the extended outrigger, itself as big as a corvette. From there it was still necessary to reach the shore. A team of laborers was unrolling the floating extension of foam plastic which would connect the concrete pier to the landing stage on the cruiser's shoreside— starboard in this case—outrigger.

The usual broad street followed the curve of the

harbor. Bulk cargo was stacked under tarpaulins or plastic film at several points along it, often spilling onto the pavement.

In the middle of the seafront was a small domed temple that looked old enough to date from before the Hiatus. Molded plaster sheathed the concrete walls. Flaking patches had been filled, but they were noticeably brighter than the sun-burnished surface.

The remaining structures were one or two stories, built from precast panels; windows ran the full height of the walls. They were painted in varying bright pastels, though, and the flowers and geometric designs stencilled on the walls gave them even more individuality.

"Ship," said Daniel, speaking into the microphone discreetly clipped to his left epaulet. In other circumstances he might've worn a commo helmet, though that was technically improper with either form of dress uniform. He preferred not to take chances in the presence of Senator Forbes, however. "I'm leaving the *Millie* in the capable hands of Mister Robinson. He'll announce the leave roster when the vessel's squared away."

Actually, Robinson would announce the leave roster as soon as the civilian brass had gotten safely out of the way. Daniel didn't want a party of rambunctious spacers to shove the governor into the harbor as they rushed toward bars at the other end of the pier. They wouldn't mean any harm by it, but folks who spent their working life in the Matrix were hard to discipline. Their attitude differed from that of civilians whose daily concerns didn't include the risk of being lost forever in a universe which wasn't meant for human beings.

"Six out, Millies!" Daniel concluded. He'd never commanded a ship with so large a complement before. He suspected that he'd have forty or fifty spacers in the local jail by morning... though it was possible that the Millies would completely overwhelm the local authorities. That would be even worse, but he'd deal with whatever happened.

"Captain?" Senator Forbes said. "Master Beckford is sending an aircar for me. It'll be able to land here aboard ship, won't it?"

Daniel's face went hard. He wasn't looking at Forbes, but he knew Adele could see his expression. There were any number of ways a civilian flying an aircar into the hold of a warship could go wrong.

"Your pardon, Senator," Adele said in her usual tone of clipped certainty. "I checked with Lieutenant Commander Robinson before I transmitted your message to Mount Marfa. On his recommendation, I directed the vehicle to wait for you on shore for the sake of your safety."

"What sort of nonsense is that?" Forbes said in amazement.

As she spoke, there was a clang and a squeal from above. A topsail yard rotated slowly across the hatchway while riggers shouted angry recriminations at one another. They were working to clear tangles, tears, and very possibly missing spars. This was the *Milton*'s first landfall after a voyage on which her captain had wrung the rig out properly.

Things did snap and fall and were dropped. Even without that, the air currents around the big ship changed as spacers opened hatches. That created a tricky environment for a pilot who wasn't used to it.

If Daniel had offered those reasons, Forbes might well have ordered him to keep the *Milton* closed up over her crew until she'd left with her friend. With the decision already made and laid to her protégé, however—

"Mister Robinson is quite right, Senator," Daniel said smoothly. "The Gods alone know what sort of ham-fisted foreigners Master Beckford found to fly for him on this benighted mudball."

He coughed into his hand and added, "Incidentally, I understand the lieutenant commander is related to you. An excellent officer, milady. The *Milton* is fortunate to have him."

Forbes looked at him, suddenly without expression. Daniel had been feeling—well, smug, if he had to be honest; smugly self-satisfied. Though he'd been *sure* nothing showed beneath his blandly professional smile.

"Captain Leary," Forbes said. Her voice sounded like a hen scratching through gravel, but she didn't raise it. "Do not patronize me."

Daniel let his face go blank. Hogg shifted; Daniel didn't glance to the side to see what his servant was doing.

"Senator," he said. He dipped his chin in acknowledgment.

The ramp boomed onto the outrigger. Clamps locked it in place with a quick *whang/whang*.

Forbes glanced over her entourage. The servants with the trunk met her eyes with the dull disinterest of draft animals. Platt, her male secretary, was tall, soft, and effete; an ageing queen unless Daniel misjudged him. He pretended to be looking at his feet. DeNardo, the senator's, well, companion, smiled back.

He probably wasn't any smarter than the two porters, but he had a sunnier disposition.

"Come along," Forbes said. "We'll wait on shore, as Captain Leary thinks best. Lady Mundy, accompany me if you please. I'd like to have someone to talk with until Prince Willie arrives. He wasn't known for being punctual even before he emigrated to this godforsaken place."

Adele turned toward her, pointedly without looking at Daniel. She slid her data unit into its pocket. "Yes, all right, Senator," she said.

She and Forbes walked down the ramp, step and step. Tovera followed a little behind and to the left of the others; her right hand was inside the attaché case.

Daniel followed Forbes's back with his eyes. "I misjudged that one, Hogg," he said quietly.

Hogg brought his right hand out of his pocket. He snicked opened the blade of his knife, then clicked it closed again.

"You got away with it by dumb luck this time, young master," he said. "But don't make a habit of it if you plan to get older."

The harbormen were sauntering back toward the pier now that they'd unrolled the floating bridge till it reached the outrigger. Woetjans and a team of spacers were lashing the free end to the landing stage; Adele noted that the connection was very loose.

The bosun glanced up at the sound of feet on the boarding ramp. She must've noticed Adele's... "frown" was too strong a word, but frown.

"The sea's calm enough now, ma'am," Woetjans said, "but if we lock the bridge in tight, she'll go under water every time the *Millie* twitches. Don't want you to get your footsies wet, right?"

Woetjans stepped aside and made a flourish with her right arm. "Clear for use, now," she said. In a different tone she added, "Get out of the bloody way, Hebart!" and aimed a kick at the backside of the spacer who was crowding the path.

Adele walked quickly down the outrigger's ladderway— as she'd learned to call stairs on a ship—and across the landing stage. It seemed solid, anchored by the *Milton's* huge mass. Only when she stepped onto the foam bridge did she have the queasy sensation of floating. It was six feet wide, with a nonskid surface and a rope railing on flimsy poles to either side.

Adele slacked her quick strides when she was well inshore from the landing stage. Senator Forbes caught up with her. The distance kept the conversation they were about to have private.

"Do you always let commoners talk to you like that?" the older woman said. Her voice would never be pleasant, but this time she was pointedly not making an effort that it should be.

Adele smiled. "Woetjans is my superior officer, Senator," she said. "I'm not political, of course, but a senator's daughter learns to appreciate the value of hierarchies."

Forbes flushed. She glared at Adele, who met the anger with an icy lack of emotion. They continued to walk side by side.

"I'm not mocking you, Senator," Adele said on the third stride. "And I'm certainly not joking. I hold a number of roles in life, as most people do. To Chief Woetjans, I'm 'ma'am' as a mark of respect granted to me and not due to my position as the *Milton's* signals officer."

The senator's expression faded to neutral. "Ah!" she muttered. She cleared her throat. "Yes, all right, I see. Sorry, Mundy."

She probably thinks that Mistress Sand placed me in the RCN, Adele realized. Not even leaders of the Senate cared to delve too deeply into Mistress Sand's business.

"You know Leary well," said Forbes as they walked on. "He's got quite a reputation, in the Navy and to anybody who follows the ordinary news."

"Yes," said Adele. "To both statements."

She said as little as she politely could until she learned where the senator was going with her observations. Daniel and the RCN were so much of Adele's life—were virtually the whole of her life—that she had to remind herself every time the subjects came up that other people didn't have the same view of the cosmos.

She smiled wryly—at herself. They were wrong, of course, but she'd understood even before the Proscriptions that other people didn't have to be right to have power over her.

"Does he fancy a political career, do you think?" Forbes said.

Adele clutched her personal data unit, still snug against her thigh. The question had been a shock. *Just as well I took the question as an informational absurdity rather than a threat.*

Smiling rather wider than before, Adele said, "He does not. I don't know a person who would be less interested in a political career. Except for myself, perhaps."

"He could parlay his naval exploits into serious votes, you know," Forbes said earnestly. "Or perhaps you don't know, Mundy, you've lived off-planet for a long time now. Take it from me, your Captain Leary could be the darling of the mob if he played his cards right."

"He's not an especially good card player, his man tells me," Adele said coolly. "Too enthusiastic, apparently."

She coughed, giving herself another moment to organize . . . not her thoughts, but how she could present those thoughts in a fashion that a politician would understand. "Captain Leary sees himself as an RCN officer before everything else."

That might not be true: Daniel probably considered himself as a spacer first and an RCN officer only as a subset of his greater role. If that meant Adele was lying to a politician, it was merely a pleasant reversal of roles.

"He's certainly capable of political maneuvering in the course of his RCN duties," she continued. "I've watched him do so a number of times, most recently in the Bagarian Cluster. But—"

"Don't forget who you're talking to, Mundy," Forbes said, though it was with bluff good humor rather than a threatening snarl. "*I* saw Mistress Sand's hand in that business."

"With respect, Senator," Adele said, feeling the edge in her tone. "Don't underestimate Captain Leary. He *is* his father's son. But you can take my word for it that they share no interests—"

Save for liking the favors of young women; but this wasn't the time for Adele to be as precise as her instinct urged.

"—whatever. Or I wouldn't be here."

Forbes laughed. She sounded like glass breaking, but Adele was reasonably sure she was really amused.

They'd led the procession all the way from the cruiser. As they neared the concrete pier, Tovera slipped between without brushing either one of them. "What?" said Forbes, too shocked to be angry.

"She'll wait for us, Senator," Adele said. She wondered if her voice showed the humor she felt. "There's some things she needs to take care of."

She watched her servant mount the metal stairs. Though they slanted out toward the bottom only by the width of each tread, Tovera didn't use her hands. On top of the pier she moved Governor Das and his aides back with a few words and an imperious jerk of her head.

Adele followed. At this stage of the tide, the pier was eight steps above the water level. The bottom two treads were slimy, but at least the stringers at shoulder height were dry to Adele's hands; they left black corrosion on her palms, though. Behind, Forbes muttered, "This is abominable!"

Adele stepped aside on the concrete. She took out her handkerchief and wiped her hands.

"Ah, Senator...?" said Governor Das hopefully to Adele. His uniform had a high collar, and his throat above it was squeezed to almost the same scarlet hue.

"She's coming, Your Excellency," Adele said, nodding toward the ladder. She refolded the handkerchief to bring clean surfaces outward.

Forbes reached the concrete. "Senator Forbes," Das said, his voice a half octave above where it had been a moment before. "Allow me to welcome you to—"

"I do not know you, sir," Forbes said, wiping her hands on Adele's handkerchief. She dropped it disdainfully into the water. "Come along, Mundy. I think I hear an aircar."

Adele fell into step. The business left an unpleasant taste in her mouth, but she hadn't liked Forbes to begin with. Das had behaved like a social-climbing toady, and by so doing he'd let himself in for a snub in front of his subordinates. That was simple cause and effect, and the victim was the cause of his own discomfiture.

She smiled wryly. It *still* left a bad taste in her mouth.

Forbes looked at her. "If Captain Leary *did* decide on a political career," she said quietly, "an alliance with an experienced politician could save him from the sort of mistakes that even a clever young man could make in ignorance."

"Senator," said Adele, "I'll deliver your message discreetly. But information is my business."

She smiled coldly. "I started to say, 'my life.' That would have been accurate also. I've told you that Captain Leary will not, in my best personal and professional analysis, ever consider a political career."

Forbes made a moue, screwing her face into even more unattractive lines. "You have a reputation for being as blunt as you're clever, Mundy," she said. "It's a wonder you've lived as long as you have."

"I'm also a good shot," Adele said. If Forbes had learned the rest, she knew that already; but stating it—bluntly—made a useful point. "That has helped on occasion."

She glanced over her shoulder. Daniel and five other officers had followed the senator's party to the pier at a polite distance. The junior officers were now returning to the *Milton*—their presence had been merely for honor's sake—while Daniel and Hogg were accompanying the local officials back to the car.

Adele gave a mental shrug. She could only hope that Beckford's aircar arrived before Das and Forbes found themselves at the end of the pier together. The governor could avoid awkwardness by dawdling, of course, which he should be able to figure out on his own. His record in Client Affairs—she'd looked Das up, of course—was good if unspectacular.

She and Forbes had reached the broad esplanade which ran in both directions around the harbor. Tractors hauled cargo wagons, many of them wooden-framed, to and from lighters. Some of the piers had derricks, but much of the work was being done by human beings. Some stevedores were women, but the gangs themselves were segregated by gender.

Forbes looked at the buildings across the esplanade. It was early in the day, but the taverns were busy. Several of the spacers staggering through the swinging doors were so drunk that they must have spent the whole night inside.

"What a *bloody* dump," she said bitterly.

"Oh, Paton isn't really so bad, Senator," said Adele, following the other's eyes with her own. "You mustn't judge a planet by its harborfront. Even Cinnabar, I'm afraid."

"You have the advantage of experience, I suppose, Mundy," Forbes said. "I'm afraid I'm going to have to learn to accept this sort of—"

She gestured toward the buildings. They were roofed with corrugated metal or plastic sheeting, and the bright paint had flaked in many places to show underlayers that from a distance had looked like designs.

"—environment unless I can somehow find a way to get back into the fight in Xenos. My whole life to date has been spent in civilized surroundings."

An aircar was approaching from the north at five hundred feet. As Adele glanced up, it dropped into a spiral centered on the senator and her entourage. It was a large, enclosed vehicle, painted light blue with swirls of pink blurring into magenta.

"I've learned I'm not very good at predicting the future," Adele said in a neutral voice as she watched the car landing. One of the things "civilization" meant to her, of course, was her sister's head nailed to Speaker's Rock; but there was no need to remind Forbes of that. "The best things that have happened to me have been wholly unexpected."

"Life has made me less optimistic than you, Mundy," the senator said. "You may be right, of course."

The aircar fluffed to a halt on the esplanade twenty feet away. The driver had landed downwind so that he didn't blow grit on the waiting passengers. If he'd been hired locally, the standard of drivers on Paton was extremely high.

Servants hopped from the vehicle's open rear compartment and opened the double doors in the middle. They wore full livery, not collar flashes, in the same blue and pink color scheme as the car.

Beckford waddled out. He was at least fifty pounds heavier than he looked in the last images taken of him before he left Cinnabar, and he hadn't been slim then. He made kissing gestures with both hands and cried, "Bessie, *dearest*!"

His costume had feathers for a theme; Adele wondered if Beckford had designed it himself. There was a range of competence in any specialty, of course, but she would've expected any professional designer to have *some* taste.

"Hello, Willie," the senator said. She didn't step closer, but she gave Beckford a tiny bow in greeting. "It's my great good luck to find you here in this—"

She lifted her hands, palms up, and gave him a false smile.

"—corner of the universe, shall we say?"

Adele stood quietly with only her eyes moving, but Beckford's attention fell on her nonetheless. "I *say*, Bev," he said. "Couldn't they find an officer to escort you? You really *are* slumming, aren't you?"

Adele realized she'd been waiting for that; waiting for some excuse, anyway. She'd known it would happen ever since she watched Forbes snub Governor Das.

Her mind was as cold as steel in the Matrix. She smiled.

"Willie," Forbes said urgently, her eyes flicking between Beckford and Adele. "You should know—"

"You are mistaken, Beckford," Adele said. There was a rasp she didn't expect beneath her drawl. Her left hand hung down at her side. "My father, who was Mundy of Chatsworth before me, didn't shun you because your people are in trade. He was quite willing to entertain tradesmen and even manual laborers when the needs of the party required it, but as a gentleman he had to maintain some standards."

She paused and smiled a little wider. "He shunned you," she said, "because you *personally* are a maggot."

"Willie...," said Senator Forbes. She took Beckford

by the right hand and half-guided, half-forced, him to turn toward the car again. "I was going to introduce you to Lady Mundy, but I don't think this is the time. Come, be a dear and get me to a hot bath and dinner at once, won't you?"

She shoved Beckford into the shadowed interior of the vehicle and followed him. "But Your Ladyship, what are we to do?" bleated Platt, stepping forward.

"Stay here until the car comes back for you!" Forbes shouted. "For Hell's bloody sake, stay here till you *rot*, you fool! Driver, get us out of here!"

The footmen closed the doors with mechanical precision, then leaped like acrobats for the rear compartment. Before they were fully in, the aircar lifted as smoothly as it'd settled to the pavement.

Tovera chuckled. "I didn't have anything heavy enough to get the driver," she said. "The windows were armored. But I don't suppose he was much of a threat anyway, do you?"

"None of them were threats," Adele said. She was trembling in response to the adrenaline she hadn't burned off in an orgy of killing. "There wasn't going to be any trouble."

"Officer Mundy?" Daniel called.

Adele turned, clenching and unclenching her left hand to work the tension out of it. Daniel, with Hogg and the three Paton officials, stood beside the official groundcar. "S-sir?" she said.

"Would you care to join us at the Governor's Palace for a discussion of recent events in the Veil?" Daniel said. "Since you appear to be free, that is."

He'll learn more without me, Adele realized. Her presence would disturb the locals, either because they didn't know why a signals officer was at the meeting, or because they *did* know. Daniel was inviting her as a way of getting her out of what must have looked like a dangerous situation.

"No thank you, sir," she said aloud. "I'll return to my duties on board, if I may."

"Carry on, then, Mundy," Daniel said, but she was already walking back down the pier. Of course she'd carry on; that's what she did.

And she'd keep on doing it until the day she died.

"I hope you won't mind if I loosen a few buttons, Your Excellency," Daniel said. He grinned across the compartment at Das and his aides, perched on the edge of their rear-facing seat. "Even these Grays are bad enough. I really should've gotten out my Dress Whites to accompany Senator Forbes, but I find them the most uncomfortable things I've worn since I was put in the stocks on Manzanita in the course of a midshipmen's cruise."

Das's official vehicle used the chassis of an armored personnel carrier. It was quite roomy, given that the present occupants weren't a squad of troops in battledress—and the furnishings were reasonably comfortable. The suspension was tuned for an additional five tons of armor, however. Jolts over potholes didn't harm the vehicle in the least, but the passengers bounced like peas in a maraca.

Das gave a sigh and unhooked his collar—as Daniel had intended he should. In fact his Whites wouldn't have been bad at all; he'd lost a few pounds on space duty, as he usually did. The governor was as miserable in *his* dress uniform as any middle-aged man would be squeezing into a closely tailored garment that he wore only rarely. Putting the poor fellow at ease was a kindness and was likely to lead to a better conversational atmosphere.

"It's part of the job," Das murmured with a self-conscious smile, "but not a part that I take naturally to."

His face dropped into bleak misery. "I needn't have bothered today, should I?"

Daniel looked out the vehicle's big side windows. The larger flying species on Paton had scaly bodies and used their hind limbs to flap wings stretched by rigid tails. A pair were curveting through a cloud of chitinous glitters drawn by a spill on the sidewalk.

"I'm afraid Senator Forbes suffered a very embarrassing political defeat recently," Daniel said, keeping his head turned to imply that his whole attention was on the wildlife. "You wouldn't go far wrong to suggest that she's in mourning for her senatorial hopes."

"I told you!" said Das's female aide. "It had to be something like that, Governor."

Well, no, it didn't, Daniel thought. *And indeed, it probably* wasn't *anything to do with Forbes's behavior. But a polite fiction, like a loose collar, made for a more comfortable ride.*

"Well, of course the ambassador was merely stretching her legs on Paton, I realized that," Das said. "There's nothing here of real importance to the Republic, or—"

His smile wasn't bitter, though perhaps it was a little sad.

"—I wouldn't be here myself, Captain Leary. Still, I like to think that although this is a small corner of Cinnabar's influence, we keep it well swept."

"You do indeed, sir!" said the young male aide. He had acne scars, and his uniform—beige with scarlet piping, apparently the diplomatic equivalent of Dress Grays—had been taken in and lengthened considerably after being cut for a shorter, fatter man. "It's an honor to be assigned to your tutelage."

Either that was blatant flattery, or the boy must have trouble in the morning deciding which foot to put each shoe on. Given that he'd been sent to Paton, Daniel suspected his Ministry instructors were of the latter opinion.

The vehicle—was it technically a limousine since that was the function it fulfilled?—pulled up in front of a long, low building similar to many of those it had passed on the way from the harbor. The walls were structural plastic, originally white but muted to a pleasant cream color by decades of sun and dust. The surface could be burnished to its original brightness, but that would just make it blindingly unpleasant in full sunshine.

The guard seated in front of the building had jumped up as the vehicle approached. He stood at attention with his weapon—an impeller carbine and not, Daniel thought, of Cinnabar manufacture—butted alongside his right foot.

"You run a tight ship here, Governor," Daniel said, surprised and amused.

Das coughed. "Well," he said, "not always. Charcot, you can relax. Senator Forbes is off on her own business, and Captain Leary here takes a reasonable attitude toward appearances."

The guard grinned and lost his stiff brace, but he didn't sit down again while Das was present. "Glad to hear it, sir," he said.

"Come in and have a drink while we talk, Leary," the governor said. "And Amos can find something for your man—"

He nodded toward Hogg.

"—if you don't object?"

"The young master doesn't object," Hogg said firmly. "Let's go, boy. And if you know where a pack of cards can be found, maybe we can try a few friendly hands of poker."

As Hogg and the youth disappeared through the front door, Daniel took a better look at the building. To the right, a number of women—several with children in their arms or clinging to their skirts—were talking with people inside. One was even holding hands. It was a moment before Daniel realized that the windows were barred.

"The jail's in that wing," said the female aide. "Mostly drunken knifings. Some theft, but that's mostly drunken too. There isn't much scope for master criminals on Paton, I'm afraid."

Daniel followed the governor through the swinging door and into a rectangular hall. It was dim after the street, because the only illumination came from clerestory windows shaded by the eaves. The air was noticeably cooler than that outside.

Half a dozen men lounged on wooden benches, apparently taking advantage of the temperature. Two were playing checkers on a board set between them. No one spoke, though several looked up when the door opened.

"We fine prisoners or sentence them to a term of labor if they can't pay the fine," Das said, leading the way down the hallway to the left. "Which they generally can't. Cone Transport buys the labor contracts, which is handy for everyone concerned."

He opened the door at the end of the hallway and waved Daniel through. A massive desk faced out from the back wall, and a modern console purred across from it. The aide moved to the console, while Das stepped behind the desk and opened a drawer.

"Have a chair, Leary," Das said. "Or—" he patted the conformal seat of off-planet manufacture beside him "—would you like this one?"

"This suits me well," said Daniel, easing himself onto one of the pair of massive wooden chairs in front of the desk. The seat itself was of braided leather and unexpectedly comfortable, but that didn't really matter for the brief period he expected to occupy it. "Ah—you mentioned Cone Transport. How much interaction do you have with Master Beckford, if you don't mind my asking?"

"I don't mind a bit," said Das, pouring an inch into each of the three glasses he'd taken from the drawer along with the bottle. Daniel's eyes were adapting to the light; he thought the liquor seemed to be cherry-colored rather than simply a dark brown. "No interaction at all, is the answer."

"We're aware that Beckford owns Cone Transport," the aide said, taking a glass and sliding a second across the table to Daniel. "But he has nothing to do with running the company or any of his companies, as best we can see. He lives on Paton by choice, not because Cone Transport is a major industry here."

"Take water to taste, Leary," Das said, rotating the water pitcher so that the handle was toward Daniel. "It's porphyrion, something of a specialty of the Veil, you know. I like to cut it by half myself, but I know you spacers have heads that an old landsman like me can't imagine."

Daniel sipped, wondering what porphyrion might be when it was at home. Adele would have her data unit out if she were here. In fact, she'd probably have started checking the instant the bottle of ruddy fluid came out of the drawer instead of waiting for Das to use the word.

"It's beet liqueur," said the aide helpfully. "Some claim that the best is distilled on Karst, but we've grown to like the flavor of the Paton product better."

If there was a flavor—and the color indicated porphyrion wasn't simply industrial alcohol—Daniel missed it, but he'd drunk his share of Power Room slash during his years in the RCN and this wasn't any worse. "Thank you, sir," he said. "Straight up is fine with me. Ah—what sort of labor does Cone Transport need?"

"Lift and carry, mostly," Das said, leaning back in his chair. "They've got huge farms, maize and turnips for greens mostly. It's heavily mechanized, but you still need human beings. Cone brings in contract labor in its own ships when they take out the crops. They're always glad of a little extra that doesn't require transport costs, though—and that's where the prisoners come in handy."

Daniel finished his drink, pursing his lips for a moment of silent thought. Das tapped the bottle and said, "Another?"

"In a moment, sir," Daniel said. He tilted a few fingers of water into his glass and drank it down to clear his mouth. Shoving the empty toward the governor, he said, "Basic subsistence crops like that usually aren't economic to transport long distances. Do you have any idea where they're going?"

"No sir," said the aide. Her tone was subdued.

"Leary...," said the governor as he finished pouring. He set the bottle on the desk with more of a thump than he probably intended to. "We carry out our duties here. We make sure that prisoners are released when their sentences are up, and we check the conditions for contract laborers generally on Cone Transport's farms."

"They're not leisure spas," said the aide. "But there's food and medical facilities. And the housing's better than what noncontract laborers who live in Hereward have, most of them."

"Master William Beckford doesn't make trouble on Paton," Das said forcefully. "People enter and leave his estate at Mount Marfa only in his own vehicles, that's true, but there's nothing wrong with that. Anybody's got the right to shut his door to other people, and if Beckford's got a bigger house than most, then he's still got the same rights."

"Captain," said the aide, "we don't borrow trouble. If Beckford came here because there's more space between him and his neighbors than there was on Cinnabar—well, there *is* more space. And he's doing nothing wrong!"

"I won't swear to that," said the governor with a half smile. He swirled the watered liqueur in his glass, then took another sip. "I won't swear that about my seventy-nine-year-old mother on Xanthippe. But I will say there's not even rumors, not beyond the sort who claims the pawnbroker down the street is an Alliance spy."

Daniel laughed, drank, and pushed his glass over for another refill. "I understand," he said. "My family's estate is on the West Coast. We don't take to officials from Xenos telling us how to do things, so long as there's no complaints...which seems the case here with Beckford. And anyway, it's no business of an RCN captain, is it?"

"I know there's a belief that all protectorate officials are corrupt, Leary," the aide said. "That isn't true, here in the Veil at least."

"There's remarkably little reason for turnip farmers to *need* to bribe anyone," Das said, lowering his reemptied glass. His cheeks and forehead had a rosy glow. He sounded more rueful than bitter, though there might've been some of both. "Cone Transport may have other interests, but not here on Paton."

"Those troops?" said the aide. She kept raising the glass to her lips, but the level didn't seem to change when she set it down again. "Not that I think there's anything wrong, but...?"

"There's something wrong, all right, but it's not the Cone factor's fault," Das said. He turned to Daniel. "There's a regiment of troops billeted here in a Cone warehouse and Factor Amberly's tearing his hair out. There's something wrong with the navigation system of the ship they're to leave on and nobody seems to be able to fix it. Amberly was here just the other day, asking if we could help."

The aide smiled at her glass. "The staff of the Veil Protectorate doesn't run to astrogators, I'm afraid," she said. "But, ah...Captain?"

She raised her eyes. Das was looking at Daniel hopefully also.

"Well, I suppose I could take a look at the problem," he said, keeping his face neutral while he thought. He didn't want to call attention to the *Spezza* and her secret mission, but under the circumstances it was going to cause more speculation if an RCN captain refused to help a unit of the Republic's troops which was having difficulties. "The senator said she planned to spend forty-eight hours on the ground before she'd be ready to leave for Karst."

He cleared his throat. He could imagine getting a taste for porphyrion, which he never would've said about alcohol bled from the Power Room hydraulics.

"Speaking of Karst," he said, "how do you—closer to the problem, that is—feel about Headman Hieronymos?"

The aide made a choking sound. She turned her head and gulped down half her drink. She wasn't faking it this time.

Das grimaced but met Daniel's eyes. "I think it's well beyond anything the Protectorate Service can fix," he said flatly. "Sending a senatorial envoy in a cruiser was a good idea. Sending a fleet of battleships would be an even better one."

He took a deep breath and went on, "And yes, I know Jeff—my deputy, Jeff Merrick—screwed up. I know it and Anya here knows it and *believe* me, Jeff knows it."

"He's a good man," said the aide, who now had a first name. She'd finished the porphyrion; the empty glass was trembling between her hands. "He's a wonderful man, smart and completely trustworthy, *wonderful*. But what does he know about spies? What do any of us know about spies?"

"Here, Anya," Das said. "Give me your glass."

As he poured, he continued, "It's really that simple, Captain. Jeff handles the customs duties for the whole region. There are never any problems—I couldn't ask for a better man. Foreign intelligence is part of the deputy's duties, but there *wasn't* any foreign intelligence, this is the Veil. By the Gods, I'm the regional medical officer! Am I at fault if a plague breaks out on Paton?"

He shrugged. Daniel suspected he'd have turned his palms up if that wouldn't have required him to put down his glass. "I sent Jeff off to Thorndyke to review the customs receipts there until I recalled him," he said. "The ministry could sack him but they won't, because bloody foreign intelligence isn't their priority either. The Gods only know what Senator Forbes might do if Jeff stayed where she could find him, though. So I got him out of the way."

Daniel weighed the options, then grinned. After all, hanging a competent financial officer wasn't going to make the situation on Karst any more to the Republic's benefit.

"Well, what do you think, Captain Leary?" said the aide in a trembling voice.

"My dear lady," said Daniel, "I think that your beet liqueur has quite grown on me. Governor, I'll have another glassful, if you please, while Anya copies all your files on the Hegemony to the *Milton*, Attention Signals Officer."

Turning again to the aide, he said, "Your console can do that, can't it?"

"Why...," she said, looking toward Das; he nodded firmly. "Yes, of course I can. I, I'll get to it at once."

As the governor refilled the glasses, Daniel said, "As you say, foreign intelligence isn't the business of the Client Affairs or the RCN either one, I'll add. I'm sure that the persons whose job it really is are hard at work right now."

He grinned. He knew that one of them certainly was.

CHAPTER 8

Hereward Harbor, Paton

Daniel had decided that they would walk rather than take a taxi or a bumboat to the *Spezza*, because he'd thought it would give him and the midshipmen a better feel for the harbor. That was doubtless true, but the morning sun seemed very bright, and every time his left heel struck the esplanade, a hot ice pick jabbed up his right nostril. Porphyrion wasn't nearly as enticing a beverage on the morning after as it'd seemed yesterday afternoon.

"Good day, sir!" he called to the watchman's shack. The gate was swung back against the chain-link fence on both sides, but he didn't think it was politic to simply walk in.

The figure within sat far enough back from the window that Daniel couldn't determine even gender without pulling up the imaging goggles he wore around his neck. Because he and the two midshipmen were in their 2nd class uniforms, they couldn't properly wear commo helmets...and they couldn't properly leave the ship in their utilities.

Under other circumstances Daniel might've been more concerned with what was practical than what was proper, but he was introducing himself to the commander of an allied military unit. And of course he had to consider Senator Forbes's presence. She hadn't been hostile to him thus far during the voyage, but she was angry enough at life and her present circumstances that he didn't want to give her an opportunity to force his superiors to crucify him.

A youngish man stuck his head from the shack to look at them. His khaki shirt had a breast patch and might've been a uniform. He didn't speak.

"We're from the *Milton*," Daniel said, gesturing back in a general way toward the cruiser's berth. "I'm Captain Leary, and these are Midshipmen Cory and Else. We were told that Captain Kelly of the *Spezza* could use our help. And Colonel Stockheim, the commander of the regiment the *Spezza*'s supposed to be transporting."

"Oh," said the watchman, nodding wisely. "They're in Berth CT7. You can't miss 'em, that's the big one."

"Thank you, sir," Daniel called as he and his officers strolled into the Cone Transport reservation.

"Why did they fence it all all like this?" Else asked quietly, as though she were afraid that the watchman would come running out after them if he didn't like the question.

"Cone Transport has all twelve berths on the east end of the harbor," Daniel said, "so it's reasonable that they'd have some sort of security here."

He cleared his throat and added, "Which, if I'd

been thinking more clearly, I would've anticipated. I hadn't appreciated the degree to which Cone Transport is involved in this operation. I'm glad my lack of preparation didn't lead to embarrassment."

In a normal voice, keeping his face deadpan, he added, "While I have the highest respect for my Millies, I wouldn't have wanted to have to shoot our way in against a regiment of the Brotherhood of Amorgos."

Cory's face worked. He managed to hold the laughter in till he saw Else's stricken expression; then it burst out in a loud guffaw, which he smothered with both hands. "Sorry, sir," he muttered through his laced fingers.

"It's all right to laugh at your captain's jokes, Cory," Daniel said. "In fact, it's generally regarded as a career-enhancing activity."

"Sir, I'm sorry," said Else, looking as though she'd just been told to choose between impalement and boiling in oil. "I mean, sir . . . Sir, I've heard the stories about you and the *Princess Cecile*. I didn't know you were joking."

"The stories are exaggerated, Else," Daniel said, making the point he'd deliberately set up with the absurd suggestion. "I don't expect to issue small arms to the crew at all on this voyage. Remember that we're carrying an embassy to a friendly power."

The *Spezza* was twice the size of the next-largest ship in the Cone reservation, so even a six-year-old landsman would've been able to identify her with as little difficulty as Daniel had. The floating bridge to her boarding ramp had been extruded from beige foam with red edges, the Cone Transport colors. There was a guard at the pier end of the ramp, which was normal; but it was a squad of fully armed soldiers in battledress, and they'd set up an automatic impeller on a tripod whose legs were weighted with sandbags.

"Isn't that a little excessive?" said Cory, showing that his mind had turned in the same direction as Daniel's. He was seeming more and more like a midshipman who was due promotion.

"Well...," said Daniel. "Brotherhood troops have a very high reputation. Perhaps they gained it by not taking any unnecessary chances, hey?"

"Like your spacers, sir?" Cory said. "I mean, not taking any chances that aren't necessary to win."

"I wouldn't have put it that way, Cory," Daniel said. "But now that you have, I don't disagree."

The soldiers hadn't been lounging before, but now most of them watched the RCN officers intently. Two had faced around to keep the bow and stern of the ship under observation, however. If raiders came around the transport while Daniel and the midshipmen were attempting a distraction, they'd be met with an immediate burst of slugs.

Only a few moments after Daniel and his party had turned onto the pier, a tall, flagpole-straight man came out of the *Spezza*'s boarding hatch. Like the guards, he wore battledress patterned in black and dark greens; only his short gray beard implied that he was a senior officer. He wasn't running, but his legs scissored at a rate that brought him to the guardpost while Daniel was still ten yards away.

"I'm sorry, sirs," the officer called. He didn't sound sorry—about much of anything. "This berth is under the control of the Brotherhood of Amorgos at present. No civilians are permitted past this point."

The guards held their automatic carbines slanted across their chests. They weren't overtly threatening, but they looked *very* ready for action.

"Factor Amberly requested the assistance of the Veil authorities with what he said was an astrogation problem," Daniel said. He halved the distance and then stopped, clasping his arms at his waist; Cory and Else halted a pace back, one to either side. "And Governor Das passed the matter on to the RCN, so we're here. I'm Captain Leary of the *Milton*, and these are two of my officers. We were to ask for Captain Thomas Kelly, but if you'd prefer that we not involve ourselves . . . ?"

The officer shook his head in disgust. "Amberly should have told me and I'd have warned you," he said. "That is . . ."

He straightened. "Captain Leary, please come aboard. I'm Colonel Thomas Stockheim of the Sixth Phratry, at your service."

A smile lifted the left side of Stockheim's mouth. "Better," he said, "I should say that I'm very glad that you're offering your services. Your male companion is welcome also, but—"

All traces of the smile vanished.

"—we cannot permit the other person aboard a Brotherhood vessel, even a hired vessel. Factor Amberly was remiss, and not for the first time. I'm very sorry if this seems a discourtesy, but I have no choice."

"Ah!" said Daniel. He *did* know that about the Brotherhood, though the fact hadn't risen into his conscious memory until he tripped over the reality. He'd been thinking of the *Spezza* and her Hydriote crew, rather than the troops who'd seemed to him to be only cargo. Clearly the troops had their own differing opinion on the matter.

"Sir?" said Else, touching the data unit cased on her equipment belt. "I can wait by the crane—"

A heavy crawler with shearlegs folded back over its hull was parked on the esplanade near the head of the pier. She nodded toward it.

"—and work on the astrogation exercises Mister Robinson set us."

Daniel gave her a quick, false smile and nodded. He said, "Yes, that's a good idea. If we're going to be any length of time, I'll contact you."

Daniel very much doubted that Else would be working on her astrogation while she waited, but he couldn't complain. It was his fault that she'd wasted the trip to the *Spezza* to begin with.

Else was addicted to the so-called novellas of her home planet, Schopenhauer. According to Adele—who of course had checked—she had brought a library of over a thousand novellas along on the voyage. They uniformly centered on strong, passionate women who were enmeshed in familial duties and the simultaneous loves of at least two angst-ridden men.

The plots were *so* uniform that Daniel would've guessed that rereading a single novella could easily have taken the place of starting a new one. Electrons didn't take up much room, however, and the critical variations that Daniel saw in the Matrix were just a blur to untrained eyes.

"Let's see what the problem is, then," he said briskly. "Colonel Stockheim, if you'll lead? And I suppose—yes, I see a ship's officer is waiting for us in the entryway."

Stockheim made a crisp turn in place and set off down the floating bridge. Daniel fell into step with him as a matter of both courtesy and self-interest.

The walkway was solid enough to support a utility vehicle, but the colonel's firm stride made it quiver. If Daniel syncopated Stockheim's steps, he would set up a rocking couple that would be uncomfortable for both of them. By good luck or intelligence, Cory too matched them step and step.

The Brotherhood of Amorgos were warrior monks, raised from birth to fulfill the obligations of their homeworld, Thebes, to the Republic of Cinnabar. There was no more gender bias in ordinary Theban society than there was on most civilized worlds—on Cinnabar, say, or Pleasaunce—where the right woman was the equal of a man.

Soldiers of the Brotherhood, however, lived apart from Theban society while they were being trained. They were then deployed off-world for their entire active careers. When they retired, they taught new recruits and lived in segregated enclaves.

The Brotherhood paid the contribution Thebes owed to Cinnabar for the privilege of being a member of the Protectorate. The Republic gained ten or a dozen regiments, phratries, of troops as good as any in the human universe.

And as for the Brothers themselves—they had a home and the respect of the only people whom they acknowledged as peers. Perhaps it was hard on them, perhaps their early training had warped them into something inhuman. But—

Daniel smiled, with sadness but also pride.

—spacers had a hard life too, and there wasn't

a man or woman on the *Milton* who wasn't proud to be one of the best of the best. Most people, the huge majority of people, had never been members of an elite. They couldn't understand that those who paid the cost of becoming a Millie or a Brother of Amorgos didn't regret it; rather, they held everyone else in contempt.

"Kelly, this is Captain Leary from the warship," Stockheim said curtly. "He's going to fix your computer."

"There is nothing wrong with my computer," the Hydriote said in a cold, angry voice that implied they'd already had this discussion a number of times in the past. "The problem is the instruction chip that you provided, Colonel. *You* provided."

He glared at Daniel. "Captain Leary, I am Captain Kelly," he said. "Come! You will see, and you will tell this *landsman* that the fault is his."

Hydriotes tended to slick, tight garments in pastel colors instead of the drab shapelessness that most spacers wore while on duty. Instead of wearing short jackets and billed caps like most merchant captains, Hydriote officers displayed their rank with crimson sashes, often with a long knife stuck through the folds. They looked barbaric, and it *hadn't* been so very long ago that Hydra had been a center of piracy; but they were skilled spacers and famous well beyond their region for the honesty of their captains.

Instead of taking them up a companionway to the spine, Kelly strode along a corridor toward the bow. To Daniel's surprise, the transport's bridge was here on the entrance level. He'd never been on a multi-decked starship before whose bridge wasn't on the highest level, the A Deck.

"It is what we do on Hydra," Kelly said, apparently reading Daniel's expression correctly. He was probably used to the reaction. "We always build ships this way. It suits us well!"

"I've heard only good about Hydra's ships and her shippers, Captain," Daniel said, which was more true than not. The Hydriotes were a clannish lot and, though famously trustworthy for their clients, had a much chancier reputation with those they sold goods to. Still, you could say that about any successful merchant.

The bridge was roomy and well appointed for a merchant vessel, with two full-function consoles. A Hydriote without the sash of office sat at the one on the port side; he didn't get up when Kelly led in the visitors.

"Get out of Captain Leary's way, Baskert," Kelly said, jerking a thumb toward the crewman. "Go on, Leary. The chip the colonel there gave me's already loaded in the system. Take a look at it and tell him!"

The crewman got up without response; indeed, his face showed no expression. Daniel slid into the bucket seat and brought the console live. It was an Emerson 3, built on Cinnabar some sixty years ago; he found it quite familiar. The short-haul traders whose refits were the bread and butter of Bergen and Associates during peacetime used exactly this sort of unit.

Daniel ejected the chip and looked it over before he accessed it. It appeared to be a standard route pack, ordinarily used by vessels with less capable computers. Preset routes between fixed points could save hours of computation time.

Reinserting it, Daniel said, "Colonel Stockheim, you provided the chip, then?"

"My orders are to hand in the old course chip to a trading house at each planetfall," the colonel said. "The factor there gives me the course for the next stage and I give it to the captain of the ship we transfer to. The phratry was carried on two vessels coming here to Paton, so I was given two chips on Raulston, the previous stage."

He cleared his throat and added, "The factor on Brightsky told me that the chip was delivered to her months ago by the courier who brought the manifests from her central office. Amberly here said the same thing."

The console purred. The data appeared to be loading normally. Without looking away from the holographic display—though for the moment that was still a pearly blur—Daniel said, "Were all the factors employed by Cone Transport, then?"

"What?" said Stockheim. "Oh, I see what you mean. No, on Welwych it was Interstellar Master Traders. And Hartman and something on Brightsky, I think. I could check the unit diary to make sure, if you like?"

"That won't be necessary, thank you," Daniel said. IMT as well as Hartman and James were owned by William Beckford, just as Cone was. There was nothing surprising about that—or even improper, really. A man as wealthy as Beckford used his influence to get contracts which made him even wealthier.

The console indicated it was ready. Daniel slid the cursor over the RUN button and banged the virtual keyboard with his usual enthusiasm. Instead of the expected course projections, the screen dissolved into pastel snow.

"You see?" crowed Captain Kelly. "It does the same

thing for him! This is garbage, Colonel, garbage. You go back to your factor and tell him so."

"Six?" said Cory, making it clear who he was speaking to while keeping the exchange informal. He'd seated himself at the other console. "Might I look at the course pack, please?"

"You think we didn't try both consoles, boy?" Kelly said. His angry history with Stockheim heightened his tone. "It's the chip, I tell you!"

"Yes sir," said Cory, calmly. "That's why I'd like to look at it."

Daniel ejected the chip again and stood to hand it directly to Cory instead of passing it through Kelly. He felt more comfortable standing anyway, given the hostile atmosphere. No, Stockheim and Kelly weren't going to start swinging at one another, but their bristling body language spun Daniel's subconscious back into the many past fights he'd been involved with.

Cory inserted the chip; he'd already warmed up the second console. Using a light pen, a much cruder version of the control wands Adele preferred, he began what Daniel thought must be a search of the chip at the physical level.

Watching a computer run was if anything slightly less interesting than the more traditional watching paint dry. "Colonel, Captain?" Daniel said, as much as anything a way to prevent the two men from glaring at one another. "Were you given any explanation for these movement orders? That is, a preset route instead of a destination? A ship as capable as the *Spezza*—"

He nodded to Kelly with a friendly smile.

"—could certainly have computed her own course,

and I'd expect that to be true of any vessel big enough to carry your regiment. Or even half of it."

Stockheim shrugged. He seemed to appreciate the reduced emotional temperature. "We're soldiers," he said. "We're used to not being told very much. Usually I'd have heard *something*, though, but not on this mission."

He offered Captain Kelly a half-smile. "Every ship's captain that carried us asked me the same thing," he said. "Kelly here did. I couldn't tell them anything. Not wouldn't, couldn't."

"Think Amberly could tell us something if we asked in the right way?" said Kelly, quirking an eyebrow.

"No," said Stockheim with a quick shake of his head. "The only solution he sees is to request further instructions from his home office in Xenos, and he's more afraid of doing that than he is of me. Unless you can fix this, Captain Leary—"

A glance and nod.

"—he *is* going to make that request. But that will take a month, I'm sure."

Daniel nodded pleasantly. Interesting to see that Kelly's "the right way" didn't suggest bribery to Stockheim. On the other hand, Kelly might not have been thinking of bribery either; the dagger in his sash wasn't a gilded showpiece.

"All right!" said Cory. He turned at the console, beaming. "Six—sirs, I mean. I found it. The chip's been encrypted, that's all."

"Why in buggering hell is that?" said Kelly.

"You can fix it, then, Midshipman?" said Stockheim simultaneously.

"Six, may I . . . ?" Cory said.

"Go ahead, Cory," Daniel said. The boy was bursting to explain, but he didn't want to put a foot wrong. "*I'm* well out of my depth."

"Sirs, there are two folders on the chip," Cory said.

"Two courses?" Kelly said. "Did they tell you that, Stockheim?"

"Sir, I don't know if they're two courses," Cory said, determinedly getting the explanation in before his seniors went off on a pointless tangent. "I don't know whether either is really course data. And the why is that I think one of them was supposed to be encrypted—"

He gestured toward the colonel.

"—maybe for the factor on the other end who'd receive it. But whoever did it was sloppy, and part of the other folder's encrypted also. I can get some of the data out of it, but not the basic parameters. It wouldn't be garbage, but it wouldn't be useful anyway."

"You can fix it, though?" repeated Stockheim. "Decrypt it?"

"No sir," said Cory. He sounded triumphant, and he looked as happy as Daniel had ever seen him. "But Signals Officer Mundy can. She's on the *Milton* now."

"Ah!" said Daniel brightly. Everyone on the bridge looked at him.

Daniel was confident that Adele would need only the course pack, but there might be other useful information aboard the *Spezza*...and besides, it suited Captain Daniel Leary to give the Brotherhood of Amorgos a little lesson in civilized behavior.

"Yes, I'm sure Officer Mundy will be able to solve this, gentlemen," Daniel said. "I'm afraid the solution comes at what you will consider a heavy price, Colonel, but sometimes that's the way. Military men like you and me are used to paying heavy prices, aren't we?"

He gave Stockheim a hard smile. "I'll summon her immediately."

The freighter's boarding ramp loomed before them as they splashed across the harbor. "Hang on tight!" called Dasi, the driver—the coxswain?—of the amphibious truck. Adele gripped her bench, but Barnes, seated inside her, reached around with both arms and clamped his hands on the sidewall.

"Yee-hah!" the two riggers cried together. The front pair of the vehicle's six wheels jolted onto the ramp in a spray of water and unidentifiable flotsam. The tires gripped and the truck continued to crawl the rest of the way up. The water-jet in the stern whirred till the middle wheels were clear also.

"That's far enough!" Daniel shouted from the entry hatch. He circled his index finger at Dasi before making a chopping gesture.

Whether or not Dasi heard the words, he knew what his captain had in mind. He swung the truck broadside to the slope and brought it creaking to a halt. The fins of the idling diesel rang like an ill-tuned wind chime.

"See, safe as houses, ma'am!" Barnes said, beaming as he stood and swung up the half-hatch behind them. "Here, let me get the steps."

"I could probably get out without breaking my neck, Barnes," Adele said with a tinge of irritation, but that wasn't fair. Probably, yes, but by no means certainly. The crew knew that their captain demanded that Adele *certainly* not break her neck.

Since Adele's earliest days with the RCN, Woetjans

had made her safety the responsibility of Barnes and
Dasi. There was no question that the common spacers respected Adele, but they also considered her—to
quote Daniel, a countryman to the bone—as awkward
as a hog on ice.

She felt herself grin as she dismounted from the
vehicle, holding her case of specialized equipment in
her left hand. Daniel caught the expression and said,
"Officer Mundy?"

"I was wondering, Captain," Adele said, "whether
I could find imagery of a hog on ice. I wasn't raised
on a farm, you see."

"Umm," said Daniel, deadpan. "I have a trained
librarian on my staff, Mundy. I'll set her to the problem as soon as she's completed her current tasks. I'm
glad to see you made it safely."

"So am I," said Adele. "Though drowning is supposed to be a relatively painless way to die."

Tovera got out on the other side. She swung down
one-handed, holding her case—which on the outside
was deceptively similar to Adele's—by the other. The
vehicle stood high enough on its all-terrain tires. Adele
had to admit that the Dasi's support really was helpful, since she didn't intend to let her code-breaking
paraphernalia out of her hand.

"I noticed that. May I ask, Dasi," said Daniel, his
tone making it clear that he *was* asking and that he'd
have an answer, too, "why the bloody *hell* you didn't
bring Officer Mundy by the concrete esplanade?"

"Chief Pasternak said there's two of these cars on
a cruiser's complement," Dasi said, grinding his right
boot toe onto the ramp. "But nobody's tried them out
on water yet, so Barnes and me thought..."

Both riggers looked off into the sky at angles.

"Use better judgment in the future, spacers," Daniel said quietly. "I know you wouldn't survive the loss of Officer Mundy, so I won't offer any pointless threats. But use better judgment."

"Sorry, Six," Dasi muttered to empty air. Barnes scowled and nodded, fiercely in both instances.

"Come," said Adele, her tone sharpened by embarrassment. "Let's get to the matter at hand."

With Daniel in the hatchway were Cory, a barbaric-looking spacer, and a very fit older man in battledress. The last wore a large pistol with a fold-down front grip in a belt holster; it was either fully automatic or it threw a much heavier slug than most handguns.

Adele smiled faintly. If you put most rounds in your target's eye, you could generally make do with a pocket pistol.

"My name's Kelly," said the spacer, "and the *Spezza*'s mine—mine and my uncles'. If you can get us on our way, Mundy, there'll be a bottle of something choice for you."

He turned and started across the entrance hold. "And you, Leary," he added over his shoulder.

"Wait a minute," said Stockheim with growing anger. "Leary, what do you mean by this? *Both* of these persons are female!"

Daniel and the Hydriote continued walking. Adele had no intention of responding—she was aboard ship by invitation of its captain and by Daniel's orders. But—

"Technically you might be correct, Colonel Stockheim," Tovera said. "But please don't let your hormones lead you into unprofessional conduct."

"What!" said Stockheim. The exclamation was no

more a question than that of a man who's set his
hand on a hot burner.

"Tovera is my assistant, Colonel," Adele said, following the two captains onto the bridge. "I choose—" she
wasn't going to lie for *this* purpose and claim Tovera's
presence was necessary "—to have her with me."

Stockheim crossed his hands behind his back. He
stood as stiffly as if he were before a firing squad,
but he met Adele's eyes. "Captain Leary has already
pointed out to me that beggars can't be choosers,"
he said. "And I mean no offense to you personally,·
Officer Mundy. It's just that we of the Brotherhood
regard women as occasions of sin."

Another spacer was seated at the right-hand console. He rose with an ill-natured grunt when Kelly
jerked a thumb in his direction, and Adele sat down
in his place.

Adele took a chip from her case and inserted it
into a slot beside the one holding the route pack. On
her way to the transport she'd been discussing the
problem with Cory over an intercom channel, using
the *Milton* herself as a base unit. She had a pretty
good idea which key would provide the solution; but
if not, she had several hundred alternatives already
prepared.

"You needn't worry, Colonel," she said as the console
worked. It was slower than a first-line RCN unit, but
no computer which could handle astrogation could be
called slow. "I assure you that I have no more inclina-
tion toward sin, as you put it, than this console does."

She patted the fascia plate with her right hand.

"So you may as well disregard my gender, just as
I do."

Having finished linking the console to her personal data unit, Adele leaned back and watched its display form. She preferred to use her wands for control; but more important in this instance, she could set the hologram so that it was focused only for her own eyes. She didn't want the others, particularly Stockheim, to know that she was sweeping up all the information in the *Spezza*'s system, but neither did she want to seem obviously secretive.

Stockheim snorted, but he didn't speak.

"You travel with twenty-three women, Colonel," Tovera said. Her voice sounded like scales rustling on a slate floor. "They're in the warehouse with your troops right now. According to the manifest, you left a twenty-fourth woman behind on Brightsky when she broke her leg in a fall."

"You hellspawn!" Stockheim said, and everything moved very quickly. Stockheim stepped forward, his right hand rising. He slammed chest-to-chest into Daniel, who hadn't been there a moment before, and bounced back.

Cory grabbed Stockheim's right arm; Stockheim twitched like a dog shaking and flung the midshipman against a bulkhead. Kelly pricked the back of the colonel's neck with his dagger and shouted, "Enough! This is my bloody bridge! All of you, *enough*!"

Stockheim turned without jerking his head away. The dagger point nicked his ruddy-brown skin before Kelly drew it back.

"Your pardon, Captain," the soldier said in a rusty voice. "You are of course right; this *is* your bridge."

"And the lady's right about the manifest," said Kelly, thrusting the dagger back into his sash with a quick enthusiasm that should've ripped the fabric if it didn't split the pelvis besides. "Which is no secret to anybody who wants to look it up at port control. So I don't see why you'd be flying hot anyhow, eh?"

Adele slipped the pistol back into her pocket, then picked up the wand she'd dropped onto the floor. She returned to the encrypted data, breathing through her open mouth. With luck no one was paying attention to her.

Well, no one who didn't know her already. She always forgot how quick Daniel was until she saw him move again in a crisis.

Tovera provoked this because she was angry, Adele thought. But she shouldn't be able to feel anger any more than she could feel love. Could a sociopath really learn to be human?

"The women, as you put it," said Stockheim, facing the empty corridor, "are a detachment of Intercessors. Their purpose, their *vocation*, is to bring the individual Brethren in touch with Godhead as required by our humanity."

His eyes swept the others on the bridge; Adele was watching through a pickup in the other console so that she didn't appear to be involved in the discussion. Stockheim was both angry and defensive, but he'd brought his emotions back under tight rein.

"The Brothers of Amorgos aren't saints," he said. "We're men as the Gods made all men: sinful. If you want to mock us for being as you are, do so. We'll continue to do our duty, regardless of laughter and insult."

"No one's mocking, Colonel," Daniel said, rubbing his chest with the fingers of his left hand. The two

men had collided like tree trunks in a windstorm...
though it was the soldier who'd recoiled. "We're here
to help you, after all."

Adele removed her key and replaced it carefully
in the attaché case. She rose from the console, aware
that all present were looking at her.

"I believe that will take care of the problem, Captain Kelly," she said, bowing slightly. "I've recopied
the navigational instructions in clear onto the same
chip. You'll be able to access them normally."

"And the other folder that your Cory said was on
the chip?" the Hydriote said. "What of that?"

Adele shrugged. "It's still there," she said. "The
material didn't appear to involve your vessel, so I
left it as it was."

"Then I think we've accomplished what we set out
to do," Daniel said, giving everyone a broad smile.
"Officer Mundy, your vehicle appears to have ample
room for me and the midshipmen as well, so I think
we'll all return to the *Millie* together."

"If I may ask a favor, Captain?" Adele said. "There's
a large public garden at the eastern jaw of this harbor;
I'd very much like to see it this morning. If you have
time, I'd appreciate it if you could give me some
pointers from your background in natural history."

"I'd be pleased to, Mundy," Daniel said. "We should
have an interesting discussion."

His expression hadn't changed in any identifiable
fashion, but something about it now reminded Adele
of the touch of her pistol's grip.

CHAPTER 9

Ravenny Gardens, Hereward on Paton

The gateway with *Ravenny Gardens* worked into the top of the arch was made to look like wrought iron, but when Adele tapped it with her knuckles, she found that it was the extruded plastic she expected. A sign beside the entrance read: A GIFT FROM THE ASSOCIATED GARDEN CLUBS OF PATON, IN HONOR OF THEIR LATE FOUNDER, DOLORES RAVENNY. This really was wood, and the paint had flaked badly.

Barnes reversed the amphibious vehicle, then snorted back down the street toward the dock area with his partner and the two midshipmen. Daniel watched them go with his usual mild smile.

"This is quite a pleasant neighborhood," he said. "Not at all the view that a spacer normally gets of a port city, I'm afraid."

"Yes, I suppose it is," Adele said. She'd checked slant imagery of the district before she picked the gardens as the venue for her discussion, but all that had really impressed itself on her was the fact it was suitably private. Out of politeness, she looked around her now.

The two- and three-story frame houses were spacious by the standards of Xenos, where land was at a premium. Each sat in its own lot, set off from its neighbors and the street by waist-high hedges or occasionally a fence of wooden pickets.

Adele returned her attention to where it needed to be. "The east edge of the gardens overlooks the open sea," she said. She was uncomfortable with what she'd just learned in the *Spezza*. It wasn't unusually awful as such things went, but she didn't know what to do about it.

The easy solution, of course, was to do nothing. That came naturally to Adele Mundy, who was more interested in knowledge than people. She wasn't sure it was the right answer here, however, so she was deferring the decision to Daniel.

Besides, Adele found herself caring more about people than she had for the first fifteen years after the massacre of her family. Either she was allowing her emotions to resurface or—

She smiled wryly.

—like Tovera, she was training herself into a series of behavior patterns which others would read as emotions. Either way, it eased life within society.

The gates were open, but a caretaker in a white—whitish—jacket got to his feet as Adele and Daniel entered. Tovera was a pace behind, moving her eyes more often than her head, but turning her head frequently as well.

"Sir?" said the caretaker. "Sorry, we're closed except for the workmen. We'll open again for the Promenade at nine."

Adele took out her data unit, casting around for a place to use it. There were benches along the path ten yards in, but if she wanted to sit without getting past the caretaker, the best alternative was moist ground covered with russet tendrils like fur. They would probably stain badly.

A lace-winged insect landed on her wrist. She flicked it off.

"Here you are, my good man," Daniel said cheerfully. He spun a florin toward the caretaker. Sunlight caught the coin at the top of its arc, flashing from the ruby hologram within the central crystal. "We won't get in the way of your people, I promise you. Setting up for the Promenade, you mean?"

"Why, thank you, sir!" said the caretaker, turning the coin over in his fingers. Adele had noticed before that Cinnabar coinage—holograms within silvery rims—had a flashy presence beyond its actual value. At that, a florin was worth about half a day's wage in the scrip passing current on Paton. "Yes, the Promenade, every tennight. Ah, if you'll be careful, then, I guess it can't hurt anything."

Smiling pleasantly, Daniel led them briskly past lest the fellow change his mind. *Tried* to change his mind, Adele suspected, but it was better to avoid a problem than to deal with one that'd arisen.

Adele grimaced at her data unit. She couldn't use it unless they stopped, which would be a foolish thing to do for no more important reason than she had now.

Daniel must have read her expression correctly— they *did* know one another well. He grinned and said, "The tennight Promenade is the major social event in Hereward. Everyone who's anyone dresses up and comes here to listen to the live band and look at one another. And nine is early evening here—Paton uses a ten-hour, daylight-to-dusk clock."

The gardens were laid out on a tongue of land. It was only twenty yards across here at the entrance, but it spread to over a hundred near the tip. To the right was the harbor; to the left, the open sea whose water was equally opaque but a clearer gray.

Circular planters, generally with a tree as the centerpiece, were spaced just inside the perimeter hedges; a graveled walk wound around them. At the end of the peninsula was a larger plaza, also graveled. Workmen were setting up a small bandstand and a dance floor, using boards from the dump truck parked on the walkway and the trailer behind it.

Daniel's eyes narrowed; then he shrugged. "I suppose they used a dump truck because they had one," he said. "That's a good enough reason, after all."

"Ah," said Adele, putting the data unit away. "Thank you."

"It's not surprising that I'd be more aware of high society in Hereward, after all," Daniel said with a chuckle. "Mind you, if I let the locals learn that my signals officer is Lady Mundy, you'll get even more invitations than I do."

Adele felt her lips squeeze into a sour bunch. "Thank you for not doing that," she said. She nodded toward a gap in the outer hedge, where a railing gave a view over the harbor. "I think we'll be adequately private here. I wasn't confident of that aboard the *Milton*, since the senator was aboard."

If Forbes—if her staff—were skilled enough, they could have set timed recording devices virtually anywhere. If the devices were designed for recovery, not real-time broadcast, they would be completely undetectable.

Though that wasn't the real reason for Adele's discomfort. She was tense and miserable because of Forbes's existence in the middle of her RCN family, not at anything Forbes was really going to do there. For all the cruiser's size, the _Milton_ wasn't a safe haven for Adele so long as there was a senator aboard.

"These gardens are full of exotic plants," said Daniel in a whimsical tone. "If you're from Paton. If you're moderately well-versed in horticulture—and I'm barely that myself—you recognize a good half of what you see as standard species which humans take everywhere they go. Many are from Earth originally—the roses, the pansies.... But the rest as well, the wagtails—"

He pointed to the clump of plants with finger-thick stems from which petals like pastel flags waved in the sea breeze.

"—are from Hinson's Rest, the bluebrights—"

He pointed to the clumps whose spiky cyan foliage overwhelmed the white florets at the center of each.

"—that they grow by the square mile on Melpomene for medicinal extracts, but you find them in gardens on just about every other inhabited world too."

He swept his hands across an arc of the plantings. "Pretty much all of them, the ones I can identify by name but I'd guess all the rest, they're off-world species. Whereas what I'd like to see is a nice slice of Paton's own plants in their native habitat."

Adele laughed, surprising even herself. She opened and closed her hands; she'd been gripping the railing so fiercely that they'd started to cramp.

"I'm sorry, Daniel," she said. "I'm angrier than I'd realized at Forbes's presence. And what I learned in the *Spezza*'s log . . . fed into it."

She cleared her throat and continued, "The Brotherhood, this phratry of it, is being sent to put down a rebellion on an agricultural world named Fonthill."

Daniel nodded. "All right," he said. "If you don't care what gets broken in the process, they're good troops for the purpose. Maybe the best."

He frowned slightly and added, "I'm not familiar with Fonthill, though."

"Fonthill," Adele said, brushing away several more of the lace-winged insects, "is owned by William Beckford. It isn't a listed world—anywhere."

Daniel frowned. A dozen or more of the large flies were crawling on his sleeves. He pinched together the wings of one and lifted it to where he could see it more easily. The slender body arched and straightened, while the four little legs paddled in the air.

"I presume there's something valuable on Fonthill," he said as he peered at the insectoid. "Minerals?"

"Fonthill is the source of shinewood," Adele said, looking toward the empty horizon. "All direct contact is through Hydriote vessels, not those of Beckford's companies. The *Spezza* has made two voyages to Fonthill in the past five years; the route pack they received from Factor Amberly is for a third, though Captain Kelly may not realize that until he arrives. The *Spezza* hasn't gone from Paton to Fonthill in the past, and the chip provides a route rather than a destination."

"That . . . ," said Daniel. He looked around them. "Here, let's walk to the harbor side, if you don't mind."

He walked around a planter centered around a tree that looked like a forty-foot coat rack swathed in streamers of thin green fabric. Around its base were plants with blue tubes which grew out of leaves the color of sunburned skin.

The foliage was covered with the winged insectoids. As Adele watched, a further cloud of them lifted over the perimeter hedge and settled to join earlier arrivals to the garden.

"Daniel," she said, though she continued to walk with him. "There seem to be more of the insects in this direction. Insectoids."

"Yes, I want to see if they're hatching from the harbor," Daniel said in an oddly lively voice. He continued, "No one's ever known the source of shinewood. I can see why Beckford would keep the location secret, since it's so valuable a product. Products, really, since there's at least a dozen identifiable species. They have nothing in common except their sheen under UV."

"The other thing that all the types of shinewood have in common...," said Adele. She brushed the railing of structural plastic clear of insectoids to that she could cross her hands on it before her. "Is that their sap is an ulcerating poison. Working with it—cutting the timber and milling it, since that's done on Beckford also—is debilitating and fatal within five years."

She gave him a cold smile, ignoring the tiny feet causing tiny prickles as they crawled over her face. "That's an average based on the number of replacement workers which the Hydriotes bring in. They have lot numbers, which permits me to extrapolate to a rough total."

"That implies very high wages," Daniel said. There was no more humor in his smile than there had been in hers. "Or that the workmen are slaves. Which would surprise me slightly, since Hydra became a signatory to the Blythe Convention over a century ago, barring its citizens from the slave trade."

He raised an eyebrow.

Adele nodded crisply. "I suspect it's a matter of definition," she said. "Beckford's companies buy labor contracts, particularly prison contracts. There are many worlds which aren't overly scrupulous about policing that sort of thing. That was the case in the Protectorate of the Veil until Governor Das was appointed, as a matter of fact. And it's still the case in the Hegemony. Headman Terl preferred to avoid public executions, but his security police were zealous in removing troublemakers."

"I see," said Daniel. "And I can't say I like it very much. . . ."

Daniel tossed the fly he'd been examining into the air and watched it vanish into the amazing swarms of its fellows. They were rising from surface of the harbor like spindrift, never more than thirty feet out from the shore as best he could judge. He thought of slipping his imaging goggles down over his eyes, but there was no call for that.

"The labor purchases are made through a variety of intermediary companies," Adele said. "The only ones that can be directly linked with Beckford are completely aboveboard, as for the Cone plantations on Paton. Separate entities recruit labor *from* those plantations with promises of wages and better conditions, but Cone and similar traders will have properly signed documents when Protectorate inspectors come by."

Daniel nodded, dislodging a platoon of the insectoids. They were fodderflies, native to Hartweg's World deep in the Montserrat Cluster. The harbor was boiling, not only with the flies but with the fish and birds which gorged on the hatching.

"And when the laborers find themselves on Fonthill at no wages," he said aloud, "there's also no recourse. Except to run into the bush."

"'Going feral,' it's called," Adele said. "Beckford's managers call it that, I mean."

She paused, then said, "I don't understand why Beckford allows the Hydriotes to know the location of Fonthill but not his own companies. I've searched the Cone Transport files here on Paton, and I find no hint in them of the world's existence. Or that Cone personnel have any idea where shinewood comes from. The shipments are brought to emporia—like Paton, occasionally—on Hydriote bottoms before being carried to secondary destinations by third parties from all over the human galaxy."

"He's rather clever in using the Hydriotes as cutouts, Adele," Daniel said musingly. Considered simply as a puzzle, it was an interesting one; rather like judging where to tap a hooked stick on the surface to bring a mudfrog from the bottom of the pond. "He can trust them, you see."

He turned and grinned at her. She was squinting and making quick brushing motions with her right hand to keep the fodderflies out of her eyes.

"The Hydriotes are a clannish lot," Daniel said. "They don't talk outside their own world. They won't try to poach the ownership of Fonthill, since Beckford would bring in the RCN before he let go of the world completely. Hydra must be making a pretty trissie on the carrying trade, which they'd lose if they got greedy. But don't you think some spacer from Cone or IMT would sell what he knew? Some *hundreds* would, I'd judge."

"One rarely goes wrong in assuming that humans will be venal, Daniel," Adele said. She held her right hand over her mouth with the fingers slightly spread, trying to prevent the flies from crawling in while she spoke. "And this business on Fonthill is an unusually striking example of venality, I would say."

"Yes," said Daniel. "It is."

He cleared his throat and went on, "I can see why Beckford would want Brotherhood troops to deal with his rebelling slaves, but I wouldn't have guessed that he had enough influence to arrange it. When word gets out, whoever signed off on the mission is almost certainly going to be executed. Such a misuse of troops in the middle of a war is treason, and there are still patriots in the Senate who won't brook that."

Adele was looking over the harbor, where the swarm had almost completed. *I'll make a log entry about the fodderflies,* Daniel thought. *Some future naturalist will be fascinated.*

Aloud, speaking to his friend's profile, he said, "My father among them, I suspect. Money was always a means to power for him, not a thing in its own right."

"The second folder has the text of the phratry's transfer orders," Adele said. She flicked her hand in front of her face to shoo away the last stragglers of the swarm. "Those state that they'll be dealing with a rebellion fomented by Alliance agents on a jungle world designated PP4/AZ—which exists but apparently was never colonized. Nobody making a cursory check of assignments would determine that, of course; and I suspect the orders were issued by clerks who had no idea that they were being manipulated."

She pursed her lips and added, "I wonder if the earlier route packs contained the orders also? Well, I don't suppose it matters."

She turned to face Daniel. That brought the plantings into her peripheral vision; she blinked with amazement. Instead of speaking, she snatched out her personal data unit before catching herself.

"It's probably simpler to ask you, isn't it?" Adele said with an embarrassed grimace. "What are these things, Daniel? They're eating *everything*."

"They're fodderflies from Hartweg's World," Daniel said. His lips smiled, but he was too caught up in the Fonthill business to really feel the humor of the present situation. "They're hatching in the harbor but not in the sea, you'll have noticed. I suspect that's because the flies' larval stage requires a hydrocarbons that they get from lubricant runoff in the harbor but not the open ocean here."

He turned and viewed the tattered remnants of the gardens. "Fodderflies take over twenty years to reach their adult stage at home; I have no idea what the cycle here is."

"I'll look it up," said Adele, stepping briskly to a bench. She swept it clear of fodderflies with her side-cap before sitting down.

The flies had stripped almost all the foliage from the garden. In the case of the Vasilyevan pole pine, they'd eaten even the bark into mottled patches; the portions covered by an iridescent fungus transplanted with the tree had been spared.

"They eat in order to lay eggs on the shore above the high tide line," Daniel said, letting his mind puzzle over questions of natural history. In the natural world, cause and effect had no moral dimension. "It'll take a serious storm to sweep them into the water, and that'll disperse them widely as well. Though here on Paton that doesn't matter, because the harbor is the only suitable habitat."

Adele looked up. "According to the Garden Club records, there was an outbreak forty-seven years ago, but that's local reckoning. It's nearly sixty Standard years."

She looked at the devastation and shook her head in wonder. "It was a terrible disaster," she said. "The creatures wiped out not only Ravenny Gardens but also many of the members' individual plantings elsewhere in the city. Just as they're doing now."

When the fodderflies descended, there'd been quite a lot of cursing and loud questions from the workmen setting up for the Promenade. That had subsided when they realized the flies didn't bite or sting; they'd resumed their work. Daniel wondered if they'd even bother to mention when they returned to the garage at the end of their shift that the gardens had been stripped.

He grinned: probably not. The citizens didn't attend Promenades to look at the foliage, but he suspected they were going to be very displeased to find it missing.

"Did you notice the grass?" Daniel said, pointing. "The ground cover, that is. That's native to Paton."

Adele followed the line of his finger. "It looks all right," she said, frowning at the feathery strips of dull orange. They showed up clearly in the absence of the more vividly colored introduced species. "Isn't it?"

"Yes, it's untouched," Daniel agreed. "So are the other native species—the vines growing up the gate arch and the hedges here, at any rate."

He carefully touched the hedge framing the vista. The upper side of the reddish brown foliage was as soft as a cat's fur, but at contact the leaves rolled inward. The undersides bore hairs as fine and irritating as glass fibers.

"Whereas the fodderflies have eaten *all* the off-world species that I can see, no matter where the plants came from," Daniel said. "They literally can't stomach the local chemistry, though it might take a lifetime to figure out precisely which enzyme or amino-acid chain was specifically responsible."

He grinned broadly. "If the Garden Club wants to get rid of the infestation, all it has to do is plant only native species until after the next outbreak sixty-some years hence; the flies will starve, then. But I'll bet they just redo everything just the way it was."

The gorged flies were rising again, circling to catch the higher breezes which they hoped would waft them to new territories. No doubt the breezes would, but the eggs would only develop in the water of the harbor, and Ravenny Gardens was probably the only food source great enough to fuel a breeding population of adult flies. It was a remarkable accidental habitat, wholly created and sustained by human beings.

"Daniel," said Adele. "What are we going to do?"

He nodded. They both knew why they'd been discussing the fodderflies—which, though fascinating, were of no importance compared with the problem of Fonthill.

Sometimes you had to act without thinking. Wise people liked to let matters simmer in the quiet darkness of their minds, however. They talked about trivia while they let their subconscious get on with the business.

Daniel shrugged. "We're RCN officers," he said, "and the RCN isn't a police force. It may be that when we're back in Xenos I'll mention the business to somebody who has a professional reason to be interested. But at this level that's politics, Adele, and I can tell you that Navy House isn't even a little amused when RCN officers decide to play politics."

He met her eyes. He'd been staring at the stark, stripped trunks and branches, all that remained of Ravenny Gardens.

"We're RCN officers engaged in an important mission," he said, hearing his words rasp. "We'll carry out our duties, and we'll ignore matters that have no bearing on those duties!"

Adele nodded. She closed down her data unit and slid the wands away.

"That's the only rational choice," she said. "I suspect that we wouldn't have to search very far back to find that both our families had been involved in similar activities. And as you say, the status of the Hegemony is of critical importance to the Republic."

She stood and put the data unit into her thigh pocket. Sweeping her eyes over the ruin, she smiled. Adele's smiles were rare and hard to interpret, but they rarely involved what most people would consider humor.

"Adele?" Daniel said.

"I was just thinking," she replied, "that it's a good thing that we don't believe in omens, isn't it?"

"I see what you mean," said Daniel.

But he wasn't sure that deep in his heart, he *didn't* believe in omens.

CHAPTER 10

Port Hegemony, Karst

"*Six, this is Three*," said Lieutenant Commander Robinson, using the command channel instead of a two-way link. "*All post-landing procedures are complete, over.*"

The *Milton* rang in a dozen different keys as elements of her hull and outriggers cooled to the surface temperature of Karst. Daniel found the most unexpected difference between the heavy cruiser and the *Princess Cecile* was how much longer—and noisier—the process of reaching ambiance after landing was on the larger ship.

"Roger, Three," said Daniel. "Break. Ship, this is Six. I'm going to open her up. You can deal with the bumboats to your heart's content—"

Hearts' content wasn't high in the list of what spacers wanted after a voyage, even the relatively short four days from Paton, but the harbor's little trading craft would provide booze and negotiable affection in sufficient quantity.

"—but liberty won't start for six hours. I need that long to get a handle on the social—"

He meant "political," of course.

"—temperature here, Millies. Those of you who've served with me in the past know that I'll give you liberty as soon as I can. Those of you who haven't, well—remember that I'm a Leary of Bantry, and I'm not even a little bit interested in your opinion. Six out."

Adele was extremely busy, which was only to be expected immediately after landing in a foreign port. All foreign ports were potentially hostile, of course, though if that were more than a theoretical possibility here, Daniel wouldn't have brought the *Milton* down to the surface.

The AFS *Merkur*, an Alliance destroyer most recently assigned to Admiral Anton Petersen's squadron in the Montserrat Stars, was already in the harbor; she was unquestionably hostile. A destroyer wasn't a threat to a heavy cruiser, of course; but the fact an Alliance vessel was here in the capital of the Hegemony would've been worrisome even without the previous reports of the new Headman's doubtful attitude toward Cinnabar.

"Mister Robinson," Daniel said, switching back to the command push manually, "you may open her up. Six out."

Robinson didn't bother to give an order. When he activated the undogging mechanism of the main hatch, the sound of bolts withdrawing echoed through the cruiser from the entry hold. Spacers all over the vessel cranked open ports and access panels in response, letting in air that hadn't been processed repeatedly from a fugg of lubricants, hot electronics, and close-packed humans.

Daniel smiled. The only reason the crew had waited this long was that they knew that Senator Forbes was aboard. They weren't going to embarrass the RCN and their captain by acting in a fashion that a civilian would consider undisciplined. And if any present crew members didn't understand that basic bit of courtesy, there were plenty of former Sissies around who'd provide the lesson with a quick boot or a fist.

An orange legend pulsed along the bottom of the command display, overlaying the schematic of expendable stores: SENATOR FORBES HAS ENTERED THE BRIDGE. Adele considered it her business to inform the captain of anything she thought he needed to know.

Forbes, her secretary, and her male bimbo had all entered the compartment. Two Marines were stationed in the hatchway, but they'd chosen not to prevent these particular unauthorized entries.

That was a good thing. If they'd made the senator angry, Daniel would've had to protect them because they *were* carrying out his orders. That would have been unfortunate.

He collapsed his holographic display and smiled brightly. "Good afternoon, Senator," he said brightly. "By local time, that is. I thought the *Millie* made a very smooth landing, didn't you? You've brought us luck on our maiden voyage."

"I believe I warned you once about trying to manipulate me, did I not, Leary?" said Senator Forbes. Her voice was as harsh as usual, and even louder than the background chorus of the starship's cooling fabric required.

"Yes, Excellency, you did," Daniel said. "The *Millie* is a big ship, Alliance-built and straight from a major rebuild. All those things mean her crew can expect trouble. I pushed her hard on the run to Paton, and then from Paton to Karst. She performed like a fully worked-up thoroughbred."

He coughed to insert the necessary pause. This was tricky, but he had to penetrate Forbes's general anger at the world. Otherwise, sure as the sun rose, that anger would find a way to crucify him in the course of this embassy.

"If you choose to be offended that I consider you a lucky charm, so be it," he said, bowing slightly. "But the *Milton*'s very important to me, Senator, and that *is* how I feel."

Forbes wore her official robes, flowing white with only the thin black hem of a back-bencher. Daniel noticed—because Speaker Leary's son noticed this sort of detail as surely as a naturalist noticed a lizard's breeding coloration—that the robes were new. When Forbes gave up her cabinet post as a result of losing the Speakership struggle, she hadn't simply removed the broad red stripe she'd worn as Minister of Finance.

Forbes's face broke into a grudging smile. "I see why you have the reputation you do with women, Leary," she said. "Well, I suppose I don't mind being treated as a woman occasionally. I trust the aircar is ready?"

The regular establishment of a heavy cruiser included an aircar when the vessel served as a flagship. In the present instance the *Milton* carried two aircars, but one was disassembled and intended as a spare in event of an accident.

"Chief Pasternak loaded it at the front of a G Level hold," Daniel said, nodding agreeably. "The driver's warming it up already."

Daniel didn't know the *Milton* well enough yet to identify the sound of ducted fans running up in a hold just above the waterline, but he'd done an optical check on the compartment as soon as they were settled on the surface. If there was a problem, he wanted to know about it before Forbes asked. Fortunately, there didn't appear to be one.

"The driver will fly it to the dock, where you and your party can board in safety." Daniel paused, coughed, and went on, "Ah, Senator? Will you want members of the ship's company with you?"

"I'll take you, my nephew, and Lady Mundy," Forbes said. "The ones who won't embarrass me, of course. Where is Mundy?"

"Remember where we are, Your Excellency," her effeminate secretary said. "An engine wiper would raise the tone of the Headman's palace, I'm sure."

"I regret that I won't be able to accompany you, Your Excellency," said Adele, seated at the signals console as usual. She was wearing utilities, which meant the senator's mind had completely disregarded her when she glanced about the bridge. "I'm not dressed for visiting."

Almost as an afterthought, she turned and looked up. She met Forbes's startled expression and added, "Duty calls, you'll appreciate."

"Oh, surely!" said the secretary. "Senator Forbes is more important than your grubby little files!"

"Hold your tongue, Platt . . . ," said Forbes. The threat was all the more credible because she didn't raise her voice. "Or I'll have it removed!"

Even senators are afraid of Adele's other employer, Daniel thought. Because it wasn't fear of Admiral Vocaine that drew such an angry response from Forbes.

"I'm ready, Your Excellency," Daniel said calmly, touching the lapel of his 1st class uniform. He was wearing his foreign medals, which tended to be a great deal flashier than those which the RCN awarded. "I'll check with Robinson, who may want to change uniform for a formal occasion."

Under other circumstances Daniel might have objected to both the captain and the first lieutenant leaving the *Milton* at the same time, but in truth the result suited him quite well. Vesey would be in charge. She wasn't a better officer than Robinson, but if the situation went badly wrong—and Daniel didn't have to see the *Merkur* seven slips away to know that it might—Vesey would defer to Adele. Given the fashion in which things were most likely to go wrong, Adele was the proper person to decide countermeasures.

"Oh, Danny's ready," said Forbes with a dismissive wave. "I told him back on Paton that I'd want you all along. Well, it goes without saying, doesn't it?"

It shouldn't have gone without First Lieutenant Robinson saying something to his captain, Daniel thought, but he merely smiled. He touched the commo bead clipped to his left epaulette and said, "Mister Robinson, join Her Excellency and myself in the entry hold, if you will. Break, Ship, the vessel will be under the command of Lieutenant Vesey until Three or I return. Six out."

He nodded to Forbes and went on, "Your Excellency, I'll lead the way if you don't mind. A ship this size is something of a maze, and you don't want to get lost on the way to the entry hold."

Woetjans waited in the corridor just outside the bridge. She'd slung a stocked impeller, but the length

of high-pressure tubing stuck under her belt reflected
her personal taste in weapons.

"Beg your pardon, Cap'n Leary," the bosun said
with what for her was unusual formality. "The car's
rated for twelve, but I figure we can squeeze in eight
of us; and more if the civvies stay here on the *Millie*
till we've checked out the locals, hey?"

She grinned at Hogg and said, "Not you, buddy,"
and then glanced down at Senator Forbes. Beyond
the fact that they were both remarkably unattractive
women, they were a complete contrast.

"And I don't mean you neither, ma'am," Woetjans
said. "You gotta come, I see that, but you'll want folks
around who can get you out of trouble if they have
to, and this poofter—"

The contemptuous thumb she jerked toward Platt
was as brown and gnarled as a briar root.

"—can't cut it."

"Chief," said Daniel sharply, knowing that he wasn't
going to be able to save the situation but trying to
anyway, "this is a friendly embassy to a civilized—"

"Leary, get this *oaf*, this *animal*, out of my sight!"
said Senator Forbes. "I swear if I see her again, I'll
have her dismissed from the service right here on
Karst! Get her out!"

"Woetjans, to the BDC, now!" Daniel said. He
pointed down the A Level corridor. "*Now!*"

"Aye-aye sir!" the bosun said. She turned and set
off for the BDC at a shambling trot. She wasn't used
to running—riggers preferred to shuffle with both
magnetic boots on the surface—but her legs were
long and they took her out of the range of Forbes's
anger before another blast issued.

Woetjans didn't argue, of course: she behaved reflexively the way any chief of rig behaved when the captain bellowed something in that tone.

And Daniel hadn't argued that a senator was out of Woetjans' chain of command and that he as her captain would make any necessary decisions regarding her punishment. Given that Woetjans was simply being zealous in the fashion that had stood the Republic in good stead many times during her service under Daniel, there wasn't going to be any punishment.

Which didn't mean that Daniel was going to baulk the ambassador's quite reasonable irritation. Forbes hadn't been the sort of places Woetjans—and Daniel—had been; just as Woetjans didn't understand that Port Hegemony at present wasn't one of those places.

Forbes glared in fury at the bosun's retreating back. It struck Daniel that it was a bad idea to insult and threaten people who were enthusiastically willing to put themselves between you and danger, even if you didn't feel that their sacrifice would be required. Indeed, that might be one of the more important differences between a man who was still called Speaker Leary, long years after he'd surrendered the post, and a woman who'd risen to a major ministry but was now fleeing her colleagues' derision.

"And Leary?" said Forbes, her eyes still glittering after she shifted them onto Daniel. "That servant of yours isn't going either."

"Your Excellency...," said Hogg, his hands jammed deep in his side pockets. The fact he bothered to get the form of address right showed how worried he was. "Look, I think—"

"I don't want that scruff anywhere near me, do

you *hear*?" Forbes said in a steeply rising inflection. She didn't look at Hogg. "We're here to impress the Headman, not convince him that Cinnabar is a haven for subnormal yokels!"

"I wonder, Senator Forbes?" said Adele, unexpectedly rising from her console. "Would you mind terribly if my servant Tovera joined your party? I'd regard it as a favor."

Tovera got up from one of the pair of jumpseats framing the hatch; the cushion thumped against the bulkhead. She wore a beige business suit. It was clean but utilitarian instead of being a marvel of tailored simplicity like the suits Adele wore now that prize money permitted her to act the part of Mundy of Chatsworth when her duties required it.

Adele made a slight gesture to direct the senator's eyes. Forbes frowned, but puzzlement had replaced the anger of moments before.

"I know which fork to use at dinner, Your Excellency," Tovera said. A spider cajoling a fly to come closer couldn't have sounded more calmly reasonable.

"What an excellent idea!" said Daniel. Not for the first time, Adele had provided a single neat solution to several problems—which in this case included punishing Forbes for her behavior to a Leary's retainers. "Not only will you be helping Lady Mundy in her duties—"

He smiled broadly to emphasize the threat.

"—but Tovera's presence will help morale."

He didn't say whose morale would be improved; in fact, he thought the whole ship's company would breathe a little easier to know that Tovera was going along with Six. He wasn't sure that anybody aboard the *Milton* really liked Adele's servant, but she was universally respected.

Hogg grinned at Forbes. When he chose to—as now—he could manage to look as though his intellect would rise if his brain were replaced by a rutabaga. "I'll tell you, Excellency," he said. "I know which fork to use at dinner too. Only with me, you'd have to worry I'd steal them, you see?"

"Shall we go, Your Excellency?" said Daniel. "I'm sure Mister Robinson is waiting."

He stepped nonchalantly through the hatch. He didn't look behind him until he reached the companionway to see if Forbes and her party were following. They all were.

Tovera was at the end of the line. She grinned when she caught Daniel's eye.

Adele was in her element. She could even have described herself as happy, if the concept hadn't seemed so foreign. She smiled into her display.

The Headman's palace was at Angouleme, in the mountains—well, the chain of moderate hills—twenty miles northeast of Port Hegemony and the commercial city sprawling around the docks. Adele was ready to use the Headman's own apparatus to eavesdrop on the embassy, but at the moment Senator Forbes and her companions were waiting for clearance to land within the palace compound.

There was no lack of things to do for those who remained aboard the *Milton*. Everybody seemed cheerfully busy, rather like the pixies in the fairy tale who bustled to clean a house while its human occupants slept.

Siegel, the armorer, was issuing small arms to some

hundreds of the crew. Inevitably there'd been accidental discharges, but there were no casualties more
serious than burns from where an iridium slug hit a
bulkhead and vaporized both itself and a divot of steel
the size of a pie plate. Well, no serious casualties *yet*.

The forty Marines had their separate arms locker
adjacent to the bridge. Their commander, Major Aran
Mull, was running them through bayonet drill in a bulk
storage hold on G Level, emptied of grain during the
voyage from Cinnabar. Despite how deep in the ship
they were, Adele occasionally heard the attenuated
snarl, "...*to kill! To kill!*" through the open hatches.

She smiled again.

"*Mistress?*" said Midshipman Cory, who must've
been watching. He was at the console siamesed at the
back with hers, but he had a miniature of her face
on his display and speaking through a two-way link.

"I was wondering if there are stories about pixies
who carry out house clearing, Cory," Adele said. "I
was too serious a child to have a really solid ground-
ing in fairy tales, I'm afraid."

Cory's image blinked at her. "Ah—pixies, as little
people who sprinkle stardust, mistress?" he said.

"That sounds like the sort of thing they might do,
yes," she said, smiling minusculely broader. The fact
that she could be whimsical was absolute proof that
she was in a good mood. "But it isn't a serious concern
at present. Go back to your databases."

Headman Terl had been a close ally of the Republic
for many years, so Cinnabar had sold him information-
handling systems as good as those in the major min-
istries of the Republic. If every clerk carried out
proper security precautions, Adele would have found

entering them by brute force to be very difficult and perhaps impossible.

Realistically, not every clerk was properly careful. While at home, Adele had browsed through the databases of finance, foreign affairs, and especially the navy as often for fun as for need. What was true in Xenos became true in spades the farther one got into the hinterlands. Karst was a wealthy, important world; but it was a very long way from Xenos or Pleasaunce.

The situation on Karst was simpler yet, however. Every data console sold to the Hegemony had a back door which allowed someone with the codes to enter it as quickly as the designated operators. Very few people even in Mistress Sand's organization knew of this facility, but Adele was one of them.

Cory went back to the task she had set him, culling data from the Headman's government. There was more than was useful even for cursory perusal, of course, but there was a rule of thumb that Adele had found worked very well when she didn't have a particular object of search: start with the items which were protected at the highest levels of security and, as time permits, work down toward open files.

She trusted Cory—certainly he would never deliberately act to harm either her or the Republic. There was no need for him to know how she'd entered the Hegemony systems, however, so she hadn't told him. She'd established the pathway and then handed it over to the midshipman to exploit.

At the console adjacent to Adele's, Sun was setting up gunnery assignments. Initially he'd prioritized every target which the dorsal plasma cannon could hit while the *Milton* floated in her slip. The first target was the *Merkur*, though a freighter from Valladolid was berthed between the two warships. Sun calculated that three 8-inch bolts at this short range would remove the obstruction, permitting a fourth round to rip the destroyer in half.

A few years ago, Adele would've thought that Sun's calculations were appalling. Now she merely found them interesting...which was also appalling, but only to a civilian. Adele Mundy was no longer a civilian.

Across the bridge from the gunnery console, Borries was choosing missile targets. The word "target" really begged the question, because there was almost no possibility that a missile launched in an atmosphere would hit its aiming point.

High Drive motors inevitably sprayed antimatter into their exhaust. Missiles were intended for use in a vacuum, where that was of no consequence. In a bath of normal matter, however, the mutual annihilation devoured the missile and probably portions of the ship it was launched from. The chief missileer and his striker in the BDC made their calculations anyway, just in case the need justified the cost.

Adele had blocked the audio of most messages, including the command channel. The inevitable chatter appeared as text blocks on the right border of her display. She'd exempted a few officers, though: Vesey and Blantyre, because of long association; Woetjans, because anything the bosun had to say was important; Cory, because he seemed to look on Adele as an elder sister and she didn't choose to treat him with the harshness that would be required to drive him away; and Cazelet, who was her protégé and therefore her responsibility.

This time the call was Woetjans. "*Ma'am?*" the bosun said. "*We're getting the boats ready for an assault, you know? Hogg said we ought to ask if you want a place in one of 'em and which one? There's three, so it'll be Blantyre, Cory, and me doing the piloting, you see? Over.*"

Adele thought, *I really don't imagine that an assault on the heavily defended Angouleme Palace would be useful or, for that matter, survivable.* Aloud she said, "In the event I'll remain with the *Millie* where the communications are better. But thank you for asking, over."

"*Yes ma'am,*" said Woetjans. "*Ah, ma'am? Hogg'll be going, and you know Tovera's already gone to the palace with Six, over?*"

"Thank you," Adele repeated, more sharply than before. "I was responsible for my own safety for many years, Woetjans. I think I remember how to go about it. Signals out."

"*Yes ma'am,*" said Woetjans. "*Sorry ma'am. Rig out.*"

The *Milton* carried three spaceboats equipped with plasma thrusters rather than High Drive. They had neither rigging to sail the Matrix nor the powerful computer that would've been necessary to control such a rig. Their purpose was simply to ferry up to twenty people apiece between orbit and a planetary surface, or in rare instances between ships in sidereal space.

The boats were comfortably appointed as they would often be carrying officers or other dignitaries. They had no integral armament nor any easy way to add weapons, and the single one-person hatch of each was completely unsuited for a combat assault. That wouldn't prevent the Millies, or at least the former Sissies among them, from trying to fly through batteries of antiship missiles and plasma cannon to capture the Headman's palace.

And if worse came to worst, Signals Officer Mundy would be jamming the fire control systems of those missiles and cannon, because the cruiser's complement included spacers and Marines who would be very nearly as useful as she was for a close-in assault. Nobody Adele had met could disrupt an enemy's defensive computers as effectively as she could.

She brushed the pistol in her pocket with the edge of her left hand, then went back to her own business. It wouldn't come to an assault.

Though if it did, Cory and Cazelet might between them manage something useful on the computers. Whereas she very much doubted that anybody else aboard the *Milton* had put as many people down with quick aimed shots as she had.

She'd given Rene Cazelet the task of gathering data from the other ships in Port Hegemony, starting with those under the Hydriote flag. There shouldn't be anything tricky about their security systems, but the nomenclature and shorthand of merchant vessels were quite different from those of the RCN. Cazelet's family—before Guarantor Porra had executed his parents—had run a medium-sized shipping line; Rene had been trained as both a spacer and as a port manager before he had to flee for his life.

If Cory or Cazelet ran into unexpected problems, they'd ask Adele for help. Unless and until that happened, however, she was opening the databases of the AFS *Merkur*, and great clouds of data were tumbling into view.

Like all Alliance—and Cinnabar—warships, the

Merkur had a separate computer for its encryption procedures. This couldn't be entered through the destroyer's communications system, and its storage was probably serving as the diplomatic pouch also. Adele couldn't touch its contents.

She could browse all the *Merkur*'s unsegregated databases, however. One of the ships captured following the Battle of the Jewel System was a light cruiser deadlined at the Alliance base. It had been powered down and its crew had been transferred to active vessels. The ground personnel who surrendered the base to the victorious RCN squadron had forgotten—or hadn't known to begin with—to set off the self-destruction charge in the cruiser's encryption computer. As a result, Mistress Sand's organization had the Fleet's daily code sets for the next three months.

Adele knew that the *Merkur* carried an embassy to Headman Hieronymos. She didn't have the details that the segregated computer would've given her, but those weren't difficult to imagine when she compared the names of the envoys with the up-to-date Fleet personnel list which was part of the kit which Mistress Sand had provided to Adele.

The leader of the delegation was Captain Stewart Greathouse. He was the cousin of Admiral Petersen, the Alliance commander in the Montserrat Stars, and acted as the admiral's aide and confidant.

The other two envoys were the Cohen brothers, Alexander and Melvin. Though Fleet lieutenants, they'd been born on Karst. Twenty years previously they'd been whisked into exile when their grandfather was implicated in a plot against Headman Terl.

Without access to the diplomatic files, Adele could

only speculate about the specifics of Admiral Petersen's embassy. More information was probably available through the Hegemony databases, but Cory was on that; indeed, unless Adele was badly mistaken Daniel and Senator Forbes would very shortly have personal experience of what the Alliance was about. She went back to the destroyer's operational logs.

The *Merkur* had been part of the Alliance fleet operating near New Harmony, the forward base for Admiral Ozawa's RCN forces in the Montserrat Stars. The two fleets were roughly equal, each comprised of four battleships and a comparable number of attendant vessels.

Cinnabar's infrastructure in the cluster, however, was very shaky. Admiral Ozawa had brought his fleet to New Harmony in large measure to keep the government of that important world from declaring neutrality or even switching its support to the Alliance.

At the bottom of Adele's screen, a text crawl read AIRCAR WITH SIX JUST LANDED IN OUTER COURT OF HEADMAN'S PALACE. Adele shifted the visual feeds from Daniel's commo unit and Tovera's case to the upper left quadrant of her display, though she left the audio in record mode for now.

Vesey had sent the alert. It was typical of that tense, thoughtful officer that she chose text rather than voice, providing the information without interrupting whatever task Adele was involved with.

It was one of Vesey's great strengths as an officer that she always thought several steps ahead of any action. It was her personal curse, however, that the options expanding from that foresight tore her apart. She never became too paralyzed to act, but sometimes she didn't act as quickly as a crisis demanded.

Adele returned her attention to the *Merkur*'s log, digging deeper into the operational files. Her mouth suddenly went dry, though she continued to read and excerpt the information that she was uncovering.

There'd been a battle off New Harmony. The log of a destroyer wasn't the best source from which to gain an overview of a major fleet action, but the general thrust of the information was clear enough.

Admiral Petersen had won a stunning victory. All four RCN battleships had been destroyed.

CHAPTER 11

Port Hegemony, Karst

"Ma'am?" said a voice.

Adele was aware of the sound in the same way that she noticed the high-frequency flicker in one bank of the overhead lights. It was a mild irritation at the edge her consciousness, unpleasant but nothing that affected her ability to do her job.

Her job at present was to observe and record events within the audience hall where Headman Hieronymos was receiving the Cinnabar delegation. She'd decided not to alert Daniel to what she'd just learned from the *Merkur*'s log. His little epaulet communicator couldn't handle real encryption, and the risk of the incoming message being intercepted by the locals and/or the Alliance mission outweighed the slight possible gain.

"Ma'am?" the voice repeated.

"Barnes, don't bloody interrupt Officer Mundy when she's busy!" said Cory.

The unwonted snap of anger from the diffident midshipman focused Adele on her present surroundings in a fashion that Barnes' own voice had not. She turned and looked up at the rigger, who stood at parade rest.

Behind Barnes was an uncomfortable-looking man whom Adele didn't recognize. The stranger wore the usual shapeless clothing common to all spacers, whether they were currently in the merchant service or naval, but there was a black armband with two red stripes on his left sleeve. That marked him as an engineer's mate—in the Fleet.

"Ma'am?" said Barnes, his tone changing now that he really had her attention. "This is Doug Triplett. I had the squad guarding the boarding bridge. He come up to us and I called Chief Woetjans. She said I ought to bring him up to you, so that's what I did. He's from the *Merkur*, you see?"

"Yes," said Adele, looking the fellow over. "I did see. You want to desert to us, is that it?"

She wondered if she ought to take the fellow to a private compartment. At this moment, she had to assume he was a spy pretending to desert in order to get inside the *Milton*. Perhaps he'd been sent to target her specifically.

Adele smiled coldly; the self-styled deserter winced. He probably wouldn't have been reassured if he'd realized that she was thinking that it was a good thing that Tovera and Hogg both were absent, because they'd be unhappy if she ordered them not to kill the fellow. And it really shouldn't be necessary to kill him.

"Sir," said Triplett. He stared at his cap as he twisted it in his fingers. Whatever Barnes had told the fellow was enough to have frightened him badly; he wasn't reacting to a junior warrant officer. "Look, I'm from the *Merkur*, sure, but I'm not Alliance. I was born in Xenos—"

"Where in Xenos?" Adele said, deliberately putting him off balance.

"Ma'am, Sydenham Ward, my dad worked for a ship chandler and for a couple years he owned a bar on the Strip," Triplett said. "Ah—I enlisted on the old *Charybdis*, and fifteen years back I deserted. I admit it, I did, but it was because the engineer thought I was seeing too much of his daughter. He'd of killed me, arranged an accident, I know it! So I jumped ship to a Kostroman freighter."

"And later enlisted in the Fleet?" Adele said, her voice as dry as a payroll clerk's. Her eyes were on her display, pretending to be bored by the whole business. She was actually watching an image of Triplett's face, though the hologram was focused only from her viewpoint.

"No sir, really that's not so!" Triplett said. "I was engineer on a customs boat on New Horizon, the *Lyn*, only listed as Kostroman because, you know, I'd deserted. When Admiral Petersen landed and the Alliance took over, all of us with ratings got transferred to the Fleet—being told, not asked."

He made a face as though he'd swallowed something bitter. "The ships're all right, I grant you that," he said. "The *Merkur*'s brand new and a lot roomier than I'd figured for a destroyer, but the crews, they're *crap*! Swept outa the slums half of 'em, not spacers at all. I could see why they grabbed up ratings like they did."

"Woetjans thought that, you know...," said Barnes. "If you said something to Six, ma'am, maybe he could square things about Triplett being a deserter, you know?"

I think I can do a great deal better myself, Adele thought, *by listing him as an intelligence agent. If I choose to do so . . .*

Aloud she said, "What was your name in RCN service, Triplett?"

"Rooksby, sir," the man said. He'd stopped wringing his hat and his expression was one of worshipful pleading. "Paul Alan Rooksby, enlisted in '92 and jumped ship in '95, the night before the *Charybdis* was due to lift from Harbor Three."

Adele already had full personnel records from Navy House up on her display. They weren't classified, exactly, but the *Milton* was probably the only ship in the RCN which had a set of them. If it came to that, Adele was probably the only signals officer in the RCN who was capable of using them to advantage—as now.

ROOKSBY, PAUL ALAN/RUN FROM *CHARYBDIS*/03/02/95

"Sir, I'll take my knocks for running, I did it sure enough," Triplett said desperately toward his cap. "But I won't fight the RCN, I'll die first if that's what it is."

Adele looked up at him directly. He was stocky and muscular; the scars she could see—he was missing the little finger of his left hand—and the black grit worked deep into the skin of his callused hands proved he was a real Power Room technician, not a Fifth Bureau agent pretending to be one.

In theory he could still be a spy, one recruited on the spot by Captain Greathouse. The likelihood that anybody found locally would be so good—Triplett's speech patterns still had touches of Sydenham, the district to the west of Harbor Three—was much slighter than that the man was exactly what he claimed: a deserter who wanted to come home.

And even if Triplett were a spy, he'd be willing to offer real information at this stage to win Adele's trust. She could use some information, so... "You mentioned that the Alliance has taken over New Harmony, Triplett," she said. "How did that come about?"

"Well, ah...," Triplett said. "The way I heard the story—from the engineer of the *Rasp* that was on orbit duty when it all happened, you see?"

"Yes," said Adele. She noticed that the bridge had become crowded. Woetjans and Hogg had arrived from the boat hold, which meant they must have started up the companionways as soon as Barnes had called the bosun to ask about Triplett. Blantyre had entered with the new midshipmen—Else, Barrett, and Fink.

Besides those officers, the A Level corridor was packed with regular crewmen who hadn't dared enter the bridge but who wanted to hear about the disaster in the Montserrat Stars. If there was bad news going around, spacers liked to learn it as soon as possible. It gave them a better chance to get clear.

Rene Cazelet hadn't left the BDC, nor had Cory risen from his seat. Both men were watching the interrogation through the signals console. If Adele for some reason blocked their access, they'd switch to the command console for almost as good a vantage point.

She smiled, faintly but with pleasure. She'd trained them well.

When Adele didn't react further, Triplett smiled shyly. He seemed proud to have an audience. He continued, "Well sir, it was the locals themselves that did it. Not the government, but some of the young men from the old families. The First Blood, they call themselves on New Harmony. The rich folks, pretty much; but not the ones in the government right now."

"Go on," Adele said. She watched the inset of the Angouleme Palace out of the corner of her eye. Nothing seemed to be happening—which itself was important, albeit bad, news. She didn't dare focus on the imagery while listening to Triplett, though, because he'd provide more detail if he thought she was interested.

Which of course she was, though there were suddenly a number of things she was interested in.

"Well, some of them were running privateers," Triplett said, "raiding shipping from Isfahan and Valigursky, Alliance worlds that're close by. It looks now like they were meeting with Petersen and the freighters they were saying were prizes, Petersen was giving them to 'em. To the First Bloods."

"I see," Adele said. She wondered if Petersen had come up with the plan himself. Reports suggested that there was a large contingent of Fifth Bureau personnel operating with his fleet.

"Well, anyhow, every time they came back from a raid—and there was half a dozen ships that went out one time or another," Triplett said, "they stopped by the customs boat before they went down to land. And there was usually something good they brought back for the customs crew, you know? Might be some brandy or, or—"

He looked a little embarrassed. They *had* been the customs service after all.

"Well, you know, something good. And we got used to it, so when a privateer came back in-system and *Rasp* had the duty, they didn't think nothing of it.

They even told the RCN patrol squadron that there'd be a right fine catch of prizes arriving soonest."

"What do you mean by 'the patrol squadron'?" Adele said austerely.

"Ozawa always kept half his ships in orbit," Triplett said. "And they'd trade off. I, well, I didn't get close to the crews when I was off-duty. I, you know, I was afraid somebody'd recognize me even after all those years. I don't mind telling you, I felt sick when a huge bloody RCN fleet showed up on New Harmony and me a deserter. But I kept low and it was all right, at least as long as it went on."

"Go on," said Adele, not giving anything away with her voice.

"So Skeeter, Skeeter Morne, he was engineer of *Rasp*, he says the locals linked a sealed walkway like usual and come across," Triplett said. He was twisting his cap again. "Only this time the packages had guns inside, and when the El-Tee—that was Goldfarb, an old guy and wouldn't say boo to a goose. But he put his hand on the control panel or they thought he was going to and they shot him, just *shot* him, poor old Goldfarb. Shot him dead."

Triplett shook his head. The results of short-range gunfire in weightlessness were beyond the imagination of those who hadn't seen it happen. Blood went everywhere. That was the thing that had most impressed Adele when all her targets were down and she had time to reflect.

"And it wasn't prizes coming in after them," Triplett said, "it was the whole Alliance fleet. But the duty squadron expected prizes, so they weren't so quick off the mark as they might've been. Even so it might've been all right, except when the off-duty squadron started to lift, a harbor defense battery nailed both battleships. With antiship missiles, you know, close enough to spit at. And then it was kitty bar the door."

Somebody out in the corridor cried something obscene about backstabbing wogs. The tone of voice was tearful rather than angry; perhaps the speaker had a friend or relative with Admiral Ozawa.

"Well, the other ships lifting, they got some guns unlimbered quick enough that the First Bloods didn't have time to reload the launchers of the battery they'd captured."

Triplett cleared his throat. "To tell the truth," he went on, his voice a little quieter, "it got pretty hairy around the harbor for a while. It was just the one battery, you see, but the ships didn't know that and they shot up most anything till they was too high to do any good. Even the poor old *Lyn* took one, but it was just four-inch and I'd guess whoever was doing the shooting was half a mile up by then. We could've been back in service in a day or two."

"And the two battleships in orbit?" Adele said. She'd found that listening closely while the subject told his own story was generally the most effective way to get information, but Triplett seemed to be slipping into a reverie on his days in the New Harmony customs service. It had been a comfortable life and must in the spacer's current troubles seem a lost Paradise.

"Yeah, well, when the *Heidegger* and *Hobbes* crashed in the harbor, there wasn't much hope for the ships already aloft," Triplett said, nodding three times in emphasis. "From what Skeeter says, whoever had the patrol squadron told the light ships to run while the *Locke* and the *Aquinas* stayed to fight. Petersen wouldn't worry about cruisers and little stuff while there was battleships launching at him. They lasted long enough for the rest to get away, most of 'em. Even the ones lifting off when it all popped."

His face scrunched into a worried frown. "On the *Merkur* I heard people talking like the survivors ran to Cacique," he said. "But they didn't know, they was just guessing. Petersen didn't chase them, he landed enough ships to put things his way on the ground. And he sent the *Merkur* off to Karst here to tell the new Headman about it. As I guess you figured."

"Yes," said Adele, "I did."

Cacique was the main RCN base in the Montserrat Stars, four or five days' travel from New Harmony. The Alliance spacers might have been guessing, but it was an obvious guess.

Adele considered. She had a great deal of experience in learning unpleasant facts. This was just another sequence of them. She smiled faintly: it was certainly an impressive sequence, though.

"Woetjans," she said, "find a place for Triplett in one of your watches, if you will. When Captain Leary returns, he may make other arrangements."

This wasn't under a signals officer's purview. Adele wasn't acting as a signals officer at the moment.

"Ah, sir?" Triplett said. "I can put my hand to most anything on a ship, sure. But I've got a Power Room rating."

"Yes," said Adele, "and very possibly you'll be transferred to the Power Room at some future point. But not at present."

"Oh!" said Triplett, wilting under her icy smile. A

saboteur in the Power Room could do a great deal of damage if he waited for the right time. "Yessir, sure. I'm not a spy or anything, but sure, I see."

Triplett left the bridge between Woetjans and Barnes. In the corridor, spacers babbled questions about the battle at him.

Vesey rose to her feet at the navigation console. She nodded to Adele, silent acceptance of her disposition of the deserter. "Back to your duties, the rest of you," she ordered sharply.

The order wasn't directed at Adele, but she'd already returned to her proper business. At the moment, that meant watching what was going on in the Angouleme Palace. Her face, already set in its usual firm lines, became a little more grim.

The Angouleme Palace, Karst

Daniel stood at parade rest, looking down the audience hall with a faint, friendly smile. The Headman's court had the gaudy enthusiasm of prism bugs swarming, or perhaps of a peasant wedding. A Cinnabar gentleman didn't take this sort of thing seriously, of course, but it made an amusing display.

"Rise, Chieftains Harry Holland and Dennis Little," said the official standing on the platform of the gilded— or even golden? Adele would know—throne. "Hear the wisdom of His Holy Majesty Headman Hieronymos."

The Enunciator's voice was piped through a public address system with a good deal of distortion. The hall's acoustics weren't impressive, since the pillars and the ceiling coffers muddied the words. Mind, in the present company it would've been a surprise if the setting were any better.

"Chieftain Holland, Chieftain Little!" said Hieronymos. He looked like a child being engulfed by a golden robe and turban, but his voice was clear and as strong as that of his Enunciator. "You may rise to hear my judgment."

The throne was on a three-step platform, gold like most of the hall's other trappings. The Enunciator was immediately below the Headman, while on the wings of the broad bottom stage sat a man and a woman on less ornate, silver-covered, chairs.

The silver-clad woman had a regal, utterly bored, expression. She was young but not, if Daniel was judging correctly, as young as Hieronymos. The plump, middle-aged man wore garments slashed with black and silver stripes. His lips smiled, and his eyes were as cruel as a cat's.

"That arrogant little *worm*," hissed Senator Forbes, who stood between Daniel and Lieutenant Commander Robinson at the back of the hall. "If he goes on like this, he may find himself the first man in three hundred years that the Republic has flayed and stuffed with straw!"

The two petitioners—Daniel didn't know what the term "Chieftain" implied, and it wouldn't be practical to ask Adele at present—had been kneeling beneath the throne, both hands on top of their lowered heads. Now they rose to their feet.

They were wearing what looked like military uniforms, but so was almost everyone else in the audience hall. Given the variety of styles and bright colors, always complemented by metallic braid, this must be civilian fashion on Karst: the Hegemony couldn't possibly have that many different military organizations.

Daniel hoped the locals standing nearby hadn't heard the ambassador's whispered reference to the execution of the Burghers of Rainham, or anyway hadn't heard it clearly. Not that there wasn't justification for her anger: when the Cinnabar delegation entered the hall, an usher had barred their way forward with his gilded staff.

Daniel's smile spread a little wider. For a moment, he'd thought Forbes was going to feed the usher his staff by the back way. After that, well, Dress Whites weren't ideal for a fight and Hogg wasn't present to watch the young master's back, but Tovera out in the anteroom would no doubt prove useful if the need arose.

The need wouldn't arise. Forbes might be harshly insulting, but she wouldn't have risen to prominence in the Senate if she'd been in the habit of brawling with servants.

"Chieftain Holland, you entrusted three thousand tonnes of dried fish to Chieftain Little," the Headman said, his tone as portentous as that of a man speaking of the world's coming doom. "Chieftain Little, you shipped the fish to Cameron on a vessel owned by your brother-in-law in accordance with your undertaking to dispose of the fish at your sole cost and expense, with half the profit to accrue to you. The ship never reached Cameron."

The chieftains were bobbing their heads in agreement. Little wore a bright green outfit with gold braid on the seams and a fourragere; Holland's jacket was black, but his kepi and trousers were puce and he had just as much gold ornamentation as his rival. The hall more reminded Daniel of an ill-arranged garden than it did a real courtroom.

"He's holding us up to discuss *fish*," Forbes hissed. But of course he wasn't: Hieronymos—or the grinning shark below him—kept the Cinnabar delegates waiting to demonstrate his contempt. He probably thought he was demonstrating power as well, but an RCN officer knew that real power wasn't a matter of words and precedence.

"After consultation with my learned advisors . . . ," the Headman said. The plump scoundrel below the throne smirked to the audience. "I have decided that because Chieftain Little didn't sell the fish, he has failed in his contract. Chieftain Little must pay the full Karst value of the fish to Chieftain Holland."

"This is unjust!" Little cried, raising his fists skyward in a theatrical gesture. He didn't sound *really* upset, however. It seemed likely enough that he and his brother-in-law knew more about where the cargo had gone than appeared in the official report. "May the Gods justify me!"

"In addition," Hieronymos said, "Chieftain Little forfeits the profit expected had the shipment been sold on Cameron as a fine to the Hegemony, as represented by my august person. The audience is hereby at an end."

"What?" said Little. "This is criminal! Scully, you took my money, you slimy bastard!"

Little lunged toward the greasy courtier. Four attendants converged on him; they wore cloth-of-gold tabards, but their electromotive carbines were quite functional. They tripped the disgruntled chieftain, then beat him silent with their gun butts before dragging him out. The woman in silver turned her expressionless face to follow the bleeding victim.

It's always a mistake to underbribe an official, Daniel thought. He continued to smile, but what he'd just seen reminded him of maggots fighting in offal.

Hieronymos murmured in the ear of his Enunciator, who straightened and boomed, "His Holy Majesty Headman Hieronymos will now hear the worshipful envoys of the Republic of Cinnabar!"

Senator Forbes strode forward, her arms crossed before her. The usher hopped out of her way a little more quickly than perhaps he'd intended to; that saved his shins a knock from the thick sole of the buskin which, worn beneath Forbes's formal robes, added three inches to her modest height.

Daniel and Lieutenant Robinson stepped off to the senator's right and left, keeping a pace behind her out of courtesy. Besides, to catch up they'd have to run, which would still further increase the affair's resemblance to farce.

Daniel had never been good at formal drill, but fortunately Robinson was. By matching his step to his First Lieutenant's thirty-inch strides, they were able to look professional, though the senator drew noticeably ahead along the fifty yards of aisle to the base of the throne. There she waited, her arms still crossed, while the RCN officers completed the necessary three further paces to flank her again.

"Headman Hieronymos!" Forbes said. "Your grandfather came down from his seat to meet the representatives of Cinnabar, as befits all who wish to retain the Republic's good will."

Her voice wasn't being amplified. The officials in front of her would have no difficulty understanding, but the audience in general was going to find her address a muddy hash. Knowing that probably made Forbes's tone even more raspingly angry than usual.

"A great deal has changed since Headman Terl's day," said the official in black and silver. "Terl was an old man, perhaps too old to properly hold such a responsible position long before he passed."

Forbes turned slightly toward the official, then back to Hieronymos with the precision of a lathe making a cut. "I am here on behalf of my government," she said, "to speak of the Headman of the Hegemony. Not with some fat flunky!"

Hieronymos continued to look straight ahead. The Enunciator, obviously briefed for this ahead of time, said, "His Holy Majesty Headman Hieronymos chooses to speak through the person of his trusted councillor, Chieftain of Chieftains Scully."

"His Holy Majesty Headman Hieronymos conveys his deepest sympathy to you, Mistress Forbes," Scully said. If his voice were any smoother, there'd have been oil dripping from the corners of his mouth. "He knows that the complete destruction of your republic's forces in the Montserrat Stars is a tragedy rarely if ever equalled since time immemorial. How your hearts must ache! How your cities will grieve, while your enemies rejoice!"

Daniel felt a sudden hot buzzing under his skin as though he were about to faint. *They wouldn't say that if there weren't something behind it.*

Forbes had no such concerns. "Where did you hear this arrant twaddle?" she demanded. Her eyes were riveted on the Headman. "Has your dog here taken leave of his senses, boy?"

"I take no offense, Mistress . . . ," said Scully. Despite the easy words, his smirk looked somewhat the worse for wear. "Since I realize you're ignorant rather than merely boorish. Captain Greathouse, will you and your colleagues come forward and inform these poor folk from Cinnabar?"

Three men in bright green and gold stepped from a doorway concealed behind the throne. Any one of them would've fit in with the crowd of courtiers in the body of the hall, but three together meant they were *in uniform*; specifically, the dress uniform of officers in the Alliance Fleet.

"Captain Stewart Greathouse," said Scully, still grinning at Forbes but gesturing toward the Alliance officers with his right hand. "And his aides, the Lieutenants Chieftain Melvin and Alexander Cohen."

Greathouse was well over six feet tall and built in proportion to his height. Though bulky, he moved as smoothly as a fighting bull. There was a long purple scar on his right cheek. It continued to the point of his chin, whitening a wedge of his otherwise-black beard. His eyes glanced across Robinson and Forbes, but they lingered for a time on Daniel Leary.

The slender, blond, Cohen brothers had girlishly pretty features. They were in their mid-twenties, but if the lighting were helpful they could pass for teenagers. They gave the Cinnabar contingent practiced sneers as they followed Captain Greathouse to the front of the throne. All three fell forward, abasing themselves as abjectly as the Hegemony citizens had done earlier.

"Rise, my brothers from the Alliance!" said the

Headman, speaking for himself. "Inform these visitors of how you crushed your enemies in the Montserrat Stars."

Greathouse rose with the ponderous grace of a starship lifting. He bowed low to Hieronymos, then turned to face the Cinnabar envoys. His eyes were on Daniel, not on Senator Forbes.

"Gladly, Your Holy Majesty," Greathouse said. Directional microphones picked up and amplified his voice, but that thunderous bass could've filled the hall without support. "The enemy was in force on the world of New Harmony. My friend and superior Admiral Petersen isn't the sort to dally. He gathered his forces and struck for the enemy's heart."

"We ground them to dust!" cried one of the Cohens. The operator of the parabolic mike picked him up in mid-phrase. "When a battleship explodes, it looks like a star, and there were four of the Cinnabar rascals exploding together. It was like the Feast of the Guarantor's Birthday on Pleasaunce!"

"Yes," said Greathouse, still watching Daniel. He wasn't gloating, but made his delivery all the more believable. "We caught the *Locke* and *Aquinas* in orbit and crushed them. The *Heidegger* and *Hobbes* tried to join the action, but they were still climbing out of the gravity well when we destroyed them. They fell into the harbor."

Greathouse shrugged. "A few of the smaller RCN ships got away," he went on, "but that's temporary; we're chasing them down now. And of course those few worlds of the cluster who hadn't already joined the Alliance did so since the victory."

That could be a complete fabrication, Daniel thought, *but the Veil is too close to the Montserrat Stars*

*for deception to last more than a few days. Unless
Petersen has a very short-term objective, the story is
basically true.*

"Well, Captain Leary?" jeered the boy on the throne.
"What do you have to say to *that*?"

"I have nothing to say to that, Your Majesty," Daniel
said. His words weren't being miked. Well, he hadn't
thought they would be.

He turned very deliberately to face the belly of
the hall. Hieronymos and his flunkies would still be
able to hear him; and if they thought they were being
insulted, so much the better.

"I am an officer of the Republic of Cinnabar Navy!"
he boomed. He'd learned to project his voice while
calling to shore from a small boat off the coast of
Bantry. He might not sound as honey-smooth as a
practiced orator, but by thunder! they'd hear him at
the back of the hall. "We're not in the habit of getting
our facts from officers of the Alliance, whom we've
defeated so many times in the past!"

"Come along, men!" Senator Forbes said. She
turned on her heel, crisply but with more vehemence
than an Academy drill instructor would've approved.
"This is no place for Cinnabar nobles who value their
reputations."

This certainly didn't work out well, Daniel thought
as they strode along. That was nothing new to a spacer,
of course. When he was outside the audience chamber,
he'd be able to start serious planning; which left the
problem of getting outside, of course.

The central aisle had seemed long when he and
Robinson followed the senator down to the throne.
It seemed a great deal longer in the other direction

with Daniel's shoulders prickling against the possibility of a shot.

Or perhaps rotten fruit. That would be even more embarrassing, though more survivable as well. He didn't suppose the Headman's petitioners attended his levees with rotten fruit, though, or that they were permitted to attend with guns. There was still a risk that Hieronymos would order his guards to shoot the Cinnabar envoys, but that was unlikely even for an arrogant, rather stupid, boy.

Daniel grinned. The usher who'd barred their way to the throne watched them from the doorway. When he saw Daniel's cheerful expression, he backed aside in growing horror.

Daniel threw the double doors open for his companions. Still smiling, he tossed the usher a salute as they went out. Generally his salutes looked as though he were trying to learn fly-fishing, but this time it was uncommonly sharp.

The soldiers, some of them probably guards, in the antechamber were just as bored and relaxed as they'd been when the Cinnabar contingent arrived. They and the civilians—aides, courtiers, and loungers who could afford good enough clothes to enter the palace—watched the envoys leave with the same mild interest that they'd have given dogs walking across the room, and a good deal less than if the dogs had been mating instead. Tovera was almost invisible among the gaily colored rabble.

"A communicator!" Daniel said, holding out his right palm. Tovera tossed him the standard RCN unit she held ready, then put her hand back inside the attaché case as she fell in behind the envoys.

They crossed the antechamber. "Signals, this is Six," Daniel said. He was taking some risk in speaking before they were at least out of the building, but he very much doubted that anybody on Karst would be able to crash whatever encryption Adele and her servant were using. "I need any information you've gotten on recent events in the Montserrat Stars, over."

"Captain, this is intolerable!" Senator Forbes said in her buzz-saw voice. "We'll return to Xenos immediately and—"

To Daniel's utter amazement, Mister Robinson touched the tips of his left index and middle fingers to the senator's mouth. "Aunt Bev," he said, "Captain Leary needs to concentrate on the safety of the mission right now."

As they exited to the courtyard where the aircar waited, Adele began recounting the disaster at New Harmony with her usual frigid calm.

CHAPTER 12

Hegemony Harbor on Karst

Daniel hadn't changed out of his Whites when he reached the *Milton*. There'd have been time and his Grays were technically sufficient as well as being more comfortable and practical, but it was just possible that the greater formality would help when he met the Hydriotes shortly.

"Captain Leary!" said Senator Forbes, storming past the Marines at the bridge hatchway. They didn't so much admit her as ignore her presence the way they did air flowing through the ship's environmental system. "Instead of dealing with this insult to the Republic, you've given the crew liberty! I want you to take me back to Cinnabar at once. At once, do you hear?"

"Your Excellency," Daniel said, rising politely from the command console. Forbes *had* changed in her compartment; Senatorial robes and the buskins she wore with them were impossible in the tight confines of a warship.

Robinson—still in his 1st class uniform—had followed the senator with tight lips and a worried grimace. The

poor fellow was between a rock and a hard place: sure
he would offend either his great-aunt or his captain.
He'd demonstrated in the Angouleme Palace that he was
an RCN officer first, but he wouldn't have any better
idea of Daniel's plans than the senator did. And certainly
if you didn't know where those plans were going, the
first stage—calling Vesey from the aircar and telling her
to give the starboard watch three hours' liberty—must
look so perverse as to be insane if it weren't instead
treasonous.

Daniel glanced around him. Rather than key the
intercom, he raised his voice and said, "Clear the
bridge! Only Senator Forbes and Officer Mundy are
to remain. Move it, spacers!"

The RCN personnel, Robinson included, reacted
immediately. Borries looked as though he might have
said something, but Vesey gripped him firmly by the
shoulder as she went past and turned him toward
the hatch.

"What's this?" said Forbes, startled but no longer
evidently furious.

Rather than answer her, Daniel said in a much
harsher tone, "Hogg, that means you and Tovera too.
Out, and close the hatch behind you."

Hogg shrugged and obeyed. Tovera gave Daniel a
sardonic grin as she followed, or anyway he thought
she did. *It's generally a mistake to anthropomorphize
the behavior of reptiles, though*. Regardless, Hogg
closed the hatch as directed.

"Your Excellency," Daniel said, "this is between the
three of us as Cinnabar citizens. I apologize in advance
for any seeming discourtesy. If I didn't respect you,
you wouldn't be here."

Adele had rotated the seat of her console so that she faced him and Forbes in the center of the compartment. Her eyes were on the display of the little data unit in her lap, however.

"Leary," said the senator, "I know your reputation. If you try to manipulate me, I'll make it my life's work to have you executed by Bill of Attainder. Even if I have to wait for your father's death to do it!"

"Yes, ma'am," said Daniel. He smiled faintly. "With that understood, I'll proceed with the briefing."

Forbes's threat was a warning. Corder Leary wasn't the sort to wait for an enemy to do something overt. Nor was Hogg, which was the main reason Daniel had sent his servant off the bridge.

"We're still taking on supplies," Daniel explained. He thought of suggesting that they both sit down like Adele, but this wasn't quite the time. "We could lift without them, but that would look like panic—and we'd be short of fresh fruits and vegetables for the voyage home."

He gestured to the astrogation display on the console behind him. "Waiting to complete loading will only take six hours," he said, "and I'll venture to shave six hours off *any* other astrogator's time to Cinnabar orbit. Giving the crew a short liberty demonstrates to the wogs—"

He chose the slur carefully.

"—and particularly to Captain Greathouse that the RCN is conducting business as usual despite the disaster on New Harmony. The delay isn't significant."

"Yes," said Forbes, frowning. "What *is* the story on that? Do you suppose there's any truth in what they were saying?"

"It's more or less true," said Adele without looking up. Her wands danced as she frowned at the holographic data forming in front of her. "The battleships, a cruiser, and a number of destroyers were destroyed or captured in harbor. The remainder of Ozawa's ships fled to Cacique, where Petersen is blockading them."

"By the *Gods*, Leary," Forbes said. She looked as though she'd been punched in the stomach. "What... what does this mean?"

Daniel gestured her to the navigation console and sat down on his own couch. When Forbes was settled, he said, "The bulk of Petersen's fleet, three battleships and attendant screens, proceeded from New Harmony to the Cacique system after the battle. Their plan is to set up a base on the larger moon and reduce the Cinnabar defenses. You'll appreciate—"

He nodded toward Adele.

"—that Lady Mundy has gained this information through methods outside the normal RCN procedures."

"Yes, Leary, yes," said Forbes. "I'm not in the habit of blurting inside knowledge to amaze strangers at dinner parties. But we have to get this information back to Xenos! There's nothing we can do about it by ourselves, surely?"

"I'm coming to that, Senator," Daniel said. "There has to be a warning sent back to Xenos, of course, but we don't have to carry it ourselves. The *Milton* is a powerful vessel, and the three of us on this bridge are—"

When he smiled, he realized how stiff his face had been. His cheeks felt like cardboard, crinkling.

"—in our different ways, important assets of the

Republic also. We're very close to the Montserrat Stars. If the Alliance is allowed to consolidate its victory, it'll require a fleet much larger than Admiral Ozawa's to dislodge them; and the RCN doesn't have those ships. If we three are willing to take risks..."

Daniel lifted an eyebrow toward Forbes. She glared at him and said, "Leary, I warned you. Just *say* it. I still don't see what this cruiser can do against a fleet with three battleships—or even the other battleship, wherever it's gone off to."

"The remaining Alliance squadron is reducing Ponape," Daniel said, shrugging. "Ponape isn't a Cinnabar ally, but it's trying to remain independent and has some naval forces."

He looked toward Adele and nodded to direct Forbes's attention to her. "Lady Mundy," he said. "Please describe the situation on Bolton to the senator."

"Bolton?" said Forbes. "What's Bolton? Where's Bolton, that is?"

"Bolton has for sixty years been the Alliance capital in the Montserrat Stars," Adele said calmly. Daniel doubted that Forbes would hear her irritation at being asked a silly question. There was no particular reason the senator should know about Alliance sector capitals, of course. "It's the cluster's main Fleet base. There are no warships stationed there, however, and the regular garrison is small."

She looked up from her display, a blur of light to any eyes but her own. "Many Alliance military retirees live on Bolton," she said, "but the weapons that would be issued to them if they were reactivated are under guard in the military reservation. The only troops presently under arms are a regular battalion of about five hundred."

"But this is a Fleet base?" Forbes said. "Surely it's defended?"

She touched the console she sat at, obviously for a moment considering bringing it live. A senator wouldn't carry a data unit herself, but her secretary would normally be at her side with one available. Daniel was coming to respect Senator Forbes...and he suspected his father respected her also.

"There's an extensive planetary defense array," Adele said, lowering her eyes to her display again. Her wands danced. "A minefield. I can't disarm it except from its control room in the citadel."

"What?" said Forbes. She was using that word and tone a great deal this afternoon. "*Is* it possible to switch off PDAs? Why, Cinnabar isn't safe if that's true!"

"I said it *wasn't* possible to disarm this array," Adele said with a waspish buzz. "But it's an older system and out of date. I may be able to adjust its coverage patterns from outside the controlled zone."

"While we were returning from the Angouleme Palace," Daniel said, leaning toward the senator, "I discussed the details of the situation with Lady Mundy. The individual warheads of a PDA can move. They have to be able to in order to close gaps swept in their coverage. Lady Mundy believes she can shift the mines outward from an axis wide enough to allow a ship to pass through without triggering any of them."

"It sounds," said Forbes deliberately, her eyes holding Daniel's, "insanely dangerous."

He shrugged and smiled. "I have more experience of Lady Mundy's skill than you do, Senator," he said.

"But if you'll look at the record of ships which I've commanded, I think you'll see that I have reason for my confidence."

"You'll also see," said Adele unexpectedly, "that the fact that a plan is insanely dangerous has never deterred Captain Leary in the past. But we expect to take risks on the Republic's behalf, since we're RCN."

Daniel didn't know how to read Adele's expression. It was cold, certainly, but it was always cold in his experience. There was real emotion underlying the analytical glare, though. It reminded him that her father, like his and like the woman here on the bridge with them, had been a senator. Was she judging the whole structure of the Republic when she spoke to Forbes?

"And I'm not, you mean?" said Forbes. She laughed, cackled anyway. "Well, I think you'd find agreement among my colleagues that I'm at least as expendable as you are, Captain Leary. And I'm quite sure—"

She looked at Adele. For a moment, the women's expressions mirrored one another.

"—that Mistress Sand would shed fewer tears for me than she would for Lady Mundy. So, Captain . . ."

Her eyes switched back to Daniel.

"What is it you need from me?"

"We need troops," Daniel said. Forbes had demanded that he be direct, but he was pleasantly surprised to learn that she really could accept directness without becoming angry or defensive. "How close are you to William Beckford?"

Forbes grimaced. "Not good enough friends that he'd give me soldiers," she said. "Besides, Captain, I don't believe that he *has* soldiers in any number. Yes, I know he's skirted the edge of legality a time or two, but I assure you that Prince Willie is the last man I know who'd try to overthrow the Republic by force. He's interested in his pleasures and in the businesses which bring in money to pay for those pleasures. That's all."

"That's not precisely what I had in mind," Daniel said. "To phrase it differently, would you object to the Republic getting troops from Master Beckford without his prior agreement?"

Forbes frowned and pursed her lips. "No," she said. "No, I don't suppose I would. Not in the present need. If there were any."

"Then," said Daniel, rising with a smile, "the next step is for the three of us to go to the Hydriote Traders' Guild here in Hegemony City, where you'll represent the Republic. I'll run over the points of the proposition while we're on route."

Adele rose also, shutting down her personal data unit. "I've called ahead," she said. "Captain Gambardella is the senior official present, and he wasn't at all happy about entering discussions with us. But he couldn't—"

Adele smiled. A pistol shot would've been warmer and held more humor.

"—refuse to meet with a senator of your stature, Mistress Forbes."

For a moment, the senator's face was as hard as Adele's. It softened suddenly and she said, "Then it's fortunate that I decided to throw in with Captain Leary, isn't it?"

As Forbes stepped toward the hatch, she went on, "Captain, tell me about this proposition."

❖   ❖   ❖

Adele preferred imagery to looking at things directly, but the best view she'd been able to find of the Hydriote Traders' Guild was a slant shot which the *Milton*'s sensors had captured as they landed in Port Hegemony. The buildings across the relatively narrow street were of three and four stories, so even with computerized manipulation there was more conjecture than reality in the scene.

Tovera drove the amphibious truck with fussy precision. She was probably a better choice than Hogg, who'd learned his enthusiastic driving style on a rural estate, but she'd scraped a number of bollards at intersections and knocked over a barrow of citrus fruit by cornering short on the twisting streets of the old city.

Daniel bent close to be heard over the truck's air-cooled diesel. "I'd have tossed the barrow boy a florin," he said, "but I don't have pockets in my Whites, and Hogg isn't here with my purse. Still, I think we've arrived."

"Yes," said Adele, staring at the facade of the Guild offices with considerable irritation. Three layers of large, gray-brown ashlars formed the foundation; the slant image hadn't gone that deep and therefore the building she'd studied was radically different from the one in front of her. She'd failed to get an accurate picture of the structure.

The ornate door with a fanlight above it was correct, though: her software had extrapolated the pilaster bases from the scrolled pediment. She smiled wryly, realizing that she was playing a game with herself and making up the scoring rules to suit her ego.

"Adele?" said Daniel, who was perhaps the only person alive who could read her facial expressions.

"I was noticing evidence that I'm human," she said. She paused, then added, "I suppose it's unfortunate that I see humanity primarily in my failings."

Daniel smiled, but she wasn't sure what that really meant.

Tovera pulled up on the shallow plaza in front of the Guild offices, ignoring the middle-aged woman wearing a severely cut dark blue tunic and trousers. The uniformed woman leaped back but rapped the vehicle's left front fender loudly with her cudgel.

Daniel swung open the rear door on his side and banged the folding steps down. "I think you'd better slide across the seat, Your Excellency," he said to the senator, who was in back with him. There was room for three on the bench, but Adele had chosen to ride with the driver. "I'm afraid that the RCN's version of ground transport is even farther from luxury than the aircar we took to the palace this morning."

The parking warden—or whatever she was—stood on the truck's running board to shout at Tovera. Gripping the door with the hand that held her cudgel, she reached inside to fumble for the lock.

"Leave," said Tovera calmly. "Or I'll injure you."

Nothing could have been more clear than the request, but Adele knew from experience that people heard tones, not the actual words. Tovera could've been mumbling about the weather for all the effect it would have on the angry warden.

"Give her a coin," Adele snapped, because Tovera knew perfectly well that the woman wasn't listening. "Give her a florin. And don't shoot her!"

Very few people—probably nobody in hearing except for Adele herself—would consider Tovera to be correct if she shot someone because they were being noisily discourteous. Adele assumed the majority was right, though she didn't pretend she really felt that way.

"Benazir!" called the man who'd come out the door of the Guild offices. "Leave the car alone. These are the visitors who've come to have lunch with me. It's all right for them to park in front of the building."

The warden glowered but dropped down from the vehicle. Adele waited to make sure the silly person had really obeyed. Early in their relationship Adele had directed her servant not to kill anyone without orders. Tovera had accepted the spirit of the command, though both of them realized that situations could arise unexpectedly.

Here there'd have been no need to kill the warden. If she'd pursued her threats, however, Tovera might easily have shot her through both wrists; and that wouldn't have eased negotiations with her employers.

"Captain, ladies," said the man who'd come out of the building. He wore a red sash and covered his head with a golden bandanna. He gestured. "I am Matthew Gambardella, whom you talked to, Lady Mundy. There's a restaurant just across the square, the Four Pipers, and we will eat there."

"I don't need a meal," Senator Forbes said, a frown in her voice. "I'm not in a mood at all for eating, to be frank. Let's go inside and talk business, if you will."

"But I will not," said Gambardella. He was a short, plump man. He had waxed moustaches and was probably bald beneath the bandanna. "Come along. We will have Karst specialties, and perhaps we will find congenial souls with whom to chat on various subjects over our meals."

"Ah," said Forbes. "Yes, when on Pleasaunce, do as Pleasaunce does."

She started across the cobblestoned square between Gambardella and Daniel. Adele hesitated a moment, then understood; she followed a few paces behind the others.

Gambardella had to do business in the Hegemony. He was therefore making sure that this meeting with the Cinnabar representatives was unofficial . . . but of course he wasn't saying that, which would negate the whole purpose of the deceit. Deceit was often necessary to smooth human interactions, whether or not the Adele Mundys of the world liked the fact.

Captain Gambardella's presence cleared a path across the crowded square, but Adele was far enough behind her companions that the hole closed behind them. That was no real difficulty; she slid past bigger, hurrying locals, adjusting her stride and course but mostly keeping her hard eyes open and letting others avoid her.

Adele felt a smile at past memories, though the expression didn't reach her lips. She'd walked alone through city streets for many years before she met Daniel Leary. Most people wouldn't guess what her left hand held in her pocket, but her clear stare discouraged others from treating her with the contempt that a lightly built woman might otherwise have received.

The restaurant had the ground-level corner of a modern building. Its facade of green-painted wood transoms framed large windows which were plastered with advertising bills. Instead of leading Daniel and the senator inside, Captain Gambardella gestured them through a wicket in the waist-high palings enclosing an open-air dining area. Three huge pillars marked the corners of the plaza, separating it from the modern square. They were the same kind of stones as the foundation of the Guild offices.

Adele reached for the data unit in her thigh pocket, but she didn't take it out yet; better to wait until she was seated. Gambardella nodded to a waiter, who lifted the wicket to admit her.

The round tables were large enough for six; one had eight locals squeezed around it, drinking clear liquor in four-ounce stemware and arguing loudly about politics. Two men—a sharp thirty-year-old with a goatee and one who looked like a skeletal mummy—rose from the table Gambardella indicated. They too wore the sashes of Hydriote captains.

"We'll have fricasseed macaca, Miguel," Gambardella said to a hovering waiter. "And raki all round."

To Senator Forbes he added as the waiter shuffled away, "The specialty of the house and a local delicacy. You'll like them, I'm sure."

Adele sat on a three-legged stool. While the others murmured greetings she brought her data unit live, ignoring the surprised looks of the Hydriotes and the scowl she drew from Senator Forbes. First things first, and here proprieties could wait on information.

"These are my friends Captains Christopher Weber and Thor Christianson—"

The goateed man and the walking cadaver, respectively.

"—whom I'm glad we've chanced upon this afternoon," Gambardella said. "Good conversation makes a meal more tasty, I've always found."

A boy came with four-ounce glasses of clear spirit. Adele ignored hers and got to work. She'd used distilled alcohol to purify water often in her life, but she had neither a taste nor the head for it.

Mistress Sand's files on Hydriote hierarchy weren't as complete or up-to-date as those on members of the Alliance bureaucracy, but Adele had already identified Captain Gambardella as the head of one of the Fifteen Families of Hydra. He was a shipper in the same sense that Senator Forbes was a Cinnabar politician.

Weber and Christianson commanded two of the dozen Hydriote ships in the harbor, but each was a member of a leading Family. The trio couldn't speak for Hydra, exactly, but its members were important enough to carry the Cinnabar position in the House of Families if they were themselves convinced.

"Did you have a good voyage from Paton, Captain Leary?" Weber asked.

"We had a topmast bend the first time it carried sail," Daniel said. "It was from stores and I suspect had been taken from a ship that was being broken up. It was the only one, so it wasn't a serious problem."

Adele looked up. Daniel was deferring to the senator, and the senator was waiting for a suitable moment. In Adele's opinion, the present moment was the most suitable.

"This area...," Adele said. She swung her head side to side, because she held the data unit's controls in both hands. "This plaza, was the forecourt of a Terran sector headquarters before the Hiatus. These pillars—"

Nodding again.

"—are well over two thousand years old."

"That's right," said Gambardella with a quizzical expression. "The foundations of our offices are made from the stones from the headquarters as well."

He coughed. "You're a historian, Lady Mundy?" he said.

"An antiquarian," Adele said primly. "And Captain Leary as a naturalist might be interested to learn that the coin-like buttons that compose the limestone are the skeletons of plankton from fifty million standard years ago. But neither of those things is the reason we're meeting here. Senator?"

Forbes looked at her with a flash of anger; it subsided into a smile of respect, albeit grudging respect. Returning her attention to the Hydriotes she said, "Lady Mundy is of course correct. Gentlemen, we wish to arrange for the transport of approximately five thousand workers. They can travel in spartan conditions, though they should be better treated than the cargoes of slave ships. Not that Hydriotes would be engaged in slaving, of course."

"Over what distance?" Christianson said, staring into his open palm. It was empty.

Forbes glanced at Daniel. He nodded and said, "I would ordinarily say twelve days for a merchantman, but you're Hydriotes. Perhaps you can make the run in ten."

He raised an eyebrow in question. "Am I able to speak in confidence?" he said.

"Yes," said Gambardella. He didn't have to consult his fellows. "Anything said at this table is in confidence."

"Good," said Daniel, bobbing his head twice in understanding. "Captains," he said, "we wish to transport laborers from Fonthill to Bolton."

The waiter arrived with three flat bowls along each arm and a round of bread on his head; his right hand clutched six spoons. He bent over the table.

"A moment," Gambardella said. "And you visitors should note that the edge of the utensil is sharpened on the back side. If you're left-handed, it behooves you to be extremely careful."

The waiter shuffled the bowls off his right arm with his left hand, serving the Hydriotes, then dropped the spoons on the table and cleared his left arm with his right hand. Finally he straightened and laid the loaf in the center of the table without either a plate or a napkin beneath it.

"Enjoy!" he said. He sauntered toward the couple rising from a table across the plaza.

"You would provide us with the coordinates of Fonthill?" Weber said. His expression hadn't changed in any way Adele could identify, but she was suddenly struck by his resemblance to a fox. "For you see, we understood these coordinates were a closely held secret."

"We'll supply the coordinates, yes," Daniel said.

Adele's wands twitched. She said, "Captain Christianson, you've been recording this conversation on the data unit in your left breast pocket. I've just transmitted those coordinates to you, so that you can distribute them to the other ships of the argosy which will be required for transport."

It was probable that all the ships which the Hydriotes picked for the operation would have made the journey to Fonthill in the past, under contract to Master Beckford. These men wouldn't have admitted their knowledge, however, if the Cinnabar envoys hadn't proved they already had the information.

"This is very interesting," said Gambardella, speaking with what was probably unexpected honesty. "But I'm very sorry, Senator. We of Hydra cannot be parties to an act of war."

"Let alone an invasion!" said Weber, his moustaches twitching. "Do you think we're unaware of Bolton's defenses?"

Adele looked at the contents of her bowl: six caterpillars, corpse-white with brown splotches, in gravy. Each worm was the thickness of Daniel's thumb. They were, at least, dead.

"This is simply a transportation contact between ports controlled by the RCN," Daniel argued. "Of course we wouldn't ask you to land on Bolton if it were in Alliance hands."

Adele locked her display and put the control wands in their carrying slots, though she didn't shut down the data unit on her lap. Following Captain Christianson's lead, she cut the end off a worm with the back of her spoon, then scooped it to her mouth. The gravy was tangy, with a hint of peppers and sage.

"I find it hard to believe that your Republic's navy will capture Bolton, at least during the lifetimes of us at the table here," Gambardella said. "I thought that even last week. Yesterday, my cousin brought his ship from New Harmony, saying that the Alliance had captured the planet after destroying the Cinnabar fleet in the cluster."

"Nonetheless, it's true," said Senator Forbes. She was forceful and sounded more certain than she had in recent discussions with Adele and Daniel. "All you're being asked to do is to land five thousand unarmed laborers to Bolton. There's no question of being involved in an invasion."

"We're here, gentlemen," Daniel said, "because

of our respect for the skill and integrity of Hydriote merchants. I would hope that you in turn hold our Republic and the RCN in what I believe should be deserved respect. Bolton will be ours before your vessels land."

Adele munched her way through the first worm and started on the second. Neither Daniel nor the senator were eating. In Daniel's case it may have been solely because he was focused on the negotiations. From Forbes's expression when she'd looked into her bowl, her lack of appetite was for other reasons.

Weber glowered; Christianson ate while watching Adele in puzzlement as she also ate. Gambardella said, "You're a very surprising man, Captain Leary. You're all very surprising."

Gambardella's gaze wavered between Forbes and Adele, then locked again on Daniel. He continued, "But I'm afraid that though technically such a charter as you propose could be considered neutral, the Alliance would have another opinion of it. By all accounts, Guarantor Porra takes a very robust view of the law."

"Unless...," said Weber carefully. Had they orchestrated this? The timing was perfect. "This were a private charter, one which didn't involve the Republic of Cinnabar. Hydriote ships *have* taken private cargoes to and from Bolton during the present war, after all."

Gambardella pursed his lips, then looked at Forbes and raised an eyebrow. "Perhaps you would care to charter the necessary vessels, Mistress Forbes?" he said. "Or could you act as agent for Master Beckford? I don't think I'm disclosing any matters that will surprise you if I say that we've carried many cargoes for Beckford to worlds controlled by the Alliance."

Forbes laughed in what seemed to be good humor. "I don't think I'll trouble Prince Willie on this," she said. "And as for chartering ten or a dozen transports at war rates—it would be war rates, wouldn't it?"

The Hydriotes looked at one another. Christianson said, "Yes, I fear that for the region you're discussing, that would be necessary. Though these would be private cargoes."

"Of course," said Forbes. "Would you accept my personal note for that amount, Captain Gambardella?"

Gambardella looked embarrassed. Not all senators were fabulously wealthy. On learning of the embassy, Adele had investigated Forbes and found that she was deeply in debt from her failed run for the speakership. She hadn't held the position of Finance Minister very long, but even so a less scrupulous person would have made a better thing of it.

"We'd discuss the matter among ourselves and with the local agents you direct us to," said Christianson. "In the normal course of business, you understand."

He too sounded subdued. His eyes were on Adele as she mopped the rest of her gravy with a wedge of bread she'd torn from the loaf.

"So that isn't practical either," said Forbes in the same bright, bantering tone as before. "Fortunately, gentlemen, before the *Milton* lifted from Cinnabar, the managing partner of the Shippers' and Merchants' Treasury summoned me for a consultation. She authorized me to pledge the full credit of her bank on such commercial ventures as I might sumble across on a mission such as this."

"Well bless my soul!" Daniel said. "Why, that's my bank! And the manager is my sister Deirdre!"

"Yes," said Adele. She cleared her throat. "How very fortunate that you'd made this arrangement, Your Excellency."

In a very different sense the Shippers' and Merchants' Treasury was Corder Leary's bank. He owned the bulk of the shares and had installed his daughter as managing partner.

Knowing Deirdre's eye for a profit, the bank expected to make a good thing out of this when the Senate approved transfer of the contracts to the public exchequer. The element of risk justified the profit, however, as the supersession of the contract by the Republic would only occur if Captain Leary's plans were successful.

Deirdre wouldn't have been able to provide so sweeping a credit without the approval of the majority partner. On principle, Daniel would never have accepted the money if he'd known it came from his father; but Adele's principles didn't require that she inform her friend.

The Hydriote captains stared at one another. Adele didn't see any type of communication pass between them, nor did her personal data unit detect anything in the electro-optical band, but clearly something was going on.

Captain Gambardella turned to Forbes. "The Shippers' and Merchants' Treasury is well known to us," he said. "Not that we doubt your word, Senator, but do you have this authorization in a form that . . . ?"

"Yes," said Forbes, pulling open the placket on the bosom of her tunic. What Adele had assumed was either a stiffener or body armor turned out to be a fitted document case. "This in the electronic form—"

She laid a chip on the table, sliding the remainder of the bread to the side. Christianson immediately fitted it to the data unit which he'd taken out at the same time.

"—and in a more colorful medium," Forbes said, handing a sheet of parchment to Captain Gambardella. It was small enough to fit in the case without folding or rolling, but even in a quick glance Adele saw ribbons, seals, and text in a tiny copperplate hand as regular as printing.

She smiled coldly. Given that the document represented a credit greater than the net product of many worlds, it *ought* to be ornate.

"This is satisfactory," Captain Gambardella said, handing back the letter of credit. "Very satisfactory. Captain Leary, when will you have the details of the contract ready?"

Adele had unlocked her data unit when she finished lunch. Her wands twitched.

"I believe Lady Mundy has just transmitted them," Daniel said, smiling. He leaned back on his stool. "Your standard commercial rates, adjusted by a fifteen percent war risk premium. Calculated time to the rendezvous and destination are there as well. I'm assuming most if not all the vessels will come from Hydra herself, but I'm also assuming that you'll send the fastest available courier there with the information."

Weber grinned, more like a wolf now than a fox. "I'll carry the information myself, Captain," he said. "And for your future calculations, I estimate the run from Fonthill to Bolton at nine days maximum, and eight if conditions are favorable. For Hydriote vessels."

"I'll travel with you, Weber," Gambardella said. "There are some matters I should take care of at home."

"And I," said Christianson. The three Hydriotes chuckled.

"Then I believe we've finished our business here,"

Daniel said, rising to his feet. "Unless you have something to add, Senator?"

"I do not," said Forbes. "Though I suppose a prayer would be proper if I believed in the Gods."

"We'll see you on Fonthill, then, good sir and ladies," Captain Gambardella said, bowing. "No doubt you'll arrive long before we do, but we'll keep our schedule."

"We need to make a side trip to US1528," Daniel said, "so I suspect the timing will be similar for both of us."

Weber frowned. "US1528?" he said. "If you need to take on reaction mass, Captain, why not do so here?"

He didn't, Adele noticed, mention that US1528 was an *Alliance* refueling station.

Daniel laughed. "As you have matters to deal with on Hydra, so the needs of the RCN are varied, fellow spacers. I look forward to our next meeting."

He turned. As Adele poised to follow him, Captain Christianson said, "Ah, Lady Mundy? If I may ask, you appeared to like the macaca worms?"

Adele shrugged as she put away her data unit. "The gravy was good," she said. "I found the worms themselves tasteless, which—"

She smiled. Christianson didn't react, but Weber straightened and his face went blank.

"—is better than some of the things I ate during the years I lived on very little money. I prefer their texture to that of hog tripes, at any rate."

As they walked back to Tovera and their vehicle, Adele leaned to speak past Daniel. "I share your doubt about the Gods, Senator," she said. "But regardless, there's a closer power at present. I've found putting my faith in the RCN to be quite efficacious."

CHAPTER 13

En route to US1528

"Your Master Cazelet tells me that the Matrix from a masthead is the most spectacular thing I'll ever see," Forbes said. "But Lady Mundy doesn't seem as convinced. Which of them is right, Leary?"

"I'm in agreement with Cazelet," Daniel said. "I suspect that if it were possible to display imagery of the Matrix on Officer Mundy's data unit, she'd be more impressed with it."

While he pulled on the stiff sections of his rigging suit, Tovera was dressing the senator in an air suit. Daniel would have been happier if the senator were wearing a hard suit also, but the gear really was impossibly clumsy until you got used to it.

Mind, he'd have been happier still if Forbes hadn't decided to take a jaunt on the hull. Rene Cazelet was right in his enthusiasm, but it wouldn't be his responsibility if the senator managed to kill herself by ripping her air suit wider than Daniel could fix with one of the emergency patches he was carrying on his equipment belt.

He grinned faintly. Adele had never managed to get used to a hard suit either. The chance that she'd awkwardly tear her suit on a sharp corner was less of a concern than that a rigging suit would make her stumble and she'd drift off into the Matrix as a miniature universe. Besides that, she'd gotten scrapes and bruises from the inside every time she'd worn a hard suit. Adele's comfort wasn't as high a priority to the RCN as her safety—neither was important to Officer Mundy herself—but when there wasn't an obvious improvement in safety, comfort had to count for something.

The same was true of Senator Forbes, Daniel supposed, though despite her being a former minister he doubted that anybody would be terribly upset if she had a fatal accident now that the embassy to Headman Hieronymos had failed. Forbes had a sharp mind, however, and when pushed didn't hesitate to do what she'd decided was necessary. Daniel had served under RCN officers who lacked both those virtues.

"Will I be able to see this Alliance base from out there?" Forbes said. "I've heard that distances aren't the same when we're in space as they are on the ground."

"Not yet," said Tovera as she stepped behind Forbes to lift the torso of the air suit. "*Now*, Your Excellency. Put your right hand into the hole first."

"Distances—constants of space and time—in the universes through which we travel in the Matrix do differ from ours, Your Excellency," Daniel said. He'd had to blank his face to avoid staring in disbelief at such a, well, *ignorant* question. "But not so that we'll be able to see US1528. We won't do that until we extract into sidereal space after another two days sailing."

Twenty feet down the corridor, Hogg was chatting

with the senator's bedmate DeNardo. The fellow had a equable temper and had proven willing to lend spacers a hand when his considerable muscles would be helpful. Obviously Forbes trusted him, though she probably wasn't one to indulge in pillow talk.

Daniel wanted DeNardo at a distance because he wasn't very bright. While he wouldn't consciously betray the senator, it wouldn't take a skilled inter-rogator to lead DeNardo to repeat any discussion he remembered. Hogg could keep him occupied; Tovera could help the senator on with her suit—what was true for DeNardo was true in spades for spacers given a chance to impress their messmates; and Daniel could chat with Forbes without concern that anyone else would hear about their discussions.

"Captain Leary?" said Tovera obsequiously. "Are you ready for me to close down Her Excellency's helmet?"

"Yes," said Daniel. He locked down his own face-plate, then patted his belt to make sure the brass communication wand was in the tooled leather scab-bard which the craftsmen of Bantry had sewn for it unasked. Wearing a hard suit he could only look down by bending at the waist, which wasn't a useful way to determine what you were wearing on a waist belt.

He smiled, gestured the senator ahead of him into the cruiser's forward dorsal airlock, and set the inner valve to close behind them as he followed her.

The *Milton* had eight locks instead of the *Sissie*'s four, and each chamber was big enough to hold sixteen riggers—or twenty, if they were good friends. It felt oddly wrong to Daniel that he shared such a volume with only one other person.

He grinned at the thought. He grinned at most things.

On average, Adele and I smile the usual number of times in a day. That thought made him grin more broadly.

The light in the chamber began to flatten as pumps drew the air out. Forbes looked first startled, then concerned. Daniel leaned close to touch helmets—the wand would be more trouble than it was worth—and said, "This is normal, Your Excellency. An atmosphere scatters light, so things look a little different. But there's no problem."

The telltale on the outer lock door switched from red to green. Daniel tugged the safety line attached to his belt, then clipped the end to the staple in the center of the senator's chest plate.

"Just shuffle your feet, Your Excellency," he said, then touched the hatch switch. The airlock swung slowly outward. Daniel put an arm around the senator's shoulders to guide as well as to reassure her. They stepped into the flaring wonder of the Matrix.

Forbes placed her right foot on the hull. She froze with her left foot still inside the lock chamber, staring upward. Her mouth opened and closed like that of a carp on the surface of a pond on a hot day. Daniel weighed alternatives, then half pulled, half lifted the senator toward him so that he could cycle the airlock closed.

The cruiser was proceeding with topsails on the port and starboard antennas, and topgallants cocked at 30 degrees on the dorsal and ventral antennas of the G and H Rings. From the airlock, just aft of the dorsal antenna of the A Ring, only the standing rigging and the antenna itself marred the view of the Matrix.

Daniel touched the communication wand to the senator's helmet. "Magnificent, isn't it?" he said.

It'd be even more magnificent from the masthead, but Forbes wasn't going to get up there unless she managed to drag Daniel along by main force. With luck she wouldn't remember—or understand—Cazelet's exact words.

"Leary, this is . . . ," Forbes said. "All those *stars*!"

"What you're seeing aren't stars, Your Excellency," Daniel said, warming to the senator due to their shared enthusiasm. "Each point of light—"

He held the wand in his right hand, so he swept his left arm through Forbes's field of view.

"—is a universe equal to our own. The colors indicate each one's energy state in relation to us. That is, in relation to the *Millie* herself, a bubble universe driven through the Matrix by the pressure of Casimir radiation on her sails. At present, we're in a much higher energy state than the sidereal universe."

Forbes turned her head slowly, taking in the full expanse of sworls and brush strokes of light. "And you control this, Leary?" she said. "You must feel like a god!"

Daniel thought for a moment. "No, Your Excellency," he said. "But I do feel—"

As he never did in a temple.

"—that the Gods are real. Surely beauty like this can't just have occurred at random?"

The senator laughed and turned her gloved palms up. "You'll have to ask a priest about that," she said. The rod thinned her voice, but it sounded less harsh than it ordinarily would. "I don't spend much time with them myself."

The dorsal antennas shook out their topsails; the hull quivered in response. On the A ring, the left half of the sail didn't descend. Two riggers scrambled up the ratlines to open the mispleated fabric.

Forbes followed the crewmen with her eyes. To Daniel the riggers moved very gracefully, but he didn't know what a layman saw. At last she said, "Captain Leary, why are we raiding a small Alliance base? What do you hope to find there?"

"A transport," Daniel said equably. "Specifically, the *Wartburg*, a three-thousand tonner out of Bankat. According to movement information from the *Merkur's* database, she's scheduled to take on reaction mass on US1528 about the time we'll arrive there."

"But we're hiring ships from Hydra," Forbes said. "Surely they can provide all the capacity we need for the invasion?"

The *Milton* was swinging under her new rig. Did Forbes feel the course change or was it lost to her eyes in the majestic, slow swirl of the Matrix?

"With respect, Your Excellency," Daniel said, "the Hydriotes aren't providing ships for the invasion. By the contract, and by the oath of a Leary—"

He didn't overly stress "and," because he was sure Forbes would take his meaning without being beaten over the head with it.

"—Bolton will be in our hands before the first Hydriote vessel lands."

He grinned, though the senator wouldn't be able to see the expression.

"Fonthill isn't a problem, of course, but I can't say the same of a major Alliance base."

Forbes touched the wand with her left hand, then turned to face Daniel. After a moment she said, "I see, Captain. I'd thought this ship herself—"

She tried to tap the cruiser's hull with her toe; the magnets in her boots made them too sticky to respond the way she wanted.

"The ship, as I say," she went on, "would capture Bolton. But I suppose I can leave those matters safely to you."

Forbes stared at the gorgeous, glowing Matrix. "After all," she said in a voice that Daniel could barely hear. "You rule the heavens, Leary."

Above US1528

"Base Control," said Adele in the accent she'd picked up during the fourteen years she lived on Blythe, working in the Academic Collections. "This AFS *Admiral Spee*. By order of Admiral Petersen, all liftoffs and landings are embargoed until further notice. Acknowledge, base. *Spee* over."

There was nothing very prepossessing about US1528. Almost half the surface was water, making it a suitable world to refill with reaction mass. The gravity, temperature and atmosphere were all within the human comfort zone. There was even life.

The problem was that the life was single celled. The most complex forms were an analogue of blue-green algae which built reefs in the tropical oceans. The land was sterile and windswept.

You couldn't grow crops without importing the nutrients, so it was simpler to process algae and bacteria into edible blocks that sustained life without providing any reason for living. The Alliance had sited its base on a temperate coastline with minimal repair facilities and a warehouse filled with nutrient blocks; immigrants, contract laborers, and the crews of tramp freighters couldn't be choosers.

"*What?*" said ground control. Adele hadn't been sure anybody would be awake at the base, so besides the standard microwave communication she'd broadcast on the 20-meter emergency frequency. That set off automatic alarms, no matter how bored and sleepy the staff was.

"*Say again*, Spee?" the controller demanded. "*This is Transit Base US1528, over.*"

"Base Control," Adele repeated. "This is AFS *Spee*! Admiral Petersen has embargoed all movements on your sand pit until we've carried out a survey. Do you copy, over?"

Adele normally tried to sound blasé during this sort of false communication so as not to raise the emotional temperature of the party she was deceiving. This time, because she wasn't available to help Cazelet and Cory oversee data from the sensors while she was pretending to be an Alliance officer, she probably seemed irritated. That was all right too.

A caret blinked in a corner of Adele's display; she opened it. Cory had located the *Wartburg*, the Alliance freighter they were here to capture. It was in orbit. Still in orbit: it had only arrived minutes ahead of the cruiser rather than having lifted off after refilling with reaction mass.

"Spee, *I don't understand*," said the bewildered controller. "*Why are we embargoed, over?*"

Cory had already transmitted the data on *Wartburg* to the command console. Just in case Daniel was in the press of other business ignoring an alert from a less-than-brilliant midshipman, Adele ran a crawl at the bottom of his display—WARTBURG IN ORBIT PREPARING TO LAND—and followed it by a duplicated link to the course data.

Cory didn't have all the skills that could be wished in an RCN officer, but his knack for communications had positively impressed Adele. She wished him well.

Openly snarling, she said, "Base, this is *Spee*! You are not required to understand, you are required to obey. Are you prepared to obey Admiral Petersen's direct order or not, over?"

The *Wartburg* was 200,000 miles out from the planet; a good approximation if her astrogator had brought her there directly out of the Matrix. In all likelihood they'd been lucky to extract in the system the first time, and getting this close had been the result of two or three additional jumps. Freighters didn't have astrogators trained to RCN standards, nor were their crews large enough for delicate maneuvering with the sails.

"Spee, *this is 2-8 Base,*" said a new voice: female and harsh with frustration. "*We're shutting down as requested. There's nothing here to shut down, Spee. This is the bloody sticks! 2-8 Base out.*"

"*Adele,*" said Daniel on a two-way link. "*Tell the* Wartburg *to hold where they are and await boarding. Tell them we'll use an umbilicus to their dorsal airlock. I don't trust them to have suits, even air suits, for all the crew—but don't tell them that. Over.*"

"Yes, Daniel," Adele said. She switched to tight-beam microwave, then reconsidered and aligned a 15.5 megahertz antenna instead. Starships used their antennas and yards to send and receive shortwave signals. Though a freighter's maintenance of microwave cones, let alone laser pickups, might be lax to the point of nonexistence, a starship in service always had some form of rigging.

She wasn't relaxed, precisely, but she felt much less pressured than she had a moment before. US1528 wasn't protected by a planetary defense array, but the base had shipkilling missiles. The battery might be unserviceable, and even if it did work the *Milton* was probably above even the extreme range of a ground-based system. Nonetheless, until Adele had bullied the ground crew into acquiescence, there was a possibility that they'd launch and get improbably lucky.

And it would be her fault. Adele was one of the people who viewed all failures as her fault. She knew that wasn't rational, but it meant she made fewer repeat errors than the large number of people who were sure that all failures occurred because someone else had made a mistake.

"Freighter *Wartburg*," Adele said, "this is AFS *Admiral Spee*. Acknowledge, over."

A buzzing rumble gripped the cruiser. Powerful magnetic levitators raised the gun turrets minusculely above their tracks and began turning them by precession. Though the rotation was without metal-to-metal contact, the inertia of armored gunhouses and the paired osmium-lined 8-inch gun tubes nonetheless made all the loose fittings in the hull and rigging vibrate like individual steel drums.

Adele had learned to recognize the sound of gun turrets training aboard the *Princess Cecile*, but the corvette's lighter battery didn't have anything like as great an effect. She smiled coldly. If the *Wartburg* had decent optics, they were getting a good look at the *Milton*'s weapons right now. Even at a hundred thousand miles, the bore of an 8-inch plasma cannon was enough to get one's attention.

"*Wartburg*," Adele repeated, hearing her voice slip into the harsh tone that was never very far beneath the surface. "This is *Spee*. Respond in the name of Admiral Petersen, over!"

She was better at using proper communications protocol when she was playing a part than when she was performing the proper duties of an RCN signals officer. She didn't know what that meant, but in the realm of human behavior Adele didn't expect to know what much of anything meant.

"*Spee, this is the* Wartburg *out of the Free City of Willowbend on Tilton,*" said an angry, frightened voice. The transmission was on the upper sideband only; because of that and compression, Adele couldn't be sure of the speaker's gender. "*You have no right to delay us. We haven't landed, we'll just proceed to another fueling point and leave you to your business, over.*"

Adele took a deep breath. A lime-green text crawl across the bottom of her display read HOLD ONE. She glanced at the inset of Daniel's image. Rene Cazelet had sent the caution, but he'd been in a discussion with Daniel and Sun while Adele argued with the Alliance captain.

"*Ship, this is Six,*" said a grinning Daniel over the intercom. "*This is a warning only. Mister Cazelet, go ahead, out.*"

"*Wartburg, this is Captain of Space Sir Helmut*

von Thoma!" Cazelet said. The *Spee*'s real captain was from Pleasaunce whereas the Cazelets were a Diregean family, but both worlds pronounced 'mut' as 'moot;' even if the *Wartburg*'s captain was an improbably good judge of accents *and* had a Fleet List handy, Rene's voice would ring true. "*You have been directed to heave to by an officer of the Fleet!*"

Daniel, grinning as widely as a Verrucan rubbermonk, dipped his right index finger toward Sun. The gunner, grinning if anything wider toward his gunnery display, stabbed the red button on his virtual keyboard. The RF filter of Adele's console blanked the spectrum-wide noise of an ion release.

Even though Adele knew it was coming, the crash of one gun from the dorsal turret made her flinch in her seat. Her previous experience with plasma cannon had been in the midst of battle, when she'd been fully absorbed with her own duties and the sound of gunfire had been lost in the general racket.

Besides that, the *Milton*'s guns were orders of magnitude more powerful than the *Sissie*'s 4-inch weapons. She'd heard Daniel say that the *Milton* was overgunned with what were properly battleship cannon. Now that Adele had been subjected to the recoil of an 8-inch gun fired from a cruiser's hull, she knew what he meant.

Plasma cannon used a laser array to detonate a bead of deuterium, sending the jolt of thermonuclear energy through the single window and down the axis of the bore. In the hard vacuum of space, the discharges spread very slowly. A bolt from an 8-inch gun was potentially dangerous to a lightly built freighter, even one as far distant as the *Wartburg* was from the *Milton*.

"Spee, *what are you doing, you animals!*" screamed the voice from the *Wartburg*. "*Cease firing, cease firing! In the name of all the Gods, we're laying to, over!*"

"Wartburg, *this is* Spee," Cazelet said, his voice dripping with aristocratic malevolence. "*We'll be joining you shortly by the Matrix. I'm sending a boarding party through an umbilicus to your dorsal airlock. If you've nothing worse on your conscience than more Chantral peaches than were listed on your manifest, you don't have to worry. We're the Fleet, not a customs barge. But—*"

Adele's dancing fingers brought up the references. Chantral was the *Wartburg*'s most recent port of call. The planet's main export was Terran peaches— actually nectarines—which formed a warmly pleasant hallucinogen when grown in Chantral's soil. Adele suspected—and Cazelet, the onetime heir of a shipping family, had obviously known—that the freighter's captain would have under-reported his cargo of so valuable a product to avoid duties.

"*—if you attempt to escape while we're in the Matrix, every one of you will go out the airlock when we catch you. And we will catch you, on my oath as a von Thoma! Do you understand, over?*"

"Wartburg *to AFS* Spee," said the freighter's chastened captain. "*We've shut down our High Drive. We'll be waiting in free fall until you link with us, Captain von Thoma.* Wartburg *out.*"

"*Mister Robinson,*" Daniel said, switching to intercom, "*pick a prize crew of twenty to serve under yourself. Mister Cazelet, I'm detaching you to accompany Mister Robinson. You have the accent and you know Alliance commercial procedures; we'll need both those things. Lieutenant Vesey, take a squad of Marines aboard the prize and escort the present Alliance crew back to the* Milton *after you've satisfied yourself that the freighter is sound and capable of proceeding. Break."*

Adele imported images from the navigation console to see how Cazelet was taking the sudden directive. The boy looked cheerfully excited. Lieutenant Vesey's face, on the other hand, was as white as a chalk bust. Her lips were pressed tight in anger or frustration.

"Ship," Daniel continued—briskly, brightly. *"Prepare to insert into the Matrix. Inserting...now!"*

He pressed a virtual button with two fingers. Adele felt the charge build, lifting the tiny hairs on her arms and neck; then she felt a reversal and cold like that of a dead planet.

The look in Vesey's pale blue eyes was colder yet.

CHAPTER 14

Above US1528

Imagery from three of the *Milton*'s hull sensors and the *Wartburg*'s single working sensor framed the schematic of the linked cruiser and freighter in the center of Daniel's display. Even so it was the astrogation computer that handled—that had to handle—the operation.

Daniel rated himself as a better-than-good shiphandler, but the stresses which worked on the two ships were so varied and so minute that the best pilot in the human universe would've found himself overmatched by the task. Use of the umbilicus in freefall was taught at the Academy, but the instructors made it clear that the system was really meant for ships close to one another on an inhospitable surface.

He could've transferred the prisoners and prize crew on US1528, but that would've taken time, and it would've meant dropping into the range of an Alliance base with ship-killing missiles. He trusted Adele to have shut down the battery, if it was in working order to begin with, and if it crossed the mind of anybody on the ground to launch—as it almost certainly wouldn't have.

Even so, remaining out of range of enemy weapons was always a better choice than hoping that those weapons wouldn't be used. Spacers took enough risks as it was.

Adele was busy with six simultaneous data fields, presumably organizing just-gathered information. It was hard to imagine anything useful coming either from a minor refueling base in the sticks or the sort of freighter which frequented such a base, but Daniel had seen her do magic with equally unpromising material.

Except for Adele, everyone on the *Milton*'s bridge was watching the operation. Daniel had set his big display omnidirectional, so several off-duty shipside crewmen were clustered in the hatchway for a better view than they could've gotten from the flat-plate terminals in their quarters.

The ships drifted nose-to-tail in high orbit. Six-inch cables linked them so that they couldn't spread wider apart, but that didn't prevent them from rotating in opposite directions around the umbilicus...which they were indeed doing, slowly but visibly even to a human eye. Daniel judged that he'd have the personnel transferred before the problem became acute, and he surely hoped he was right. The least touch on a plasma thruster would reverse the spin, not cancel it. Even with the computer in charge, that meant a real chance that the next Alliance warship to pass would find the *Milton* and *Wartburg* still locked in a tight cocoon of cable.

"*Repeat that please, Vesey,*" said Adele's voice. "*Ah, over.*"

Daniel leaned past his display to look at her. That showed him only the back of Adele's head; he switched to the message icon on the screen and learned from the history that she'd just cut him in on what had been a direct query from Vesey, now aboard the freighter.

"*Officer Mundy, could you join me for a few minutes on the* Wartburg, *over?*" Vesey said. She was using the optical communications fiber woven into the umbilicus, but despite the broader than usual bandwidth her voice sounded clipped.

Adele didn't look up from her console, but the miniature of her face on Daniel's display expanded. The image raised an eyebrow in question; Daniel nodded approval with pursed lips.

"*Yes, all right, Vesey,*" Adele said in her usual professional tone, cold disinterest. "*I'll be over as soon as I get my suit on. Over. Out, I suppose.*"

"*Mistress,*" said Vesey urgently. "*Bring a helmet and air bottle against emergencies, but you shouldn't need even that. We'll just be a few minutes, over.*"

Daniel was nodding even as Adele lifted her eyebrow again. He thought he knew what Vesey wanted, but he didn't need to brief Adele on how to handle it.

He smiled. For a person who claimed to have no more insight into personal relationships than she did into crystal growth, Adele had shown herself to be quite a good counselor. There were worse forms of understanding than what one got from dispassionate study.

Adele unstrapped and rose from her couch. Tovera was already upright, anchoring herself in the weightless conditions by hooking a toe under the signals console. She held two breathing rigs in her left hand and had slung a full-sized sub-machine gun from the cruiser's armory under her right arm. Her usual satchel was strapped to her back.

Tovera saw Daniel look at her and gave him a smile of sorts. He smiled back, which he probably wouldn't have done a year ago.

He still didn't think Tovera was human, but she made an obvious effort to act as though she were. And besides, there'd been times that the pale little snake had come in bloody useful.

Daniel had ordered the umbilicus to be attached to the cruiser's forward dorsal airlock which opened onto the rotunda beyond the bridge hatch. The Marines there presented their sub-machine guns even before their officer hopped out of the lock from which he'd been watching and snapped an order.

Tovera stepped in front of Adele and eased her safely against a bulkhead. The *Wartburg*'s crew swam out of the airlock one at a time. They were a scruffy lot, though no more so than any other collection of spacers. They were dirtier than the off-duty Millies eyeing them, but that was because they'd lacked RCN discipline rather than any difference in the basic material.

The Marines who'd chivvied the prisoners off the *Wartburg* followed them into the rotunda. Daniel felt a glow of pride that brought another smile to his face.

He loved the *Princess Cecile*, his first command and a corvette which had done more harm to Guarantor Porra's Alliance than most RCN battleships... but captaincy of the *Milton* was a promotion, and the degree of promotion was evident simply in her greater size. Twenty Alliance spacers and the equal number of Marine guards fit in the cruiser's airlock rotunda; there wouldn't have been room for them to stand comfortably in the *Sissie's* whole A Level corridor.

Adele and Tovera slipped out the airlock after the last Marine had returned to the *Milton*. Despite Tovera carrying equipment in both hands, she was guiding her mistress. Daniel had seen his friend wind her way through tight-stacked books and paper without brushing any of the piles into collapse, but in any other environment she seemed not so much clumsy as oblivious of her surroundings.

Daniel used the lip of the hatchway as a dais from which to look onto the gathering of prisoners and guards. "Fellow spacers!" he said, "I'm Captain Daniel Leary and you are my prisoners."

The words drew eyes to him. Until then the Marines had been glowering at the captured crewmen, and the crewmen had—quite understandably—been staring at the muzzles of the guns pointed toward them.

"You've been captured by the RCN through a legitimate ruse of war," Daniel said. "You'll not be harmed. Those of you who choose to join the RCN will be welcomed into the complement of the *Milton* here, a crack ship and a lucky one."

He grinned broadly. "As you yourselves can testify, can you not, spacers?"

He'd hoped to get a grin or even a laugh from some of the prisoners, but they were too cowed to respond to his humor. Maybe it was being held at gunpoint by uniformed Marines instead of sailors wearing slops like themselves.

The Marines had properly anchored themselves to bulkheads or fittings so that recoil wouldn't spin them in all directions if they opened fire. A sergeant with three chevrons on her collar tabs had even extended her sling to loop the airlock's manual dogging wheel.

"Major Mull!" Daniel said, more sharply than he'd meant. The commander of the *Milton*'s Marine detachment had personally led the squad aboard the *Wartburg* and was the last man back from the prize. "Order your troops to put their guns up, if you will. I trust there'll be no trouble here that requires a gun to finish."

Mull and his personnel—two were women, a lower percentage than would be found in an equal number of spacers—probably differed on the need to keep their guns pointed. They began to lower or even sling them even before Mull relayed the order which Daniel had properly issued through him, though.

"Those of you who don't want to serve on the finest ship in the RCN . . . ," Daniel continued, grinning to make the statement sort of a joke. He was pleased that this time half the prisoners smiled in return. "Will be set down on the first Alliance or neutral world the *Milton* touches on. I'll give you a month's pay out of my own pocket to replace the bindles you've had to leave behind on the *Wartburg*. I'm a Leary of Bantry, and we don't hold it against common spacers that they have a brute like Guarantor Porra for their master."

In normal operation, the inner and outer hatches of an airlock couldn't be opened at the same time. With the umbilicus in place, the cross-locks had been disconnected—electronically on the cruiser's bridge and mechanically at the hatch by a tech in Robinson's prize crew.

The current of air which Daniel felt was a reminder that the seals and even fabric of the umbilicus were leaking, but hatches leaked anyway and ships were equipped to replace lost atmosphere. This slight extra wastage wouldn't be a problem.

"You'll be taken aft now to the BDC, where Lieutenant Blantyre will enroll and assign watches to those of you who want to join the *Millie*," Daniel said. "Those of you who claim advanced ratings will have a chance to prove it. If you satisfy the chief of your department, you'll receive the higher rate at your first pay parade."

"What about officers?" asked somebody—Captain Mike Martin, the freighter's commander almost certainly, the black-bearded man who was holding his cloth cap in front of his mouth to conceal the fact that he was speaking.

"The RCN grants master's warrants to qualified astrogators," Daniel said cheerfully. "And a master with skill and ambition can receive a commission even without Academy training. It's happened often—"

That was a bit of an overstatement, but allowable under the conditions.

"—Captain Martin. When I have a bit more time than I do at the moment, I'll talk to you about the details."

Things were going well. When people were discussing terms and conditions of employment, they were no longer so frightened that they were likely to do something desperate. Daniel wasn't worried that the prisoners would suddenly capture the *Milton*'s bridge, but if his own Marines opened fire with their sub-machine guns to prevent a rush, there'd be a real problem.

Maybe he'd have been wiser to use spacers for guards. Wrenches and lengths of pipe weren't going to ricochet lethally off steel bulkheads.

"Any questions?" Daniel said brightly. Without allowing time for anyone to take up his offer, he continued, "Maor?"

One of the Power Room techs was standing in the corridor to watch. He jumped to attention when Daniel called his name.

"Take these spacers, our fellow Millies I hope shortly, to the BDC, if you please."

He paused, grinning, then sobered and went on, "I know, fellow spacers, that this wasn't the day you expected when you got up this morning. Nonetheless, if you play your cards right, you may find that it's the luckiest day of your life. Dismissed!"

"All right, spacers!" Mickey Maor said, his voice cracking with enthusiasm. He was an engine wiper, the—lowly—equivalent of a landsman on the Rig side. He didn't get many opportunities to lord it over other people. "Lively, now. You're getting a chance to join *the* crack ship of the RCN, you are, and serve under the best captain anywhere!"

The prisoners, whom he did hope were on the way to becoming recruits, paddled down the corridor behind him. Major Mull looked at Daniel with a worried expression. He didn't know how to proceed, and he didn't want another sharp—though unintended— rebuke for heavy-handedness.

"Follow them with a squad, Major," Daniel said, making an effort to sound cheerful. "I doubt there'll be a problem, but we can't have strangers wandering about the ship unattended in Alliance space, can we?"

In all truth, he needn't even have bothered with a prize crew. It probably would've worked out all right if he'd left the crew on the *Wartburg* and told them that they were to obey the RCN officers he'd put aboard. Spacers tended to identify with their profession or at most with their planet of origin, not with the aims and ideals of the political body where their ship happened to be registered.

Half the *Wartburg's* personnel had probably been born outside the Alliance, and there were doubtless several who'd been subjects of Cinnabar. They'd likely choose to keep that quiet—even if they weren't, as Triplett had been, RCN deserters—but it was a reality of star travel that every captain, whether naval or civilian, knew and accepted.

Having said that, there *were* fanatics. The new enlistees would be watched a little closer than usual, but all good petty officers kept an eye on new personnel anyway, to make sure of their competence.

Daniel looked up through the airlock. The umbilicus curved enough to hide anybody twenty feet beyond the cruiser's hull, but there came Vesey in a rigging suit with the right arm painted silver. Beyond her were other figures, likely Adele and Tovera.

"Excellent timing, Lieutenant!" Daniel called. "Take charge of detaching and stowing the umbilicus, if you will. I want to get under way as soon as I've checked the course I'm transmitting to Mister Robinson."

"Aye aye, sir!" said Vesey, turning quickly but carefully so as not to bump Adele with the stiffened fabric of her hard suit. Her voice had the animation which had been so signally lacking when she called Adele to her.

"Well, Leary," said Senator Forbes, at his side. She'd come out of her compartment when the prisoners and Marines cleared the rotunda. "I listened to your little speech. You're your father's son, I can see. But...?"

"Your Excellency?" Daniel said, since the pause required something.

"How much of it was true, eh?" Forbes said archly.

Daniel smiled. "Well, Your Excellency," he said, "I don't claim to know Truth with a capital letter; I'm not a priest. But if you mean, 'What do I believe?' *I* believe everything I just told those spacers."

Shall I? Yes, because she's pricking me and she needs to know that a Leary can prick back.

"And if you heard what Maor said...," Daniel said. His smile was just as hard and mischievous as that of Tovera, following Adele out of the airlock. "He believes that too. So far as it touches on the ship, at least—my oath as a Leary that he's right!"

The outer airlock hatch clanged closed; Vesey was on the job. It might be a while before Daniel learned what had happened between Adele and the lieutenant in the privacy of the umbilicus, but it had been good enough.

Adele drifted into the umbilicus. The fabric bulged slightly outward so that the ridges of the stiffening helix were ideal for batting oneself along in freefall.

Adele knew that she was better off letting somebody else—here Tovera—direct her. Initially her clumsiness in freefall had been an embarrassment and an irritation, but over time she'd come to the conclusion that she should concentrate on things she did well rather than trying to train herself in skills she utterly lacked.

The spacers she served with didn't mind; they didn't even laugh. Maybe they'd at least have smiled if it weren't for the other stories. *Lady Mundy keeps a pistol in her tunic pocket, and she never misses with it....*

Vesey waited thirty feet up the umbilicus with the

helmet of her hard suit latched open. She seemed worn. Her short hair, a nondescript blond at the best of times, now looked as though somebody had layered wet straw on her scalp.

Adele glanced about and nodded with approval. Even if there were other people ahead or behind in the umbilicus, she and Vesey wouldn't be overheard. The ridged, flexible tube was nearly perfect for deadening sound: it would drink normal voices from even a few feet away.

Tovera gripped the back of Adele's belt and eased her to an upright halt. When she'd turned her head, her body had started rotating in reaction; Tovera straightened that out too.

"Vesey?" Adele said, realizing that her face and tone were as hard as steel plate. Adele didn't like to stand as close as she was to the lieutenant. That was likely Tovera's plan for security rather than the awkward mechanics of freefall, but it was still uncomfortable.

Vesey swallowed, but she met Adele's eyes. "Mistress," she blurted, "why doesn't Six trust me to command the *Wartburg*? I've done this before, I brought the *Rainha* in on Mandelfarne Island, didn't I? You were with me! Why doesn't he trust me now?"

Adele nodded to give herself time to process the information—what she'd just been told, and what that implied. She didn't like commo helmets and wasn't wearing one now, but as a result she was out of touch with the currents of information flowing about her. That was an irritation, which was good. It meant she was concentrating on that trivial matter instead of dwelling on the huge problem Vesey had just posed her.

Adele smiled wryly. Vesey was using displaced anger

as a safety valve in the same way. If she weren't angry, she might start to cry. And that, of course, was the key to the problem.

"Does Daniel's action strike you as unfair?" Adele said, using her friend's first name deliberately. It got Vesey's attention as effectively as slapping her face would have done, and it was—humor really did spark Adele's tiny smile, though she might be the only one who would realize that—more to her taste than the other.

"I don't—" Vesey said; but of course she did. "Well, I suppose—"

"Fairness had nothing to do with it," Adele said, as crisply as a pistol cycling. "Fairness never has anything to do with Daniel's decisions. He doesn't care about fairness."

"Captain Leary isn't unfair!" Vesey said. She clapped her heels together by reflex, then started rotating sideways around her navel.

"Of course not," Adele snapped. "I said fairness wasn't a criterion by which he framed his professional decisions. He decides on the basis of what will best achieve his ends, which because of who he is means the ends of the RCN and the Republic itself. And because he always decides by the same criteria, his decisions are *always* fair—without fairness ever having been considered. Do you understand?"

Vesey pinched a strand of the stiffening coil between the thumb and forefinger of her left gauntlet, bringing her slow spin to a halt and then reversing it. She was really quite strong to have been able to do that; and the physical effort was a useful way of burning off the hormones which anger had spilled into her bloodstream.

"But mistress?" she said. "I *did* do a good job with

the *Rainha*, capturing her and then landing her on Mandelfarne. Why wouldn't C-c..., *Six*, not let me have the *Wartburg*? Mister Robinson's a good officer, a very good one, I agree—but I've *done* this."

Adele raised an eyebrow. "Is there anything so very difficult about taking a transport from point to point and landing it in prepared harbors, Vesey?" she said. "Not that I could do it, of course; but for somebody with training—"

She paused to set the hook properly. Logic was a game; but then, so was a duel with pistols. She was rather good at both.

"—like Cory or Cazelet?"

"Oh," said Vesey, stiffening upright again. She blushed. "No, mistress," she said, "not the shiphandling, of course. But this will be an enemy base, like Mandelfarne Island."

"Yes," said Adele. "It'll be very dangerous, I'm sure. But I don't think we need worry about Mister Robinson's courage—"

"By the Gods!" Vesey said. "I didn't mean that! Of course his courage is above reproach!"

"And as for you having a chance to risk your life, Vesey," Adele continued dryly, "I'm sure Daniel will oblige you in some other fashion. Personally, *I* haven't found any lack of danger during my association with him."

Vesey smiled, her first sign of relaxation since Adele met her here in the umbilicus. "No, I haven't either," she said. "Mistress, I'm sorry, I just—reacted. I'm sorry."

And part of the problem is that Rene Cazelet will be aboard the transport, Adele thought. She didn't say that out loud, though, because it would lead to the next problem: that Vesey no doubt suspected that Daniel was trying to separate her from the midshipman with whom she'd been ... socializing, call it.

Vesey was quite a clever young woman, but people constantly imagined that they and their actions were more important to those around them than common sense would've dictated. Why in heaven would Daniel care? He hadn't objected to Vesey's association with the late Midshipman Dorst, had he?

This wasn't the time to discuss an inflated sense of importance—because that's what it amounted to, despite Vesey's self-effacing personality; Adele doubted there would ever be a time for that. And there were more important things to cover now.

"Daniel sent you aboard the *Wartburg*," Adele said. "What did you do there?"

Adele knew perfectly well what Vesey had done. The lieutenant's helmet sensors had been transmitting the whole time, so Adele had dipped into the imagery—and that of the other members of the boarding party—as a matter of course while it was going on. She hadn't had a specific reason to do so other than the general one of liking to know things, but she'd never needed a better reason than that.

"Well, I checked the reaction mass and the consumables," Vesey said, frowning slightly. She didn't see the point of the question, but she knew that there had to be a point if Lady Mundy was asking it. "There was a risk that they'd be too low to reach Fonthill, so we'd have to top off here or on the way. The volumes were fine, a twenty percent margin on food and probably better than that on air and reaction mass."

Adele nodded. "But you didn't check by the gauges and inventory," she said. "You *looked* at the lockers and the tanks."

"Well, Rene, ah—"

"Rene is fine," Adele interrupted, smiling a trifle less harshly.

"Ah, yes, mistress," Vesey said, lowering her eyes. "Midshipman Cazelet and I did look at the gauges, of course, but we also made a hands-on inspection the way Six taught us. It's just a matter of opening hatches and thumping the side of a tank to see how it rings."

"Right, you did what Daniel knew you'd do, because as you say, he's trained you," Adele said. "He didn't train Lieutenant Commander Robinson, Vesey. So he made sure you'd board the ship. That way he avoided a potential problem without embarrassing a subordinate by appearing to be checking up on him."

Vesey swallowed. "I'm sure Mister Robinson would've made a physical inspection," she said. "In fact, he thanked me for saving him time when he saw what Rene and I were doing. But do you think . . . ?"

"Yes," said Adele. "I do. *And* there's the other matter: who's the *Milton*'s First Lieutenant now?"

Vesey's face went flat. "Mistress," she said, "I'm *not* a better officer than Mister Robinson. Thank you for what you're trying to do—"

"Be quiet, Vesey," Adele said. Her voice snapped, which was useful for her purposes but quite natural under the circumstances. It was all right for people to leap ahead of her actual words, but they should *not* assume that Adele Mundy was about to say something patently stupid.

Vesey stiffened again. She didn't lose her hold on

the umbilicus, so she remained in place. "Sir!" she said reflexively.

"I'm sure either of you has the skill set required for the First Lieutenant's duties," Adele resumed, back to her normal flat delivery now that the flash of anger was gone. Not that there was anything abnormal about her being angry. "What you personally will do is keep out of Daniel's way in a crisis. You'll anticipate and without direction solve all the problems that occur around the edges, but you won't try to fight the battle when that's in the hands of the best fighting captain in the RCN. Daniel *trusts* you."

Vesey's face remained blank for a moment. "Mistress," she said, her eyes shifting away. "I apologize."

For a moment Adele thought she was going to explain why she was apologizing, but Vesey really *was* sharper than that when she let intellect rather than her emotions direct her. Instead she said, "If Six were incapacitated in action, mistress, I would handle maneuvering and damage control myself. But I'd hand off battle direction to Lieutenant Blantyre, who has more of a talent for it."

"Thereby demonstrating why the best captain in the RCN wants you for his First Lieutenant, Vesey," Adele said; smiling also, but stating the flat truth. A compliment was always more effective when people knew that you said what you meant, no matter what that was. "Now, can we get back to our duties?"

Vesey looked at her with an odd expression. "Mistress," she said, "I don't think you've ever done anything *but* your duty. As you said about Captain Leary and fairness. But yes, our standing out here won't get these ships to Fonthill."

She exchanged a glance with Tovera, then led the way back toward the cruiser's airlock. Adele, sandwiched between her servant and the lieutenant, found herself smiling.

That was a very nice compliment indeed. For someone like me.

CHAPTER 15

Fonthill

Daniel breathed deeply as he looked up toward Base Alpha, the primary facility on Fonthill. The nearest structures were a few hundred yards from the harbor, as close as you could build something that wasn't raised on pilings. They were low, constructed of sheets of beige structural plastic with pillars of the same material. Someone familiar with colonial buildings would notice immediately that these didn't use the abundant local wood.

Daniel had learned it was good to get used to the local atmosphere quickly, because you couldn't avoid it except by wearing an airpack. Given that a voyage between stars could be thought of as weeks or months in a giant airpack, it was pleasant to get out into something different even when that involved decaying vegetation and smoldering mudbanks.

The usual rot and organic haze were profusely abundant on Fonthill, but there was also an undertone that set its claws in Daniel's throat when he sneezed.

The sap of Fonthill shinewood was corrosively poisonous. Apparently the trait was evident even as far down the evolutionary ladder as the algae growing in the water of the harbor.

"Gods!" said Senator Forbes. "Great Gods, this is worse than I dreamed! What sort of *stinking* hellpit is this, Leary?"

"A pretty standard one for undeveloped worlds, Your Excellency," Daniel said, considering the network of interlinked ponds surrounded by lush vegetation. "The smoke from things our thrusters set alight during landing will clear. Though it's still going to be hot and humid, of course."

He wondered how many shades of green there were within immediate sight. To his left, the prickly seedhead on a waist-high stalk was a particularly striking chartreuse.

The only color that wasn't black or green came from the underside of a bird—well, a flying lizard—which shot out of a clump of bushes on the bank and began circling. Its wings appeared to have three folds, and their underside was pink.

From orbit, the temperate and equatorial expanses of Fonthill's sole continent had seemed to be a huge bog. Now that he was here at Base Alpha, Daniel saw no reason to change that assessment. Because the water table was so high, even a landing on an area that wasn't covered in open water would've been cushioned by steam rising from the marshy soil.

A pair of men were coming from the group of buildings on a hill above the pond which the *Milton* now filled. Daniel had landed easily enough, but the berths here on Fonthill hadn't been intended for ships the cruiser's size. The locals each wore a white brassard on the right arm, presumably uniforms.

The lower end of boarding ramp was set on firm ground, rather remarkably. Ordinarily harbors were placed on large bodies of water, and for safety ships landed far enough out from the shore or quay that some sort of extension was necessary to reach land.

Major Mull and his detachment had double-timed down the ramp even before it quite touched the ground. Four Marines carried an automatic impeller and its tripod.

Heavy though the latter was, it wouldn't by itself anchor the weapon for bursts of more than two or three rounds. The Marines were furiously shoveling dirt into sandbags to weight the gun's legs as well as to shelter the crew. The soggy soil oozed back through the sides of the bags almost as soon as they'd been filled.

"They'd get a better field of fire from a hatch, like the spacers're doing," Hogg said in a derisive tone. "From down there they can't see aught but the bloody brush."

"I think Major Mull is concerned to control movement onto the ship, Hogg," Daniel said. He'd never had Marines under his command before, and he was learning that they *weren't* as much under his command as he might have wished. Mull had his own way of doing things. He seemed to regard suggestions from a spacer—even the ship's captain—as being either amusing or blasphemous, depending on how firmly the suggestions were put.

"Well, I'm more concerned with getting on with the job," said Senator Forbes. "That's the headquarters up there?"

She nodded toward the nearby buildings. In consideration of the terrain she wore a zebra-striped business suit with practical looking boots. She and her effeminate secretary weren't armed, but DeNardo and the two muscular servants carried sub-machine guns.

"Right," Daniel said. He paused a few heartbeats to decide how to phrase the next statement, then decided to simply go ahead with it. Forbes claimed she wanted the straight truth, and she seemed willing to make that more than lip service.

"Your Excellency," he said, "the quicker we get to the compound, the better. I'd like you there from the beginning so that we're agents of the Republic instead of rival gangsters, but that means walking. It'll take an hour at best to deploy the truck and longer than that to set up the aircar."

"Yes, all right," Forbes said with a moue and a toss of her head. "It's what I expected, after all."

Which was probably true, given the way she'd dressed. Daniel grinned and said, "All right, Woetjans. Lead on—and remember that we're the stern but just forces of law and order, not the Shore Patrol breaking up a drunken brawl."

The bosun, waiting farther back in the hold with a detachment of armed spacers, grinned and said, "What would I know about the Shore Patrol, Six? Except being on the other side, I mean."

Laughing, she slapped her left palm with the length of high-pressure tube she carried. She'd slung a stocked impeller over her right shoulder, but Daniel doubted she could hit anything useful in the unlikely event that she tried to shoot.

For this duty Daniel had directed Woetjans to dress

her party in new utilities, issued from the ship's store and charged to the RCN's account rather than paid for by the spacers themselves as they normally would be. In its new uniforms the detachment looked less like a band of pirates than it would have in its usual shabby, grease-stained slops.

"Let's go, then," Daniel said. Though Woetjans was treating the warning as a joke, he knew she and her unit had understood him. Spacers didn't have the formal discipline of Marines, but neither were they out of control.

"Move it, spacers!" Woetjans said, her harsh voice echoing in the big compartment. "And remember we're going to a reception, not a bloody riot!"

Led by Woetjans herself, half the detachment double-timed around the senator and Daniel. Some were shouting, "Hup! Hup!" or similar things, and the clatter of their equipment added to the drumming of their boots on the steel ramp.

Each carried a sub-machine gun or stocked impeller, but almost all had a club, knife, knuckleduster, or similar personal weapon as well. Daniel didn't see any pistols, for which he was thankful. Despite training, most spacers were more enthusiastic than skilled with projectile weapons. Pistols greatly increased the risk of accident that was inevitable even with long-arms.

"Great Gods," Forbes muttered in amazed horror.

"They'd follow Captain Leary to Hell, Senator," said Adele primly. Daniel started; he'd expected her to be on the bridge. "In fact, they've done so a number of times in the past and come back from it."

"These have, at least," said Hogg, grinning broadly. "Good folks to have with you in a hard place, for all that they don't clean up as good as a lot of prissy house-servants."

"That will do, Hogg," Daniel said quietly, but he hadn't forgotten the senator's contemptuous dismissal of his servant on Karst either. "Though what he says is correct in my opinion, Your Excellency. Shall we go?"

The only weapon Hogg carried openly was a stocked impeller. If there was a better marksman with such a weapon aboard the *Milton*, it was Daniel himself. Hogg's pockets bulged and clinked, though.

They started down the ramp. Daniel let Forbes and her entourage get a little ahead because he wanted a chance to talk to Adele. He would've told Woetjans over the helmet intercom to slow down if he'd needed to, but the senator kept up a good pace and spacers—unlike soldiers who were used to marching—weren't likely to stride away from you anyway.

"Carry on, Major Mull," Daniel said as they passed the Marine outpost. The gunners were trying to spike their weapon's trail to the ground with entrenching tools, since the sandbags wouldn't hold a sufficient weight of the available soil.

Mull muttered, "Aye aye, sir," but he watched the spacers pass with open frustration. He'd announced that his troops would secure the head of the ramp after landing—and Daniel, instead of arguing that he thought his usual squad of spacers would be sufficient, had simply agreed.

Daniel preferred having an escort of spacers anyway, because he knew they'd obey without question no matter how stupid Six's order seemed. He didn't doubt the Marines' courage, but he knew they didn't trust him like the former Sissies whom Woetjans had picked for this duty.

That was an added incentive not to screw up, not that Daniel needed more reasons not to screw up. He grinned and whistled the chorus of "Down in the Valley": "*A rolling stone gathers no moss, so they say, but a standing stone gets pissed on.*"

Judging Forbes was out of hearing, he turned to Adele and said quietly, "I thought you were going to stay aboard, Officer Mundy?"

Adele shrugged. "There's at least one database up there—"

She nodded toward the compound. The two men who'd started toward the cruiser were now going back up the hill at an accelerating pace.

"—which isn't linked to any kind of a network, so I have to be on site to examine it."

The *Milton* began to squeal and complain. Sun, predictably if against what had almost been a direct order, was rotating the dorsal turret to bear on the dull buildings. His excuse would probably be that he'd thought that the locals' flight from a band of armed men meant that they were hostile. In truth he just liked to play with his guns. The 8-inch turret set up stresses in the hull as its great mass shifted.

Daniel looked at his friend. "Well," he said, "I'd trust your judgment on any other opinion you offered. I'll therefore trust it on this."

But I'd much rather you'd stayed where it's safe, he thought. *Which here on Fonthill, the bridge of a heavy cruiser really ought to be.*

Very possibly Adele understood what he was thinking,

because her lips seemed to twist on something sour and she said, "They're not going to fight us, Daniel; I was able to listen to the control-room conversation through their satellite receiver. They're all atwitter, as you might imagine, but they were in the process of locking their weapons in the shipping container that serves as an armory. They didn't want any chance that they'd be mistaken for hostile."

"And if anybody does point a gun in our direction, young master...," said Hogg with a self-satisfied smile. "Before he shoots, he'll have a hole in his forehead and a bloody sight bigger hole in the back of his skull, where the brains all splashed out. Not so?"

Tovera laughed. "Unless Sun gets ahead of himself," she said.

The trees started ten feet out from the pond and grew taller as the increasing slope reduced the likelihood of floods. Many species had strongly conical trunks, but a number of quite different varieties rose in corkscrews which their branches repeated. Daniel had noticed similar patterns in shinewood panels, but he'd assumed that the grain was artificial.

"Spread out!" Woetjans rasped to her section. "Keep your eyes open but *don't* bloody start the trouble!"

Then, presumably over her shoulder, "Six, we're outa the woods. Nobody's showing at the windows, but there's an enclosure and a couple guys without clothes looking out through the wire."

"Those are prisoners, captured rebels," Adele said. She was using a commo helmet for the moment, but she would probably set it on the floor as soon as she'd found a place to settle and bring out her personal data unit. "The administrators call them ferals."

She frowned and added, "Don't let the administrators kill them if you can help it. We'll need them."

"Woetjans!" Daniel called. "Secure those prisoners! Do what you need to keep them safe!"

He thought for a blink of time, then said, "Come on, Hogg! Dasi—"

The bosun's mate commanding the rear guard.

"—stay with the senator. I'm going forward!"

They jogged past Forbes and her aides. She looked startled and concerned. It was hard to tell how much she'd understood of the shouted conversation with the advanced guard.

It was uphill and spacers don't get a lot of practice running, but it wouldn't be far. Daniel burst out of the trees, allowing Hogg to get ahead as he couldn't on the narrow path. Unless he'd been willing to clout the young master out of the way, of course—a plan that he'd probably considered for the young master's own sake.

The vegetation on the hundred feet remaining between the woodline and the nearest of the three buildings was blackened and dead, killed by herbicide rather than fire. Burning it off would've released a lethal cloud of the toxins that the staff was trying to keep away from their quarters.

"Base Alpha, this is Captain Daniel Leary, RCN!" Daniel called as he trotted forward. "We are taking control of this facility in the name of the Republic and of Senator Beverly Forbes!"

He was trying not to wheeze and also trying not to fall on his face. Quartz outcrops in the coarse laterite and the twisted remnants of vegetation made the footing treacherous, but he didn't dare take his eyes off the buildings he was running toward.

He wore a pistol on his equipment belt, more as a badge of rank than a weapon; he wasn't a good pistol shot. The holster slapped his thigh as he ran.

"If you resist," called the public address speakers under the eaves of both buildings, "you will infalli- bly hang as rebels against the Republic of Cinnabar! Depend on it!"

It took Daniel a moment to realize that the threaten- ing voice was Adele's. He should've expected that, he supposed; she'd said that she'd been listening in through their communications system. That meant, being Adele, that she could take control of it as she wished.

"I surrender!" someone cried shrilly from inside the nearer building. "Don't shoot! I surrender!"

The twenty-odd spacers of the advanced guard had spread around the buildings and were pointing their guns at whatever seemed most threatening to each individual. *Nothing* seemed very threatening to Daniel, but his spacers were determined not to miss a bet.

Woetjans was poised to kick in the front door, which was dull red plastic and contrasted with the beige walls. Since it opened outward, she'd probably fail— and then somebody would shoot the latch off without bothering to see if it was locked in the first place.

Daniel grimaced. This wasn't at all the placid stroll to the door and presentation of credentials that he'd hoped for before they'd landed, but there wasn't any help for it. He certainly wasn't going to come without an armed escort; and even if he had, the *Milton*'s enormous bulk would probably have put the wind up the locals' tails.

"Please, please, don't shoot!" the voice squealed. The door quivered as someone grabbed the handle from the other side.

Woetjans tensed. Daniel tapped her on the shoulder and gestured her back forcibly.

"Come out, then!" he said. "You won't be harmed so long as you turn over control of the facility promptly."

The door opened. The man who came out was fat besides being tall. Though balding, his moustache flowed into the beard that covered his neck; the facial hair was intensely black. He wore a white shirt and a shoulder sash of red silk.

"I'm the, ah ...," he said. His voice was higher pitched than his bulk suggested. "That is, my name's Disch. Please, we've put up all the guns and we only have them for the ferals anyway. We'll do anything you say!"

Looking down he noticed his sash. He tugged violently without being able to tear the cloth, then lifted it over his head and threw it onto the ground.

A barefoot woman wearing a brown shift stepped out of the door behind Disch. She held a frying pan before her.

"Right," said Daniel. "Now, Master Disch, how many staff members do you have—"

The woman brought the pan up and around in both hands, slamming the edge into the base of Disch's skull. The cast iron rang dully, but the sound of crunching bone was sickeningly audible as well.

Blood splattered, a drop splashing Daniel's cheek. Disch's eyes rolled upward; he pitched forward on his face. Daniel stepped to the side to avoid the big man; he grabbed the woman by both wrists.

"Let me—" she shouted; then her taut muscles relaxed. She let go of the frying pan. Meeting Daniel's eyes, she said, "There's five of us, and him."

She kicked Disch's thigh with her heel. Though she

was barefoot, her soles were callused like hooves; the stroke would have hurt if the fallen man had been conscious. He was breathing in great snorts.

Adele stepped around her to get to the doorway. She was holding her data unit and the wands in her right hand; her left was in her tunic pocket. Her utility trousers were stained by the dead vegetation she'd been sitting on, though that wasn't obvious on the black-and-gray mottled fabric.

"Mistress!" said Tovera.

Woetjans gripped Adele's sleeve, pulling her back; Tovera entered the room with her sub-machine gun ready. Adele looked up with an expression as cold as the blade of a guillotine; the bosun released her.

Adele smiled faintly. "Yes, I take your point, Woetjans," she said, taking her left hand out of her pocket. "But be careful, please. Sometimes I just react when I'm thinking of other things."

Barnes and four other armed spacers entered the building; Adele followed them. Close up, Daniel could see that algae with a faintly orange cast was creeping over the structural plastic, softening its lines but probably making it dangerous to touch.

"He's just a trustee," said the girl Daniel held. She prodded Disch with a toe—not a blow but a disparaging reference. "No different from the rest of us, but he thinks he's god because the off-planet staff lets him act like one. *They* won't stay here, so Disch does what he pleases."

She half-smiled. "Did," she said.

This would be a more unpleasant place to live than many of the apparently harsher worlds which Daniel had seen. You could move normally on the surface, unlike some iceworlds, but that surface would inevitably begin to devour you. The woman had a rash beneath her chin and on the inside of both arms, and a line of sores circled the neck of the sprawled Disch where his collar rubbed.

Forbes and her aides stamped up from the woods. Dasi had kept his spacers from rushing forward when Woetjans charged the compound with the lead section; he deserved a pat on the back for that, which Daniel would see he got as soon as things quieted down. Not quite yet, though. . . .

"In the name of the Senate and people of the Republic!" the senator said. "I declare the entire world of Fonthill under martial law. Cinnabar forever!"

Spacers cheerfully shouted, "Cinnabar forever!" and, "Up Cinnabar!" Some of the most gleeful weren't, as Daniel knew from their enlistment records, even Cinnabar citizens.

Daniel shot a sharp glance at the woman he was holding. She was much younger than he'd judged, no more than eighteen. Her arms and legs were badly bruised, and he suspected there were more bruises on the places that her loose shift covered.

"Are you going to be all right if I let you go?" Daniel said. He could get one of the spacers to watch her or even tie her up, but he didn't want to do that if he could avoid it.

She laughed without humor. "I'm fine," she said. "If you mean, am I going to hit that bastard again—"

She jabbed Disch with her foot.

"—no, don't worry. Though I don't know why you bloody care. He's not worth anybody caring, believe me."

Daniel *did* believe her, but he was a naval officer and the matter didn't fall within his remit. If Forbes wanted to set up kangaroo courts, he as the ranking RCN officer would provide the civil authorities with support as required. Until then, he'd maintain order among the local population so long as that was consistent with his naval duties.

Forbes was trying to get into the headquarters building, which *was* part of Daniel's duties. The senator's two servants were about to try pushing through the spacers who clogged the doorway, and that wasn't going to end in a good way.

"Poindexter!" Daniel said, stepping between Forbes and the spacers' backs. "Smolich! Get your asses out of Her Excellency's way. Woetjans, I want all personnel out of the control room *now* except you and two others. Put the compound in a posture of defense!"

He paused while the room emptied. There'd been a dozen spacers inside, along with the Adele, Tovera, and the Fonthill officials—trustees, the woman had said, as though this were a prison. Which it obviously was, in the minds of everybody who was involved with it.

Daniel and Hogg followed Forbes into the control room. The building didn't have climate control, and though the large openings under the roofpeaks provided ventilation, they did nothing for the mugginess.

The officials were three men and an older, heavily tattooed, woman. The men stood with their backs to the wall while the woman leaned against it, supporting her weight with her arms. She glared over her shoulder at Tovera, but Tovera's smile was considerably more threatening.

Adele was speaking into a modern communications console. She looked up when Daniel entered.

"The rebels are dealing with interloping traders,"

she said. "Hydriotes, I'm sure, moonlighting between runs to Fonthill under contract to Beckford's companies. But that means they must monitor the shipping frequencies, so I've been calling the local rebel commander, Earl Wiley."

"Carry on, Mundy," Daniel said. "Excellent!"

He turned to the captured officials. The men appeared harmless, cowed and frightened. The tattooed woman—well, she was harmless with Tovera watching her over the muzzle of a sub-machine gun, but it might be as well to transfer her to the prisoner cage outside.

"Right," Daniel said. "First, I'll want the location of all the labor camps here on Fonthill. Who'll find that for me, hey?"

"I schedule the runs," the eldest of the three men said. His left arm was shrunken, though all the fingers moved; Daniel wondered whether it was a pre-existing injury or reaction to the endemic poisons of this hellworld. "I can show you on the other computer, the one in there."

He nodded toward the room to the left. The doorway was arched and closed with a screen of glittering plastic ribbons.

"But it won't be quite up to date on where they're cutting, because the satellite link's been out for the past week."

Which explained why Adele couldn't access it from the *Milton*: bad maintenance instead of exceptional security. If all the personnel on Fonthill were slaves, the chances were that bad maintenance was the only maintenance there was.

"We'll see if we can't get that working shortly," Daniel

said, wishing that he'd brought Cory along. Well, they'd sort it in good time, he was sure. "For now, show me the unit. And what's your name, my good man?"

"Daniel!" Adele said. "I have contact."

That wasn't according to RCN protocol, but none of the spacers present looked startled. They didn't think of Adele as a signals officer, and however Lady Mundy spoke to Six was fine with them. Lieutenant Commander Robinson might've had conniptions, but he was smart enough to keep his mouth shut—and anyway, he and the *Wartburg* were still in orbit.

"Who is this that calls to Comrade Wiley, over?" said the console's speakers; Adele must have cut them on when she got the signal.

"I'll speak," said Forbes, stepping in front of Daniel in the assumption that he would give way. As he did, because this wasn't a tactical situation; but he felt his face harden slightly.

"Go ahead, then," said Adele, looking up. Her face was blank, but again Daniel had the realization that the senator might want to be more careful about what she said and how she said it.

"This is Lady Beverly Forbes," the senator said, striking a pose unconsciously. "Senator of the Republic and Ambassador Plenipotentiary to the Veil and neighboring worlds. I'm here to bring Fonthill under direct Cinnabar rule and to right any wrongs which may have been done here. I want you to come to Base Alpha immediately so that we can negotiate an arrangement which will greatly benefit you and your followers."

She stopped. "Over," said Adele, more punctilious as intermediary than she ordinarily was with her own communications.

"Are you mad, woman?" the console replied. The cackling laugh that followed suggested that the man on the other end of the conversation—Comrade Wiley himself—wasn't too tightly wrapped either. "Wiley does not come to Base Alpha or anywhere else. If you wish Wiley, you come to him! Over."

The Fonthill authorities—if that wasn't too grand a description—must be completely lacking in military skills and equipment if the rebel chieftain was willing to communicate directly. Whether the sender was broadcasting or bouncing his signal through the satellite net, Adele certainly had a fix on the location. A missile or a company of Marines could be on top of it within an hour if that were the plan.

Which it wasn't, of course.

"Don't get above yourself, Wiley," Forbes said sharply. "Of course I'm not going off into a swamp to meet a run slave. You have my word that you and your followers will be safe when they come to Base Alpha."

Instead of adding the closing protocol, Adele said calmly, "I didn't transmit that, Senator. I'll take it from here."

"What?" said Forbes.

"Quiet down the tattooed lady if she moves, Woetjans," Tovera said, shifting her stance. She'd hung the sub-machine gun under her right arm in a patrol sling; now the waist-high muzzle pointed at the senator's aides. The men with guns merely blinked, but Platt squealed and dropped the briefcase he'd been clutching to his chest on the hike from the *Milton.*

Hogg chuckled. He'd slung the impeller and was holding a folding knife with a knuckleduster grip. It was made for close quarters like this, but Daniel had seen Hogg throw the weapon fifteen feet to put the point through the eye of a flying lizard and into the creature's brain.

"She's too smart to do that," Hogg said. "Isn't that so, sweetie?"

The woman snarled a curse, but she didn't try to straighten from her off-balance position.

"Comrade Wiley...," Adele said. She'd made her initial contact behind an active cancellation screen, but she left that down now so that everyone else in the room could hear her conversation. "This is Lady Adele Mundy, Senator Forbes's colleague. We've freed two of your fellows, Comrades Jarrod Selsmark and Fred Gibbs. I'm going to put them on in just a moment."

As she spoke, Barnes and another rigger, Jimmi Laursen, chivied the two prisoners down the short hallway from the cage. They were stinking and emaciated, and despite their attempts at bravado they were obviously afraid of what was going to happen next.

"I want you to set up a rendezvous with them," Adele continued. This hadn't been planned; but Adele had a quick mind and didn't bother discussing things she considered obvious. "I assume you have some kind of code. The Republic will provide your colleagues with whatever form of transportation they wish, and my secretary and I will accompany them to you. Then we can go over the Republic's offer in person. Over."

She gestured the—former—prisoners toward her. Barnes prodded one at the base of the spine with the muzzle of his impeller; they both lurched forward.

"This is not enough!" cried the console. "I am Wiley! I will meet with the senator!"

"You'll meet with Mundy of Chatsworth, Comrade

Wiley," Adele said, "and if you know anything of Cinnabar history you'll feel honored. Now, I'm turning the console over to your colleagues. Comrade Selsmark—"

She pointed at the nearer prisoner. He was tall and must once have been powerful. His red beard was in two braids, though they had frayed into a tangle.

"—see if you can convince your leader that it's in his best interests to deal with me as a friend."

"You're on," she said, chopping her index finger down.

In a quiet aside to Daniel, Adele added, "Because he *is* going to be dealing with me."

Adele sat beside Selsmark on the forward thwart of the square-bowed skiff, balancing Tovera and Gibbs with the control wheel in the stern. The motor sang with high-pitched enthusiasm, but it wasn't really big enough for the twenty-foot vessel, even with only four people aboard. They were travelling up the sluggish watercourse at what ordinarily would've been a walking pace.

It wouldn't have been possible to walk so quickly along this route, however, or for that matter to walk at all. Sideways the skiff could've spanned the stream at its widest, and the vegetation to either side wasn't so much a wall as a ragged 200-foot cliff.

Though a number of the trees shared common features—corkscrew trunks and an orange undertone to the bark were the most visible ones—Adele wouldn't have sworn that any two were the same species. Daniel might be able to judge which were age states or genders of a particular tree, but Adele was lost without a database. If Master Beckford's scouts had bothered to log that sort of information, it hadn't reached files which Adele could access.

Something in the forest called, "Coo! Coo! Coo!" It was very loud, but Adele couldn't tell which side of the stream it was on. She thought it might be a signal, but the feral beside her paid no attention.

Adele's data unit was in her lap, though she'd resisted bringing it live. It had nothing useful to tell her and would've been better in its thigh pocket, but she took comfort in its open presence.

"We ought to be getting close," Selsmark mumbled through a mouthful of protein ration taken straight from the packet without rehydration. He seemed to be speaking to himself anyway, though Adele could understand him when she concentrated. "*Bloody* hell, I don't like this, I don't like it a bit!"

Cory on the *Milton*'s bridge was tracking her through the data unit, but the satellites that guided Fonthill's logging crews saw only the top of the triple canopy. Cory could follow the barge's progress, but he couldn't give warning of what might be waiting beneath the curtain of foliage. Branches interwove from both sides, hiding the stream from above.

Four-legged, four-winged, insectoids swarmed up from rafts of algae and landed on the passengers. They didn't bite or sting, but the touch of their feet itched and might raise welts in the course of time. Since all the vegetation was poisonous, the creatures that ate it were likely to transport the toxins also.

The ferals ignored them, and Adele avoided brushing the insects away also. If they were poisonous, spreading their juices over her body wasn't going to help the situation.

Selsmark finished the ration packet and threw it into the bottom of the skiff. Adele said, "What do you eat in the jungle?"

"Bloody little," the feral muttered. He scanned the green tangle to either side with nervous flicks of his eyes. "Whatever we can plant, corn and squash mainly. Nothing local, it'll rot you from the inside. What we steal from the camps, what we trade to the ships that slip in from Hydra, but they pay us crap for logs. Not near as good as they pay Beckford, but we've no choice. And mostly we buy guns."

He looked over his shoulder, his mouth twisted in a snarl. "Gibbs!" he said. "Can't you get this bloody thing to go faster?"

The animal—or bird—boomed a single brassy, "Coo!"

The mudbank ahead was so fresh that its surface was only vaguely iridescent with algae. Six men stepped out onto it. Four were naked except for breechclouts made from rice sacks. Two had crossbows, while the other two carried spears with plastic shafts and blades made from kitchen knives. Their skin was both freshly ulcerated and scarred from old injuries.

"Wiley!" Selsmark cried, rocking the skiff as he spun around. "I was afraid you wouldn't come."

Park rotated the small wheel and pulled it back. The skiff lost way and nosed toward the bank as the little electric motor groaned to silence. Adele slid the data unit away with her right hand.

"Is that what you were afraid of, Selsmark?" said the feral chief. "Then you really are a fool—but I knew that already, from the fact that you came to me."

Wiley was small and delicate, scarcely bigger than Adele herself. Incongruously he wore a gray business suit and a peaked hat of a style that had been fashionable on Blythe five years ago; there was a yellow quill in the hatband. He was unarmed.

The skiff nosed softly into the mud. Selsmark rocked forward, then leaned back on the thwart.

"I'm your friend, your soldier, Wiley!" he cried. "What do you mean? I've escaped, of course I come to my leader!"

"Help him out of the boat, Dapp," Wiley said harshly. "Selsmark, do you think I don't know you told Disch where we'd cached the last shipment of arms?"

"No!" Selsmark said. "I was a prisoner! The Cinnabars can tell you, they freed me!"

The sixth man was huge, taller even than Disch and muscular rather than fat. He was naked save for a spiked leather jockstrap and bandoliers over both shoulders, but his skin had been painted red and orange and white. Two pistols and six knives dangled from the bandoliers, and he held a stocked impeller at the balance in his left hand.

Leaning forward, he seized Selsmark by the neck with a right hand that looked like a huge orange crab and jerked him up from the thwart. The skiff rocked; Adele didn't move.

"We moved the guns before the soldiers came, fool!" Wiley said. "As you should've known we would, fool and bastard of a fool! But we waited in the bush and watched the soldiers searching. Of course they threw you back in the cage! But you did not lie to Disch, you lie to Wiley now!"

Selsmark wheezed but no words could force a way past the bodyguard's choking grip. His face was turning dark.

Wiley spit at the man he'd condemned as a traitor. "Finish him, Dapp," he said cheerfully.

The big man tossed his impeller to a spearman. With his now free left hand, he drew a carving knife with a ten-inch blade. Selsmark thrashed even more wildly, but Dapp held him out at arm's length so that his bare feet couldn't reach him. He thrust the knife beneath Selsmark's breastbone. He shoved it forward till the point came out the victim's back, then ripped the blade down till it grated on the pelvis.

Dapp pulled the knife out; Selsmark's intestines spilled onto the mud in long pink coils. Laughing, Dapp wiped the blade on Selsmark's bare shoulder; his teeth had been filed to points. He tossed the dying man to the side and sheathed his weapon.

Selsmark landed on his back. His eyes had glazed, but his hands made several fumbling attempts to stuff his intestines back into his belly before a tetanic convulsion wracked him as he died.

"Now . . . ," said Wiley. "Which of you little ladies thinks she will offer terms to Comrade Wiley, hey?"

"I will," said Adele, rising to her feet. She paused till the skiff's bow had settled firmly again, then got out. She had no choice but to step onto mud covered with a wash of Selsmark's gore, but at least she was able to avoid the loops of entrails.

The *Milton*'s gig rumbled across the high sky, carrying Daniel on his portion of the operation. That would be difficult also, though not—Adele smiled—in the same fashion.

"I'm Lady Adele Mundy," she said. "Mundy of Chatsworth that is, and this is my servant Tovera."

CHAPTER 16

Base Amorgos, Fonthill

The *Milton*'s gig had four plasma thrusters. A single moderate-sized unit would've provided sufficient output to propel the little vessel, but safety and controllability at low altitude required the larger number.

Daniel grinned. Because gigs were expected to carry senior officers and dignitaries, safety was a greater concern than might otherwise have been the case. He'd landed anti-pirate cutters of about the same size, and that had been exciting every time.

Cass McDonough, the coxswain, hadn't served in one of Daniel's commands before; Daniel had never before had a command that rated a gig or a cox. The clearing, projected on Daniel's face-shield was rushing up at a pace that made him want to grab the controls, but McDonough caught them on a cushion of vectored plasma and rotated the gig back for front without the hop it would have taken if Daniel had been at the controls.

McDonough had been Admiral Trelawney's cox for

the twelve years before Trelawney retired. Nonetheless, Daniel never really trusted a specialist till he'd seen him perform, and if it was a specialty Daniel knew something about, he was a very hard judge.

The gig settled with a *rasp/bump/rasp* of the thrusters, a delicacy possible only because of the four lightly loaded nozzles. The touchdown was smoother than many aircars would have managed.

"Very well done, McDonough," Daniel said, releasing his straps to rise. "Woetjans, open the hatch, if you will."

The cox was in fact a great deal better than her captain would've been at the controls of the gig. She should have been, of course, but Daniel was—he grinned again, wryly this time: cocky was the term he'd heard frequently at the Academy—cocky enough to think he could give anybody a run at almost anything having to do with a spaceship. Senior Motorman McDonough had just defined one of the "almosts."

Daniel lifted his face-shield. While greeting Colonel Stockheim with a polarized ball instead of a face was proper in the military sense—he was in utilities and this was a combat zone—it wouldn't advance the spirit of friendly professionalism that he hoped would prevail during the negotiations.

"Sir?" said McDonough, turning her head as best she could while still strapped into the control console; she was prepared for an emergency liftoff, as was a proper if unlikely concern. "You might want to give the atmosphere a minute or two to clear."

Woetjans ignored her, cycling the inner and outer hatches together. The gig's tiny airlock would take two people in airsuits or one rigger, but it was normally going to be opened on the surface or a pressurized bay. It didn't have the safety features that the locks of a starship would.

"I don't believe we're senior enough to be prostrated by a lingering whiff of ozone, do you?" Daniel said, adjusting the holster on his equipment belt and the hang of his uniform. No doubt McDonough meant well, but Daniel wasn't a porcelain admiral who needed a coxswain to fuss over him. "I'll lead, Woetjans."

Camp Sixteen, the northernmost of Fonthill's logging camps and the site Colonel Stockheim had chosen for his base of operations, was the wasteland Daniel had expected, but to his surprise it hadn't been clear-cut. Hundred-foot spikes, some of them with streamers of foliage still fluttering from the top, were scattered at intervals from fifty to a hundred feet. They'd make landing the *Wartburg* trickier than expected, though it should be easy enough to bring them down with belts of explosive.

Assuming the colonel agreed, of course.

Daniel tramped down the gig's ramp; Hogg and Woetjans flanked him a pace behind. Stockheim and two aides stood at parade rest thirty feet away. The colonel looked furious, but Daniel couldn't tell whether that was because the bosun was female or just his general attitude to the situation. Certainly the situation deserved a scowl or worse.

Great stumps dotted the interior of the base, but the trash of branches and scraps which Daniel had noticed in two camps the gig overflew had been bulldozed into the earthen berm which now ringed Sixteen. There were bunkers as well, ready to defend against attack even without the armored personnel carriers now facing out from the berm.

The APCs were air cushion. Except for them and the aircars aboard the *Milton*, transport on Fonthill was by boat or by the great hydrogen-filled blimps which hauled logs to Base Alpha.

Impeller slugs had twice ricocheted from the gig's heavy plating on the way here. The blimps were easily patched and their lift gas was hydrolyzed from the abundant water, but a slug through an aircar motor or even a fan blade wouldn't be survivable. The pilots in blimp gondolas didn't have an easy time either, though the captured officials said there was competition for the job because extra rations were a perk of it.

Stockheim saluted. He wore a slung sub-machine gun, and unlike Daniel's pistol it wasn't for show.

"Captain Leary," he said. "I didn't expect to see you again."

His craggy face lurched into a smile as grim as a landslide. He added, "To be honest, after we learned the situation here, I didn't expect to see anyone I could consider a representative of the government of the Republic."

Daniel returned the salute, though not well. Generally he didn't care, but he hoped Stockheim didn't feel the clumsiness implied a lack of respect.

"Colonel," he said, "you've had time to go over the material that Officer Mundy transmitted to you on my behalf?"

"Yes," said Stockheim. The syllable was as uncompromising as the slam of a cell door. "Let's go to the TOC. We've got maps there, and besides—"

There was slightly more humor in his grin this time.

"—I feel naked standing out here, even though the

ferals don't have heavy weapons that we've encountered as yet. They don't even snipe very often."

"There's no point in giving wogs a chance to get lucky," Daniel said with a smile, falling in with the Brotherhood troops as they crisply went about face and strode toward the Tactical Operations Center—three trailers dug halfway down into the purplish soil, with layers of sandbags covering the exposed walls.

"We'd begun to suspect something of the sort ourselves, sir," said the younger aide, gesturing Daniel ahead of him down the steps of plastic-sealed earth. The three soldiers could have been son, father and grandfather, so close was the resemblance. "Otherwise, I don't think we'd have been able to believe the documents you transmitted."

"If I may ask, Captain Leary...," said the older aide. "How is it that you came by the material?"

Each of the trailers held a console, a smaller version of the units on the bridge of the *Milton* or any other starship from a developed world. Two were manned, but the operators didn't look up when Stockheim and his companions entered.

The area in the center of the trefoil had been dug down further and shaded with a tarpaulin. A book of three-foot-by-three-foot acetate maps of the region lay on the simple folding table there.

Daniel crossed his hands behind his back. "As I understand it, gentlemen," he lied, "it was pure accident. An employee of Cone Transport misdirected an internal file to Governor Das. He sent it to his ministry, which passed it up to the Senate. Because Senator Forbes was already in the region, her colleagues requested her to investigate—which brought us here."

To the best of Daniel's knowledge, there wasn't a word of truth in what he'd just said. Daniel had no intention of answering the Brotherhood officer's impertinent question. Saying so wouldn't have helped achieve the ends of Captain Daniel Leary and of the Republic of Cinnabar, so he'd invented a believable lie instead.

And it *was* an impertinent question.

The Brethren positioned themselves on three sides of the map table; Daniel by default took the place across from the colonel. Stockheim ruffled the map sheets, his face as harsh as that of the legendary boy whose belly was chewed open by the fox he'd stolen.

"Captain Leary," he said, "granting the truth of documents you've provided—and I *do* grant that, they explain matters that made no sense before—there's still the question of our honor. We have our orders."

Hogg and Woetjans stood in the empty trailer. They talked in low voices, but their eyes never left the group around the map table.

Daniel grimaced. "Colonel Stockheim," he said, "you've seen the secret attachment to the orders posting your regiment to Fonthill. If you like, I can probably get you a copy of the encryption key so that you can decrypt the attachment on your own console here. That is, you can if you had the common sense to make a copy before you handed the chip over to Administrator Disch."

He hoped that Adele would provide some sort of emasculated key if necessary, but he hoped even more that it wouldn't be necessary. Daniel had met officers who seemed to have nothing but the Military Regulations between their ears, but in the present case even the regulations were on the side of common sense.

"Colonel," he said urgently, "your orders were illegal.

Senator Forbes represents the Republic to which your honor is pledged. Her authority has been accepted by Headman Hieronymos, so I can't imagine what problem *you* can have with it."

"Women are the lesser vessels," the young aide said. He'd been looking down at the acetate-printed maps, but now he glared straight at Daniel. "We of the Brotherhood do not accept orders from women."

"Really, Lieutenant?" Daniel said. He didn't have to pretend that he found the situation funny, though he knew there were other possible reactions to this stiff-necked idiot's words. "But you don't have any problem taking orders from Prince Willie Beckford, apparently—and I assure you, he's not a man in any sense that *I* recognize."

The boy blushed, indicating that even the Brotherhood of Amorgos had heard stories about Prince Willie's revels.

"Regardless," Daniel continued breezily, "the question doesn't arise. A senator doesn't have any military rank, so you'll be taking orders from the senior RCN officer in the region. Me."

He beamed at the three Brethren. "I hope you don't question my manhood, Lieutenant?" he added mildly to the young aide.

The boy blushed even darker. "No sir," he whispered toward the maps. "I didn't mean that at all, sir. Sir, I'm very sorry."

"I checked your record after we met on Paton, Leary," the colonel said. His smile wasn't wide, but it seemed sincere. As with Adele, one got the impression that his face might crack if his lips spread too broadly. "I'm not in doubt about your manhood."

He swallowed; his face wrinkled as though what had been in his mouth was sour. "While I realize that my business as a soldier is to take orders, not to question them, has any provision been made to protect the laborers after the regiment is withdrawn?"

"The ferals are beasts," the older aide said. He didn't raise his voice, but harsh emotion trembled in his tone. "I know how Beckford has treated the laborers on Fonthill, but the fact remains that the ones who've run—the ones who survive in the wild—aren't human any more."

"And you mustn't think that they'll spare the laborers who're still in the camps," said the younger man earnestly. "They hate the ones who haven't run even worse than they do the administrators, or they seem to. They *eat* laborers they capture, as if they were cattle!"

"We'll be taking the laborers away with us," Daniel said. If Adele had been here, she would've commandeered one of the consoles to create a visual display; perhaps she'd have shown the Hydriote fleet which would be removing the former slaves. Still, his verbal description seemed to be holding the Brethren's attention. "And that includes your ferals, if my colleague Officer Mundy can convince them to go with us."

"Are you joking, Leary?" Colonel Stockheim said, his voice getting colder and harsher with each syllable. "What could you possibly offer the ferals? They're not human any more, we've told you!"

"I'm offering them a cash payment to be determined later, plus citizenship on Bolton," Daniel said. "Or rather, Officer Mundy is, in the name of Senator

Forbes. The same offer that's being made to all the other laborers on Fonthill. They can stay here, of course, but I can't imagine why they would want to."

"Bolton?" said the young aide, frowning as he tried to get a mental grip on the statement. "Sir, the only Bolton I know is an Alliance world in the Montserrat Stars."

"Right," said Daniel, "at the moment. But they're about to become Friends of Cinnabar. That's why we need the labor force from here. The ordinary workers will patrol St. James Harbor, where about half the planet's population lives. That will be peacekeeping so long as there's enough of a garrison from the start to keep the lid on. Out in the countryside, though, where there isn't that kind of control—well, that's work for the ferals. They'll find the conditions better than they are in the jungle here, and from what you tell me—"

He met the eyes of each of the Brethren in turn. Their faces were gray. Daniel was smiling, but someone who knew him would have noticed that his cheeks were set in hard lines.

"—they'll find anti-partisan work more congenial than you or I would."

Nobody spoke for a moment.

"I told you I'd read your file, Leary," Stockheim said at last. His face and voice were without expression; his fingers riffled the maps again. "I'm just a soldier, but I've seen things; I can read between the lines of a report."

"Yes sir?" said Daniel, meeting the eyes of the older man.

"I read about what you'd done in the Bagarian

Cluster," Stockheim said, "and I thought, 'He's as hard as his father, and his father was as hard as the Speaker's Rock.'"

Daniel heard a whisper of sound, though it was so faint that the landsmen probably didn't notice it. A starship was tearing through the upper levels of the atmosphere, coming in for a landing.

"Colonel," he said carefully, "we're at war. And we've both taken oaths to defend the Republic against her foreign enemies."

"Yes," said the colonel. "But I'm glad my duties involve these."

He patted the receiver of his sub-machine gun.

"The work is cleaner, in my opinion."

"The Republic is fortunate to have soldiers of your quality, sir," Daniel said. "And certainly I'm fortunate on this operation."

"Captain?" said the young aide. "If I may ask—what do you foresee as the Brotherhood's role in your operation? You haven't said."

"Ah!" said Daniel with a nod. His face shivered into his familiar grin, like ice breaking up in the rush of a spring freshet. "Yes, I mentioned that Bolton would shortly be joining the Friends of Cinnabar?"

The Brethren nodded, their expressions all to a degree guarded.

"Well, gentlemen," Daniel said. "Your regiment and my *Milton* are the instruments which are going to make that happen."

Even if the soldiers had wanted to reply, the thunder of the *Wartburg* dropping down to land beyond the berm would have drowned them out.

West of Base Alpha, Fonthill

The innate goodness of the Lower Orders of Mankind was an article of faith with Adele's mother, Evadne Rolfe Mundy. Apparently the Lower Orders—Evadne capitalized the words—had a simple purity which brought them closer to Nature and therefore to The Good.

After the Mundy estates were confiscated during the Proscriptions, Adele had spent many years as a member of those Lower Orders. She therefore viewed them without her mother's blinders of ignorance. Adele had no great affection for civilized Man, but Man in a state of nature stank.

That was particularly true when—she gave Wiley a cold smile—one member of the Lower Orders had just disemboweled another member on the mud bank beside you. She said, "Senator Forbes has arrived at Base Alpha aboard the RCS *Milton* and begun to bring Fonthill under proper Cinnabar government. As part of that process—"

Adele moved sideways to allow Tovera to get out of the barge without stepping in Selsmark's reeking entrails. The other freed captive, Gibbs, remained seated at the transom. He was still holding the control wheel, and his face was as stiff as if he'd died of strychnine poisoning.

"—Senator Forbes has granted all current Fonthill residents an amnesty for crimes committed before her arrival."

Tovera toed the corpse's thigh. Daniel had provided the freed ferals with trousers from the *Milton*'s slop chest before they set off in the barge. The long knife had severed Selsmark's waist cord, so his pants had fallen to his knees before Dapp had flung the body down.

"I'd say this was an internal organizational matter, not a crime Lady Mundy would have to report," she said. She held her attaché case slightly open in her left hand, but her right hung at her side. "Still, it might be a good idea not to repeat it, all right?"

She smiled at Wiley.

Wiley's other four supporters had retreated minusculely when Dapp executed the adjudged traitor. They backed farther now, glancing between Adele and Tovera in amazement.

"Do you laugh at me, lady?" Wiley squealed. "I *eat* pretty ladies like you! Do you *hear* me? We going to deal, yes, but I make the deal! Your people pay plenty to get you back, pretty lady!"

"Comrade Wiley," Adele said sharply. She reached into her tunic pocket. "This is an extremely good offer from your viewpoint. If you refuse it—"

"Dapp!" said Wiley. "The little pale one has a smart tongue. You fix her like Selsmark. Then the pretty lady knows we mean business!"

Dapp laughed, baring his filed teeth. He reached for Tovera's throat. Tovera didn't move, but Adele brought out her pistol.

"*Wah!*" Dapp said. He jumped back.

Adele shot him twice in the right eye. He was so close that a blob of clear jelly splashed her cheek. His left arm and leg flailed convulsively. Wiley tried to jump out of the way, but Dapp's fist clouted him on the cheek and knocked him down.

Adele waggled the pistol out at her side to cool it;

even two shots seriously heated the barrel. To drop
the weapon back in her pocket immediately risked
charring the lining and even giving herself a blister.

A feral lifted his spear. "*Put* that down," Adele said.

The feral threw it to the ground and vanished into
the jungle behind him. His three fellows followed an
instant later, one of them dropping his crossbow as
he ran.

Dapp fell onto his back. The knives on his bandoliers rattled as his body shuddered. His mouth and
left eye were open, and pinkish brains oozed from
the crater of the right one.

Adele grimaced. Wiley rested on his elbows with
a dazed expression.

"Get up," she snapped. She put the pistol out of
sight to encourage him; by now the coil-wrapped
barrel was only vaguely warm.

"What will you do to me?" said Wiley, rising with
a careful expression. He was judging whether he'd be
better to run or to jump the pair of small women,
calling for his henchmen to return.

Tovera took out her little sub-machine gun. "Stay
and listen, little man," she said. "You'll like that better
than the other ways this could go."

"I'm going to make you a fair offer and return to
Base Alpha, just as I've been saying," Adele said. She
had a good deal of practice at restating the obvious,
but she'd never come to like the experience; that was
one of the reasons she found dealing with Daniel to
be such a pleasure. "I have neither the desire nor
the ability to force you to take it, but common sense
should be enough."

She was suddenly dizzy. *The stench*, she thought,

blinking angrily, but it wasn't Dapp's voided bowels. It wasn't even reaction to the adrenaline that a few instants of violence hadn't burned out of her system. *Some day one of them will kill me instead, and then the dreams will stop.*

Wiley rose, eyeing her warily. *Did he notice that?* But the feral probably hadn't seen anything wrong, and anyway it couldn't matter.

"You're welcome to stay on Fonthill if you like," Adele said, drawing a handkerchief from her breast pocket and wiping her cheek. "We'll be taking all the laborers and staff off with us, though. Perhaps you can arrange for food with Hydriote traders, though for the immediate present their ships are going to be fully occupied in other matters. And nobody else has the coordinates of Fonthill, of course."

Wiley straightened slightly. He didn't relax, but neither was he on the verge of suicidal action. "And if we go with you, we ferals?" he said.

"There'll be fighting," Adele said. "Quite a lot of the civilians where we're going won't like the change of government we're imposing. You'll have modern small arms and the overall direction of the campaign will be by RCN officers."

"The civilians will have guns?" Wiley said.

Adele nodded. "Some of them certainly will," she said. "And many will be retired military personnel. They won't be organized, but individually they'll know what they're doing. Better than you and your personnel will, I dare say."

Wiley sniffed. "Maybe in a battle they would," he said. "From what you tell me, this won't be a battle."

The feral chieftain should have looked ridiculous

standing against a wall of jungle in his mud-blotched suit. He didn't.

"Yes," said Adele. "I take your point."

She cleared her throat as a pause to collect herself. For a moment, her mind had been other places.

"In return for your services to the Republic," she said, "you and your personnel will gain Friendly Citizenship. That is, citizenship on a world classed as a Friend of Cinnabar. You'll be able to vote in planetary elections but not—"

Her smile was dry.

"—for Senators of the Republic. Besides the cash stipend—whose amount has yet to be determined—I have no doubt that despite RCN oversight, your military activities will provide you with ample opportunities for pillage and rape."

Wiley shrugged without speaking. His eyes didn't leave hers.

"In case your comment about cannibalism was more than just boasting," Adele said, "I strongly recommend you drop the practice. Quite a lot that happens during a war will be ignored, but cannibalism will not."

Wiley tugged his trousers around to glance at the seat, but he didn't try vainly to brush away the drying mud. "I can't be everywhere," he said.

This time Adele shrugged. "I'm offering you choices, Comrade Wiley," she said. "What you do with the offers is your own business."

"How much time do we have?" Wiley said. "I'm not saying I accept, but if I do?"

"The last ships will be loading at Base Alpha in four days," Adele said. "After they're gone, the remaining residents will have Fonthill to themselves for months or perhaps years. I suspect that when the Republic returns, it will do so with proper military forces and sufficient ships to enforce its revenue regulations, but that's beyond both my knowledge and my interest."

She looked down at Dapp and Selsmark. They were veiled in insects, and worms or perhaps root tendrils were squirming from the mud to nuzzle them.

"We'll leave you now," she said. She stepped carefully into the skiff, trying not to make it wobble too badly as she worked her way back to Gibbs in the stern. Tovera waited on the mudbank until her mistress was seated on the thwart.

When Adele looked again, Wiley had vanished. Something had raised its wedge-shaped head from the water and was tugging at a coil of Selsmark's intestine. Like the feral chieftain, the creature was small and rather pretty.

From the length of its paired fangs, it was probably poisonous as well.

CHAPTER 17

One light-hour above Bolton

The *Milton* was accelerating at 1 g to maintain the illusion of gravity, but Adele didn't care. She never noticed the discomfort of freefall when she had work to do. At present, she had a great deal of work.

Bolton's planetary defense array was even older than the *Merkur's* log had led her to believe, a Type 30 instead of the expected Type 32. That made marginally easier the task of deriving its codes.

The other thing that she'd expected—not counted on but expected, the way she expected to awaken in the bunk where she'd gone to sleep the night before—was that the array would be poorly maintained and that twenty or even thirty percent of the individual mines would be unserviceable for one reason or another. Instead, the serviceability rate was above 95 percent and perhaps as high as 97 percent.

Adele smiled wryly. If the entire garrison of St. James Harbor was as good as the Defense Systems Officer, the Cinnabar forces were facing a very long day which might not have a happy ending. Recriminations would only matter to the survivors, however, and she had no intention of surviving a disaster.

The mine tender *R11* was exchanging signals with the *Wartburg*, which had extracted fifteen minutes previously. The transport was a comfortable distance from the PDA's coverage area, waiting for the tender to pass her through. Captain Robinson had the normal commercial codes, and the *Wartburg* was, after all, exactly what she claimed to be—save for her crew and cargo. There shouldn't be any problem with her clearance.

The trick was getting the *Milton* through, and that was going to be quite a trick. *That's why I'm paid the big ten florins a week*, Adele thought with the same grim smile as before. Plus prize money, which for spacers under Captain Daniel Leary had in the past amounted to considerable amounts. The ones who survived, of course.

A ship was already in the process of landing. It had arrived an hour ahead of the *Wartburg*. Adele frowned, wishing she'd been—distantly—present when it was signalling the tender, so that she could identify it.

The ship began to drop out of orbit. As it did so, the sensor image twinkled as it spoke to the controller below with a modulated laser that wouldn't be smothered like the radio frequency band by the roaring plasma thrusters.

There was good luck and bad luck; and unless you were prepared, all your luck was going to be bad. Adele was prepared. She ran the signals through a decryption program.

The code was Alliance Fleet, not commercial, which

in itself was important to know; but it was intended only for low security communications, shiphandling and docking instructions, so it wouldn't have taken long to defeat even if the particular code set hadn't been included in the updated package Mistress Sand had provided before the *Milton* lifted from Harbor Three.

The aviso *Zieten* was acknowledging St. James Control's directions to land in Fleet Berth 14. That wasn't important in itself, but the fact it was a courier vessel rather than a heavier warship was critical to the success of the operation. Adele transmitted the information as a text crawl at the bottom of Daniel's display.

If by great ill fortune the *Milton* had arrived on Bolton just after an Alliance battleship landed, there would be virtually no chance of accomplishing the operation. Even a destroyer whose captain reacted instantly to the situation would have made success problematic.

Adele didn't for a moment imagine that they would have aborted the mission, of course. "Virtually no chance" had in the past been chance enough, when Daniel was in command.

The cruiser's 8-inch turrets began to rotate, setting up as many competing vibrations as a rainstorm lashing a pond. Adele scowled and lifted her feet from the deck plating. Her console's cushions couldn't smother the tremblers completely, but without competing inputs from the deck she could control her wands with adequate precision.

R11 signalled the *Wartburg* to wait while a path through the defense array was cleared. Adele had hoped that the tender would simply switch off the mines for the time required for the transport to pass through the swept area. That would be easier for the tender's crew, quicker for all concerned, and under ordinary circumstances would be perfectly safe.

Ordinary circumstances didn't include an RCN cruiser waiting to swoop down on the base like an avenging angel. Well, after seeing the array's high state of readiness, Adele hadn't expected good news on the procedures either.

The mines were small thermonuclear weapons. In the instant of dissolution they generated a magnetic lens which channeled the blast in much the way that a plasma cannon did the explosion of its smaller charge. Each mine had a propulsion system, here a simple reaction motor, which allowed it to shift orbit as required by circumstances.

The *R11* sent coded signals to create a dynamic gap in the array, allowing the transport to pass through on a precisely calculated course. If they did this often—and they probably did—the mines would have to be refueled regularly, but the practice eliminated the risk that an interloper would slip in while the array was shut down.

Adele smiled as her equipment translated the tender's signals and passed them through to the astrogation computer for processing. She had to find or deduce the keys to 218 separate mines rather than that of the single signal which would shut down the array. If she made a mistake, she and everyone else aboard the *Milton* would die before they knew it.

If they didn't die, Adele would ask to see the Alliance Defense Systems Officer after Bolton had been conquered. If that officer was alive, she supposed she'd shake his or her hand.

But it would be perfectly all right with Adele Mundy if that careful *bastard* had died in the fighting.

Above Bolton

"Extracting in thirty, that is three-zero, seconds," said Daniel, his right index and middle fingers poised over the virtual EXECUTE button. A light-hour's hop was short, even by the standards of merchant vessels with doubtful astrogators and crews too small to handle a suit of sails capable of real subtlety.

Even so, it concentrated the mind to maneuver toward a planetary defense array which would infallibly destroy a ship that extracted too close to it. "Extracting—now!" Daniel said and hammered the button.

The flip-flop from the Matrix to sidereal space was never pleasant and not infrequently nauseating. Experience didn't help: Daniel knew spacers with forty years experience who regularly emptied their stomachs of bile, though they'd learned long since not to eat before an extraction.

Which left the question of why they hadn't found another line of work. Well, no spacer found that question easy to answer, as Daniel knew from looking into his own heart. Spacefaring was either in the blood or it wasn't, but those who'd caught the infection weren't cured simply because they couldn't keep their breakfast down.

In the present case, extraction meant that Daniel felt a red-hot knife flay his skin away in strips, starting at his scalp and working down. It can't have gone on for more than a second or so. His display flickered as each color switched to its complement, then switched back as the transition became complete.

Instead of a pearly glow, the main screen was a Plot-Position Indicator centered on the *Milton* herself.

Daniel had brought the ship out within three thousand miles of the planned extraction point, excellent work if he did say—well, think—so himself.

"*PDA Control, this is AFS* Luetzow, *requesting permission to land at St. James Harbor with dispatches from General Command,*" said Midshipman Cory. "*Over.*"

The boy's Florentine accent would pass for that of half a dozen Alliance worlds, especially through a single-sideband transmission. Daniel thought Cory's voice was a little higher than usual, but if anything he was drawling his words rather than rattling them out nervously.

Adele usually oversaw the work of her subordinates, especially when they were handling commo. This afternoon—ship's time; it was six in the morning at St. James Harbor—she was wholly focused on manipulating the mines of the defense array. The wands danced in her hands, and a stranger would have taken her set expression as one of cold fury.

It was really just the resting state of her face. Daniel was uncomfortably aware that his friend's resting state might really *be* cold fury, however.

Daniel had left the bridge hatch open even though he expected the *Milton* to go into action shortly. There'd be plenty of time to seal the ship's internal divisions, unless they were caught in the pulse of a mine; and if that happened, the internal divisions would vaporize along with the hull and its whole contents.

The A Level corridor and its bow rotunda were crammed with suited riggers; some had even locked down their helmets. If the cruiser had to reinsert into the Matrix, Woetjans wanted both watches on the hull as soon as possible to adjust the sails. That would be an emergency and no mistake.

They had to remain aboard for now, though, because the sidescatter of the 8-inch cannon would be lethal to personnel anywhere forward of the muzzles. The bosun was willing to take the risk—and she'd have been there with her people, of course—but Daniel was not.

"Luetzow, *this is Bolton Defense*," said the female handling the *R11*'s signals said. "*Transmit your identification codes, over.*"

The signalman probably wanted to ask what the oddball cruiser was doing in the Montserrat Stars, but even a rating on a mine tender knew that such a vessel probably carried an admiral or a high-ranking political delegation. Smart people kept a low profile when folks of that sort showed up unexpectedly.

The *Milton*, originally *Scheer*, had been the attempt of Alliance designers to get battleship performance out of a heavy cruiser hull. Like other something-for-nothing schemes, it was unsuccessful; only three ships had been built in the class. The other two were still in Fleet service, however, and it was no more unlikely that one of them would be arriving on Bolton than that it would be anywhere else.

"*Transmitting codes, over*," said Cory. He'd been trying manfully to learn to manipulate control wands the way Adele did, but he was using a virtual keyboard now since the situation didn't permit any errors. His index finger stabbed, sending the queued message.

Daniel nudged the Port 1 High Drive motor. The brief impulse would start the cruiser swinging to starboard with the slow inevitability of planetary precession. Three seconds after the initial touch on the throttle, he stroked an identical burp from Port 8. That would—if he'd judged correctly—cancel the swing without reversing the change in the vessel's attitude.

"*Bloody hell*, Luetzow!" the mine tender said. "*You've sent last week's codes! Send the current codes* now, *over.*"

Cory had sent the most recent codes he had—those in use when Adele entered the *Merkur*'s log on Paton. The code generator was separate on a Fleet—or RCN—warship, so not even she and the software from her other employer could predict the regular changes from past examples.

"*Wait one, Bolton,*" Cory said. "*I'm checking to see what's the matter. Just bloody wait, over!*"

He sounded agitated, which was perfectly appropriate for a signals officer who's been told that he's transmitted the wrong information. It was *so* appropriate, though, and Cory's face appeared so calm by contrast, that Daniel suspected that the nervousness was acting. The boy had certainly blossomed under Adele's tutelage.

The *Wartburg* was braking to enter the atmosphere; she'd be floating in a berth in St. James Harbor before long. *I wonder if Robinson would be able to pull it off without the* Milton? Probably not, but Daniel hoped that Robinson and the Brotherhood would at least try. It'd be nice to go out on a success, even if he weren't alive to know it.

"Luetzow, *what the bloody hell is going on?*" R11 demanded. This time the voice was male and sounded to be on the edge of panic. The vessel's captain—on a net tender, that would be a junior lieutenant—had taken over from his signalman, though she was probably older and more experienced. *"Either send the right codes or withdraw from the system until you can, over!"*

"Bolton, this is Luetzow!*" Cory said. "Transmitting, transmitting! These are the only codes the bitch will give us! By all the Gods, man, let us land or at least send a systems specialist up from the base to work on this poxy bitch, over!"*

Normally a vessel's plasma cannon—and even merchant ships were armed if they expected to venture off the best-patrolled trade routes—were locked fore-and-aft unless they had been cleared for action. The *Milton's* guns were still at zero elevation, but Sun had rotated the turrets in opposition while the ship was still in the Matrix. The dorsal guns pointed at 30 degrees to the forward axis, while the ventral weapons were at 210 degrees.

"Luetzow, you are not cleared!" R11 said. *"Get out of the system at once! You do not have the right codes, you are not cleared to land! Get out! Over!"*

"Daniel," said Adele, cool as spring water over a two-way link, *"the array is opening. You may proceed on your planned course in thirty seconds."*

As she spoke, a countdown clock—starting at 27 SECONDS—appeared in the lower right corner of Daniel's display. He checked to be sure that the propulsion commands were queued to go. They were, of course, just as they had been before the cruiser extracted from the Matrix.

Normally the mine tender would send a course through the array to the vessel wanting to land. It was necessary to work backward this time: Daniel had designed the entry course and Adele was, with the very powerful support of the *Milton*'s astrogation computer, maneuvering the mines away from it.

"*Daniel, they've noticed the mines moving,*" Adele said with what for her was considerable urgency. "*They're preparing to command detonate one of them in our direction. I don't know if I—*"

"Sun!" Daniel said over the command push. "Take out the tender *now*, over!"

Daniel realized he was expecting the crash of the dorsal 8-inch guns; instead he heard the deep groan of the elevation screw. He'd tried to align the cruiser so that the forward guns, cocked to clear the dorsal antennas, would bear by apparent accident. He hadn't been quite successful, so the gunner had to make an adjustment before he could fire.

The charged particles spewed from a mine explosion were dangerous even to a heavy cruiser at many times the range at which it would ordinarily detonate. The blast might not destroy the vessel, but it would shred rigging, weld the joints of yards and antennas, and strip away external communications gear. If the operator aboard *R11* was able to command detonate one of the mines before Sun—

Dorsal Right fired. For a heartbeat Daniel thought the *CLANG!* was a mine destroying the *Milton*; then Dorsal Left fired also. He was alive, and the *Milton* had a clear path to her goal.

Daniel grinned. One thing about concentrating on what the enemy may do is that it prevents you from worrying about whether your own people were doing their jobs. In the present case, Sun certainly had been.

"Cease fire!" Daniel ordered. "Ship, prepare for course change. Changing course... *now*!"

The High Drive motors resumed their grating snarl. Daniel had gimballed them to send the cruiser through the minefield instead of skirting it as before.

Both plasma bolts struck the mine tender squarely, though the second had really just roiled the expanding gas ball created by the first. Most of the vapor was hull metal, but some was the mortal remains of thirty-odd Alliance spacers who'd been doing their jobs rather well up to the instant of their deaths. Which had at least been instantaneous.

"Woetjans, get the rigging in soonest so that we can land," Daniel ordered, using the general channel that fed through the PA system as well as to all commo helmets. "The Brotherhood of Amorgos is on the surface by now. The RCN can't let pongoes fight the battle all by themselves, can we? Six out!"

"Cinnabar forever!" spacers shouted. Probably every spacer on the *Milton*, including the considerable number who weren't Cinnabar citizens.

"Cinnabar forever!" Daniel shouted. Every spacer on the *Milton* . . .

CHAPTER 18

Above Bolton

The bow dorsal airlocks opened as Adele found the electronic keys to the substation at Bahnson Peak, on Bolton's less-inhabited western continent. She wouldn't have noticed that any more than she did the rest of the cruiser's chaotic activities, except that Woetjans was bellowing, "Out out out, line up in the bloody corridor and count off *now*, you bloody turtles, *now!*"

Watch commanders always counted their riggers before landing, making sure that nobody'd gotten tangled in a cable where they'd hang till the violence of reentry whipped them to a pulp and tossed the corpse away. This was a landing with the added urgency of a ship rushing into battle. When the bosun meant to be heard, you heard her no matter how busy you were.

The *Milton's* snarling High Drive braked her into orbit, and Adele was awash in data. Her first task wasn't the information, however, but to keep the information flow open when the cruiser's descending course took her across the planet from St. James Harbor.

Bolton had a very sophisticated communications system, as was to be expected on a world that had been an Alliance regional headquarters for two generations. Nobody on the ground had thought to shut down the communications satellites, but they *might* do so. Adele was creating a cable pathway as backup.

It was possible the Alliance officials didn't realize how vulnerable their satellite communications were. More likely, though, they had other things on their mind at present. The fighting on the ground wasn't Adele's job, but she was using real-time imagery of St. James Harbor as the background to the columns of numbers which she manipulated to take over the landlines.

The harbor was a natural embayment on the coast of East Continent. The jaws of the land were more than half a mile apart, but they were extended by artificial moles whose ends interleaved. There was a passage for surface ships at right angles to the harbor's axis.

In addition to the planetary defense array, the harbor had a concrete-walled missile emplacement at the base of each mole. In an atmosphere, an anti-starship missile greatly outranged a warship's plasma cannon. No vessel could hope to land in the teeth of those batteries.

A bubble of orange flame licked the face of the southern missile pit. Adele had set the imagery to highlight motion, so a white caret traced a speck wobbling several hundred yards before splashing into the sea: one of the armored leaves of the gate into the site. The current magnification couldn't pick out individual Brotherhood soldiers, but their actions identified them clearly.

Relays flopped in the Bahnson Peak Substation. Adele didn't really know where the communications node was: all she had was a schematic with names which might be outdated or might not have had real geographical meaning in the first place.

In one sense the answer mattered, because she wanted to know all there was about everything with which she came in contact. But for now Adele Mundy had complete control of Bolton's electronic communications systems. That would do.

"*Six, all watches reporting,*" Woetjans said over the command net. "*All rigging is stowed for landing and all personnel are off the hull, over!*"

The southern margin of St. James Harbor was a military reservation surrounded by a fence with guard towers. Most of the latter were unmanned now, as generally according to the roster in Command Headquarters. Ranks of brick barracks capable of holding ten thousand troops in total marched along the western edge of the perimeter. On the other side of the fence were civilian subdivisions which had expanded to enclose the reservation.

Barracks began to disintegrate in what looked like rusty smoke. Adele knew from experience that she was seeing the dust of bricks pulverized by bursts from automatic impellers.

Great rips appeared in the roofs of civilian houses beyond; the swimming pools in their back yards scattered light as they danced in the rain of debris. Half-ounce osmium slugs accelerated by the phased coils of the impellers' barrels kept going a long distance after they'd shattered walls, and they carried along a great deal of what they'd destroyed.

Adele began searching for a path into the northern missile pit. It was possible to isolate batteries so that they couldn't be controlled by anyone outside the emplacement, but that meant leaving defense to a junior officer at the site. More often they were under control of director, generally in the Combat Operations Center.

She couldn't find a connection here, though. That might mean there wasn't one, but equally it might be a closed circuit which she couldn't control without being physically present. The battery shouldn't launch on a starship which simply happened to be landing, but who knew what would happen in the middle of a firefight?

"*Ship, we're going in,*" Daniel said over the general channel, competing with the increased roar from the High Drive motors. "*Keep her closed up till I tell you. Don't worry, Millies, I'll turn you loose! Six out.*"

Adele's imagery took on a specious sharpness: the actual signals had degraded, so her computer was enhancing them to a clarity which the real thing never had.

There had to be a way to control the missile pit! She'd switched off the sensor antennas feeding it, but a crew that knew what it was doing could launch using optical sights. A heavy cruiser hovering to provide fire support made a very big target. There *had* to—

A sulfurous cloud jetted up from the emplacement the Brotherhood had captured. A spike stabbed north from it, so close above the bay that the shock wave parted the water to the stony bottom. Although the Brotherhood was a light infantry unit, somebody in it knew or had learned how to control an anti-starship battery.

The missile struck the center of the northern emplacement. The round used kinetic energy rather than a warhead to destroy its target, but much of the missile's fuel remained unburned at the moment of impact. A fireball lifted momentarily from the target, then sucked in to be replaced by smoke the color of rotten urine. The cloud expanded over the whole harbor, thinning but remaining a presence no matter how far it spread.

Adele switched her attention to identifying strong points still in Alliance hands. Her own taste was for subtle work, but years in the RCN had taught her to value well-placed brute force as well. She would compliment Colonel Stockheim when she next saw him, assuming they both survived.

The upper levels of Bolton's atmosphere began to buffet the heavy cruiser. They would be down in the midst of the fighting shortly.

Though Adele had a great deal of information to process, she touched her pocket just to make sure that the familiar weight was where it should be. It didn't seem to be the kind of battle in which a pistol would be of any importance.

But then again, it might be. And Adele Mundy would be ready.

The *Milton* roared toward St. James Harbor from the east with Daniel at the controls. He grinned even more widely as he fought the throttles: "roared" was very much the word for it, because every part of the big ship was making a thunderous racket.

His main display was a panorama of the surface beneath their course as he braked the cruiser into a slant onto the target. Daniel had entered the atmosphere with the display set to show the next thousand miles, but he reduced the scale as their track carved down toward the surface. When St. James Harbor rose above the horizon line to become visible to the ship's real-time sensors, it served as the terminus of the rapidly swelling image.

The long descent had scrubbed off orbital velocity, so the plasma thrusters were driving and supporting the ship. Airspeed had dropped to 220 miles per hour, and they were holding a 3,000-foot altitude as closely as Daniel's skill permitted—which was *not* as closely as he thought he should have been able to manage.

"*Six, this is Guns,*" Sun said. "*I'm deploying the turrets at the ordered airspeed, over.*"

As he spoke—before he spoke, really—hydraulic jacks began driving the turrets up into their extended position. When a warship was in harbor or in vacuum, the gun turrets were raised to provide more internal volume. For liftoffs and landings in an atmosphere, however, they were recessed within the hull.

A starship couldn't be streamlined, even with its telescoped rigging snugged against the hull. Unless the turret armor was brought as close as possible to the vessel's center of mass, however, the chance that buffeting would set up an uncontrollable roll became very high.

Daniel had told Sun to keep his plasma cannon stowed until the cruiser's airspeed had dropped to 200 mph. Predictably the gunner had decided to ready his weapons for action early; and because he was experienced as well as determined, he'd set the process in motion before he'd announced what he was doing.

Sun deserved a rocket for disobeying orders, and maybe he'd get one later. But Daniel had to admit that the cruiser's terrible handling in an atmosphere wasn't made worse when the turrets rose into the airstream.

The *Wartburg* had landed in her assigned berth on one of the civilian quays; to do otherwise would have been to—literally—set off alarms early. Daniel was slanting the cruiser in over the water close to the military reservation, which would have been proper had she still been the *Scheer* as she'd been launched. In any case, the course was unlikely to raise the garrison's suspicions further in the midst of a battle.

Carets, wavering between orange and purple depending which gave greater contrast to the background, sprang to life across the terminus of the course panorama. Adele was indicating major Alliance targets. The data would be copied to the gunnery screens as soon as the turrets could bear on the port.

"Ship, this is Six," Daniel said, throttling back and adjusting the thrusters' attitude to ease the big ship toward a hover. "You can open her—"

Even before he got the words out, hatches being undogged all over the vessel clanged a raucous alarm. Although the cruiser's forward speed was dropping, the windblast through scores of hull openings lifted anything loose and whirled it in the corridors. The thrusters were deafening as they pounded at high output.

"—up, but targets on the south side of the water only. We've got friends down there, spacers, and I don't want pongoes to be saying the RCN is more dangerous to its friends than the Alliance is. Don't disappoint me, Millies! Six out."

The hull shuddered as Sun rotated his turrets to bear on opposite beams—ventral to starboard, dorsal to port. The harbor wasn't in sight yet, but it would be in less than a minute.

Daniel sneezed. Even up here on A Level, the sharp claws of ozone from the exhaust curled in with the noise of the thrusters.

Hogg sat on the jumpseat of the command console. He held a stocked impeller, but he'd slung a submachine gun as well. Presumably one was for the young master in the event they made a ground assault.

That might be extreme preparedness rather than wishful thinking on Hogg's part, but the longing glances he cast toward the hatch on the port—south—bulkhead of the bridge was genuinely hopeful. Hogg liked shooting things, and if the targets were men shooting back, that just made it more interesting.

That wasn't going to happen this time. Daniel's worst enemies wouldn't call him a coward, but his task right now was to maneuver the *Milton* so that her firepower could aid the ground forces in capturing St. James Harbor. The mission wouldn't be helped by a chance slug or two entering through an open port and ricocheting around the bridge.

"Gunner, you may fire when—"

WHANG!

The blast of an 8-inch plasma cannon slammed flat all the previous sounds of wind, thrusters, and the ship working in an atmosphere. The ship torqued noticeably on her axis and the bow kicked to port. The jet of charged particles ripped a thick saffron line through the air.

Two miles away, what had been the Planetary Police Headquarters vanished in an iridescent flash. Seven seconds after the thunderclap of the plasma bolt's track closing came the deeper, distance-muted thump of the building exploding.

Marines and spacers at the open hatches on the port side began to shoot furiously in the direction of the military facilities. The slant range was over a mile, and the likelihood was that half the projectiles struck low—the harborfront danced—or sailed over not only the reservation but even the civilian subdivisions beyond. It made the crew a part of the action, though, and it certainly didn't do any good to Alliance morale.

So long as the individual marksmen—and the automatic impellers which were even now being clamped to hatch openings—fired at the enemy side of the harbor, they couldn't do any harm. The police building was on the north, but Adele must have determined that the Brotherhood troops hadn't advanced that far. There had been only two careted targets on that side, the police headquarters and the planetary government buil—

WHANG!

The second plasma bolt hit at the base of the Albert Robida Government Office Building, a slender, pyramidal structure some fifteen stories high. It had been built up rather than outward: for show presumably, because land couldn't have been at much of a premium even in center of St. James City.

For show also, the building was beige stone instead of concrete or some utilitarian cast synthetic. Daniel realized that when the whole thing lifted on the vaporized contents of the ground floor, then shook itself into a rain of ashlars. They cascaded down, dishing in the fronts of the flimsier structures on all four sides.

There were now no suitable targets for heavy weapons on the north side of the harbor. It was possible that

the Brotherhood would run into a pocket of resistance
that they wanted the cruiser to eliminate. So long as
it was adequately marked, the job would be both safe
and simple. Given the way Colonel Stockheim's men
had stormed the missile battery, however, that didn't
seem the way they thought.

Daniel minusculely boosted the output of the leading
pair of port thrusters; the cruiser's track straightened.
He'd sent the projected course to Sun so that the
gunner could plan his fire missions as soon as Adele
provided the targets. He'd been a little surprised that
Sun had started with the civilian installations, though
that had probably cleared the flank of the friendly
infantry so that it could—

WHANG! WHANG!

The shock of two bolts at minimum separation—the
right cannon had fired the instant the left tube had
returned to battery—was momentarily stunning, even
to Daniel. The fact that this time they were firing at
maximum depression from the dorsal turret—which
was in addition offset toward the bow and therefore
bridge—made the effect even worse.

Daniel didn't think anybody could get used to
8-inch plasma cannon; certainly he didn't expect to.
The weapons really needed the 60 to 100 thousand
tons of a battleship's hull to anchor them. Sturdy
though the *Milton*'s frames were, he guessed that if
the cruiser saw action as frequently as he was used
to in the *Princess Cecile*, she would warp herself to
scrap in less than ten years.

But by the Gods! What the powerful bolts did to
their targets was a treat to see—if you were at the
breech end of the gun when it happened.

Brick walls didn't burn, but the roofs were corrugated sheets of structural plastic. They ignited at the sun-heart temperature of a plasma bolt. The bedding, wood floors, and the bodies of any troops and dependants who happened to be inside simply exploded.

A fire-shot cloud of brick rose skyward, spread into an anvil, and rained down for a half mile in every direction. Daniel even heard the clunk—it was too dull to be a slug—of a fragment hitting the *Milton*.

What Sun had very cleverly done was to wait to fire into the military reservation until the angle let him enfilade a row of ten company barracks with each bolt. The Brotherhood had been chewing up the two-story structures with their automatic impellers from across the harbor, but they hadn't known which of the buildings were occupied by the garrison among the much larger number which were empty and available for transients.

Adele—or perhaps Cory?—had looked at power meter records to determine the question. In general, the *Sissie*'s faster-firing 4-inch guns would've been better for support in a sprawling camp like this one, but Sun's careful aim had allowed him to use the 8-inch weapons to their full effect.

The *Milton* had reached the harbor moles. Daniel began to swing her cautiously, holding the cruiser at a steady five-hundred-foot altitude. Even a corvette like the *Princess Cecile* was too big to fling around like an aircar.

In the middle of a battle, Daniel's intellect had to fight the adrenaline coursing through his system. Feeding in too much thrust was likely to start the ship rolling, spinning, or diving uncontrollably toward the surface which at the moment was scarcely her own length below.

An automatic impeller began raking the cruiser. Daniel might not have noticed it if a slug hadn't ricocheted through the field which provided real-time imagery forward: his electronic equivalent of a window to look out the bow. The neon-bright streak of osmium bouncing at high velocity from steel was unmistakable if you'd seen it before, as Daniel certainly had.

Once he knew it was happening, he registered the *cling-cling-cling* of short bursts, three to five slugs each, that continued to rain on the cruiser. The hull was impervious and it wouldn't be a matter of real consequence either if a spacer or spacers were killed by a round through an open hatch.

Daniel had accepted the likelihood of a few casualties when he decided to let the crew use their small arms during the attack. They wouldn't have much effect on the enemy at this range, but it helped the crew's morale if they were a part of the battle instead of waiting blindly while giants slugged it out.

A slug that hit a thruster's Stellite nozzle would put it out of action till it was replaced. That too would be a hassle, but there was bound to be damage during a battle. This single impeller was no more real danger to the *Milton* than a wasp was to the crew of an armored vehicle. But like the wasp it was irritating and insistent, and it might cause Daniel to make a mistake. There was nothing he could do about—

"*I have him,*" said Adele sharply on the command channel. "*Her. Can somebody deal with her? She's knocked out one of my sensor arrays. Over. Out?*"

The general display highlighted a guard tower on

the southern edge of the military reservation. It had been unmanned at the start of the attack, but an Alliance soldier had put it into action, probably on his own initiative.

Daniel touched the icon beside the caret, bringing up a greatly magnified view of the tower's interior. The four-sided roof sheltered an automatic impeller on a central pintle. A grimly determined woman crouched behind the weapon, her hands on the spade grips. It was a pity that the mounting allowed the gun full rotation rather than just the ability to sweep the area beyond the fence line. She was aiming across the reservation, an obviously dangerous practice if anybody less skilled had been doing it.

A fluorescent haze spurted from the impeller's muzzle: the aluminum driving bands vaporized by the flux that accelerated the projectiles up the barrel. Instants later, Daniel heard another *cling-cling-cling*, then *bwow-w-w!* as the last slug of the burst skidded from a hull plate on its own wild course.

He didn't allow himself to adjust the throttles to tighten the turn the way he wanted to do. The tower was a mile and a half away, but when the ship's side was toward the reservation again there was a reasonable chance that massed luck if not marksmanship would put an end to the irritation.

WHANG!

A ventral plasma cannon had fired. Dust lifted from a graveled parade ground and swirled about the track of the bolt slanting low across it. The inset guard tower was a white flare. A three-story tenement in the civilian district beyond exploded outward, flinging brands in all directions. Other buildings began to burn.

Daniel hadn't expected that Sun would have a clear shot with either turret. He'd done a very nice piece of work, stabbing the bolt between a pair of empty barracks to clip the top of the guard tower beyond. One could call it a surgical job, though the civilians who'd been downrange of the target probably wouldn't have been so positive about the result.

WHANG!

The sidewalls of a large building, probably a garage, blew outward. The roof of extruded plastic fluttered down like a dark red blanket. Secondary explosions lifted the roof in tatters, belching gouts of orange flames. A truck wheel flew up like a flipped coin, then spun back into the pall of black smoke which rippled to cover the remains of the roof.

WHANG!

On the harbor side, fifty yards of perimeter fence blazed white and vanished, including a pair of guard towers. The turf for twice that distance beyond was blackened and the woven-wire fencing sagged. Sun had timed his shot to sweep as much of the fence line as he could. Though nobody had been shooting from the towers he'd destroyed, soldiers spilled from others. Some threw away their guns as they ran.

Armored personnel carriers had been driving off the *Wartburg* while squads of Brotherhood infantry fanned out to eliminate anything that might have been a threat on the north side of the harbor. The empty vehicles raced to shore over the water itself, each sending up a great roostertail.

There were two ramps up from the water in the warehouse district. The APCs climbed them, then glided purposefully along the esplanade to the infantry which had double-timed to shore along the floating walkway from the transport's entry hold.

WHANG!

The bolt hit a domed amphitheatre in the military reservation. Such structures served for assemblies during bad weather and as additional barracks space when needed, as well as for entertainment purposes. It was probably empty at the moment, but because it was the largest building on the post it made a spectacular target.

The benches and even the paint on the interior concrete walls flashed into a flame which the slanted ramps channeled upward. The orange bubble shot a thousand feet into the sky and vanished into itself with a loud bang. It was even more stunning than the jet of plasma which had brought it to life.

The spacers and Marines were firing with renewed vigor through the *Milton's* hatches. Daniel knew how hard a stocked impeller recoiled. Excitement was keeping the spacers going, but in the morning the shoulders of many would be too bruised for them to make a fist with that hand. Most would be lucky to hit a house at this range, let alone a human target, but the rain of slugs out of the sky would dispirit any Alliance soldier who hadn't been left numb by the 8-inch plasma bolts.

APCs laden with Brotherhood troops started around the harbor by streets a block in from the water, moving in pairs. They were simply battle taxis, not fighting vehicles, though each mounted an automatic impeller to provide covering fire while its infantry squad cleared buildings with grenades and sub-machine guns.

"Daniel, they're surrendering!" Adele said on a two-way link. *"Commodore Donald Harmston, the Base Commander, is offering to capitulate to avoid further*

bloodshed. He's asking for medical help for his aide-de-camp. Ah, the aide's name is Harmston also. Over."

"Cease fire!" Daniel ordered on the general intercom channel. Taking no chances, he used the command console to lock out the main guns' firing circuit. "All personnel, cease fire immediately. I mean it, Millies, cease bloody fire or there'll be court-martials!"

The crew had its blood up, and there were bound to be Alliance troops on the ground who hadn't gotten the word and would by shooting give the Millies justification. Fortunately, the fighting—the shooting, at least—had gone on long enough that as soon as the spacers stopped, they were going to notice the throbbing pain of their bruised shoulders.

Likely enough there'd been a few broken collarbones as well. Inexperienced shooters often held the stock a half inch from their shoulder, thinking to reduce the shock. Instead the weapon, recoiling without the body's additional mass to slow it down, hit like a hammer instead of like a heavy medicine ball.

"Signals, inform Colonel Stockheim that the enemy is surrendering," Daniel said as he adjusted his thrusters to bring them to a hover. "And inform the Hydriote ships in orbit that they'll be able to begin landing within the hour. Six out."

He took a deep breath. "Ship, we're about to land on Bolton, the newest possession of the Republic of Cinnabar. Fellow spacers, the Republic thanks you, and I thank you from the bottom of my heart! Up the *Milton!*"

"Up the *Milton!*" shrieked hundreds of voices, till the thrusters licked the harbor's surface into a deafening thunder of steam.

CHAPTER 19

St. James Harbor, Bolton

"Captain," said Vesey over the command channel, *"this is Three. The transports will be landing at two-minute intervals starting in seventeen minutes. I've assigned the ships berths in both the civilian and the naval portions of the harbor, but I can't determine billets for the personnel until we have an inventory of how many barracks remain undamaged, over."*

The *Milton* clanked and sizzled in her slip. Most of the A Level hatches remained open though Daniel had ordered the marksmen away from them, so steam continued to boil in. The mugginess carried the usual stench of burned muck.

"Roger, Three," Daniel said, suppressing his smile in case Vesey was watching an image of his face and thought he was mocking her. For an extremely able officer, Lieutenant Vesey seemed often to be on the verge of tears. "Well done. I think the Fonthill Militia—"

That was the name he'd come up with to regularize Master Beckford's former slaves.

"—can sleep for another night aboard their transports if necessary. Six out."

"*Six, this is Five,*" reported Pasternak from the Power Room. "*The ship is secure. All thrusters are shut down but operable. There's no problems there, though one of the High Drive motors apparently took a slug during the fighting. I'll have her changed out in an hour after things have cooled down, though being one motor short won't affect our performance if we have to lift, over.*"

Daniel started to reply but had to cough instead to clear the sharp dryness at the back of his throat. It felt for a moment as though he'd tried to swallow a mouthful of burrs. There was smoke in the air as well as steam.

The Gods alone knew what all was burning. Anything that could combine with oxygen would do so when hit by a plasma bolt, including all metals and some rocks.

Daniel swallowed his phlegm, then resumed, "Roger, Five. One of the Alliance soldiers was bound and determined to die for the Guarantor, and it seems that she did some damage before Sun obliged her. Get us shipshape as soon as you safely can, but I'm not expecting to lift for several days."

He coughed, this time as a pause in which he could word his thought correctly. "Chief Pasternak?" he said. "The Power Train operated without a hiccup during our low-level approach and the firing passes. The thrusters gimballed smoothly, and the flow to each nozzle remained precisely where I set it. My regards to your personnel, and please inform them that they can all expect a drink on their captain when next we have a chance at liberty. Which I'm afraid won't be any time soon, however. Six out."

The topgallant section of the Dorsal A Ring antenna locked in place with a *cling* which vibrated through the ship. It was a familiar sound in the ordinary course of things—but not in an atmosphere. Here it had a deeper, richer tone than when the ship was preparing to insert into the Matrix.

"What's that?" demanded Senator Forbes as she entered the bridge. DeNardo, showing his usual bovine calm, and Platt, who seemed on the verge of frightened tears, were with her, but the pair of servants/bodyguards were not. She was in a cream business suit with shoulder flounces rather than senatorial robes, the sort of thing she might wear during office hours while the Senate was in session.

"I've raised an antenna because the sensors at the masthead will give us a twenty-mile panorama," Daniel said, looking up with a smile. Things had gone very well thus far, but from the senator's sour expression she wasn't sure of that. "If we have to lift off too suddenly to bring it down properly, it'll go by the boards. But that's unlikely, and in that event I'm sure we'll have worse problems."

Fires were burning all over St. James City. Most were in the military reservation—Vesey had been right to wonder if there'd be barracks for the laborers-become-garrison—but six or eight spots on the north side of the harbor licked flame into the smoky haze. Unless some were coincidental with the attack, the heavy plasma charges had flung blazing debris up to a quarter mile from the impact sites.

"I've been watching through the display in my suite,"

Forbes said, seeming to warm slightly. She'd had sense enough to keep out of the way during the fighting, but it would have rankled her nonetheless to be on the sidelines. "I won't pretend I understood much of what was going on, though, except that apparently we weren't all about to die the way the noises made me expect. That *is* correct, isn't it?"

"The worst noises were us shooting at Alliance positions," Daniel said, encouraging his smile to widen. "I've arranged a meeting with Commodore Harmston to formally accept his surrender of the planet. I hope you'll accompany me?"

The senator really was doing very well for someone who was used to thinking of herself as one of the dozen most important people in the Republic of Cinnabar. If she got peevish, she was nonetheless behaving better by an order of magnitude than Corder Leary would've done in similar circumstances.

Daniel didn't care if Forbes preferred to sit in her cabin and twiddle her thumbs—or DeNardo, for that matter. What he really hoped was that she'd be pleased at the invitation. Since the meeting was between military commanders, she couldn't demand to be present by right.

The senator's eyes narrowed, but after a moment she smiled wryly. "In fact I was *hoping*, shall we say," she said, "to be present. Which is why I'm in this—"

She pinched the ruff over her right shoulder.

"—instead of something less ornate."

Major Mull, wearing battledress and holding his sub-machine gun at the balance instead of slinging it, stamped into the compartment. He'd lifted the face-shield of his helmet.

"Sir!" he said, quite clearly ignoring the civilians. "Request permission to put a squad of marksmen on the hull for security before we lower the boarding ramp!"

Daniel's eyes narrowed. "Major Mull," he said. He didn't raise his voice unduly—the Marine was just short of shouting—but it snapped nonetheless. "I will remind you that the bridge is the captain's territory, and that at present the captain is in conference with Her Excellency, Ambassador Forbes. *Is* that understood?"

Mull slammed to attention. "Sir!" he said, focusing his eyes on a spot on the bulkhead. "Understood *sir!*"

He's older than I am, and this—Daniel had checked the major's record—*is his first shipboard command, though he's served as a junior officer on two battleships before his promotion.* Mull didn't have a chip on his shoulder, but he was an unimaginative man who had never before taken orders from someone outside the Marine hierarchy.

"At ease, Major," Daniel said aloud. "And yes, that's a good idea, but I'll want twenty of your people to accompany the senator and me when we take the surrender of the—"

"*Daniel, mine tender R16 in Fleet Berth Four is preparing to lift off!*" said Adele, speaking through his commo helmet.

"Belay that, Mull!" Daniel said as he dropped onto his console again. He hoped Senator Forbes wouldn't feel offended, but that wasn't his first priority anymore.

"*Six, I'm on it!*" cried Sun on the command push. The bone-deep rumble of the dorsal turret—the ventral turret had been withdrawn for landing and was now below the harbor's surface—would have made that obvious anyway.

"All personnel get off the hull!" boomed Vesey's voice from the PA system and the ship's outside speakers. "Prepare for gunnery exercise! All *Milton* personnel get inside *now* or you'll be fried. Move it, Millies!"

Vesey was on the ball too, as expected, though Daniel wouldn't have been surprised to learn that it had been Cory who cut in the external speakers. He wasn't sure he'd have been able to manage that unusual task so quickly himself, though of course he'd never have to with Adele as his signals officer.

Just as he didn't have to worry about directing his next transmission. "*R16*, this is RCS *Milton*. Shut down or you will be destroyed. Shut down and acknowledge, over!"

There were scores of ships on the civilian side of St. James Harbor, several of them freighters bigger than the *Wartburg*. The naval base to the south was almost empty by contrast, though the extensive docks were built to handle a fleet including battleships. The *Milton* was by far the largest ship present, but the harbor facilities dwarfed her.

A pall of steam rose from a slip near the eastern end of the naval harbor. From ground level the vessel floating there wouldn't have been visible over the quay at this stage of the tide, but Daniel's masthead sensors let him peer down on it. Another hundred-foot mine tender like the one the *Milton* had destroyed in orbit was trying desperately to escape and warn Admiral Petersen of the disaster.

"*R16*, this is Captain Daniel Leary!" Daniel said. "Shut down immediately! You will not escape, you *cannot* escape. Shut down now and avoid dying for no purpose, over!"

Text crawled across the bottom of Daniel's display: VOLTAIRE 6, THIS IS TIGER. GET YOUR PERSONNEL BENEATH OVERHEAD COVER IMMEDIATELY, REPEAT, SEEK OVERHEAD COVER, OUT.

Voltaire 6 was Colonel Stockheim's call sign, while Tiger was the *Milton*. Adele was keeping Daniel informed of her transmission without interfering with what he was doing.

"*R16*, this is suicide!" Daniel said. "You *must* shut—"

The gush of steam from Berth 4 redoubled, concealing the mine tender for a moment. Then the hull with its minimum rig rose slowly from the cloud. *They probably don't even have stores aboard for an interstellar voyage!*

"*Six, I've got her, over!*" Sun cried. He was hunched over his console, his right hand poised over the EXECUTE button.

"Gunner, you may fire one round only," Daniel said, his face hard. Taking risks and ordering others to take risks were major parts of a naval officer's duties. This sort of pointless bravado disgusted him.

WHANG!

The shot came quicker than Daniel had expected. Because of the *Milton*'s greater height, Sun had managed to get an angle while the tender was still largely within her slip. From the masthead sensors, Daniel saw a wedge of the top of the quay blaze white as the lower margin of the bolt touched it, reducing the concrete to quicklime and shattered gravel.

Most of the plasma struck the *R16*, however, and ripped her in two. In a breathable atmosphere, steel heated to the temperature of a star became fuel. The central portion of the little vessel didn't just vaporize as it would have done in space, it burned.

An iridescent fireball filled the slip, then paled as it lurched upward. When it burst high in the air, diamond-bright droplets rained down.

R16's bow dived into the slip, driven by two working thrusters. A double blast followed when water bathed the hot Stellite nozzles. It would have been impressive if it hadn't been upstaged by the plasma bolt itself.

The last ten feet of the tender's stern accelerated skyward in a steep curve while Daniel watched in amazement. The fragment hurtled several hundred feet up before the thruster driving it ran out of reaction mass. It spun, flinging out lesser debris which seemed to include a pair of human bodies, and plunged into a subdivision. There was no explosion, but more houses began to burn.

"The *bloody* fool," Daniel said. That was as much of an epitaph as *R16*'s commander would get or deserved.

He took a deep breath, furious at the waste. "Ship, this is Six," he said. "All clear, all clear. And Gunner, that was a fine piece of work. Six out."

Calm again, Daniel turned back to Senator Forbes. "Sun, that's our gunner—"

He gestured left-handed toward the gunnery console.

"—caught the mine tender while it was still in its berth. If it had had time to get up to a thousand feet or so it would have been an easy target because of the reduced deflection, but the falling debris would've done all manner of damage. That was *very* good work."

Daniel didn't know what if anything Forbes made of what he was saying, but the fact that Sun heard his captain praise him to the senator was important. Sun had done a very good piece of work. Most of the lives he'd saved were those of local civilians, but there would've been losses among the Brotherhood infantry too.

"Yes, I see," said Forbes in the tone of somebody who would have preferred not to have been interrupted. "When were you planning to meet the Alliance commodore?"

There was a dull *bong* and the cruiser rocked slightly. Forbes and her aides might not even have noticed it after the violence of the plasma cannon, but it announced to Daniel that the boarding ramp had lowered until it butted firmly. The naval berths in St. James Harbor were as well appointed as those of Harbor Three on Cinnabar; instead of floating catwalks, metal extensions unfolded from the dock on cantilevered supports.

"Yes," he said. "If you're ready, Your Excellency, we'll be heading for the command bunker in about five minutes when the utility vehicles come up from the hold. I'd have used the aircars—"

"Except that the turbulence which the ship creates makes them too dangerous a risk to my life?" the senator said. Her tone was so dry that Daniel wasn't sure whether she was joking or still angry over his previous manipulation.

"No, Your Excellency," he said. Forbes had a right to be angry, and this would be as good a time—in the middle of a major victory—as he could imagine for her to let it out. "Because it's too dangerous to put anybody up in the air when hundreds of Alliance personnel are loose and haven't been disarmed. I'll take my chances—our chances, if I may say so—with the odd slug flying around, but it's easier than you might think to shoot an aircar right out of the sky. And it's very hard to dodge gravity if that happens."

Forbes sniffed and looked down at the cream sleeve of her jacket. "I should have worn gray," she said, as much to herself as to anybody. "This will be all soot by the time we get to this bunker."

"Well, think of it this way, Senator," said Hogg in a raspy voice. "So long as you haven't shat your trousers, you'll be better dressed than the local brass you'll be meeting."

Forbes stared at him, then turned to Daniel. He let the smile ease from his lips and waited with a neutral expression.

"Your man has a smart mouth, Leary," she said. "Does he know how to handle those guns he's carrying?"

"Hogg is a very good shot, Your Excellency," Daniel said.

"I thought he might be," Forbes said. Her face crinkled into a slight smile. "And I dare say he's right about how our opposite numbers reacted to being on the other end of those bloody great cannon. Well, whenever you're ready. Do you have to change clothes?"

Daniel glanced down at his utilities. "No, Your Excellency," he said. He took the sub-machine gun which Hogg offered. "This is a useful reminder to Commodore Harmston that we're a fighting force."

The first of the Hydriote transports was rumbling down from the stratosphere with a load of the Fonthill Militia. Blantyre was in charge of them. Before they'd even lifted from Fonthill, she'd used maps of St. James City to set up patrol areas. Each unit would be commanded by a petty officer from the cruiser. There'd have to be adjustments—there would have been adjustments even if a tenth of the city hadn't been destroyed in the assault—but Blantyre would take care of the problems without bothering her captain about them.

"As soon as we're sure the Alliance forces understand that they've surrendered," Daniel said, "I *will* change—at least into my Grays. The prisoners from Admiral Ozawa's squadron are in a quarry north of the city. Freeing them is my next priority, and they deserve the respect of a dress uniform."

Forbes nodded crisply. "I'll join you," she said. There was no question at all in her done.

"I hoped you would," Daniel said truthfully. "Now, let's deal with Harmston."

He glanced back at the panorama as he started out of the compartment with Hogg, Major Mull, and Senator Forbes. Armed spacers were trotting down the *Milton*'s boarding ramp. That would be the cadres for the Militia as well as the cruiser's own security party, as expected. But among them—

Daniel looked at the signals console; it was empty, though Cory was doubtless handling communications from his station. He'd been right to think that the two slim figures leaving the ship were Adele and Tovera. They'd left the bridge while his attention was on Senator Forbes.

What in heaven is Adele doing now?

Though being Adele in the present chaos, the question might better be phrased, *What in Hell?*

While Adele, Tovera, and Dasi clung to the pivot where a lowboy would normally be attached, Barnes drove the tractor along the esplanade toward Fleet

Berth 74 where the *Zieten* was moored. There was plenty of room on the deck of the bright orange vehicle, but passenger amenities were conspicuous by their absence.

Something fell on the back of Adele's neck. *Rain?* she thought, but when she patted it absently with her right hand the fingers came down black. It had been a blob of ash—oily ash.

She grimaced and wiped her fingertips on the back of her trouser leg. Quite a lot of the things burning around St. James Harbor this afternoon were human bodies. The smell was unmistakable if you'd been exposed to it before.

The tractor jounced over a length of pipe—plastic and therefore not a mast section, but it didn't deform under the small, solid wheels. Dasi's left arm was around Adele's waist; she was as safe as she'd have been if she were attached to the pivot by a safety line. That didn't make it a comfortable ride, though, even at a modest eight miles per hour which was as much as the low-geared electric motor could manage even without a loaded trailer.

"We could've gotten something with springs," Dasi said glumly. His partner seemed to be having a good time at the control yoke, but Barnes also had the tractor's only seat. "There was a couple little trucks in the shed two berths over. All we'd have had to do was lift the roof off them and I'd bet we could've got one of them to run."

Something exploded to the right. Adele jerked her head around, but she couldn't tell where the blast had come from; it might not even be within the military reservation. There'd been several random shots since she and her *ad hoc* escort set off from the *Milton*, but nothing that sounded like real fighting.

"The Brotherhood of Amorgos has the reputation of shooting first and not bothering to ask questions at all," Tovera said with a touch of gentle mockery, about as close as she usually came to displaying humor. "Armed people driving toward them in a truck with Alliance markings are likely to be stopped by the quickest means available. In this case that would probably be an automatic impeller, though they could doubtless take care of us with personal weapons."

"Lieutenant Alderman expects us," Adele said. "But I too thought that the tractor was the best means of transportation at present."

Three transports had landed, all of them in the military reservation, and a fourth was now thundering down from the heavens. The former slaves had to be armed from the Alliance arsenal here—Daniel didn't have sufficient RCN weapons.

"Ma'am?" Dasi said. "Is something wrong?"

I must have smiled, Adele thought. *At least I would have meant it for a smile.*

Aloud she said, "I wonder if we'll be equipping the new militia with Cinnabar weapons? Admiral Petersen would have captured quite a quantity of small arms on New Harmony, and it's likely enough that they would have been shipped here to the main base in the cluster, just as the prisoners were."

Dasi laughed gaily over the jingle of the wheels grinding debris into the concrete pavement. "Say, you're right, ma'am!" he said. "That'll teach 'em, won't it?"

Adele didn't respond save for a another neutral smile. Dasi took the reversal as an Aunt Sallie, a toy

which inevitably bobbed upright on its weighted base
after it had been slapped down. Adele's own image was
that of a wheel: the Alliance had rolled to the top at
New Harmony, but the wheel had turned again here
at Bolton. The wheel was still turning, and it would
turn until the end of time.

The tractor rolled and rattled into the warm cloud
surrounding a recently landed freighter. Adele couldn't
see farther than the control yoke. She expected Barnes
to switch to infrared viewing, then realized that he wasn't
wearing a helmet or goggles that would allow him to.

They trundled into the sunlight on the same line
that they'd entered a hundred feet earlier. She supposed spacers got used to working in blurred light
and darkness.

Adele tapped her personal data unit, though she
didn't take it out of its pocket on so jolting a ride.
The gray haze was too much like the hours before
dawn when faces returned to her in an almost-dream.
She knew that was only a trick of her mind, for their
features were clear. For the most part they'd only been
pale blobs above her gunsights during the fractions
of seconds she'd seen them in life.

"They're waiting for us up there," said Barnes. His
hand rose from the control yoke to point.

Tovera reached around from behind him and pulled
his arm down. She said, "Let's not do anything our
friends in the infantry might misunderstand."

Barnes grunted. "Got it," he said.

"You should've let me drive," Dasi said peevishly
to his partner. As best Adele could tell, Dasi didn't
really mean he wouldn't have pointed while approaching keyed-up men with guns; he was simply seizing

the opportunity to complain again about something that had rankled throughout the ride.

A hundred yards ahead, sixty-odd spacers lay like rolls of carpeting on their backs along the edge of the esplanade. A dozen or so at the far end wore field-gray Fleet utilities.

A Brotherhood APC was parked its own length from the prisoners with its nose toward them. That was too far for anybody to decide to be a hero by rushing the vehicle. The impeller in the cupola and the troopers' personal weapons were stained gray at the muzzle by vaporized aluminum from firing.

Several Brotherhood soldiers crouched behind cover, following the tractor with their guns. Adele didn't know where the rest of the squad was—probably controlling the other approaches. It wouldn't be a good time to bring out her data unit and get a precise answer from satellite imagery.

"Halt where you are!" boomed a loudspeaker on the APC. "No vehicles are allowed closer than you are right now!"

Barnes obediently pushed the control yoke forward, bringing the tractor to a jingling halt. Adele hopped down, as glad as not to leave the hard orange deck.

"I'm Officer Mundy!" she said, wondering if anybody in the vehicle could hear her. She walked forward, taking her usual quick, short steps. "I need to speak to Lieutenant Alderman!"

"I'll talk to them, ma'am," Dasi said apologetically, striding in front of her.

They'd reached the nearest Alliance prisoners; some twisted their heads to follow the newcomers with their eyes, but many remained as stiff as logs or as corpses. A Brotherhood soldier with a sub-machine gun knelt at the base of the gantry Adele had just passed, watching events silently.

"Now look, you pongoes!" Dasi bawled. "We're from the *Millie*, so put them bloody guns up now or Cap'n Leary'll show you what *real* guns is!"

Adele grinned despite herself. She'd expected Dasi to politely request to meet the Brotherhood lieutenant, albeit more loudly than a librarian's lungs were capable of. After the fact, the notion seemed absurd. She knew riggers, and in particular she knew Barnes and Dasi—which was much of the reason she'd asked them to escort her to the *Zieten*.

That didn't mean it was the right way to approach the Brethren, who were reputed to have their own outlook on honor and propriety. Once you'd devoted your life to the State through its Gods, you were likely to disregard merely human regulations.

Adele stepped forward, her hands raised at her sides. "Lieutenant Alderman, I'm Officer Mundy," she called. At least between them, she and Dasi had confused the troops enough to get within speaking distance. "I'm the one who requested your unit to take charge of the ship and its crew. I gather you've done so?"

Two soldiers stepped out from between a pair of room-sized shipping containers. Both carried sub-machine guns, but the older man behind wore a commo pack which would boost the signals of the small helmet transceivers which all the infantry wore.

"You're female!" said the younger man. Combat troops didn't wear insignia, but he was obviously Michael Alderman.

"Yes," said Adele, lowering her hands. *If you must*

state the pointlessly obvious. "I spoke with Colonel Stockheim, who gave you your orders. Have you carried them out?"

"Mistress, please remain where you are!" Alderman said forcefully. He was either angry or nervous because he was faced with an unexpected situation. "I need to check with the colonel."

An older soldier rose from the APC's hatch. He said, "Sir, that's the RCN officer who got the astrogation gear working on Paton."

Ignoring his noncom, Lieutenant Alderman began speaking into his helmet microphone. His sound-cancellation field was up. *You little puppy*, Adele thought; but after her mental rebuke of the rigger, she didn't say that aloud.

The noncom met Dasi's eyes and shook his head, one enlisted veteran to another. He didn't look at Adele, though.

Alderman stiffened abruptly, his eyes focused straight ahead as they would if he were being dressed down face-to-face instead of just over the radio. Adele hadn't warmed to Colonel Stockheim, but he seemed to be better at ordering priorities than this junior lieutenant was.

Swallowing, Alderman turned to face Adele squarely and saluted. "Your pardon, Officer Mundy," he said. "The crew of the ship *Zieten* is here as you wished—"

He gestured with the muzzle of his sub-machine gun. He carried the weapon with the ease of long practice. However poor Alderman's judgment might be, Adele had the impression that he would give a good account of himself in a gunfight.

"—but the ship is closed up. Ah—should we blow

it open? The colonel was clear that we were to extend you every facility."

"I'll take it from here, Lieutenant," Adele said. She was furious, but the first order of business was to correct the problem.

She turned to the Alliance officers, the prisoners wearing uniforms instead of ordinary spacers' slops. She said, "Corvette-Captain Friedman—"

She had the *Zieten*'s roster from her databanks.

"—stand up if you please!"

The pudgy man on the end lifted his head but didn't otherwise move. Goodness only knew what sort of threats the Brethren had offered anyone who didn't lie flat.

"Now!" Adele said.

The pudgy man rose to his elbows, watching Alderman, then carefully got to his feet. "I'm Peter Friedman," he said. "Look, we're prisoners of war. You can't just shoot us."

He didn't sound very sure about that. Adele grimaced. "Of course not," she said. She nodded to the supine row. "Is your whole crew here?"

"Mistress, we're a courier ship," Friedman said. Adele didn't bother to say that she knew that; he was nervous enough already. "All my crew is here, yes. We obeyed the, ah, Captain Leary's orders. It'd be crazy to think we could fight a heavy cruiser!"

"That's very much what Captain Leary said after he destroyed the *R16*," Adele said, emphasizing the point which obviously the Alliance officer was already aware of. Tovera and Barnes moved up to join her and Dasi. "But why is the *Zieten* still sealed?"

"Look, mistress, this isn't our doing, I don't want you

to think that," said Friedman, speaking in a breathless monotone. His eyes kept dancing around as though everything they lit on seared them. "But like I say, we're a courier ship and there were a couple Courier Service people aboard with the pouch."

Lieutenant Alderman stared at Tovera with the fascination of a small animal facing a viper. Tovera usually—Adele couldn't see her face at the moment—smiled back in such situations, making the metaphor even stronger.

"So they stayed aboard when the rest of you marched out?" Adele said, deciding to prod a little. She ordinarily let a subject tell the story his own way, then rearranged the bits later in a logical sequence; she'd learned that expecting logic from most people was as vain as expecting them to be skilled astrogators. Here, though, time might be getting short.

"Courier Alfreda, that's the officer, she carried the chip to Base Headquarters," said Captain Friedman. "But Ken Wilson, he's Support Staff, he stayed with the database. One of them always does. I mean the Courier Service database, it isn't linked to the ship."

Friedman swallowed. He turned his head from side to side, then stared at his boots. "Look," he said, "one of my engine wipers is a friend of Wilson's. She stayed aboard with him. I mean, what was I supposed to do? I got everybody else off, that's what's important, right?"

The just-landed freighter shut down its thrusters. In the near silence Adele heard five quickly spaced shots from across the harbor. The dull *whoomp* that followed was probably a vehicle's fuel tank bursting.

The most recent freighter had landed at the far end of the Fleet docks, but the next one would probably be nearby. Well, there were even better reasons to handle this quickly.

"Wilson and this woman are armed?" Adele said.

"I guess," Friedman said miserably. Adele wanted to slap him, but it wasn't the Alliance captain's cowardice that was really making her angry.

"All right," she said. "Barnes, Dasi—can we get into the ship from here or do I have to go back to the *Milton* to enter the command console electronically?"

She would have done that before they left the cruiser if she'd known. She *should* have known, it was her *job* not to make mistakes!

"We can blow it open, mistress," Alderman said with false brightness.

Ignoring the soldier, Barnes shrugged. "Sure," he said. "There's a hand wheel on each hatch. There's gotta be for when she's sitting in the yard with her fusion bottle pulled."

"And the bloody relays can fail," Dasi said to his partner. "Remember the old *Calydon* above Rubin?"

Barnes nodded. Dasi shrugged and added, "It'll be a bit of work, but at least we don't have to worry about our air giving out."

"All right," Adele repeated. With the two riggers in the lead, her party started down the quay toward the moored aviso.

Lieutenant Alderman trotted out in front of them. "Mistress," he said. "There are armed m-men aboard that ship. It's my duty to remove them from the vessel."

Adele looked at him. They were already half the hundred yards out from the esplanade. Odd; she wouldn't have thought they'd come so far.

"Yes, Lieutenant," she said. "It *was* your duty, and

you failed to accomplish it. Please get out of the way. The RCN will take care of the problem now."

Alderman froze, gray-faced. None of his men had followed him.

"Hey, pongo?" Barnes said. "There's something you can do after all. It'll make turning the wheel easier if we got a come-along, and your gun barrel's just the right diameter. Give me your gun."

"We might need to use our own," said Dasi, patting the receiver of his stocked impeller. "We're RCN, you know."

The riggers weren't ordinarily cruel men, but they were fighters. Alderman had insulted Mistress Mundy. Now that Adele had knocked him down, they were putting the boot in.

Without speaking, Alderman lifted the muzzle of his sub-machine gun and held it out to Barnes, who gripped it at the balance in his free hand. The riggers sauntered around the lieutenant to either side; Adele and Tovera followed Dasi to the left.

The riggers began whistling the chorus of a song which Adele had heard in the past: *"Here we come, full of rum, looking for boys who peddle their bum...."*

That was bravado, of course; they knew what they were getting into, or anyway they thought they did. But bravado had taken more than one RCN ship down the throat of a powerful enemy and out the other side.

Adele glanced back over her shoulder. Alderman remained where they'd left him. He looked like a statue of despair.

The *Zieten* had been down for more than an hour, so the steam of its landing had cooled to condensate soaking the quays. The riggers trotted on ahead, unconcerned about the slick metal surfaces of the dock extensions.

By the time Adele and Tovera arrived at a more sedate pace, the cover plate on the hinge side of the airlock was unbolted. Barnes stuck the barrel of the borrowed sub-machine gun through the six-inch wheel there and began cranking it around.

"Can we talk to the people inside?" Adele asked Dasi.

"Sure," he said, "once we get the lock open. There'll be an intercom."

Adele nodded. "I'll speak to them before we enter, then," she said.

Dasi smiled without real interest. While his partner turned the wheel, he pointed his impeller toward the widening crack. Both riggers were big men. Barnes worked swiftly, but Adele realized that even with the gun for greater leverage it was a real job. What must it have been like while wearing rigging suits in orbit above Rubin?

"That's good enough," Dasi said. "Gimme the pongo's gun and I'll take the inside one. Ah—unless you..."

"Be my guest," Barnes said as he tossed Alderman's sub-machine gun to his partner. Dasi slipped into the empty airlock through what was, to Adele's surprise, a wide enough opening for him.

"I want to speak with the people inside," Adele said sharply.

"Don't worry, ma'am," Barnes said, stretching out the stiffness of his recent exertion. "It's not going to happen quick. It's as much work on the inside hatch and it's cramped besides."

The lock would hold eight spacers in rigging suits. Some airlocks had clear panels in the inner door; this one didn't, but an intercom was in the chamber's wall as the riggers had said.

Tovera stepped between Adele and Dasi. The submachine gun she'd taken from the cruiser's armory was pointed at what would become the opening when the hatch moved; she wore her own miniature weapon in a belt holster like a pistol. Dasi began to crank.

The intercom switch was a slide. "Master Wilson," Adele said, "and all of you Fleet personnel aboard the *Zieten*, this is Officer Mundy of the RCN. Surrender immediately and don't put us to the trouble of killing you. You and all your fellows will be treated according to the normal usages of war. There's obviously no escape for you, so you may as well be reasonable and live."

Another Hydriote ship was landing. Adele put her ear close to the speaker plate, but she didn't think there was a response.

In Alliance service, dispatches were downloaded into a discrete database aboard the vessel carrying them. When the vessel reached its destination, the courier copied the dispatch onto a chip which was physically carried to the recipient; information was never transmitted electronically. The database was then wiped.

Complete clearing of a database required specialized facilities, however. St. James Base might have such equipment, but there hadn't been time to bring it to the aviso. If Adele could get to the database, she would have all the information that it had carried since its last thorough clearance.

"Wilson, you don't want to die and we don't want to kill you!" Adele said. "And if you're not thinking of yourself, what of the friend you've got with you? Do you want *her* to die?"

A heavy male voice, perhaps rougher for the intercom's bad transmission, said, "Put Officer Alfreda on. If I can talk to her, I'll give up."

If you talk to her, she'll tell you to empty an impeller into the database, which would also be a thorough way of destroying its data, Adele thought. She said, "Alfreda was killed in the fighting. Unless you surrender immediately, you and your friend will join her for no reason at all. Don't be a fool, Wilson!"

The hatch was open a hand's breadth and spreading further in the steady increments of sand dripping through an hourglass. Adele didn't know whether or not Alfreda was alive. If she was, she'd almost certainly triggered the miniature charge in her pouch and reduced the data chip to powder. The *Zieten's* database was the only sure path to the dispatches.

"I gotta speak to Alfreda!" Wilson said. "And stop opening the door, I'll shoot, I swear I'll shoot!"

"Come on, Wilson," Adele said, trying to sound soothing. She doubted that she succeeded; it wasn't something she was good at. "There's no need for shooting. Just put down your gun and you can relax for the rest of the war."

Dasi continued cranking. A shot from inside banged into the hatch and howled deeper into the vessel. The hatch was opening toward Wilson. He'd tried to shoot—probably with a service pistol—through the crack on the hinge side.

"Don't shoot!" Adele snapped to her companions. A slug bouncing around the aviso might hit the database that Wilson apparently hadn't been smart enough destroy deliberately.

"Barnes, take care of this," Tovera said. She drew

the miniature weapon from its holster while her left hand stretched back with the armory sub-machine gun. Barnes reached past Adele and took it.

Adele drew her pistol. The opening was almost wide enough for her to slip through. She said, "Tovera, I'll lead."

"You've got to leave!" Wilson cried. "I'll kill you all! Send Officer Alfreda!"

Tovera poised. "Hold on to her, Barnes," she said. The rigger reached around Adele's torso with his right arm and clamped her left shoulder like a seat restraint.

"I'm warning—" Wilson said.

Tovera was through the hatchway like a wisp of fog. Her sub-machine gun stuttered, echoes muddling the snapping discharges. Wilson fired an instant later. His heavy slug bounced twice, each time deforming further to sing in a different key.

"I give up!" screamed a female voice. "I give—"

Tovera's weapon crackled out another three-shot burst. A body thumped into a bulkhead, then the deck. Heels drummed briefly before there was silence.

"All clear!" Tovera called. "All clear!"

Barnes released Adele and stepped back. Dasi stood beside the hatch mechanism, swallowing with unaccustomed nervousness.

"Do you know who you laid hands on?" Adele said. "I'm Mundy of Chatsworth! I can have you flayed, you little worm!"

"Yes ma'am," Barnes said, staring at the bulkhead above her head. "We know that. Ma'am, you do what you want to do. But I'm not going to look at Six and tell him that you got killed because we let you be stupid."

"Ma'am?" said Dasi. His hands were knotting together; Adele had a sudden vision of a little boy unable to save his drowning puppy. "I'd have done the same. Ma'am, Six wouldn't ream us out, he'd *cry*."

Adele felt a cold knife sinking into her heart. Her lips pursed to speak, paused; pursed to say something else and paused again. At last—and it was only a few heartbeats delay—she said, "Captain Leary is well served by his crew."

She shook herself, dropped the unused pistol back into her pocket, and said, "Tovera, we're coming through."

Tovera stood in the hatch opening, watching the exchange. "Mistress," she said with a nod and stepped out of the way.

Adele hadn't even been angry at her. Tovera wasn't fully human; she would do whatever she decided was right in a given situation, regardless of what any individual or society as a whole said. And in this case—

Adele's thin smile was self-mocking.

—Tovera *had* been right, by any standards one could reasonably apply. Lady Mundy had been about to act irresponsibly, so her colleagues had correctly restrained her.

The airlock opened into a rotunda much like that of the *Princess Cecile*. Across it, a brawny man lay on his face, his legs back in the compartment adjacent to the bridge. There was no sign of blood, but his body must have frozen at the instant of death; the pistol gripped in his left hand was slightly raised from the deck.

A woman sprawled against the wall of the compartment behind him. She'd been short and vaguely pear-shaped. Her face was flushed and bulging. Adele could have covered with two slim fingers the trio of holes above the bridge of the woman's nose.

"The courier database is in the compartment with them," Tovera said, gesturing with her left hand. "It wasn't damaged."

"I thought I heard her surrender," Adele said in an even tone.

Tovera shrugged. "Mistress," she said, "it's hard to hear anything like that after the shooting starts."

Adele stepped over Wilson's legs. "Barnes," she said. "Get these bodies out of the way. I'm going to be here till I've downloaded the dispatches, and I have no idea how long that will be."

She swung the bunk out of the wall and seated herself on it, then took her personal data unit from its pocket. She threw a switch on the side of the dispatch computer. The action settled her mind almost magically.

Adele began working. Now that she'd opened the data port, it really shouldn't take very long.

Barnes lifted the woman by the throat of her tunic and carried her out of the compartment. That was just as well. Adele didn't notice her surroundings once she'd become lost in a project, but both corpses had voided their bowels when they died. The ship's atmosphere had been close after a long voyage besides.

CHAPTER 20

The Travanda Quarry, Bolton

The aircar paused at the top of the ramp which zigzagged into the quarry some thirteen miles north of St. James City. Daniel got out.

"Good luck, Your Excellency," he said, waving to Forbes. As the words came out, he wondered if he should have said, "Break a leg," instead. The car slid down the ramp in ground effect, followed by the APC whose external speakers would amplify the senator's speech.

Travanda marble was the color of whipped butter and remarkably free of inclusions. Before the Battle of New Harmony—the New Harmony Massacre—it had been Bolton's only export except for governmental directives. Now the quarry was full of RCN prisoners, the survivors of the ships trapped on New Harmony when Admiral Petersen arrived.

Ranks of shelters as irregular as teeth in a human mouth striped the quarry with as much order as possible on a floor laid out by stonecutters rather than architects. Alliance administrators had provided sail fabric and pipes from which the prisoners could create their own living quarters in a man-made cavity. That wasn't harsh treatment but an acceptance of reality: the authorities on Bolton couldn't pull secure housing for five thousand out of the air.

"You're Leary?" said the fiftyish man who led the contingent which had climbed to the top of the ramp to await their rescuers. He saluted. "I'm Haugen, Commander Kenneth Haugen, and I've been camp commandant till now. Ought to thank you, I suppose."

Haugen had a full beard and moustache, but his hairline receded steeply. The Alliance authorities had allowed each prisoner a single set of utilities without rank markings, but Haugen had made replacement insignia from bits of ration cans. He'd been first officer on the battleship *Heidegger*, according to the information Cory had waiting when Daniel returned from accepting Commodore Harmston's surrender. Originally he'd been an Engineer, but he'd taken astrogation courses and successfully sat for his commission.

"Yes, I'm Leary," Daniel said. He returned the commander's salute, hoping the effort didn't seem too perfunctory. "We'll begin transferring you to billets in St. James City shortly, using the stone trucks."

He grinned. "It won't be luxurious," he said, "but there'll be proper rooms and beds at the end of it. Right now, though, Senator Forbes wants to make what amounts to a stump speech, so I thought I'd keep out of the way till she's done. She's the planetary administrator, after all."

"Yes, well, I suppose that's proper," Haugen said with a tinge of disappointment. He looked down on the rows of shelters and went on, "Rather good, isn't it? Did it ourselves, you know. Better quarters than the enlisted ranks had on shipboard, if you want to know the truth."

"I'm sure they are, Commander," Daniel said. The man was twice his age and probably a very useful officer in his way, but the Gods forefend that Navy House ever appoint him to an independent command! "But we're going to need the quarry here for Alliance prisoners, you realize."

"Ah!" said Haugen, who obviously hadn't thought that far ahead. "So you're staying here, then? On Bolton, I mean?"

"Yes, Commander," Daniel said dryly. "We've captured the planet, and we intend to hold it for as long as it takes Navy House to get reinforcements here."

"My fellow citizens!" Senator Forbes said, insulting even those freed captives who happened to be from Cinnabar. A citizen was a landsman, while these folk were spacers—an altogether higher form of existence, so far as they were concerned.

Not that anybody really cared. This was a happy occasion so far as the spacers were concerned: a high dignitary was addressing *them*, even if they couldn't hear her—the quarry's jagged angles made the acoustics abysmal.

"Cinnabar grieved at your misfortune," Forbes said. "You must have known that your motherworld would waste no time in redressing the harm done you on her behalf!"

She stood on the deck of the aircar, speaking through a lapel mike. The APC parked on the second dogleg above the car amplified the signal. Forbes's voice then boomed through the APC's cupola speakers and rattled down the quarry's twisting hollowness.

"You really think you can do that, Leary?" said Haugen, tugging at the left brush of his moustache. His face was scrunched in honest puzzlement, like a dutiful child listening to a lecture on tensor calculus. "I mean to say, Admiral Petersen is a lot closer than Cinnabar; and as far as Cinnabar goes, Harbor Three was looking pretty picked over even when we lifted back at the beginning of the war."

Forbes's secretary scrambled around the car, holding an imagery recorder and trying to get his mistress from every angle. This was the real purpose of the speech: it wasn't for the spacers but so that crowds back on Cinnabar could see Senator Forbes freeing thousands of stalwart RCN spacers.

If Forbes had expected a photo opportunity like this, she'd have traveled with a proper public relations crew. As it was, even the bumbling Platt could gather enough raw material for professionals in Xenos to cut and polish into useful shape.

Daniel grinned. Capturing Bolton had given him an appreciation for the problems that Admiral Petersen had faced when he unexpectedly took New Harmony. Though the conspirators who'd aided the Alliance were now the planetary government, they had many personal political enemies in addition to the portion of the populace who supported Cinnabar or opposed the Alliance.

It wasn't safe to imprison thousands of RCN spacers on New Harmony: they would become a shock force of counterrevolution if one party or another managed to arm them. The high RCN officers—Admiral Ozawa and his staff, and all surviving ships' captains—had been sent to Pleasaunce, proof of and an ornament to the triumphant victory which they announced. Quite a number of common spacers had no national allegiance; Petersen simply enlisted them in his squadron.

The remainder—the officers, warrant officers, and Cinnabar citizens—had been sent to the nearest Alliance base where the civilian authorities and the Fleet's rear echelon would deal with them. They were a serious problem on Bolton, but they'd stopped being Petersen's problem.

Though that might be about to change. Daniel smiled more broadly.

"With any luck, it'll be some time before Admiral Petersen gets word of the change of government here, Commander," Daniel said. "No ships left the system during the attack, and with the exception of the two prizes I'm sending to Cinnabar, none will lift for another few days until I've got cargos together for them. The planetary defense array is just as useful to enforce an embargo as it is to fend off a hostile fleet, you see."

The Hydriotes who were bringing in the Fonthill Militia weren't going to be happy about the situation, but that couldn't be helped. They'd be paid for the unexpected delay in harbor—the volume of Alliance stores captured here would make even the *Millie*'s common spacers rich for the months it took them to carouse it away—but nobody was going to get a fat reward for bringing Admiral Petersen word of the disaster in time to retrieve it.

"The PDA is still in place?" Haugen said. He blinked three times, trying unsuccessfully to get his mind around the concept. "How the bloody hell did you get through it, Leary? I don't understand!"

"It was a matter of good luck and very careful timing," Daniel said, a truthful if incomplete explanation and as much as Haugen was capable of absorbing. Daniel thought of the child facing calculus again.

"Well, I'll be buggered," Haugen said. He shook his head carefully, apparently hoping the information he'd just been given would sort itself into a form he could understand. "I *will* be buggered."

Senator Forbes was talking about the debt which the Republic owed her brave spacers and Forbes's own pride at being the person who was joining with Captain Leary to pay that debt. Daniel would just as soon that she didn't use his name so frequently in material which she planned to spread all over Cinnabar, as it wouldn't make him any friends in Navy House. On the other hand, even his worst enemies in the RCN knew not to take a politician's blather seriously.

"Cargos, though, you said?" Haugen went on. "Ah—Captain? I know your record and of course—"

He patted his laboriously created rank tab.

"—it's not my business to question a senior officer. But, ah—you're a young man, Leary. I know things go on, I've seen things go on. But it might be best to be careful about what you say to a stranger. There are officers who, well, might not be as broad-minded as I about captains engaging in trade."

Daniel laughed in delighted amazement. *I hadn't thought of that interpretation!*

"Your concern does you honor, Commander," he said, speaking quickly so that Haugen wouldn't think he was being mocked. "But these cargos are very much proper RCN business. Besides you and your fellow prisoners—"

Daniel gestured toward spacers crowding about the rows of shimmering tents to get closer to the dignitary on the aircar.

"—Admiral Petersen put his hostages here on Bolton. I'm sending them back to their home planets."

That would have an additional benefit, because Hydriote shippers carried out commissions in an absolutely trustworthy fashion. Each captain would make his contracted voyage before he set off for New Harmony. That would add at least a week before the news about Bolton reached Admiral Petersen.

"Hostages?" said Haugen. "What sort of hostages?"

"There are a hundred or two people from each of the important worlds in the Montserrat Stars," Daniel explained. "They're here on East Continent. Generally they're the sons and daughters of the most prominent citizens, that sort of thing. Officially they're being educated to fit them for high office in the Alliance, but—"

He shrugged.

"—the parents weren't given the option of refusing this honor. Fifth Bureau officials—" Guarantor Porra's personal secret police "—gathered them up."

"They're treacherous bastards, the whole lot of them," Haugen muttered. "But I didn't know anything about hostages. We're all RCN here, and all taken on New Harmony."

He shook his head. "A bloody awful thing that was," he said. "*Bloody* awful. We weren't but ten feet up when bang! and we went down again and broke poor *Heidi*'s back on the quay. The *Hobbes* hadn't even gotten her outriggers out of the water. Bloody awful. I didn't have the faintest bloody notion what had happened, just trying to get everybody off before the fusion bottle failed. Which it didn't, thank the Gods, but you can't count on that."

"No, you certainly can't," said Daniel, who suddenly liked Haugen a great deal more than he had a moment before. As executive officer, damage control was in his care. With the ship a hopeless wreck, he'd immediately made the correct decision: getting the crew to safety.

"And it was the wogs stabbed us in the back," the commander said in amazement. "Can you imagine that? Well, they've got themselves to thank for whatever Porra and his Fifth Bureau monkeys do to them, and there'll be plenty done I don't doubt."

The fact that the battleships had been destroyed on the surface explained why the bulk of their crews had survived. The *Locke* and *Aquinas* had fought the hugely superior Alliance squadron to give their lighter consorts a chance to escape; their crews wouldn't have been so lucky. But spacefaring and war were dangerous, and war in space was many times dangerous.

Daniel could feel good about the many spacers below him in the quarry. They might just as easily have been protoplasm drifting around New Harmony.

"I hope that by returning the hostages to their home planets," he said with quiet pride, "we'll encourage those worlds to think well of Cinnabar. If that also has the effect of sparking a rebellion or two against Guarantor Porra's flunkies, so much the better. And at the very least—"

Daniel beamed at Commander Haugen.

"—it removes the problem of feeding and administering some thousands of civilians at a time when all Cinnabar personnel on Bolton should be concentrating their efforts on keeping Petersen from recapturing the place. Eh, Commander?"

"By the Gods, Leary!" Haugen said, shaking his head again. "You're a deep one, no doubt about it. Well, you give me my duties and I'll get on with them the best I can. I always have, if I do say so myself."

Senator Forbes seemed to be running down, though it was difficult to be sure. A good speaker always repeated her points, because his listeners couldn't glance up the page to see what they'd missed. In the particular case the speech was going to be recast completely by editors, so there was even less reason than usual to expect the speaker to be succinct.

Nonetheless, Daniel assumed it was about time for him to say a few words to the crowd, explaining that they'd be trucked to St. James City to await developments. Whatever ships Navy House managed to send to Bolton would be short-crewed, so the unexpected bounty of trained spacers would greatly help the defense of the planet.

If Navy House could only get *something* to Bolton before Admiral Petersen—

"*Daniel,*" said his commo helmet in Adele's voice. "*I need you back here as soon as possible. Can you hear me?*"

She's excited. Adele spoke with her usual disdainful calm, but she wouldn't usually ask if they were connected.

"Yes, Adele," Daniel said, raising a hand in bar and stepping away from Haugen. "What's the problem, over?"

The Brotherhood APC which amplified the senator's speech also acted as a satellite downlink for the helmet intercom. Blantyre, her head out of the vehicle's cupola, was looking back at Daniel. She couldn't hear the signal, but she knew it was coming through—and that emergency communications were never good news.

"*I've been going over the dispatches which the* Zieten *was carrying,*" Adele said with her usual disregard for protocol. "*Some of them are for the squadron detached under Captain Varnell to take possession of the Ponape System. It includes at least one battleship.*"

Down on the quarry floor Forbes had raised her hands high; the spacers were cheering her wildly. If things had gone as planned, Daniel would shortly have spoken his own few words to them.

"*From the way the dispatches are worded,*" Adele continued, "*Captain Varnell is expected on Bolton in no more than two days.*"

"I see," said Daniel. "In that case, the senator and I will be back as quickly as the aircar can bring us. Six out."

He started down the ramp, taking long strides. It looked like Lieutenant Blantyre instead of Captain Leary would be representing the *Milton* to the liberated spacers. That was all right—they'd understand that things came up.

They were RCN, after all.

St. James Harbor, Bolton

"Captain Leary's coming up the companionway, mistress," Tovera said. "And Senator Forbes is with him."

"Mmm," Adele muttered. "Well, I still have more

to learn, but I suppose that would be true no matter when they arrived."

She brought herself fully back to the present; she'd been sunk deep in the aviso's database. The *Zieten* had been in the heart of Petersen's fleet throughout operations in the New Harmony system and then following.

"I certainly hope I'll continue to learn things for the rest of my life," Adele said primly to her servant. "I see very little point in life if that were not true."

And sometimes she saw little point in life, period. Right now, though, she was feeling exhilarated by the challenge of ferreting out and organizing the necessary data from the *Zieten*'s log and dispatches. Exhilarated because she was succeeding, of course; but as a matter of course she expected to succeed.

Every situation of this sort was new and presented new difficulties. Here Adele was guessing what Daniel would want to know; which meant that first she had to guess what he would want to *do*, which in turn depended on the factual situation which he would learn from the information she presented to him. It was a lovely circular problem with an infinite number of wrong answers and no certainty of any right one.

Beaming, Adele turned to the hatchway as Daniel entered. It was the sort of problem that people gave to Officer Mundy, because nobody else could handle it as well.

Forbes followed Daniel up the companionway, but she did so in a chair-sling carried between her two brawny servants. The pair eased sideways from the armored tube and stood like tree stumps while she got out. Their faces were set in the same deliberate stolidity that they would have maintained if their mistress were on a chest of ease: *they* weren't present at a scene of embarrassing weakness.

Civilian vessels sometimes had elevators to move passengers between levels, but warships never did. The process of slipping between universes twisted the fabric of a starship and could bind an elevator in its shaft. A warship not only transitioned more violently than the civilian norm but might also be hammered by plasma or kinetic weapons. What was a doubtful choice in the civilian context would have been absurd on a naval vessel.

Adele looked back to her data, smiling faintly. Lady Adele Mundy, whose fellow spacers preferred to carry her through any situation in which a misstep might be dangerous, wasn't going to mock an older woman who needed help climbing slick metal stairs.

"Eh?" said Daniel, squatting beside her console.

"I'm rather good at steps," Adele said, stating the thought behind her smile without explaining it. "The elevators in the Academic Collections worked poorly when they worked at all, and the levels of the stack area didn't correspond well to the floors in the support structure anyway. I climbed openwork metal stairs as frequently as a midshipman goes up and down the antennas."

"Indeed you are," Daniel said, smiling also. "I certainly wouldn't want to race you up a companionway. But now—"

Senator Forbes entered the compartment, followed by her attendants and finally Platt. She was scowling, but that could have been for any number of reasons.

"—what's the situation? And—"

Daniel looked around, his face suddenly set. "Clear the bridge," he ordered.

The RCN personnel rose as one and shifted toward

the door with the apparent organization of sand dripping through a timing glass. Nobody argued or hesitated: Daniel had done this before, so his Millies were
prepared for it.

"Hogg, you and Tovera too," Daniel added sternly.
There must have been hesitation in the look one or
the other servant gave him, because he said, "If Her
Excellency causes trouble, I can club her senseless
with my commo helmet."

The senator's expression became if anything more
sour, but she didn't sound angry when she murmured,
"You *will* have your joke, Leary."

Hogg chuckled as he touched each of Forbes's
attendants on an elbow and said, "Come on, boys,
we'll wait in the hall. D'ye play poker, by any chance?"

"I'll follow," said Tovera. She smiled also, which
ended any chance of an attendant deciding to argue.
She closed the hatch behind them.

"I could have moved," Adele said, embarrassed by
the fuss. "We don't have to be on the bridge."

She wasn't even sure that the crew shouldn't know
everything she was about to say. Though thinking
about it—and Daniel had of course thought about
it—it probably wasn't a good idea to show them how
decisions affecting their lives were really made.

The Millies knew that Six was brave, and at least
some of them probably understood that Lady Mundy's
unconcern for her personal safety went beyond mere
fatalism. It might disturb them to realize that their
own lives would be spent as a matter of conscious
planning if the Republic required that choice, however.

"We'll use the large display," said Daniel, "which I
think Her Excellency will find easiest to grasp."

He stepped to the astrogation console and rotated the couch to face the center of the compartment; the latch was simple but not intuitively obvious, and Forbes would never have used one before. He smiled and said, "Please make yourself comfortable, Your Excellency. Officer Mundy will put information where we can all see it."

"After Petersen captured New Harmony," Adele said, "he divided his force. He send a squadron under Captain Varnell—"

She'd waited until Daniel was in the command console and could watch before she threw up the first visual, images of the battleship *Direktor Friedrich* and its accompanying cruisers and destroyers. A viewer could open tabular data on each ship by touching an icon with the pointer in each console. Forbes probably didn't know how to do that, but neither did she need any information save the hulking mass of the battleship.

"—back to Bolton to refit, but by way of Ponape where there'd been a rebellion of sorts. Captain Varnell's ships were in relatively poor condition but they were thought to be capable of overawing rebels, especially since news of the disaster to Admiral Ozawa's fleet would have reached Ponape by way of merchants whom the locals would trust."

"It would appear that we owe a vote of thanks to the courageous citizens of Ponape," Daniel said in a tone of irony. "I'm not sure exactly what would've happened if we'd reached Bolton just after a squadron that size had arrived, but I'm confident that it wouldn't involve us controlling the planet."

"Based on my knowledge of how the Alliance deals

with rebels," Adele said, "I doubt that any of the really courageous citizens are alive to thank. You may think it proper to pray for their souls, of course."

She paused to recover the thread of her exposition, then said, "Petersen took the remainder of his force—"

A much larger body headed by three battleships replaced the imagery of Captain Varnell's squadron. Forbes's eyes narrowed as she watched, but she didn't speak.

"—to Cacique, which had been Admiral Ozawa's base of operations. He assumed that the surviving elements of Ozawa's fleet would have fled there, and that they would quickly surrender when he arrived in overwhelming force. Cacique has a planetary defense array, but—"

This explanation was for Forbes. She knew Daniel was up to date on all naval resources in his area of operations, both friendly and hostile.

"—beyond that the facilities are rudimentary. Don't imagine something like you see here, Senator. Stores are transferred by lighters, not docks and cranes."

Forbes slammed the side of her fist on the console's armrest. Nonetheless it was in an even tone of voice that she said, "So Cacique has fallen also? Then there's no world among the Montserrat Stars which isn't under the Alliance or ready to go over to the Alliance as soon as Admiral Petersen gets around to taking its submission?"

"No, Senator," said Adele.

"No, Your Excellency," said Daniel. They had spoken simultaneously and at once.

With a cold smile, Adele nodded the precedence to Daniel. He bobbed his head twice.

"Twenty-odd ships including three heavy cruisers

escaped from New Harmony," he said. "They may not all have gone to Cacique, but that would be the default choice of any RCN captain under the circumstances. It's the nearest friendly world with a defense array, which is the only present safety from a fleet the size of Petersen's."

He shrugged. "And they won't surrender, Your Excellency," he said. "Whoever's the senior captain will take command. He may not be much good—there are captains in the RCN that I wouldn't trust with organizing three other people into a bridge game. But whoever takes charge *will* be RCN. He won't surrender, and if he even suggested it, his fellow captains would hold a drumhead court-martial and have him shot on his own bridge."

Daniel rapped out the final words with a vehemence that obviously surprised him when he stopped and realized what he'd done. He coughed and straightened.

"Sorry, got a bit carried away, I'm afraid," he muttered.

"Regardless, Senator," Adele said, "Captain Leary is correct in how the forces on Cacique behaved. The prime reason that Admiral Petersen sent a courier to Bolton was to countermand his previous orders and order Captain Varnell to rejoin him off Cacique immediately. Having judged the situation, Petersen feels that he wants all the force he can muster to prevent the RCN squadron from inflicting embarrassing reverses on his blockaders."

"Since we *are* in control here on Bolton," Senator Forbes said, leaning forward slightly, "you think we can hold out against this Captain Varnell? Long enough for Cinnabar to get reinforcements to us?"

Adele turned to Daniel and lifted an eyebrow. She thought she knew the answer, but it wasn't her place to speak for the military commander.

"Yes, Your Excellency," Daniel said, "I think we could hold out for a very long time. A planetary defense array can't be swept quickly at best, and the warehouses here on Bolton include several hundred additional mines which we could use to replace those the Alliance clears."

He waved a hand dismissively.

"But I don't intend to fend off Captain Varnell's squadron," he continued. "I have a very different plan."

He smiled. Seeing his expression, Adele realized for the first time the similarities between Daniel and Tovera.

CHAPTER 21

St. James Harbor, Bolton

Daniel was in the head of his space cabin when the summons came. He was wearing his commo helmet, but for this he wanted the big display.

"Go ahead, *R12*," he said, tugging his trousers up as he ran—well, stumbled—toward the bridge. "Over."

Whoever was on duty in the BDC rang the deep bong of Action Stations over the PA system. Hatches began to clang against their coamings, a process that would continue for some while since the *Milton* had been completely opened up to the pleasant day outside.

"*The heavy cruiser* Treasurer Johann *and the destroyers* Z44 *and* Pigafetta *have extracted approximately one and a half million miles from Bolton*," Adele's voice stated. Communications algorithms which were designed to counteract the effects of sideband transmission and atmospheric distortion had the odd result of making her sound livelier than she would have been if she'd been giving Daniel a similar report face-to-face. "*There are indications that at least a dozen more ships are following.*

Full data is being streamed in accordance with Alliance standard operating procedures. R12 over."

Daniel threw himself onto the couch of his console; it synched automatically with his commo helmet and came live. "Roger, *R12*," he said. "We're awaiting developments here, out."

He raised his buttocks and hitched his trousers the rest of the way up. They were still skewed and he'd misaligned the fly when he sealed it, but they'd do for now.

You could say that this had been the most awkward possible instant for the Alliance squadron to arrive, but it hadn't really mattered. Action with the enemy was what an RCN officer lived for, and it was certainly what Daniel Leary lived for. He could've been just reaching the short strokes with the most beautiful woman in the human universe, and he'd still have run for the command console.

Daniel grinned. *I'd regret that more afterwards, though.*

Sun ran down the corridor, carrying with him the rigging suit that wasn't issued equipment for a gunner—or a Power Room technician, for that matter, which is what he'd been before he'd struck for the specialist rating. If the *Milton* took the sort of damage that required her crew to suit up, Sun was willing to trade its stiffness and weight for greater protection than an air suit would provide. He was a veteran who'd learned both how to find things that hadn't been offered to him and how to store them in the limited volume of a starship.

The alarm continued to ring. Pasternak was a methodical man who didn't act without communicating his intent, but things could go wrong. "Power Room," said

Daniel over the command channel as incoming ships continued to spill onto his display, "this is Six. Do not, I repeat, do not light the thrusters. We can afford a few extra minutes getting under way if it helps convince our Alliance friends that everybody down here is asleep. Six out."

Senator Forbes entered the bridge on the gunner's heels. Daniel didn't grimace, but he certainly wished that his august passenger had joined Lieutenant Robinson in the BDC as she'd done in the past. Apparently Forbes had come to regard him as an associate, not just a glorified chauffeur. In many respects that was a positive development, but the start of an engagement with the enemy Daniel would just as soon have been left alone.

He reached for his cursor to shut off the bell. Before he reached it, somebody in the BDC beat him to it. The hatches continued to ring through the cruiser as they closed, but the sound was almost restful to men and women who'd become spacers because they were ensorcelled by the thought of far worlds.

"Is this what we're waiting for?" the senator said. She stood beside the command console and stared at the display with a look of frustrated puzzlement. "They're coming, I mean, this Captain Varnell and his ships?"

In truth, Daniel didn't have much to do at the moment besides gather information, and retailing that information to Forbes if anything aided his concentration. He glanced at her, smiled, and said, "Yes, Your Excellency. The Alliance squadron has arrived, or anyway most of it has."

After a moment's consideration, he displayed the

data in the form of a Plot-Position Indicator centered on the *Milton* in harbor. Ordinarily one would use the PPI for lesser volumes and only when the ship was itself out of the atmosphere, but it seemed the most effective tool with which to lay things out for a civilian.

"Here's their flagship, the *Direktor Friedrich*," he explained, highlighting the Alliance battleship with red. The dot was invisible at this scale, but the letters FRI and three numbers identified the vessel even without calling up the full imbedded particulars.

Captain Varnell's squadron seemed badly scattered, but Ponape was seven days distant, and they'd probably made long reaches to get here. The officers no less than the crews would be looking forward to liberty in St. James City. Well, if things went as Daniel hoped, they'd get complete release from naval duties very shortly.

"She's accompanied by three heavy cruisers—"

More highlights, this time in magenta. The *Johann* and *Eckernferde* had extracted within ten thousand miles of the flagship, but the *Arcona* was a hundred thousand miles away, more distant than most of the freighters.

"—and a squadron of originally ten destroyers according to the dispatches on the *Zieten*—"

The highlights this time were pink. *Adele would be pleased with how much I've learned from seeing her work.*

"—but there's only seven present now. I don't know if that means the other three were left on Ponape or if they're just a trifle later—ah, there's eight! And nine as well."

Though he continued cheerful and smiling, mention

of Adele reminded Daniel of her circumstances. He wouldn't need the recent examples of the *R11* and *R16* to inform him of what a heavy plasma bolt would do to a 90-tonne mine tender—but he had those examples.

"But there's more ships than that," said Forbes. "The white ones."

Then, hopefully, she looked from the display to Daniel's face and said, "Are they ours? Are we getting reinforcements after all?"

Daniel's expression went instantly blank. The question was completely unexpected, as much so as if the senator had suggested that they begin to pray to the Gods to grant victory to the forces of Justice and Cinnabar.

It was rather fortunate that he *was* taken aback. If he'd understood from the first instant what Forbes was saying, he'd probably have blurted something in a tone that would have to be considered insulting.

"Ah, no, Your Excellency," Daniel said, carefully keeping his eyes turned toward the great holographic display. "The blush dots—"

They weren't white, but he might not have emphasized that if he hadn't been so appalled by the senator's misunderstanding. Only desperation could have led her to such a ludicrous fantasy.

"—are freighters travelling in company with Captain Varnell. There should be seven in all, six of them—ah, there's the other two and the last destroyer as well."

He cleared his throat, still looking at the display, and continued, "Six of the transports originally carried materials for the base which Admiral Petersen constructed in the New Harmony system during the siege. They've probably been sent here to carry additional supplies to

Petersen's main force which is now off Cacique, but I won't know that until I can examine their orders."

"And the last ship?" said Forbes—evenly, but with a hint of cold displeasure. She had apparently sensed how Captain Leary really felt about her hopeful suggestion. "Since I believe it's colored blush, like the other transports."

Daniel grimaced and met her eyes. "Yes, Your Excellency," he said, "but it isn't a Fleet vessel or even under Fleet command. The Fifth Bureau, that is—"

"I know what the Fifth Bureau is, Captain," Forbes said. "I've known what the Fifth Bureau was since before you were born."

Daniel dipped his torso in what he hoped was a submissive gesture. It was as close to a bow as he could manage while seated at his console.

"Just so, Your Excellency," he said. "Guarantor Porra sends his inquisitors along with every expedition so that they get in on the ground floor, so to speak. My expectation is that this ship, the *Oswestry*, will be carrying the offspring of the locals whom the Alliance has installed as the rulers of New Harmony."

"Rather than pro-Cinnabar leaders?" Forbes said, surprise finally overcoming her pique.

Daniel shrugged. "That's what we would do on a recently...," he said, then paused.

He gave Forbes a lopsided smile and resumed, "A world recently welcomed to the Friendship of the Republic, I should say. Based on what I've seen of Alliance practice, the people who had been ruling New Harmony in friendship with Cinnabar are now either dead or being tortured back on New Harmony. The *Oswestry* will be carrying hostages from the present ruling elite, much like the others whom we recently freed from the prison colony on East Continent."

The senator's nostrils flared. "I see," she said.

Daniel looked at the display. The Alliance squadron was reforming. The ships would reenter the Matrix for a brief hop closer to Bolton. They could make the run in sidereal space, of course, but that would take days or weeks.

They'd been reasonable in erring on the side of caution when they made their first extraction in the system, however, especially since there were merchantmen in the convoy. A navigation error that put a ship too close to the planetary defense array would mean instant destruction.

Daniel turned to Forbes again. He was embarrassed at what he was about to say, but he decided to say it anyway.

"Your Excellency," he said, "I'm not a philosopher, I'm an RCN officer. It's my duty and my honor to carry out the Republic's policies, not to worry about whether they're correct in some abstract way. But I've seen what it's like on the edges, a long way from Cinnabar and Pleasaunce . . . and Your Excellency? However much they may grumble, people are bloody lucky to be paying Cinnabar taxes and reporting to Cinnabar bureaucrats, because I've seen what the choice is. *Bloody* lucky!"

"As you may have guessed, Leary," Forbes said, "the Senate doesn't concern itself with such abstract questions either. But I suspect you're right, and I'm pleased at the realization. Though it obviously doesn't affect our own actions."

She coughed. "Having said that," she went on, "what do we do next?"

"We wait, Your Excellency," said Daniel, returning to the display. The Alliance vessels were vanishing into the Matrix; shortly they would reappear just outside Bolton's minefield, waiting for mine tender *R12* to pass them down to the surface. "We wait for Lady Mundy to carry out her task, which she will do with the perfect competence she has exhibited in all her previous duties."

And we'll hope that Adele and the spacers with her are lucky, Daniel thought. *Because her skill guarantees success, but it doesn't guarantee survival.*

Above Bolton

"Squadron Command, this is *R12*," Adele said, watching her screen coordinate the squadron which was appearing with the ships the *Zieten*'s dispatches had led her to expect. "Bolton Control has changed its procedures. All vessels in your squadron will be passed into landing orbit together, then the array will be reactivated. Please confirm that you understand, over."

Her sidebar list of Alliance ships as listed in the *Zieten*'s dispatches was in white print. Those names were quickly turning black on a white background. Another blip appeared on the main display; the last name on the sidebar changed. All present, and no extra vessels. The number—whether less or greater—of vessels didn't matter, but it pleased Adele to have everything occur according to plan.

"*R12, this is* Friedrich *Signals,*" said the voice which had made contact by laser communicator when the battleship reentered sidereal space a few minutes before. *"Hold one, please, I'm passing this up to Squadron Operations, over."*

The mine tender's bridge was cramped. Vesey was controlling the vessel from the signals console, a flat-plate display which left the command console and the vessel's only holographic display to Adele. Tovera sat at the third bridge station, her face placid and her eyes empty as usual.

Adele had never been sure what her servant thought about. A spider's brain had no room for anything but a hunger to kill; were Tovera's thought processes that simple?

Tovera looked up and smiled. Adele stiffened in shock, instinctively afraid that Tovera had read her mind. Though—

Adele returned the smile wryly. It didn't really matter what Tovera knew or thought. She was a loyal dog; or perhaps better, a loyal spider.

The *R12* had been holding the usual 1g acceleration. They staggered suddenly and began what would have been a tumble if Vesey hadn't caught them immediately.

Adele frowned, wondering if they wouldn't have been better to give Vesey the command console and herself control the minefield from the signals station. The latter required complex work to be sure, but Adele was sure that she could handle it with the display of her little personal unit if she needed to.

On the other hand, Vesey seemed perfectly comfortable at the two-dimensional screen. Her fingers moved with calm certainty across the virtual controls. She didn't, perhaps, make adjustments like a musician as Adele had often watched Daniel do, but she moved like a chess player confident in her game.

Adele nodded approvingly, though the brief tick of her head would probably have gone unremarked even if the lieutenant hadn't been absorbed with her duties. The tone of the High Drive motors grew harsher, a feeling rather than an audible sound; the ship steadied.

"*PDA Control, this is Squadron Three,*" said a gravelly, forceful, male voice. The squadron ops officer would ordinarily be a full captain, but in the present case he might be a senior commander instead. "*What's this about not dicking us around for half a day in orbit as usual? Has Commander Stemphill come to her senses, over?*"

Adele's smile was cold as a knife edge. "Squadron Three," she said, "I can't speak regarding Commander Stemphill. The present Defense Systems Officer, Commander Wohner, is responsible for the current SOP, over."

The operations officer might be perfectly willing to accept his good luck and bring the whole squadron into the minefield without concern or further comment. On the other hand, he—or someone younger and smarter on the staff, or even Captain Varnell personally—might think twice about it. News that Commander Stemphill, whose punctilio was apparently well known in the squadron, had been replaced should allay any suspicions.

As it did. "*Roger, PDA Control,*" said the voice. "*I'll be transmitting our course data in a couple minutes. But just to be sure, shut the array off right now. We've got civilians in this convoy, and the* Arcona *had a partial failure in her astrogation computer so she's running at half speed. Unless we want to wait for the cows to come home, we'll have to accept a greater margin of error than you'd usually get from a timber freighter, over."*

"Roger, Squadron Three," said Adele. "I am disarming the planetary defense array. No ships will be allowed to land until the entire squadron is present, however."

She paused. The array was already on manual control, but there was no way for the Alliance ships to learn that.

"The array is disarmed," she said. *"R12* out."

"Squadron out," said the voice.

Adele took a deep breath. Vesey, who'd been watching her, said, "We're on plan, sir?"

"Yes," said Adele. Vesey ranked her by virtue of a commission as well as command of the mine tender, but it was doubtful whether even Daniel's direct order would have caused her to act as though that were true. "We'll be getting their planned extraction point shortly."

"I'm sorry about the trouble with the motors," Vesey said apologetically. "We refitted the High Drive in a hurry, and I can't hold either of the bow motors steady. I'd been operating with the starboard unit angled to balance the stern pair, but I've had to shut it down too. We can maintain attitude and acceleration with two motors if we have to."

She smiled with a pride she wouldn't have shown in the long months following the death of her fiancé, Midshipman Dorst. *"Since* we have to, I should say," she added.

"It only has to last for another ten minutes," Adele said. The humor of the situation struck her and she added, "Or even less than that if one of the Alliance ships calls what it thinks is our bluff."

Tovera giggled. A moment later Vesey smiled also and said, "Just so, mistress. But I'll plan on nursing the motors for the entire ten minutes."

They'd been lucky to get the *R12* into orbit at all. Because of the necessary destruction of *R11* and the suicidal foolishness of *R16*'s captain, *R12* was the only ship of her class on Bolton; she'd been undergoing a full refit when the *Milton* arrived. Though any ship could have been modified to control the minefield, the incoming squadron would expect a dedicated mine tender.

Daniel therefore made the tender's repair his first priority, but that had meant pulling the High Drive motors from a freighter captured in harbor. The motors themselves were fine according to David Reuben, the engineer's mate running the Power Room, but cavitation in the feed lines was causing the front pair to stutter.

The problem probably couldn't be repaired in orbit. According to internal exchanges which Adele monitored as a matter of course, Reuben and his crew were nonetheless trying to do so while the motors were shut down. Daniel had given the mine tender a crack crew for this mission, starting with Vesey as captain.

An INCOMING DATA icon flashed on Adele's screen. As she twitched a wand to open it, the ships of the Alliance squadron began to vanish from the display. They were withdrawing into the Matrix. They would hop close enough to Bolton that they could maneuver the last of the way to orbit in sidereal space.

Adele opened the Alliance course data and plotted it on a large-scale image of Bolton and the space well beyond. Varnell was bringing his ships in as though the defense array didn't exist.

That wasn't unreasonable; the tender controlling the array had said it was shut down, after all. She had the suspicion that Daniel would've been a little more careful, however. He knew—and Adele certainly knew—that hardware, software, and bored junior officers all could make mistakes. Daniel wouldn't want to be remembered as the captain who led twenty-one ships to destruction in a friendly minefield.

As a reflex, Adele also copied the data to Vesey: that was what she would have done if Daniel were commanding. Vesey opened the file and set it to plot, then gave Adele a look of suppressed concern.

"Mistress?" she said. "What would you like me to do with this?"

"What?" said Adele, surprised into allowing herself to sound irritated. "Oh—it's just informational, Vesey. There's nothing either of us—any of us—can do with it."

She cleared her throat, embarrassed because she *had* been a little sharp. "If they can extract where they're supposed to, then we'll be able to relax in less than the ten minutes I'd estimated. But in a good way."

"Yes, mistress," said Vesey, obviously relieved not to have made a mistake. "Still on plan."

Adele turned toward the display again. She kept her face blank, but she was frowning internally as she thought about Vesey.

An officer who thought she was incapable of making a mistake was a boneheaded fool—and the RCN had its share of the type. But officers had to *act* as though they were incapable of error; otherwise they frightened everyone around them. If Vesey couldn't learn that sort of theater, she wouldn't be fit for command of a warship.

Ships began to extract above Bolton. Most of them were well within the minefield. *It's working. . . .*

Adele manually keyed the microwave link to Daniel's console rather than use a verbal cue. She didn't want to leave anything to the whim of an unfamiliar—and third-quality—computer.

"Bolton Command, this is *R12*," she said. "I estimate that Squadron Varnell will request landing instructions in three minutes, thirty seconds. All vessels noted in the dispatches are present. Over."

She was being extremely formal. Though intercepting the coded signal was within the capacity of any warship's sensor suite, isolating it from the clutter would be beyond most, maybe all, of the signals personnel in the Alliance squadron. Nonetheless this wasn't a time to cut corners.

The form of a message could tell a great deal to someone knowledgeable and careful, even if the contents couldn't be deciphered in the available time. Officer Adele Mundy was knowledgeable, careful—and competent. She wasn't willing to assume that her opponents weren't all those things as well.

"*Roger*, R12," replied Daniel. "*I'm transmitting instructions on the order in which the squadron is to land. Command out.*"

The Alliance ships continued to extract close to the planet, tripping the sidebar that now recorded vessels which had reached the immediate neighborhood of Bolton. None of them had too badly handled the final short jump. Naval officers tended to sneer at the astrogation ability of civilian skippers, but these freighters were under contract to the Fleet; their officers were obviously competent, and the ships themselves were well found and reasonably up to date for equipment.

Even the *Arcona*, the cruiser with computer problems, extracted within three thousand miles of the *Direktor Friedrich*. That may have been luck, of course, but it was good luck for Adele. A powerful cruiser had to be within the trap before it was sprung, but too long a delay for landing instructions would have provoked a confrontation.

Though in theory planetary control officials had complete authority over landing operations, Captain Varnell had the same rank as Commodore Harmston and carried the far greater prestige of a space appointment over a ground-based one. The length of time Varnell would twiddle his thumbs on Harmston's say-so was indefinite but not great.

Adele let out her breath with a gush of satisfaction. She hadn't realized that she'd been holding it. "Bolton Command," she said, "this is *R12*. Squadron Varnell is in position. I'm ready to relay your directions to Captain Varnell, over."

"Officer Mundy," said Daniel, *"this is Bolton Command. There'll be a lag and the possibility of interference if you relay my transmissions. Handle the matter yourself in my name, copying me as you go. Six out."*

Adele weighed the plan. She supposed this way was as satisfactory as the other, though she certainly wouldn't have suggested it herself.

"All right, Daniel," she said. She smiled. That wasn't the correct form, but the time for trickery was over. "Break. Squadron Three, this is *R12*. Emergency, emergency. Order all ships to hold their current heading and acceleration. There's a problem with the planetary defense array. Confirm immediately, over."

"PDA Control, this is Friedrich *Signals,"* said the first voice. *"Repeat your most recent transmission, over."*

"Squadron Varnell, this is an emergency," Adele said. She knew she didn't *sound* as though it were an emergency; she never did. When things were at their worst, she spoke even more slowly and distinctly than usual; and things were potentially very bad now. "Captain Daniel Leary of the RCN has captured this minefield."

She didn't know whether Daniel's name would mean anything to the Alliance officers listening to her. Even if it didn't, the very specificity of her statement was its own confirmation.

"You are in great danger," Adele said. Perhaps she could shout and pretend to be angry? But she just wasn't an actor. "The mines around you are in suspense for only as long as they receive a signal modulated by an encryption program on the *R12*. If the *R12*'s transmitter should fail, the minefield would destroy your entire squadron."

She took a deep breath, then concluded, "Hold your course and acceleration, over."

Signals passed in growing alarm among the ships of the squadron, but for nearly a minute nobody on the flagship replied to Adele's transmission. When someone finally did come on, it was a third male voice saying, *"R12, this is Varnell. Who's your captain, over?"*

"Captain Varnell, I'm Officer Mundy of the RCN," Adele said. "Mundy of Chatsworth. Please observe the *Oswestry* in your squadron, over."

"Mundy or whatever your name is," said Captain Varnell, *"I can only assume you've gone mad. Hand*

your command over to the next senior officer before I'm compelled to end this farce myself."

Adele expanded her minefield control screen. It was entirely text and numbers, the ship names and codes in place on a white background. She highlighted the *Oswestry*, then keyed the DELETE icon.

"We're going to begin landing in St. James Harbor," Varnell said, *"where I'll sort this out with Commodore—"*

CONFIRM COMMAND the screen said. Adele touched DELETE again. *Oswestry* OSW791 disappeared; the seven names and codes farther down the alphabetical list hopped up one place each.

"—Harmston, and we'll—bloody hell, they what? What?"

The transmission broke off. Presumably the last of it had been Varnell's response to the underling babbling about what had just happened 14,000 miles from the flagship.

Adele called up the imagery. She knew what she would see; she'd seen it before, after all. But she felt that she should always look at the consequences of her actions, lest she begin to find it easy to do the sort of things which her various duties required.

Besides, there was time. Varnell was going to have to discuss what had just happened before he accepted her offer. Or called her "bluff," of course. If he did that by blasting the *R12* the way the *Milton* had destroyed the tender in orbit when they arrived, then Adele wouldn't be around to watch the Alliance squadron vanish a few heartbeats later.

The *Oswestry* was a largish freighter whose chunky design increased the internal volume on a given tonnage. It had been a Cinnabar vessel initially, but an Alliance privateer had captured it some years before the recent interval of peace. Not that it mattered.

The mines of a planetary defense array were thermonuclear weapons with sensor and communications suites. Its magnetic lens squeezed the discharge into a line, much the way a warship's plasma cannon did. The differences were that the mine destroyed itself completely in the first usage... and that the mine's jet of ions was orders of magnitude greater than that from a cannon.

In normal time the propagation wave was so fast that the *Oswestry* simply disappeared, replaced by a swelling gas ball. Slowed down by a thousand, the freighter bulged noticeably. Seams ruptured to gush fire, but only for an instant even at the greatly magnified interval. The fusion bottle had burst on the spike of ions, turning everything into an iridescent bubble.

It was more beautiful than any pearl, if you viewed the thing itself as separate from the cause.

"Mistress," said Vesey. "Mistress. That was the ship with the hostages!"

"Yes," said Adele. She turned to meet Vesey's eyes. "I chose it for the earnest of intent because according to the manifest, there were eighty Fifth Bureau personnel aboard. Mostly low-level, of course."

"*Mistress*," Vesey said. "I... you *can't*..."

Adele shrugged. "Varnell has to understand that we, that *I*, can and will destroy his squadron unless he surrenders unconditionally," she said. "If I hadn't proved that in a fashion he couldn't doubt, he or someone in the squadron would've tried to get out of the situation by destroying us. Then they would all have died."

She smiled coldly. "And us as well. But we might not have known that, depending on what they hit this tender with."

Vesey simply stared. Adele shut down the insert in which the *Oswestry* exploded in a continuously looping image; she studied the PPI again. It would be at least five minutes before the ships which were headed away from Bolton reached the fringes of the minefield. One had been going in that direction when she sprang the trap, but the other two had changed course in defiance of her orders. She readied the field.

"What the mistress isn't telling you, girl," said Tovera, "is that before the *Oswestry* surrendered, they'd have put the hostages out an airlock. That's Fifth Bureau SOP, you see—you never permit hostages to be taken alive. When word gets around that trying to rescue hostages means that they're all killed, there aren't so many rescue attempts. Besides—"

Adele looked at Tovera, who was grinning.

"—it's fun. Speaking as a former Fifth Bureau agent."

"I didn't know that," said Vesey. She swallowed. "Mistress? Lady Mundy? Why didn't you say that instead of . . . ?"

"I gave you my reasoning, Vesey," Adele said sharply.

"Perhaps she thinks that you're too soft for this—" Tovera said.

"Tovera, that's enough," said Adele.

"No, mistress, it's not," said Tovera. The pupils of her eyes were trained on the lieutenant like pistol muzzles. "Too soft for this job, because sometimes it means killing. If you can't kill, you can't be a good RCN officer. You can't even—"

"Tovera!"

"—be a piss-poor RCN officer. What do you really want to be, little girlie?"

"*R12, this is Captain Kendall Varnell,*" said the voice from the Alliance flagship. "*You said you were Mundy of Chatsworth. That is, Lady Adele Mundy, over?*"

Adele frowned. "That's correct," she said. "At present, I'm Signals Officer Adele Mundy, acting for Captain Daniel Leary. Do you unconditionally surrender to the RCN, Captain Varnell, over?"

"*I know who you are,*" said Varnell. "*I don't know how you did this unless you really are in league with the devil, but I won't throw away the lives of my crews.*"

There was a pause, followed by what seemed to be a deep intake of breath. Then Varnell said, "*I tender the surrender of the ships under my command, on the condition that the crews will be treated as honorable prisoners according to the law of nations, to be exchanged if agreed by the parties and to be released upon termination of the present hostilities, over.*"

"Your surrender is accepted on the terms stated," Adele said formally. "I'm transmitting *now—*"

Her wands twitched, forwarding Daniel's landing instructions to the Alliance commander. The freighters would go down first, one at a time; then the destroyers, followed by the cruisers. The *Direktor Friedrich* would remain within the minefield's kill zone until the remainder of the squadron had been boarded and disarmed by Daniel's forces in St. James Harbor.

"—directions on how you are to proceed. If I may add my personal caveat to the general orders? If the *Eckernferde*, *Z40*, and *Insidioso* don't begin braking into landing orbits around Bolton within the next ninety seconds, their crews will shortly have a chance to exchange greetings with the crew of the *Oswestry. R12* out."

"*Received and understood*, R12," said Varnell. "*Squadron out.*"

The cruiser and two destroyers which were headed outbound immediately reversed their thrust. Adele watched to make sure that they weren't simply feigning obedience. When they continued to brake hard, she gave a sigh of relief and rubbed her forehead hard with her fingertips.

After a moment, she cued the two-way link again. "Daniel," she said, "they're coming down. It seems to have gone all right."

"*Of course it did, Adele*," said Daniel. His voice sounded thick, but that might have been the form of transmission. "*I had my best officer in charge of the operation. Bolton out.*"

Adele stared at the display, exhausted and empty. A captured freighter, the *Conestoga*, would lift shortly under Midshipman Cory to take over control of the minefield. The *R12* could land then, having completed its mission.

A ball of plasma, rippling with all the colors of the rainbow. Perfectly beautiful, in an inhuman way....

"Mistress," said Lieutenant Vesey. "I'm an RCN officer. I won't disappoint you."

Adele looked at her. *Disappoint me by acting human?* she thought.

But aloud she said, "Very good, Vesey. Captain Leary will be as pleased to hear that as I am."

CHAPTER 22

St. James Harbor, Bolton

"Fellow spacers!" Daniel said, standing arms akimbo on the reviewing stand. He paused to let his voice roll back to him from the additional speakers Woetjans and Cazelet had rigged at the rear of the drill field. "I'm Captain Daniel Leary of the RCN. For those of you with guts and a real desire to get rich, I'm the best thing that's ever happened!"

The crowd murmured, spacers talking to one another or muttering to themselves. Many were probably afraid.

Daniel grinned. They were *all* probably afraid. Spacers liked to know what they were getting into, and this lot didn't have a clue. It wasn't every day that a twenty-ship squadron was captured and the crews were mustered under enemy guns.

"Do you see the warrant officer down there at the front?" he continued, pointing toward the panel truck from which the PA system was being controlled. Cazelet was inside and Hogg was driving, not because he was particularly good at it, but because he liked

388

to drive and Daniel didn't see any reason not to let him. "That's my bosun, Chief Woetjans."

Woetjans stood on top of the truck in a rack knocked together from tubing. That would let her climb to any of the pole-mounted speakers which malfunctioned during the speech. She wore her liberty suit for the event. The fluttering ribbons made a colorful display when she waved.

"When we get back to Cinnabar, she'll be able to buy a mansion and staff it with a hundred of the prettiest boys in the Republic!" Daniel said. "She's bosun on a cruiser, and she'll have a bosun's share of the prize money of a captured battleship! Think of it, spacers, a share of a battleship! Do you know how much liquor that'll buy on the Strip?"

There were various ways to get a spacer's attention. Offering money was a good one, but money was an abstract to many of the men and a number of the women who crewed starships. For that segment of his audience, Daniel had gone straight to the heart of the matter: sex and booze.

Pointing out that Woetjans—with a body like a tree trunk and the face of a camel—could have her choice of bedmates underscored the sex option perfectly. She waved again, this time with both hands.

There were, of course, spacers who wanted nothing more than to retire to a farm or small shop, or perhaps to own a ship instead of working for wages. They tended to be those with warrants or at least ratings, solid folk whom you wanted in your crew.

The speech worked for them as well. They saw money as an object in itself.

"Now you ask...," Daniel boomed through the PA

system. "'Can Captain Leary promise *me* that kind of prize money too?' And the answer is, I can't!"

The ideal place for this assembly would have been the great domed hall at the south end of the military reservation. *Would* have been, until Adele highlighted it during the *Milton's* attack and Sun converted it into startlingly impressive rubble.

Daniel wasn't about to complain about that decision, because he wouldn't have been addressing anybody if the Alliance garrison hadn't been stunned into almost immediate surrender. Blasting the largest structure on the planet to instant ruin had been an important part of that process.

"But I didn't promise it to Woetjans, either, spacers," Daniel said, "and *look* at what she's got! Look at what every single spacer on the *Millie's* got, right down to the wipers and landsmen. They're rich because they sailed with Captain Daniel Leary; and I'm giving you the chance to do the same!"

There was a scattering of cheers from the crowd, then a louder and more enthusiastic one. He'd sprinkled eighty crewmen from the *Milton*, former Sissies who'd been with him for years, across the crowd. They weren't so much a claque as nuclei of good feeling toward the RCN and the captain giving a recruiting speech on the reviewing stand.

The remainder of the thousands on the drill field came from the crews of Squadron Varnell. There weren't many fanatics who would be willing to sabotage a starship while they were aboard—but there were some. Thanks to Adele's ability to open the ships' files, probably faster than the Alliance clerks themselves could have done, that risk had been minimized. All

Equals—the Alliance equivalent of adults with full Cinnabar citizenship—had been sent directly to the Travanda Quarry, as had personnel from any Alliance world who ranked above warrant officer's mate.

What remained was the bulk of the common spacers. They wouldn't do alone—they wouldn't do *well*—as a warship's crew, but they were the perfect addition to the senior spacers and Cinnabar citizens who'd been sent here from New Harmony.

"Now, I know that some of you served under Admiral Ozawa recently," Daniel said. "And here you are, having taken Guarantor Porra's pay. You're wondering if that's going to be a problem."

He stared across the assembly with a stern expression. He already knew the names of spacers who'd switched sides on New Harmony. He could have separated them with an hour's time and a company of the Brotherhood to provide muscle. If the people below hadn't been worried before, they certainly were now.

"No, of course not, fellow spacers!" Daniel said. "What choice did you have? I'd have done the same thing if I'd been in your place!"

He wouldn't have, of course.

"But I *will* give you a choice," he continued. "If you return to the RCN, I'll credit you with the wages you were owed at the time your ships were lost on New Harmony. I'm Captain Daniel Leary, and I swear it!"

The first cheers were timid, but they built to real enthusiasm. Daniel waited for them to die back.

"Now, I'm not threatening you," he said. "Nobody *has* to join the luckiest captain in the RCN and have a chance to get filthy rich. You can stay here on Bolton, eat as well as you will in space and just sit on your butts without a bit of work or danger either one!"

He was warming to his subject. It wasn't hard to be enthusiastic, because he really was telling the truth. Sure, he was polishing it up till it was fit for an admiral's inspection, but it was the truth nonetheless.

"But for those of you who really are spacers, the ones that a fighting captain *wants* serving with him...," Daniel said. He'd been speaking loudly enough that there was distortion from the speakers at the distant rear of the field. He lowered his voice a trifle; the howl was disquieting at an animal level, and he wanted to build enthusiasm instead of subliminal fear. "Then look at the tables down in front of me."

Midshipmen Else, Barrett, and Fink; Gunner Sun; and Dasi and Barnes, the bosun's mates, each stood by a folding table with a pile of florin coins, a personnel roster, and a technician holding a retinal scanner. Behind every enlistment table was another where a husky rigger guarded a demijohn of rum. A four-ounce stainless steel tumbler was chained to the handle of each liquor jar.

"This is your chance, spacers," Daniel said. "*Here's* your opportunity to walk into a bar on your next liberty, richer than anybody else in it—but you not having to buy a drink yourself, because *you* sailed with Captain Leary and everybody wants to hear your stories. If you'd rather be a rich hero instead of a space bum waiting the war out in a quarry on bloody Bolton—take the Republic's florin and have a drink on me. Join the RCN!"

Cheers followed. More important, spacers surged toward the tables to enlist. The folk who were willing to be in the front of the assembly were the ones who were least afraid of what was going to happen. Daniel had a row of Millies in liberty suits ready to calm congestion, but the crowd's self-selection left them with nothing to do.

Besides, spacers were used to moving in tight places. A pileup in a hatch or an airlock during a crisis meant that people and maybe the ship would die.

Colonel Stockheim had offered troops to keep order. Daniel was afraid that his response, though technically polite, had conveyed the disgust he felt at the notion of a captain who needed ground troops to control spacers.

Major Mull and his Marines were drawn up in two ranks in front of the dais, wearing dress uniforms. They had a right to be present, but Daniel had made it clear that they were a guard of honor, no more.

Behind the dais waited the cadre of the fourteen new vessels of the RCN, ready to gather in the recruits which would fill out the ships' companies. Daniel had parcelled out the former prisoners in the Travanda Quarry, keeping crewmen of the same vessels together where he could and putting them under familiar officers.

Lieutenant Commander Robinson came up the steps at the back of the stand. Daniel smiled over his shoulder, but he continued to look out over the assembly.

"A brilliant speech, sir," Robinson said. "I wouldn't be surprised if you got them all."

"Thank goodness for Officer Mundy," Daniel said, nodding toward the crowd. It was moving now like a single entity, a vast amoeba. "She eliminated everybody who might have been a problem, so this is no different from a recruiting expedition back on Cinnabar. Records are wonderful things if you've got somebody who can access and interpret them."

Robinson shook his head in smiling amazement. "We'll have the first RCN ships with full crews in my lifetime. Maybe in all time!"

"Well, they were ready to join us," Daniel said. "What spacer wants to sit in a prison camp without anything to drink but water, hey?"

"I wouldn't have known how to speak to them, not that way," the First Lieutenant said, shaking his head again. "I will now, though."

He looked at Daniel and added, "We're not as well set for commanding officers, though, I'm afraid."

Daniel laughed. "I wouldn't say that, Robinson. This is scarcely the first time in the history of the RCN that a ship's executive officer has succeeded to the command. Not infrequently the change of command has occurred during a battle, in fact."

"Yes sir," said Robinson. "But I don't know that it's happened before that no captain in a squadron has ever commanded so large a ship before. Except for you, of course, since you're staying with the *Milton* instead of taking the battleship."

There was a question on Robinson's face if not in his words or even tone. Daniel shrugged and said, "I've tried to keep ships' companies together, or in the case of the *Friedrich* I've seen to it that she's crewed by the combined crews of the *Heidegger* and *Hobbes* who're used to serving on a battleship. Which I'm not, unless you count the *Swiftsure* back in training."

He looked at the *Direktor Friedrich*—it wasn't his

place to rename his captures; that would be done by the proper committee on Cinnabar—then back to the *Milton*. "And besides," he said, "the *Millie*—and the Millies—and I have gotten to know each other since we lifted from Bergen and Associates. It's more efficient all round to keep our company together and put Commander Rebecca Pimental back aboard another battleship."

"I've got more respect for what they do at Navy House since I spent yesterday and most of this morning roughing out the crew lists for you, sir," Robinson said. "Respect, but I assure you not liking. It's like a jigsaw puzzle. Well, like fourteen jigsaw puzzles, and the pieces all jumbled together."

He cleared his throat. "Ah, Captain Leary?" he said, lowering his voice. "I, ah . . . I'm very pleased that you gave me command of the *Insidioso*. I, ah, I'm aware that there are officers senior to me who aren't in command slots."

"If anybody asks, you can tell them that you were a midshipman on the *Dardo*, which was built on Pantellaria like the *Insidioso*," said Daniel. "But—"

"Sir?" Robinson blurted. "You knew that?"

Daniel grinned. "I told you that records are wonderful," he said. "At least for those of us who have Officer Mundy to go over them for us. But as I started to say, that's a polite lie anyway. The truth is, I thought you were the man for the job, so I put you in it. I didn't need to go over any records to decide that."

Robinson's face was slender and aristocratic. He blushed, an event as out of place as Dress Whites on a pig.

"Sir . . . ," he said. "Sir. I'll . . . thank you, sir."

Daniel returned his attention to the thinning crowd. "We might get them all, just as you say," he said. "There's a point when deciding to hold out takes more courage than being the first to move. Thanks to Officer Mundy, there was nobody down there who'd try to convince the others that they *shouldn't* join the RCN."

"Officer Mundy is indeed an asset, sir," Robinson said. "I'd heard stories, of course, but I didn't fully credit them until I had the privilege of serving with her."

He looked around, frowned, and then said, "I suppose there's no reason she should be here for this. Just a waste of her time."

Daniel smiled. "Well, perhaps," he said. "Officer Mundy says she doesn't need to be told when she does a good job—that it should be enough that *she* knows. I'd just as soon that she be present when something works out perfectly because of her actions."

Especially something that doesn't involve sprawled corpses who she's shot, Daniel thought, suddenly saddened. He doubted that any of the crew, even Sissies who'd been with Adele throughout her service in the RCN, knew what it cost her to do the things she regularly did for the Republic and for her shipmates.

Forcing the smile back, he said aloud, "In fact she told me she had business to discuss with Senator Forbes. And though you wouldn't think of asking, Robinson, I'll tell you flatly that I don't have any idea of what she was planning to discuss. The person who informed me was *Lady* Mundy, who isn't under my command."

Robinson looked startled, then cautiously blankfaced. "I see, sir," he said.

"I don't," said Daniel. "But as you noted, Adele is an asset. I'm sure we'll learn what she's doing when there's some reason for us to know."

"Daniel swears by the view out here while the ship is in the Matrix," Adele said as Senator Forbes looked about them. She gestured upward. "Actually, he prefers the view from the top of a mast."

"But you don't, Mundy?" said the senator. From here on the spine of the *Milton* they could look down on most things in the harbor and the city beyond, but the battleship half a mile away swelled like a steel cliff. Distance blurred the rust and scars on its hull, leaving jeweled shimmerings and soft shadows.

"Daniel is religious," Adele said. "I'm not. And I find that I process information better at second hand than I do directly."

Somewhere in the western distance was the drill field where Daniel was addressing the captured crews. It was probably out of sight beyond the *Friedrich*. Adele could tell for certain by viewing satellite imagery through her data unit, but—her right index and middle fingers caressed the thigh pocket—that would be inappropriate. Quite a lot of what she liked to do was inappropriate when she was being forced to interact with other human beings.

"Religious?" said Forbes. She was wearing a dark blue suit. It seemed to be as comfortable as business dress ever was, but she was fiddling with the cuffs and the collar, obviously ill at ease.

"Well, not formally, though he'll wear his Whites to the temple if he's on Cinnabar during a High Feast," Adele said. She didn't pay much attention to her own clothing; so long as it had pockets for her data unit and pistol, fit and color didn't matter to her. "But he believes in something greater than himself. He certainly wouldn't *say* that the Matrix is the face of God, but I think that somewhere in his heart he feels that it is."

A haze still lay over portions of St. James City. There had been considerable looting by locals, who felt the arrival of Cinnabar forces gave them license to settle scores and improve their fortunes. Oftentimes fires had resulted. Things were quiet now, but it had been almost ten hours after the battle that the Fonthill Militia, armed from arsenals here on Bolton, fanned out across the city to keep order.

"What do you believe in, Mundy?" Forbes said, facing her directly. The senator was even shorter than Adele herself, though her fiery energy gave her presence. "The Republic?"

Adele sniffed. "The same way I believe in this ship," she said, tapping the hull with her toe. "It exists and the Republic exists, so of course I believe in them. If you mean in the sense of what do I have faith in—I believe that I'll die, mistress. And beyond that, I believe that the universe will end."

Also I believe in a few human beings, she thought. *One, at least.* But that wasn't any of Forbes's business.

Forbes looked away, then turned back to Adele. "You didn't ask me to join you here to discuss philosophy," she said. She arched an eyebrow and went on, "You know, when you asked me—summoned me, might be a better phrase—to join you on the hull, I wondered if I ought to bring my bodyguards."

"Good heavens, woman!" Adele said. "I didn't bring

you out here to kill you. I want to discuss politics. And anyway, what possible difference did you imagine that bodyguards would make?"

The thought of the two hulking servants trying to prevent her from shooting their mistress was funny enough to bring a smile to Adele's lips. Forbes looked even more disconcerted, but the smile seemed to relax her somewhat.

"Politics are a subject on which I have some expertise," the senator said. "Though after my debacle in the speakership election, you might wish to quarrel with that claim."

Adele's smile widened slightly, though if anything it became colder as well. She said, "I think you have some ways to go before your political misjudgments reach the level that my father's did. But I had nothing as complex as the Cinnabar Senate in mind. Here in the Montserrat Stars, you're the representative of the Republic's government."

Forbes pursed her lips, then said, "No one is likely to argue with the assertion," she said. "My appointment as plenipotentiary was to the Veil and Adjacent Regions...which this cluster can be claimed to be."

Her smile was suddenly as hard as Adele's own. "The governor on Cacique is an Administrator Grade Three named Richard Flanagan," she said. "He wouldn't argue the point even if he were able to get a message out through the Alliance blockade. But why does that matter to you?"

The *Milton* shuddered; a blanket of steam rose from around the stern. Forbes started for the forward airlock. Adele frowned and said, "That's all right, Senator. Chief Engineer Pasternak polished the throats of four stern thrusters. Apparently he's testing them now, but it won't be more than an irritation."

"Just as you say," Forbes said doubtfully, but she came back to Adele as directed. She gave their immediate surroundings a sour look and added, "Though I still don't see why we're here in the first place."

Adele looked around also. The antennas and yards were telescoped to minimum length, then folded tightly to the hull so that the cruiser could lift off on the shortest possible notice. The rig was therefore as neat as a starship could be, without the webbing of cables and sails shaken out in differing states and attitudes.

It was far more orderly than a garden or a park, as a matter of fact; but orderliness wasn't to everyone's taste. Well, it wasn't Adele's present concern either.

"We're here for privacy," she said crisply. "Daniel hasn't informed me of his plans, but I'm going to speculate on them and I don't want anyone else to overhear me."

"I see," said Forbes in a guarded tone. "I'm surprised to hear that Leary hasn't confided in you, however, Lady Mundy. As you're obviously friends."

"Yes," said Adele, "we are. But Daniel rarely consults anyone about military subjects. He'll ask me for information, and he may ask me for help in executing his plans. He probably will, in fact. But that hasn't happened as yet, and I'm therefore speculating."

Forbes was actually frowning. "*Would* he tell you?" she asked.

The steam from Pasternak's brief touch on the thrusters—touches, really, because he'd cycled through all four individually—had almost dissipated. Adele could still feel the tingle of an occasional ozone molecule at the back of her nose when she breathed, but that was as normal a part of shipboard life as the smell of lubricant.

"Yes," Adele said, "he would. But because I *haven't* been told anything, I'm free to speak to you without violating a confidence."

She coughed. "I want you, in the name of the Republic, to appoint Daniel—to appoint Captain Leary—to the brevet, that is temporary, rank of Rear Admiral. The civil representative of the Republic has the authority to do that in an emergency. I've checked the regulations."

Ádele smiled wryly. "I'm not, thank my good fortune, a lawyer," she said. "But information is information, even when it's clothed in the most remarkably turgid and repetitive language."

Forbes looked relieved, to Adele's great surprise. "I see," she said with a knowing smile. "You want to raise your friend's rate of pay for the time we're here in the Montserrat Stars. And perhaps you're hoping that Admiral Leary will see fit to pass some of the temporary largesse to a valued friend."

Adele chuckled, though she was glad that she'd guessed where the senator would go with the information. Otherwise she was likely to have said things that the senator would find as difficult to overlook as Mundy of Chatsworth did an accusation of corruption at a piddling level.

"During the years I've served under Captain Leary, Senator . . . ," she said, her tone just short of a sneer. "I've had occasion to learn a certain amount about prize money. The value of the squadron which the *Milton* just captured makes the incremental value of an admiral's pay over a captain's insignificant to Daniel, to me, and even to the ordinary spacers."

Adele coughed delicately into her hand, then looked toward Forbes with her head still slightly bent. She said, "But I hope you won't repeat that silly suggestion to anyone, even as a joke. My family, as you may know, has a reputation for being tender about its honor."

"I understand," Forbes said; her stiff expression suggested that she really did understand how serious the consequences of her verbal misstep could have been. "Lady Mundy, why do you think Captain Leary should receive a temporary promotion?"

"So that his rank is clearly superior to that of other RCN officers whom we meet during operations here in Montserrat," Adele said. "I believe that Captain Leary is the best officer to command our forces, but he's very junior."

"I agree that he's the best man," Forbes said carefully. "I, ah, would accept your judgment on the matter even if I hadn't had personal experience of his skill. And I'll certainly brevet him or whatever the term is if you'll provide me with the proper form to use. But ... ?"

Adele nodded curtly, giving permission to proceed. The senator was determined not to put her foot wrong again. Adele's father Lucius was *not* quarrelsome, but he'd made sure that his whole family, even his little daughter, were known to be dead shots. That prevented those who objected to his political views from deciding to silence him on the field of honor.

Senator Forbes probably remembered that. Even if she didn't, somebody in the *Milton*'s company would to have told her about Adele's personal reputation as a pistol shot.

"Because Admiral Ozawa's staff and all the commanding officers in his squadron were transported to Pleasaunce, milady," Forbes said, "Captain Leary is already the most senior officer on Bolton. There are officers who are older than he is and no doubt many who've been in the navy longer than he has, but none of them are of the rank of captain."

"Ah," said Adele, turning to watch a handful of leather-winged birds lift heavily from the surface of the water. Busy ports were good foraging for fish eaters who weren't finicky about pollution. Every time a ship landed or lifted off, it boiled a portion of anything which had swum in from the open sea.

Adele didn't care about natural history, of course; not unless Daniel asked her to look something up. The birds provided a useful delay while she chose her next words, however.

"Captain Leary is the highest-ranking officer on Bolton," she said, following the birds as they circled higher. She would much rather have been speaking into the images—any images—she summoned from her data unit, but that wasn't an option. "I don't expect him to remain on Bolton now that he commands such a powerful squadron. It appears that several cruisers escaped to Cacique, and their commanding officers will almost certainly be senior to Captain Leary in length of service as well as time at the rank of captain."

"I don't . . . ," Forbes began. Her face hardened. When she continued, her tone gave no sign that she was still concerned about how Adele would react: "Mundy, a few days ago we were in a captured Alliance base, hoping that reinforcements would arrive before Admiral Petersen ground through our defenses and retook the planet. Providentially, reinforcements *did* arrive, though in the form of ships which we've captured. They will enable us to hold the planet until additional forces come from Cinnabar, whereupon we may *possibly* be strong enough to challenge Petersen for control of the Montserrat Stars."

Adele met Forbes's eyes at last and gave her a lopsided smile. "Senator," she said, "that's a reasonable plan and one that most people, most RCN officers even, would choose to follow. I don't believe Daniel Leary is one of those people, however. Based on my past experience of him, I expect him to set off within a day or two to attempt to raise the siege of Cacique."

"That's absurd," said Forbes. She sounded amazed rather than angry. "Mundy, you don't simply walk aboard a ship and rush off in it to do battle. Why, the crews won't even know where to sleep yet!"

"Ideally I'm sure Daniel would prefer to spend a week working up the ships and their new complements," Adele said, quirking another smile. She was actually feeling cheerful now that she saw that the senator was taking this business well. Better, at least, than Adele had been afraid that she would take it. "It's a voyage of some days to Cacique, however, and I suspect that time will have to suffice. Needs must when devils drive, you know."

"There's no bloody need at all!" Forbes said. "The need is to hold Bolton, and that's what I'll order Leary to do if he really is as great a fool as you say!"

"You'll recall, Senator," Adele said, "that Navy House directed Captain Leary to give you all possible assistance in your mission to Karst. That's in the past, however, and Captain Leary is now in an independent command. I hope you won't embarrass yourself by giving him orders which are beyond your authority and which he will certainly refuse if they conflict with his professional judgment."

Forbes stared. She opened her mouth, closed it, and then broke into a sort of smile.

"*This* is what you brought me out here for, Mundy," she said. "You didn't care about making Leary an admiral or any other bloody thing. You were just warning me not to interfere so that I wouldn't lose my temper when Leary springs his plans on me!"

"I think it is important that you grant Daniel the brevet rank," Adele said judiciously. "Beyond that..."

She drew herself up straight. "Senator," she said, "part of my job is to gather information, but it's equally important to provide that information to those who need it. I've found that sometimes I do better to use an indirect approach. In both activities."

Forbes took a deep breath. "You know, Mundy," she said, "if Leary himself had said all that to me, I might think that he was bluffing. I don't think you ever bluff, do you?"

Adele considered the question and shrugged. "I don't believe I ever have," she said. "It seems much easier just to tell the truth. As you say, Daniel might come to a different determination."

She gestured across the harbor. "You needn't be concerned about your safety on Bolton, Senator," she said, "at least in the short term. The minefield will keep even a large Alliance force out at least for months. And even if Daniel—if Admiral Leary's attack doesn't succeed, I'm confident that it will be some while before Admiral Petersen is ready to mount a serious attempt to retake Bolton. Navy House will send you reinforcements if it's humanly possible to do so, and there'll be plenty of time for them to arrive."

"I'm glad to see that the prospects for the Republic retaining Bolton are good," Forbes said. "It doesn't affect me personally, however, since under the circumstances I'll be accompanying Leary. Admiral Leary, as you say."

Adele blinked. She'd considered a wide range of ways that the senator might have reacted, but this wasn't one of them.

"Senator Forbes," she said, "this will be a naval operation in which you have no part. Your business is here, not on a warship where you'll only get in the way."

"Officer Mundy," said Forbes, "I've recently been reminded that I should consider what was and what was not within my authority as a senator and envoy of the Republic of Cinnabar. That was good advice. I recommend you also follow it."

Adele looked at her, smiled faintly, and bowed. That was probably against regulations while she was in uniform—she was wearing utilities—but there was a great deal about this conversation which would raise eyebrows if it became public. Which it wasn't going to do.

"I take your point, Senator," she said. Neither an RCN officer nor a private citizen like Mundy of Chatsworth had any business telling Forbes how to carry out her duties. "May I suggest, however, that you're uniquely qualified to set up a civil administration here on Bolton, while the only thing you'll do by accompanying the squadron is to risk being killed for no reason."

Forbes sniffed. "You might think there's no reason, Mundy," she said, "but your father would have known better. I'm not going to have it said that I hid behind a minefield while the courageous Captain Leary fought the Republic's battles."

"That's...," Adele said. The word on the tip of her tongue was "silly" which was true enough but probably not a good choice. "...not right. No one would think you were a coward because you carried out your proper duties and let the RCN get on with its own."

"Your father would know better," Forbes repeated, this time with a smile that Adele couldn't read. "And besides, Mundy, *I* might think that I was a coward."

Adele frowned but didn't speak. It was as though the senator had begun babbling in some self-created ecstatic language.

Forbes laughed. "You really can't imagine what I'm talking about, can you?" she said. "You've never doubted your own courage."

"We may as well get inside," Adele said. "I have work to do on the bridge, and I suppose you have duties also."

She made a moue, then said, "As for your question, Senator, I think it would be better to say that the question has never arisen. I believe that courage of the sort you mean requires that one be afraid of dying. On a good day—on most days since I joined the RCN, I suppose—I no longer wish I were dead. But that's a long way short of saying that the prospect of death frightens me."

"As you say, Mundy," Forbes said, walking toward the open airlock, "we both have duties."

She paused and turned. "Speaking as your shipmate on the coming operation, however," she added, "I very much hope that you survive at least for the immediate future."

CHAPTER 23

En route *to Cacique*

"The astrogation computer," said Lieutenant Cory—promoted when Lieutenant Commander Robinson took command of the *Insidioso*, allowing Vesey and Blantyre each to rise a step aboard the *Milton*, "would take us from M631 to M637."

Cory held the brass communications rod between his helmet and Daniel's with his right hand, so he pointed his left arm. Daniel noted that he'd correctly identified first one, then the other bubble universe against the glowing haze of the Matrix. Both were greenish, but M637 was much closer to the yellow range than the musky blur of M631.

The cruiser's port and starboard antennas began to rotate, by 13 degrees according to the semaphore not far from where Daniel and Cory stood. Daniel checked the process reflexively, turning his body because the rigging suit limited what he could see with movements of his head alone. Nonetheless he kept his helmet firmly against the rod so that he continued to hear Cory.

"But if we go from here to G224," Cory said, when he realized that Daniel was still listening, "then we can go to G213 and get a better increase without overstressing the ship, even though the first step isn't quite as far."

"And after G213?" Daniel asked. Six months ago, Cory could no more have picked individual universes out the Matrix than he could have flown. Six months before that, Daniel wouldn't have trusted him to read the astrogation computer's solution correctly. The boy really was coming along.

"Well, G171," said Cory, pointing to a universe whose energy state relative to that of the *Milton* at present made it appear a dull saffron. "And then... oh. Oh, I didn't..."

"Right, there isn't a good step from G171," said Daniel. "You're right, there usually would be, but for some reason the T-series is well down into the blue from here at present. I've only rarely seen a drop-off from the norm this sharp; but it does happen, and you need to keep an eye out for the possibility."

He eyed the Matrix judiciously. "I'm afraid that the book solution is the best choice," he said. "Much though I'd like to save another fifteen minutes."

"Sorry, sir," mumbled Cory. "I should have... Sir, I'm sorry."

Daniel grimaced, feeling as though he'd just kicked a loyal dog. "Nothing to be sorry for, Cory!" he said in a determinedly cheerful fashion. "Your solution would've cost us... seven, I think, minutes over the book, but it had the possibility of gaining us more than double that. And you checked it—with me instead of running it through the computer, but you would have used the computer again if I hadn't been here."

Or at any rate, Cory would know to do that the next time. He still had a great deal to learn, but he was learning. That was all you could expect, in astrogation or in life more generally.

They'd extracted from the Matrix a light-day out from Cacique, then reinserted. Normally Daniel would have come much closer before extracting, but this time he wasn't taking a star sight to check his astrogation. Rather, Adele needed to gather data about present activity in the neighborhood of Cacique.

In about fifteen minutes by ship time, they would extract again at three light-hours from the planet. By comparing the previous slice of information with one from closer in, Adele could make a prediction. There was still a dangerous range of variation, but it would give them *a* view of the tactical situation.

The final extraction would be one light-hour out, and this time the entire squadron instead of just the *Milton* would return to the sidereal universe. Daniel would have an attack plan prepared to transmit to the ships under his command, but if necessary—if Adele changed her predictions radically on the basis of the third point in time—he'd rip it out and replace it with a new one as quickly as possible.

And might the Gods grant that that would be quickly enough. Daniel needed to arrive at Cacique before the light of the squadron's presence did. Admiral Petersen was expecting Squadron Varnell, but if his force sighted ships in the offing, they would prepare for battle. There was no harm done if the newcomers were from the Alliance as expected, but they'd be prepared for the possibility that the RCN would try to throw reinforcements through the blockade.

Daniel smiled, though Cory wouldn't be able to see the expression through the helmet of his hard suit. "Let's get back on the bridge, Lieutenant," he said. "We have about enough time to get our suits off before the *Millie* dips into and out of our universe. As soon as that happens, Officer Mundy will start giving us information, and we'll turn it into attack plans."

They moved toward the forward dorsal airlock, the magnetized soles of their boots brushing over the cruiser's steel hull. Daniel tilted his head to look up at the Matrix, seeing it this time as the magical tapestry that made his heart leap rather than a series of bubble universes through which he threaded a ship.

Cory stopped also. Daniel gestured the boy forward, then followed him into the lock chamber. It would be interesting to see how good a tactician Cory was, given that his astrogation had become distinctly respectable.

Three data streams coursed down Adele's display like a divided waterfall. Under normal circumstances she would've said that this was more than she—even she—could handle properly, but time was short and she herself was part of the flow.

"Fellow officers," said Daniel from the command console. "This is a squadron council of war. We don't have time to do this by real-time link in sidereal space."

He grinned broadly. "Let alone by bringing the other captains aboard and discussing matters over sherry in the Admiral's Stateroom," he said. "Quite apart from the fact that Senator Forbes wouldn't be best pleased to be ousted from the quarters which I've assigned her."

Adele's wands danced and wove. She supposed this

was like running full-tilt down a steep hill: so long as she didn't stumble, she'd be fine.

She *was* fine. She didn't recall ever before feeling more alive.

"Therefore I've assigned each of you a role to play," Daniel said. "You can think of this as amateur theatricals, if you like, but it's dead serious: you're to view the coming operation from the standpoint of the captain of the ship in our squadron which I've assigned you."

He gestured with his right hand and left. "Cory and Cazelet each command a flotilla of five destroyers for this exercise," he said. "You've all done this in the Academy. Most of you have, that is."

Rene Cazelet hadn't graduated from the Academy like the other officers. He'd been getting a double portion of tactical training from Vesey, however, since he was more than adequate in shiphandling and astrogation. By setting him battle exercises, Vesey also strengthened her own abilities in an area in which she had a decided lack of aptitude.

Daniel had warned Adele that he planned to speak to his officers directly instead of using the ship's intercom; if he hadn't said something, she'd have amplified the council as a matter of course. Using unaided voices was workable because the ship was in the Matrix; neither the thrusters nor the High Drive motors were hammering the hull. Adele wasn't sure that this really made the discussion more friendly and collegial the way Daniel hoped it would, but she wasn't about to argue with him on a question of social interaction.

The bridge hatch was dogged shut. Although the captain's voice would have carried over the varied echoes rattling through the *Milton's* corridors, those of some of his junior officers would not.

"Sir?" said Midshipman Barrett. "What if the other captains, the *real* captains, object when they learn what happened? I, well... Commander Kiesche of the *Arcona* is bound to feel insulted when he learns that I was pretending to be him."

Adele's lip curled. Barrett's comment was based on a number of unstated assumptions, not least being that he and Commander Kiesche would survive the coming action. The reality of a space battle was that lives could vanish as quickly and utterly as the specks of light which indicated ships on a Plot-Position Indicator.

"The answer to your question, Midshipman...," Daniel said. He didn't raise his voice, and his tone was mild. "Is that Commander Kiesche is an RCN officer who accepts and obeys the orders of his superiors. You've raised a more serious question, however."

Odd, thought the disengaged fragment of Adele's mind. *His voice hasn't changed and he's still smiling, but it feels as though the temperature has dropped twenty degrees. His smile doesn't go very deep just now, but most people's smiles don't go very deep.*

"That question being," Daniel continued, "why an RCN officer would be concerned with social niceties instead of carrying out his assigned task? Perhaps you should consider a career as a social secretary instead, Barrett."

He coughed. "Officer Mundy will now—"

"Sir!" said Barrett, leaping to his feet. He'd been seated at the gunnery console, which Sun had vacated for this council. "I—"

Cory and Blantyre sat adjacent to him, at the lead

and backup couches of the missile console. Cory grabbed Barrett by the waist belt and slammed him back in his seat; Blantyre leaned closer and snarled, "Sit *down* and shut *up!*"

"Officer Mundy," Daniel said, "please give an overview of the tactical situation."

"Cacique's inner moon—which they call Inner—lacks an atmosphere," said Adele. She started her display with the planet in the center and tiny Outer, 600,000 miles away, at the edge of the image area. After a moment to establish scale, she shrank the image down to Inner alone. "There's fossil ice at both poles and gravity at a little over an eighth of a standard g. Inner isn't normally inhabited, but it makes a very suitable base for Admiral Petersen's fleet blockading the planet below."

She was using the cruiser's large-scale astrogation display, placing the holographic imagery in the central area of the bridge. Ordinarily those who wanted to watch on their own consoles could have done so, but Daniel had directed Adele to lock everything but her own system. This was to be a group experience, centered on him.

"That base is in a crater near the north pole," Adele said, shifting the imagery to what was really a computer's best approximation rather than a real picture. "The four missile batteries are mounted on the plain outside, however, with three reload trailers supporting each, or in one case four."

The slant image from a light-day out had been pasted onto mapping data from the *Sailing Directions*, then sharpened by the software. In this case, "sharpening" really meant replacing blurred shadows with stock images of Alliance weaponry and inflatable domes. In the three light-hour data, the north pole was concealed behind Inner's curve; the more distant shot was the best view they would have until minutes before Daniel launched the attack.

Because he was certainly going to attack.

"The missile batteries are dug in and on full alert in both views," Adele said. She didn't magnify the imagery again, because it was already a work of fiction. "They use passive optical sensors until they go into launch targeting, but the batteries are linked by microwave repeaters on the crater rim. The signals traffic indicates the batteries' status."

"Sir?" said Else, seated at the back of the astrogation console. A signals officer wouldn't normally rate "sir," from a midshipman, even though technically the middie didn't have a commission either. "Can you really decipher low-power microwave signals at this distance?"

"Yes," said Adele, "I can."

Vesey had rotated the couch of the astrogation console to face the central display. She looked over her shoulder at the midshipman behind her and said, "If Lady Mundy tells you she's reading your mind, Else, you'd best hope that you're not thinking anything that you didn't want her to know."

"You'll notice that there are twenty-seven civilian vessels in the crater," Adele said as she tightened the focus slightly to concentrate on the interior of the crater instead of the batteries spaced around it. "Ten are prizes from New Harmony. There are seven more prizes in Cacique orbit in addition to the three dedicated minesweepers which have Fleet registrations. Petersen is using prizes as makeshift minesweepers. He loads their holds with crust material broken into coarse gravel and expells it in vectors toward individual mines."

"Does that work, Officer Mundy?" asked Blantyre. She was probably being a little more formal than she would have been if she and Cory hadn't just reduced Barrett to a quivering jelly.

"I can't tell," Adele said. "It appears to be dangerous work—there's outbound wreckage which could be a similar freighter which came too close to a mine about forty hours ago. But it may be that Petersen thinks the effort will dispirit the defenders and convince his own personnel that there will be a good result soon. Blockades are surprisingly hard on the morale of the blockading squadron, as I learned from Alliance prisoners taken from the fleet which was besieging Diamondia in the Jewel System."

"Captain?" said Midshipman Fink. "That was you that freed Diamondia, wasn't it?"

"It was all over the Academy last year when it happened," said Else.

"It was all over Cinnabar," murmured Barrett, his crossed hands hiding his lips.

"It was *not* me who broke the siege of Diamondia," said Daniel with deliberate harshness. "Many of your present shipmates were with me on the *Princess Cecile*, the smallest vessel in Admiral James' squadron when he sortied from Diamondia and defeated the Alliance forces with a masterful tactical display."

He cleared his throat. "But that's not germane to the present discussion. Please continue, Officer Mundy."

Many thousands of spacers had played a part in Cinnabar's victory in the Jewel System, Adele thought as she switched to imagery of the Alliance dispositions above Cacique. The vessels were dots with six-digit designators on the PPI, but a sidebar gave details on them. *No one else had anything like the importance to the result as Captain Daniel Leary, and the ones who came closest were all aboard the* Princess Cecile.

But as Daniel said, that wasn't germane.

"This is data from our one-light-day view of Cacique," Adele said, switching to the next image. "The red lines are the courses of the Alliance warships visible, with the dotted continuations at either end extrapolated from the sample. Since the sample was of thirty-seven seconds, those extrapolations should be treated with great caution."

She smiled grimly. Though she used the words, she knew the assembled officers—most of them—wouldn't listen to her. Instead they would treat the dotted lines as real events, just because they could see them. Sometimes she considered not providing information which she knew could be misused, but it would be the next thing to a lie to censor what she told people whom she thought were fools.

I think most people are fools. Daniel is the only one here who matters, and he won't misuse the information.

Adele's smile spread a little wider. Anyone watching her would have thought she was pleased. Perhaps she was.

"The two battleships," she continued, surrounding two of the dots with a white haze, "are the *Heimdall* and the *Helgowelt.* They're accompanied by these two heavy cruisers—"

She highlighted two more dots, this time in pale pink.

"—and four light cruisers."

Indicated by gray cross-hatchings.

"The other seventeen orbits are destroyers, which I'm not going to highlight for this purpose," she said. "You'll have noticed that the plotted courses don't group into any formation."

The mass of lines looked more like a skein of yarn. This had disturbed Adele initially, since it implied that she was missing some crucial piece of data. If nothing else, traffic control required that the Alliance vessels keep to *some* formation; otherwise, that many ships maneuvering in a relatively small volume of space would create a serious risk of collision.

"The later imagery demonstrates what was going on in the initial view," Adele said, displaying Cacique from three light-hours out. A single battleship—the *Helgowelt*—was accompanied by the heavy cruisers *City of Hoboken* and *Kiaouchow* and seven destroyers. They formed a loose chevron back from the battleship, sweeping in a plotted circle some 280,000 miles out from the planet. That put them safely clear of the minefield but still in position to crush sorties by the survivors of Admiral Ozawa's fleet.

"This is consistent," she said, "with Admiral Petersen dividing his heavy ships into three patrol groups, each led by a battleship, and his eighteen destroyers into two groups, of ten and eight ships. A destroyer from the second group is still on the ground. If the patrol shifts overlap by a half hour, one shift would always be fully capable of facing an enemy. By good fortune, our first view of the situation coincided with a shift change."

That was good luck. The division of the heavy ships into three groups and the destroyers into two would have been obvious from any two time slices—or even from one, since Adele knew the strength of the Alliance squadron. She couldn't have determined when they changed, however, and knowing that allowed Daniel to choose whether he wanted to attack one-third or two-thirds of Admiral Petersen's force.

"Though there shouldn't be another scheduled patrol change for three or perhaps four hours after what Captain Leary gives me as our expected time of arrival," Adele said, "the remainder of the squadron is under orders to lift within ten minutes if the force on Cacique sorties again. That happened twice in the week before Admiral Petersen sent Commodore Varnell revised orders, directing him to rejoin the main force at Cacique as soon as possible. We won't ourselves have warning of another sortie either."

The dispatches summoning Captain Varnell hadn't said anything about the aggressive stance which the besieged RCN ships were taking, but the aviso's own log had given full particulars. The first time, four cruisers had lifted but had broken off their ascent when the Alliance patrol put itself in position to launch missiles into the gravity well as soon as the cruisers were out of the shielding atmosphere.

The second attempt had looked identical. This time when the patrol maneuvered to meet the cruisers, however, eight destroyers had lifted high enough to attack the flotilla of minesweepers. A missile had destroyed a converted transport, and the destroyers' plasma cannon had done significant damage to all three Fleet-registered minesweepers. Four-inch plasma bolts wouldn't have been effective on most warships, but the minesweepers were lightly built.

Adele examined her notes, then nodded. She'd covered everything she reasonably could. "Captain Leary—" she said.

It struck her that she ought to be facing Daniel instead of looking at the tiny image of his face inset onto her display. Turning, coldly furious with herself for forgetting the human courtesies which, like clothing, were absolutely necessary for those who lived and worked in civilized societies, Adele resumed, "Captain Leary, I have no further information which I think has immediate bearing on the situation."

"Before I outline my plans," Daniel said, "are there any questions about what you've just heard?"

"Sir?" said Barrett. Adele noted that almost all the interjections came from the new midshipmen, not the officers who'd served with Daniel in the past. "We're going to outnumber the Alliance, then? The ships that're up, I mean."

"That's correct," said Daniel. "If our luck isn't bad, and if we get in and out quickly. More important, we'll arrive ready to launch, while the Helgowelt Squadron will identify us as the reinforcements which they expected."

He looked around the circle of his subordinates. In a pointedly challenging voice he said, "Are there further questions?"

And a heartbeat later, "Since there aren't, this—"

Adele projected the *Helgowelt* leading its wedge of companions over Cacique, roughly opposite the calculated position of Inner.

"—is where I expect the Alliance duty squadron to be when we extract," Daniel continued. "We'll be on a reciprocal course, roughly ten thousand miles distant from them and well clear of the planetary defense array. Our launch tubes will be open but we'll keep our gun turrets in their travel positions, aligned with the axes of the ships. Alliance observers would notice the position of the turrets immediately, but the fact the missile tubes are unshuttered is likely to pass as a shadow effect until we launch."

The other officers watched in silence. Cory and Else had personal data units out and were making notations. Adele didn't watch over their electronic shoulders—she had enough on her plate—but she recorded the transactions to view later.

Daniel might not be pleased that his subordinates were circumventing his intention if not disobeying his orders... but Adele would have done the same herself, and Cory and his friend Else were probably modeling their actions on what Officer Mundy would have done. If necessary Adele would say a word for the boy—for both officers; but Daniel could make the same analysis, so that probably wouldn't be necessary.

"The squadron will extract together above Cacique," Daniel resumed. "The *Helgowelt* and her heavy cruisers will expect to be on duty for the next three hours, and the destroyers with them will have six hours to go before they're replaced. Neither they nor the off-duty vessels should be in a particularly high state of readiness."

He paused and nodded. "Yes, Vesey?" he said.

"Sir," said Vesey, making an effort to speak loudly enough to be heard. "The Alliance squadron will assume the *Friedrich* is the flagship. Unless you want Captain Pimental to handle communications between squadrons before we unmask, it might be better for the *Milton* to extract a few minutes early."

Adele called up a crew list for the *Friedrich*, though she didn't need it. Ordinarily on a battleship—or for that matter, on a cruiser—significant communications were handled by a commissioned officer, with the signals officer dealing with only the mechanics of the business. Adele didn't know any of the *Friedrich*'s officers well enough to judge whether they could handle the necessary deception, but she was quite certain that Signals Officer Snooks himself could not.

"I decided against that," Daniel said, nodding twice in approval, "because I don't want them focusing on us immediately. We'll be claiming to be the *Luetzow*, but our antennas include provision for t'top-gallants, though we won't be flying them, and the turrets are ovoids instead of being true ovals like the Alliance ones they replaced."

He chuckled. "It's one thing to fool an ensign on a mine tender," he said. "It's another to have the watch officers of an entire battle squadron staring at us. If we're part of the squadron that they're expecting, I think we'll get away with it for the short length of time we need. We—and by that I mean Officer Mundy—"

Daniel nodded toward her. She dipped her head slightly, but she didn't turn to acknowledge the others. She had her duties, and they didn't include social niceties.

"—will announce that we're Admiral Hill, sent to supersede Admiral Petersen who's being recalled to Pleasaunce with immediate effect."

Cory barked a laugh, then smothered his mouth with his left hand.

Daniel grinned at him. "Yes," he said, "I believe that will give Petersen a great deal to think about besides getting his forces in order to engage the RCN. And for that matter, his senior captains are likely to be thinking about their careers rather than their immediate duties also."

Adele smiled coldly and threw onto the display a sidebar which listed general-grade officers in the Alliance Fleet and Army whose careers had been cut short by prison or execution under Guarantor Porra. Some of them had failed miserably in their duty, but half a dozen of the victims had been political. That included General Wayne Sumter, governor of Rickett's Hope, who'd put down a rebellion almost solely by his own charismatic leadership.

Navy House was riddled with politics and the Navy Board was certainly capable of acting whimsically... but losing favor in the Republic meant forced retirement rather than being shot in the back of the neck. Except in circumstances as extreme as the Three Circles Conspiracy, of course, and the RCN had by and large remained aloof from that. Guarantor Porra's brutal vagaries had various bad effects on his military, though what was about to happen at Cacique wasn't one of the more easily predictable of those effects.

On cue, Adele projected Force Anston, the code name Daniel had given his ships, onto the display with the Helgowelt Squadron. Anston was in a similar forward-pointing chevron but on a reciprocal course, ten thousand miles from the Alliance formation and closing.

"While I hope we'll come out in good order after a one-light-hour hop...," Daniel said, "we all know that things can go wrong. That would be true even with familiar ships which had worked up together properly."

Adele began running various alternative sequences which Daniel had prepared. The chevron became a ragged globe, a greatly expanded globe, and finally a scatter from which a number of the vessels were missing.

"I'm not going to push our luck on remaining unidentified," Daniel said. "Whether or not all our ships are in position, we'll launch no more than two minutes after the *Milton* extracts—and I may decide to launch even sooner on command."

Adele had already programmed the commo clusters to handle that. The *Milton* would be transmitting by laser a time hack to each ship of the squadron as they extracted. That was the only way the later-arriving vessels could count down precisely.

"Sir . . . ?" said Barrett. His forehead gleamed with sweat, but he kept his voice steady. "I notice you show the *Arcona* failing to arrive off Cacique. With the computer from the *Lykewake* and Commander Kiesche as Astrogator, her extractions have been within thirty seconds of the *Milton*'s and within two thousand miles at both legs of this voyage. Sir."

"I stand corrected, Barrett," Daniel said. By the end of the short sentence, his slight smile had spread much wider. "I'd been thinking of the cruiser's problems under Alliance command, but you're quite right: Fred Kiesche doesn't need a naval-grade computer to thread a ship through the Matrix. My uncle Stacey trained him, you know."

Adele wasn't an astrogator, but all she was being asked to do here was to move data. Well, constructively she was being asked to do that though Daniel hadn't used the words; he might not realize that she could correct the . . . error was too strong a word. That she could modify the choice he'd made when he created the examples.

Adele switched back to the previous screen, captured the blue bead slugged ARC441 and transferred it to the final demonstration. To make the point, she placed it slightly closer than any other ship to MIL101, also light blue but scintillant rather than a simple bead.

"The *Helgowelt* is our primary target," Daniel said. "We should be able to overwhelm her, even with the hasty attack plans which the situation requires."

Adele adjusted the display, adding the missile tracks. Rather than simply placing them on the existing screen, she created fine blue lines which spread progressively from the *Direktor Friedrich* and the four heavy cruisers to intersect the Alliance battleship and the cruisers accompanying her. They traced a complex net.

"Sir?" said Vesey. "Please explain why the ships are all splitting their salvos instead of concentrating them. Ah, so that I'll know the next time."

She isn't pretending that she's asking on behalf of the midshipmen, Adele noticed. *Nor is she simply obeying orders without embarrassing herself by admitting ignorance.* Vesey had all the virtues necessary for an RCN officer except, perhaps, killer instinct.

"We don't really know what our formation will be at time of launch, Vesey," Daniel said. Adele, unasked—but when had she ever needed to be asked to do her job?—switched the display through alternate formations again, each time adding the missile tracks. "And we don't know how the equipment of our captured ships is going to behave, either. While I hope that the attack boards and the missiles themselves will perform up to specification, by splitting each ship's salvo between the *Helgowelt* and a cruiser, we vastly increase the likelihood that all three Alliance heavy vessels will take killing blows."

"And incoming from all directions is going to make it harder to avoid, won't it, sir?" Blantyre said. She frowned. "Though programming two attacks is going to be a lot harder than programming one, especially with time short."

"True on both counts, Blantyre," Daniel said. "It's all the same to the attack computers, of course, but the Chief Missileers themselves will have to hand off one target to a subordinate."

He grinned again, lighting the room. "Of course on the vessels where one of the commissioned officers fancies himself as a missileer, that permits the warrant officer in the slot to do the job he's trained for anyway," he said. "I'm confident that Chief Borries here on the *Milton* will be pleased at the prospect."

What would I do if Daniel tried to take over my communications duties? Adele wondered. It wouldn't happen, of course, but if it did?

But there was a difference between that and the way Daniel regularly usurped the attack boards. Borries was a ship chandler's son who'd gone to space and, because he was a bright lad, had been apprenticed to a missileer in the Pellegrinian service. Adele was Mundy of Chatsworth.

"And Alliance defense and maneuver will certainly be compromised, yes," Daniel went on, grinning even more broadly. "That's particularly true if we come out widely spread—"

Adele switched screens to the loosest extraction yet,

one which showed Anston scattered about the Alliance formation, rather like a handful of gravel tossed onto a tile floor. She was careful to place the *Arcona* close to the *Milton*, however.

"—though I'd nonetheless prefer that we appear close enough that our targets have minimal time to react."

The fictional missile tracks wove an attractive pattern, rather like glowing spider webs. There was a cleanliness to space battles, at least for the victors: a phosphor dot vanished, nothing more. Even the best optical sensors showed only expanding gas balls with at most a section of hull or a gun turret riding the shock wave.

The truth was close to the image. Bodies vaporized instead of burning or were torn to shreds instead of dying in slow agony from belly wounds.

Adele smiled without humor. That was Daniel's province. He'd killed far more people in his naval career than she had, but he'd never been drenched with blood from someone he'd shot in the throat nor stepped through feces which his victims had voided when they spasmed into death.

If Adele wanted, she had sufficient connections now to become an assistant director at the Library of Celsus. She wouldn't have to carry a pistol, and her whole life would be surrounded by collected knowledge and by people who'd never imagined killing another person.

But she'd have to give up her RCN family. That price was too high.

"For the same reason, our destroyers will also launch at the heavy ships," Daniel said. "Even taken all together, the Alliance destroyers only equal the throw weight of a single cruiser, and they're too maneuverable to make hits probable if we attack them ship by ship with our own destroyers."

Adele dutifully added pale blue threads from the destroyers, four apiece. That was a pious hope, but she knew as well as the commissioned officers that it was unlikely any of the captured ships from the *Friedrich* on down would manage a full salvo.

"Ships which are in range will use their plasma cannon on the Alliance light craft," Daniel said, "but I want our destroyers to concentrate on the minesweepers if at all possible. Four-inch—well, ten-centimeter—guns aren't going to have much effect even on other destroyers, and if we aren't able to break the siege entirely, the minesweepers are more dangerous enemies anyway."

"Sir?" said Cory. He cleared his throat. "I wonder if ships—destroyers, that is—who happen to extract in a suitable position might not fire on the Alliance base? On the antiship batteries there, I mean."

"Well, I'll be buggered," Daniel said in a conversational tone. "You're right, there's no atmosphere to dissipate the plasma, and even a fairly dispersed charge will heat the missile bodies enough to deflagrate the fuel. Maybe even detonate it! Very well done, Lieutenant Cory!"

Daniel looked around the bridge, beaming, then nodded toward Adele. Toward the back of her head, of course, but he knew she'd be watching on her display. No one else in the compartment might understand the gesture, but Adele did.

Cory had been . . . not her protégé, precisely, but her project. The boy had barely graduated from the

Academy and initially hadn't distinguished himself in active service either. He'd shown a real flair for communications, however. When she realized how much he was learning just by watching her, she began to actively train him in her field.

From that start, Cory had blossomed to the point of noticing a tactical possibility that Captain Daniel Leary had missed. Granted, the close-in defenses of Admiral Petersen's temporary base weren't likely to be significant in this action, but it was still a clever piece of work.

"One salvo and then we insert," Daniel said. "We regroup a light-day out, back where we made our initial extraction to observe the situation. One destroyer, the *Insidioso* under Captain Robinson, will extract a light-hour out, observe the Alliance reaction, and then rejoin us with a report."

He cleared his throat. "If the *Insidioso* is unable to carry out those duties, then they devolve on the *Z31* under Captain Kenlon. I've briefed both officers on what information I'll want, though it's obvious enough."

In a manner of speaking, Robinson—or Kenlon—didn't have to do anything except bring their ships back so that Adele and her team, Cazelet and Cory, could sift their sensor recordings. Daniel was probably right to personify the activity rather than to point out that brave, skilled RCN spacers were simply a means to allow machines to do the necessary work.

"Any further questions, then?" said Daniel. "If not, return to your duty stations. We'll be extracting one light-hour from Cacique in ten minutes ship's time."

"Sir?" said Fink. "What do we do after we've attacked and regrouped?"

Daniel shrugged, but he was smiling. "Well, I could say that the answer to that depends on the situation, Fink," he said, "and so it does, of course. But I'll expect all ships to reload their missile tubes as quickly as possible, because I don't think we're going to sweep all the Alliance forces from the Cacique system with that one pass."

"And we're not going to quit...," said Adele, rotating her couch to look at the others for the first time since the council began. She was the only one present besides Daniel who'd really been in this place before, and she had a right to speak by virtue of who she was, not her rank. "Until we *have* run the Alliance out of the system."

She gave her colleagues an icy grin.

"Or we're dead."

CHAPTER 24

Above Cacique

Adele was reviewing the notes Cory and Else made during the council ahead of the one light-hour observation when Daniel announced on the intercom, "*Extracting in thirty, that is three-zero, seconds.*"

She didn't have any particular concern with the notes, but it gave her something to focus on after she'd organized for Daniel the sensor data from the final preparatory dip into the sidereal universe. People—including Adele—sometimes had hallucinations in the Matrix. She'd found that if she was absorbed in something, that was less likely to happen...though once in the midst of a long voyage, she'd seen a slit-pupilled eye watching her from the other side of a display of RCN personnel records.

Senator Forbes, wearing her formal robes, nodded her way past the Marine guards and walked across the bridge. She knew she didn't belong here, so she'd timed her arrival so that no one would have leisure to stop her.

Adele thought of turning to grab Forbes. Shortly Signal Officer Mundy would be very busy, but for the next twenty seconds she had nothing to do but wait.

Twenty seconds wouldn't be enough time. I could shoot her, of course, but that would be more disruptive than letting her stay on the bridge. Probably.

Chief Missileer Borries was in the Battle Direction Center. At the missile console was his striker, Seth Chazanoff; the rear couch was empty.

Instead of sitting at the missile console, Forbes walked to where Hogg and Tovera sat against the starboard bulkhead and flipped down the jumpseat they'd left vacant between them. She gave Adele a nod and a curt grin. It was just possible that the senator understood the options which had sequenced through Adele's mind.

All the options, because Adele had no governor which said, "But of course we couldn't do *that*."

Adele smiled faintly. Senator Forbes was unpleasant, but the woman had intelligence and an impressively pragmatic outlook.

Lieutenant Cory was on the other side of the signals console, and Rene Cazelet backed Vesey on the astrogation console. Ordinarily Vesey as First Lieutenant would be in the BDC, but everyone accepted that Blantyre was the better tactician. If an Alliance missile tore off the *Milton*'s bow, far better that Blantyre rather than Vesey be in the separate armored control station in the far stern.

"Extracting!" said Blantyre from the BDC.

For a moment Adele felt herself being cut apart at each joint. It wasn't painful, exactly; more like a hundred icy bands jerking tight around and through her body. Then the bridge lighting sharpened, her console display switched automatically to real-time sensor readouts, and Adele was back to work.

Six RCN vessels had extracted ahead of the *Milton*, and as Adele's display brightened to life it highlighted a distortion in space-time which quickly resolved into the *Direktor Friedrich*. A microwave cone on the *Helgowelt*'s bow was already rotating toward what the Alliance commander assumed was the flagship of Squadron Varnell.

Adele alerted the command group by an icon on each officer's console or face-shield. She cued Cazelet electronically, but she also nodded toward his image inset on her display, knowing that he would watching her through her own console.

This timing was perfect beyond anybody's ability to plan. If one believed in personified Luck, then it would shortly be balanced by a corresponding disaster—perhaps a missile striking the *Friedrich* or the *Milton* itself. If one were religious, then the Gods were fighting for the Republic as they had done so often in the past according to devout historians.

Adele Mundy believed in doing her job as well as she could. On a vessel commanded by Daniel Leary, she could expect that her shipmates would have the same priority.

"*Alliance forces . . . ,*" Cazelet said, sending via directed microwave and on 15.5 megahertz. One pole of the *Milton*'s 20-meter beam was directed toward the *Helgowelt*, some nine thousand miles distant while the other pole pointed to within 20 degrees of the Alliance base. There'd be sufficient dispersion across the much greater distance to Inner for the

communications staff there to read it clearly even if
something was wrong with their microwave pickups.
"This is AFS Luetzow, *flagship of Squadron Hill. Hold
for orders from Admiral Hill, break."*

Rene Cazelet had been born on Blythe and raised
on Pleasaunce. In the course of on-the-job training in
his family's shipping firm, he'd acted both as ground
controller at a spaceport and as signals officer on a starship. There was no pretense in his accent or delivery.

Adele waited a beat of three. Ships continued to
coalesce out of the Matrix. Predictably the later they
appeared, the farther they were from their assigned
locations . . . but none of them was very late or very
far out.

"All Alliance units receiving this signal," said Adele,
broadcasting in clear. "This is Admiral of the Fleet
Holly Hill."

She'd decided to pronounce "units" as "oonits" in
Pleasaunce fashion. She didn't have a voice recording
of Hill, so she had to hope that a hint of the general-
ized accent of the admiral's home world would pass
muster for at least a brief time.

"By order of His Worshipful Majesty Guarantor Jorge
Porra," she said, "I am superseding former Admiral
Petersen with immediate effect. Admiral Petersen is
to remain in his quarters—"

Adele didn't know whether Petersen was aboard
the *Helgowelt* or on Inner. The *Heimdall* had been
his flagship at New Harmony, but a battleship under
way at 1g acceleration would be more comfortable for
most purposes than a moon base whose gravity was
an eighth of that. He might well be with the patrol
squadron on every other leg.

"—until I arrive. All Alliance citizens are directed to enforce the Guarantor's orders on pain of summary court-martial. Over."

The most interesting thing about what happened next was that for more than thirty seconds *nothing* happened. Then a hoarse male voice said, "Luetzow, *this is* Helgowelt. *Will you repeat the last communication, please, we received a garbled signal. Over.*"

He'd switched to a laser communicator, perhaps to suggest that the "missed message" really was an electronics failure. More likely, Captain Thomas Ridgway of the *Helgowelt* wanted the greater privacy of laser. He was using the squadron's one-day code also, no problem for Adele because the code generators of Varnell's ships had been synched with the rest of Petersen's command before they separated.

Ridgway was probably as fearful of being accused by his fellow captains of questioning the Guarantor's orders as he was of not making *some* effort to check if this were somehow a subtle provocation by Petersen— perhaps in concert with the Guarantor. There was almost nothing too paranoid and convoluted to have come from Porra's fevered brain.

It's all right for a leader to be ruthless, Adele thought. *He shouldn't be whimsical, though, and he especially shouldn't be whimsically ruthless.*

She smiled faintly. No one had ever accused her of being whimsical, though she would make an extremely bad leader for other reasons.

"*Helgowelt*, this is Hill!" Adele said harshly. "If Petersen is aboard, confine him to quarters and land immediately at your base. *Is* former admiral Petersen aboard your ship, over?"

Adele had chosen to impersonate Hill—it was her choice, of course—because the admiral had risen by virtue of being trustworthy rather than for her dashing ability. She was the only woman among those whom Porra might have sent on a political mission of this sort. An alternative would have been for Adele to act the part of an Alliance signals officer with Cazelet portraying a male admiral, but even with communication distortions his youth might be noticed. This seemed to be working.

"Admiral Hill, this is Captain Ridgway," said the hoarse voice from the battleship, confirming Adele's presumption. *"Admiral Petersen is not aboard the* Helgowelt. *To the best of my knowledge—"*

"Prepare to launch," said Daniel. He spoke over the intercom, but as planned Cory copied the warning through the communicators feeding a time synch to the other RCN ships.

"—he's in his quarters at Liberty Base. The Helgowelt *will continue patrolling to prevent the enemy from making a sortie, another sortie that is, from—"*

"Launching four," Daniel said, his tone calm but bright with emotion.

The *Milton* rocked with multiple hammer blows. The cruiser's size and stiff frame permitted her to launch four missiles at a time without fear that they would interfere with one another because of exhaust and the shock of launching.

Captain Ridgway was still chattering, making excuses to stay as distant as possible from the arrest of his commanding officer and its political repercussions. Adele ignored him as she transmitted full particulars on what was happening to the RCN forces on

Cacique. She used RCN codes, though by now there wasn't much to conceal from the enemy beyond what multiple missile salvos were making abundantly clear.

The miniature clock inset in the center of Daniel's display clicked from 59 to 60, then 61 and onward in red block letters. It was counting out the seconds since the *Milton* extracted into sidereal space.

He had the Plot-Position Indicator on the top half of his screen and two attack boards splitting the lower display. The *Treasurer Johann* had finally arrived, three thousand miles out of position but with a fortunately good angle to sweep the Alliance formation—if the cruiser's Chief Missileer were better at his job than Commander Kevin Rowland was as an astrogator. Rowland would *not* be confirmed in command of the *Johann* if Daniel had anything to say about it.

Daniel grinned. For his opinion on the subject to matter, he and Commander Rowland had to survive the next few hours. Daniel never bet against himself, but he was intellectually aware that both were significant variables.

The right-hand board echoed Borries's display. He was setting up the attack on the *Helgowelt* in the BDC. Borries had control of two four-tube sets on both the *Milton*'s upper and lower belts. Daniel wouldn't step in unless he saw something critically and obviously wrong with the Chief Missileer's proposal. That wouldn't happen unless Borries had a stroke in the middle of the process, and even then his deputy Chazanoff would doubtless complete it properly. Daniel glanced over the proposed attack anyway.

Senator Forbes sat against the bulkhead. She as

calm as she'd been when seated across a dinner table from Commander, as he then was, Leary in Xenos less than two years before. Forbes hadn't been wearing her senatorial robes then and she shouldn't be wearing them now—this wasn't a civil function by any stretch of the imagination—but it would look good in her campaign presentations.

Forbes hadn't attempted to bring a flunky to record her presence on the bridge, but she obviously knew that the ship's internal systems did so automatically. No doubt she believed that for the right incentive some member of the *Milton*'s technical staff would arrange for her to get a copy of what was intended to provide evidence for a court-martial or an accident inquiry.

Irritated as he'd been when Forbes breezed in, Daniel might give her the copy himself. She'd seated herself between two servants who had no more proper business on the bridge than she did...and who would without the least hesitation kill her if they decided that was a good idea. That meant she was smart and also that she had guts, virtues that the Senate could do with more of.

Daniel's own target was the heavy cruiser *City of Hoboken*, on her first commission and far more modern than the cruisers which Captain Varnell had surrendered above Bolton. The saving grace was that new Alliance ships were likely to be crewed largely by drafted landsmen with only a leavening of experienced personnel released from hospital—or prison. The draftees wouldn't have had time to work down into real spacers, not without a better cadre than the Fleet could provide.

A warship's computer could launch missile attacks

with no human oversight beyond identifying a target, just as the same computer could direct the ship from star to star within the Matrix. A ship without a trained astrogator would take a very long time to reach its destination, and missiles launched by the computer were unlikely to strike home.

Well, if it came to that, missiles launched by the greatest bloody genius of a missileer mostly vanished into distant vacuum as well. Here, though, the range was short and the enemy both unsuspecting and on a closing course. Those factors, and an initial salvo of in the neighborhood of two hundred rounds, made the odds a good deal better.

105 read the clock. 106 107 108.

"Prepare to launch," said Daniel, hearing his voice echo from the bridge loudspeaker. The missileers of the *Johann* and one or two of the late-appearing destroyers might not have refined their attack plans yet, but the delay might prove an advantage: a second wave that would paralyze defenders with indecision.

"Launching four!" Daniel said.

"—*ing four!*" said Borries over the intercom. His missiles syncopated Daniel's by a half beat, steam slamming each multi-tonne projectile from its tube.

Missiles were driven by High Drive motors, and some antimatter always escaped in the exhaust instead of being annihilated. Starting the motors within a vessel would eat away the launch tube and shortly the hull itself. Instead, reaction mass flash-heated by a jolt of electricity became live steam in the tube. That shoved the missile into vacuum where it could safely light its High Drive.

The clock read 128. "Launching four," Daniel

repeated. The cruiser's sturdy construction allowed him to sequence the launches within each set more closely than he would have dared do on a destroyer.

The *Milton's* interior was pandemonium. The thick-walled launch tubes withstood the slamming steam discharges, but the violence made the hull ring. When they came eight at a time in close succession, the whole ship rang. The hull set the rig aquiver in turn. Since the antennas and yards were steel tubes whose sections telescoped within one another, the sound of them shaking together was overwhelming and indescribable.

As soon as missiles banged from their tubes, reloads began rumbling down rollerways from magazines close to the cruiser's center of gravity. Against any background save that of combat, the process would have been deafening.

A crew under the Chief Engineer was responsible for guiding the reloads, clearing stuck or misaligned rounds and—if something went wrong with the launch—winching the massive projectiles back to the magazines and stowing them. It was a brutal job and accounted for most of the casualties aboard ships which had survived a battle.

The *Milton's* gun turrets had been in resting position until Daniel ordered the launch. Now their mass rotated into firing position, creating its own varied clangor. If the situation had permitted, Daniel would've been echoing the gunnery displays—and been tempted to take control.

The cruiser rated not only a full gunner but a gunner's mate, a dour man named Ragi Sekaly who'd been previously been mate and acting gunner on a destroyer.

He was in the BDC with independent command of the ventral turret for as long as the plasma cannon were being used as offensive weapons. Their primary use was to deflect incoming missiles, however. When they reverted to that, Sekaly would become backup while Sun directed both turrets as a unit.

133 seconds.

"Launching four," said Daniel. He pressed the red EXECUTE button again with his index and middle fingers.

This time the *whang/whang/whang/whang!* from his tubes was complete before Borries announced, *"Launching four!"* and his missiles began to clang out of the ship. The missileer was being more gentle with his equipment than the captain was.

Daniel treated the missiles, the guns, and the *Milton* herself as tools to be used as efficiently as possible but not to be considered for their own merits. To Borries the equipment was not only his life but his faith, the naval equivalent of the way a devout priest viewed the statue in the sanctum of his temple.

That was inevitable, but Daniel was the captain. He wouldn't come down hard on Borries for being a trifle slow in sequencing his salvo, but he'd mention it when they had time to reflect.

Missiles were leaving all fifteen RCN vessels, including the *Treasurer Johann*. Force Anston was rather bunched toward the starboard wing because of the way ships had extracted, but the *Johann* was well out to port and created a useful balance. As such things went, things were going very well.

"Launching four," said Daniel and pressed EXECUTE for the final time in this salvo. He was wrong, though, because there were only three notes, *whang!* and a stutter *whang/whang!* The missile in set Starboard A hadn't left its tube.

The failure was in the launch mechanism itself: either reaction mass hadn't been injected into the steam crucible—a failed relay? corrosion or a break in the feed line?—or the electrical charge had failed to heat it for one of a similar series of reasons.

The *Milton* had a crack crew and, unlike the captured Alliance vessels, had been lovingly refitted by the captain's own workmen before she lifted on this cruise. Everything made by human beings could fail, however, and all human beings could fail as well.

A cannon in the ventral turret fired, making the cruiser squirm like a fish. The bead indicating the Alliance destroyer *Heinz Zwack* blurred momentarily. She was closer to the *Milton* than most of Force Anston was, and an 8-inch plasma bolt would have been devastating. Part of her internal atmosphere had vented through her ruptured hull.

The controlled nuclear explosion from the plasma cannon was greatly the loudest individual noise on the *Milton*. While not lost in the general cacophony, it certainly didn't stand out as vividly as it had when the cruiser was shooting at ground targets on Bolton.

Daniel instinctively waited for the second ventral gun to fire. Instead the dorsal turret crashed, shuddered through a triple beat while the tube returned to battery, and crashed again from the second tube.

Sun and Sekaly—and the other gunners in the RCN squadron—were hampered because their ships had just extracted from the Matrix and the rigging restricted their guns' fields of fire. They fired only when they could safely. There were plenty of targets, but lack of clear lines of sight reduced the rate of engagement sharply.

Petersen's ships had been operating entirely in sidereal space with their antennas telescoped, their sails furled, and the entire rig clamped against their hulls. Though Force Anston's attack came as a complete surprise, the Alliance gun crews were on alert for fear of a sally by the Cacique defenders. Their plasma cannon began nibbling at the incoming missiles much more quickly than Daniel had hoped would be the case.

"*Launching four!*" said Borries. His final quartet of missiles began to *whang!* out of their tubes.

Time for us to leave too, thought Daniel. Aloud he said, "Ship, prepare to insert. Inserting—"

The second ventral plasma cannon fired, the shock stunning because Daniel had been concentrating so completely on his own task. Sekaly's target, the destroyer *Z43*, was too distant to burst the way the *Heinz Zwack* had, but specks which had been rigging tumbled away on the PPI.

"Cease fire!" Daniel said. "Cease fire! Break, inserting in fifteen seconds, over."

A vessel entering the Matrix had to balance the electrical charge over all her external surfaces, which was impossible to do while her guns were spurting ions. At the velocity the *Milton* brought with her into normal space, however, fifteen seconds should be more than enough time to clear the cloud of disruption.

"Inserting," Daniel said, "now!"

His displays flickered as the *Milton* slid shuddering back into the safety of the Matrix. The last thing Daniel saw was the tracery of lines on both attack boards as the cruiser's missiles neared their targets.

CHAPTER 25

One light-day from Cacique

One of the reasons Daniel had chosen Robinson's command for data gathering was that Pantellarian optics were famously good. Pantellarian thruster nozzles often had casting flaws and their missiles were inferior to those built on fringe worlds with a lower level of culture and technical accomplishment, but Pantellarian imaging equipment was at or better than RCN Standard.

Daniel looked at the first sequence of images which the *Insidioso* had transmitted as she extracted. They were good, but they were impossibly good.

"*Daniel, I was concerned about the high quality of the imagery,*" said Adele without preamble. "*I've examined the background star map, however, and it appears that the data was gathered from fourteen light-minutes from the battle area, not one light-hour in accordance with your directions to Captain Robinson.*"

"Ah!" said Daniel. It was good to have a staff which answered questions before you got around to asking them. "Well, we can trust the images, then. As for

Robinson, I'll discuss the business with him at leisure, if we're both still around. Over."

He'd had good reason to order Robinson to extract a full light-hour from Cacique. Closer in, the infuriated Alliance commander might notice the destroyer and send a cruiser out to deal with her. Daniel needed imagery more than he needed highly detailed imagery.

But Senator Forbes's protégé—

He glanced sideways at the senator. She was peering at the images as if she understood them. Which just possibly she did, since she'd surprised him in the past.

—had gotten away with his gamble. Admiral Petersen would have feared—expected, even, given what had just happened to his patrol squadron—that a lone destroyer was bait to lure more ships into a battleship's salvos.

There was also the fact that Lieutenant Leary, as he'd been not so long ago, would likely have made the same decision. And the detailed imagery *was* nice to have.

The *Milton*'s officers were analyzing the performance of individual ships of the squadron. Cory and Cazelet divided the ten destroyers as they'd done during the pre-battle briefing. Daniel gave his attention to the overview.

The *Helgowelt* had taken a dozen hits from several directions. Missiles were designed to separate into three pieces when their reaction mass was expended. Each chunk weighed a ton and a half and was travelling at a noticeable fraction of light speed. Because of the short range most of the missiles hadn't reached burnout, so they'd gnawed great chunks from the battleship instead of vaporizing even larger chunks.

Regardless, the *Helgowelt* was a hopeless wreck.

There was nothing left worth salvaging except one or two hundred of her crew of nearly a thousand.

The first missile that struck the *City of Hoboken* was bow-on and ripped her sternward. She'd opened up like a melon hit by a bullet. A trio of projectiles then quartered the cloud of gas and debris, stirring whorls which intermingled. There would be nothing left of the ship and her crew that couldn't be covered by the palm of a man's hand.

The remaining cruiser, the *Kiaouchow*, was both well-handled and lucky. Her captain reacted to the attack a good twenty seconds before any other Alliance vessel did, braking with both High Drive and plasma thrusters at maximum output. Their combined thrust was close to 4 g. It would have ripped off any rigging that had been set—none was—and must have strained the hull badly enough to spring hatches and depressurize several of the cruiser's compartments.

The good luck was that only four of the sixteen missiles that the *Direktor Friedrich* aimed at the *Kiaouchow* actually left their tubes. They bracketed the Alliance cruiser, but the rounds which should have filled the interior of the group didn't fire.

Skill and luck had saved the Alliance cruiser for ninety-three seconds, until the first of the *Eckernferde*'s thirteen missiles arrived. They were well spread in a circular pattern. Its center was the point the *Kiaouchow* would have been had her captain braked with his High Drive alone, so only two projectiles rather than as many as ten struck the Alliance cruiser.

One of those spent itself on the retracted starboard outrigger. It exploded into a white fireball, taking with it half the *Kiaouchow*'s High Drive motors. The impact and unbalanced thrust from her portside motors rotated her. There wasn't time for the cruiser's course to change, however, before a second projectile spiked her Power Room. The fusion bottle didn't vent, but the hit nonetheless left the *Kiaouchow* a hulk slowly tumbling out of the planetary system.

Eight of the nine Alliance destroyers were wrecks as well. Multiple hits from the *Friedrich*'s 20-centimeter guns had torn the *Z31* and *Z34* apart. *Z43* and *Sharon Pigott*, which Sun and Sekaly had hit at extreme range, had lost most of their rigging and propulsion, and the 15-centimeter guns of the *Johann* and *Eckernferde* had pummeled the *G99*, *G105*, and the old *D10* beyond economic repair.

The *Arcona* puzzlingly hadn't fired at the *S152*, however, and the *Eckernferde*—two of whose turrets were assigned that target also—didn't have an angle because the *Helgowelt* was in the way. Daniel suspected that the *Eckernferde*'s gunner was more pleased than not at a chance to rake a battleship instead of a destroyer, but on the facts Daniel couldn't fault his decision.

And speaking of the *Arcona*, where the bloody hell was she? Had her computer—

Space-time rippled as a ship began to extract into sidereal space only two thousand miles away from the *Milton*. Both the dorsal and ventral turrets groaned to bear on the potential target; Chazanoff—and doubtless Chief Borries in the BDC—bent to plotting courses. Their launch tubes had been reloaded, and they were perfectly willing to expend their missiles on a target even if it happened to be barely beyond knife distance as space battles went.

The disruption was the *Arcona* rejoining the squadron. *And about time!* Daniel thought, till he glanced, then stared, at the visuals of the old cruiser. Eight of her port and dorsal antennas stood like lightning-stripped trees, and there was heavy damage to the rigging of the other antennas of those rows. Tags of sail fabric and cable dangled from the yards.

CDR KIESCHE OFFERS HIS APOLOGIES read Adele's crawl across the bottom of his display. She—correctly—didn't believe the information was worth connecting the *Arcona*'s commander with Daniel, but she thought he should know about it.

"Signals," said Daniel, "convey my regards to Commander Kiesche and my congratulations on being able to rendezvous after such severe damage, over."

Plasma expended its energy on the first object the ion touched. Thus even a very powerful plasma cannon was a short-range weapon in an atmosphere, and a starship's sails protected her hull from bolts. The *Arcona*'s plating hadn't received so much as a sunburn from· the short-range hits by an Alliance destroyer in the moments before the destroyer herself was crushed by RCN gunfire.

Two bolts had by bad luck hit antennas rather than sails, Dorsal Four and Port Three, reducing them to stubs. A 10-centimeter plasma cannon might gouge a divot from a cruiser's hull, but the thick plating would absorb the charge without structural damage. Antenna tubing had vaporized into shock waves of gaseous steel which acted as secondary missiles.

The fireballs had stripped sails away like scythes on grass and had plated the antennas and yards. The rig couldn't be adjusted until each welded joint had been laboriously knocked free. Commander Kiesche had indeed done well to rejoin the rest of the squadron so quickly, since all of his prepared astrogation programs would have to be redone. It also explained why the *Arcona*'s turrets, sealed in molten sail fabric, hadn't engaged the *S152* during the few seconds that were available.

Daniel switched to a brief close-up of the base on Inner, which *V67* and *T63* had raked on Cory's suggestion. Adele's software had adjusted the image: the *Insidioso* had only a flat slant angle on the polar crater, so it was a computer's best guess or nothing.

T63 had been built on Zuiderdamm before that world had grudgingly joined the Alliance; she mounted five 5-inch guns in single turrets. Daniel disagreed with the design philosophy, but under the present unusual circumstances—firing at extreme range at very flimsy targets—the heavy guns had been ideal. The three launchers and most of the reload pallets had been destroyed by their own missiles. The crater wall had shielded the fourth battery, but alone it couldn't protect the base from most low-level attacks.

"Cory," Daniel ordered on the command channel, "report, over."

"*No ships damaged,*" Cory said, referring to the five destroyers for which he was responsible. He piped the first syllables, but his voice settled quickly into normal range. "*Thirteen of twenty-two missiles launched, that's none at all from Z12. TA14 hit the City of Hoboken, or anyway a missile passed through the debris cloud, over.*"

"Cazelet?" said Daniel, "over."

If there'd been more time, he would have taken

reports from his captains. It was only human for those officers to want, to *need*, either to brag about success or justify their failure. Filtering the information, both verbal and visual, through his own officers was much quicker and possibly more accurate.

"*Twelve of eighteen launched,*" Cazelet said. "*The Z44 had a missile light without ejecting so both tubes of that set are gone. Captain Grief says there's no structural damage, though. Ah, and no hits, over.*"

Half of the destroyers in Admiral Petersen's fleet—including those of Captain Varnell's captured squadron—were either old or foreign-built. Their gun and missile armament was likely to be lighter than that of new Fleet elements, as well as being in a poor state of repair.

"Else, over?" Daniel said.

"*Sir!*" Else said. Her image looked tense and her voice was noticeably high-pitched. "*Twenty-four of twenty-eight rounds launched, two hits each on* Kiaouchow *and* Helgowelt. *Many gunfire hits on battleship* Helgoland. *Sir!*"

"Fink, over?" said Daniel. Else had glided over the fact the *Eckernferde* hadn't engaged the *S152* as directed, but he already understood the situation.

"*Treasurer Johann launched twenty-one of thirty-two missiles!*" the midshipman said. "*A near miss on the* Helgowelt, *and two very near misses on the* City of Hoboken! *Over!*"

A bit too much enthusiasm, Daniel thought. *Fink sounds as though he were the cruiser's real captain instead of his proxy.*

He grinned. *Given how poor Commander Rowland's astrogation has been, that might not be a bad choice.*

"Barrett, over?" said Daniel.

"*Sir, the* Arcona *made a perfect one light-hour extraction,*" Barrett said, his jaw muscles bulging with determination. "*She was in the process of launching when two plasma bolts from the* Pigott *struck her. Nonetheless she got away twenty-seven missiles and scored a hit on the* Helgowelt."

He cleared his throat. "*Despite extensive rigging damage,*" he resumed, "*she can navigate over short distances without a significant time penalty, over.*"

Daniel kept his smile from reaching his lips. Barrett was being an advocate also, but that was fair. An RCN officer *should* take his duties personally...at least if he expected to get along with Captain Daniel Leary.

"Blantyre?" he said. "What of our battleship, over?"

He'd decided this time that having his officers at their stations was more important than the collegiality of gathering the council in the captain's presence. Though he knew Adele would just as soon be on another planet from the other parties to a discussion, emotionally Daniel would still rather have been sitting around a table with them.

He glanced at the lieutenant's image on his display. Somewhat to his surprise, she was scowling.

"*Sir!*" Blantyre said. "*The* Direktor Friedrich *launched eighty-one of ninety-six missiles. Three shutters didn't open, a bank of four missiles hadn't been filled with reaction mass, and one missile appears to have been rusted solidly into its tube. B Turret didn't fire, they're not certain of the cause yet, but both gunnery targets were eliminated by the remaining turrets.*"

Bloody hell! If that's the standard of a crew made up largely of spacers from Admiral Ozawa's battleships, then there may have been more involved with the New Harmony disaster than treachery and bad luck!

Blantyre's face worked, then relapsed into a sour, "Over."

"Say the rest, Lieutenant," Daniel said, "over."

"*Sir,*" said Blantyre, her voice glowing with suppressed fury, "*under any other circumstances I'd recommend removing the* Friedrich's *captain, first lieutenant, and chief missileer. As a start. But we can't, can we? There isn't time. Because we're going right back in, over.*"

How many junior lieutenants would have realized we were going to resume the attack? Daniel wondered. In truth, quite a number would; the Academy trained cadets in the traditions of the RCN as surely as it did in the technical skills an officer would need. But not all of them would be as eager as Blantyre was.

"Yes, we're going back," Daniel said mildly. "I trust that Captain Pimental will at least be sure that her missiles are fueled this time. And I hope for her sake that her defensive armament is fully functioning."

Several of the Alliance destroyers had launched missiles during the initial engagement, but Force Anston's hit-and-run tactics ensured that Daniel's squadron had inserted into the Matrix long before they could arrive. This time Admiral Petersen would have ample warning as his opponents started to extract. It would be a battle, not an ambush, and the odds were heavily on the side of the Alliance.

"And Vesey?" Daniel said, smiling again. "How did the flagship perform, over?"

Vesey turned at the astrogator's console to face him. "*Sir!*" she said. "*The* Milton *launched thirty-one of thirty-two missiles. The failure to launch resulted from a feed line which fractured during the most recent series of insertions and extractions. It's been repaired, though unfortunately not in time to launch with the remainder of the salvo."*

She coughed delicately to insert a pause, then continued, *"Fortunately, the missiles which did launch scored three hits including the first one on the* Helgowelt, *and three more hits on the* City of Hoboken, *though after the cruiser had been struck head-on by a projectile from the* Friedrich. *This is the highest percentage of hits in the squadron and reflects great honor on the* Milton's *captain and company. Over."*

"Thank you, Lieutenant Vesey," Daniel said dryly. He chuckled and added, "I believe that even observers less biased than we are would agree with your sentiments."

He hadn't excepted her reference to the *Milton's* captain from his endorsement. After a victory like the one just gained, false modesty would make him sound like a mealy-mouthed twit. By the Gods! they'd stuck it to the Alliance.

"Break," he said. "Ship, this is Six. Fellow spacers, we've defeated a powerful enemy. Those of you who've served with me before know what happens next: the Alliance has some ships that we didn't get the first time, so we're going back to finish the job. I expect it to be a hard fight, but we're the RCN so the fight's going to be harder for the wogs on the other side. RCN forever!"

RCN forever/Up Cinnabar/Hurrah for Captain Leary and a score of variations on the sentiment rang through the *Milton's* corridors. That was as it should be.

Daniel sighed. He had two tasks. The second and in some ways the simpler, was to defeat the remaining Alliance ships in the Cacique System. But the first—

"Signals," Daniel said. "Link me with the rest of the squadron and I'll deliver my orders. Over."

Adele set the link from Daniel to Force Anston as Receive Only. The other vessels could call the *Milton*, of course—their captains were doing so with enthusiasm. They just couldn't get through to Admiral Leary unless Signals Officer Mundy decided that they should, which hadn't happened yet.

The lieutenant commanding *T63* was particularly importunate; when Daniel didn't respond to her messages via modulated laser, she'd begun transmitting on microwave and the 20-meter band, ADMIRAL'S EYES ONLY. Adele supposed that dogged determination was an asset in an RCN officer; but shouldn't it be coupled to a modicum of intelligence?

"Fellow officers," Daniel said. Adele had wondered how he would begin this briefing. All the commanders and most of the lieutenant commanders in Force Anston had more time in service than Daniel did, and they wouldn't be human if they didn't feel at least a touch of resentment at his rapid promotion.

"We've certainly begun well; now it's time to finish the job. I'm transmitting—"

Adele had waited till Daniel used the words to send the packets to the rest of the squadron. She sent them as clear text; normally they'd have been in the squadron's code of the day, but the cipher equipment in the other fourteen vessels was of Alliance manufacture.

There was no reason the signals officers couldn't have learned to use the unfamiliar hardware quickly and properly in the days they'd had to practice—and perhaps all of them had. This wasn't a time to take chances, though. The risk of an Alliance scout gathering information a light-day from Cacique in time to affect the coming engagement was too small to consider.

"—*my battle orders. I'd like you all to look at your assignments, then tell me if for any reason you think your command may not be able to execute them, over.*"

Eight of the captains responded immediately; Adele continued to block the transmissions. Quite obviously, if they were chattering they weren't reviewing their orders.

Senator Forbes unlatched her seat restraints and started to get up. Hogg was holding a stocked impeller, as he generally did when the ship was about to go into action. He thrust it crossways in front of the senator like a waist-high railing, then shoved her back down.

The jumpseat hadn't flipped back against the bulkhead because Tovera was holding it. Adele didn't imagine that Tovera's quick understanding had affected the way Hogg proceeded.

She ought to be thankful she hadn't taken a seat on the other side of the compartment, Adele thought. Hogg still would have stopped her, but she'd have been slammed against the bulkhead from a longer distance.

Forbes looked at Hogg, shrugged acceptance, and pointed with her left hand toward Adele. Their eyes met briefly. Adele felt her lips tighten, but—

She nodded. For Daniel's sake and the mission's, it was desirable to humor the senator when it was possible. Hogg lifted the weapon and waved Forbes free with a mocking flourish.

Captain Pimental of the *Direktor Friedrich* hadn't—somewhat to Adele's surprise—been one of those who'd wanted to jabber before she'd read the orders. When she called now, *"Friedrich Six to Anston Six, over,"* Adele responded, "One moment, Friedrich," and transformed it to a text on Daniel's display. As she'd expected, he opened the message immediately.

Forbes knelt beside Adele's couch. She wouldn't be able to stay here when the cruiser began maneuvering, but that wouldn't happen until they extracted above Cacique again.

"Admiral," said Pimental, *"Direktor Friedrich will carry out your orders without excuses. I've sacked the Chief Missileer and his mate and replaced them with two commissioned officers who've programmed missiles in combat on destroyers. The problems with the missiles have been corrected and we've put jumpers around the rotten wiring harness of Dorsal B. I, ah, I'm getting together jumpers for the remaining turrets, as I expect they're in a similarly bad state of repair. Over."*

Blantyre would say that was a good start, Adele thought. It did at least indicate that Pimental wasn't trying to brazen out her command's obvious deficiencies.

"Mundy, what's going to happen now?" Forbes said. Her voice was steady and no louder than it had to be to be heard over the High Drive, but the skin across her cheekbones was tight.

Daniel was discussing alternative targets with Captain Pimental in case the battleship extracted badly out of position in the Cacique System. It boiled down to the fact that there *were* no alternatives: all his heavy ships were to split their initial salvo between the two Alliance battleships regardless of circumstances.

Pimental apparently didn't want to hear that, but for some reason Daniel was being patient with her. Perhaps the squadron had a great deal to repair, flaws which had remained hidden until the stress of the initial engagement. Certainly the saw—or perhaps a drill?—screaming on D Level wasn't a normal part of the *Milton*'s routine.

Satisfied that her part of the business was under control, Adele glanced at the senator and smiled faintly. "We're going to attack Admiral Petersen again," she said. "To cover the obvious: yes, we'll be outnumbered about two to one, and yes, they'll certainly be prepared for us."

Daniel signed off with Captain Pimental, politely but firmly.

"Break," Adele said, dropping into communications protocol though she was speaking face to face with Forbes. She kept an eye on the display but she didn't actually have to intervene: Daniel simply opened the icon for the *Treasurer Johann* and began speaking to its captain.

She looked back to the senator, who sighed and said, "Those things weren't obvious to me, Lady Mundy, which I suppose shows my naivety as well as my ignorance. Will we win?"

Adele thought about the question. There were many temporizing answers she could honestly offer, but she saw no reason not to state the flat truth.

"There's a good chance that we'll do enough damage that Admiral Petersen will withdraw, breaking the siege of Cacique," she said. "I suppose one could call that a victory—Daniel would, certainly; that's why he's attacking. But rationally we must expect to take heavier casualties than the Alliance squadron will."

Daniel had switched to the captain of the *Eckern-ferde* and was delivering personal congratulations on the ship's exceptionally good missile performance. The *Eckernferde* was an old cruiser built on the Cinnabar ally Ghent and captured by the Alliance decades past. Her present crew had been transported almost complete from the *Exeter*, scuttled in harbor on New Harmony.

"Will we survive, then?" Forbes said. "*Can* we survive, Mundy?"

"We can survive...," Adele said, her lips pursing as she considered the question. "I've informed the RCN authorities on Cacique, and of course they've observed what happened when we first arrived. They'll have cued the minefield to pass us through, so there'll be easy sanctuary for even badly damaged ships to flee."

That wasn't quite as certain as she'd made it sound: it would require that the people on the ground were alert and competent. Adele would have liked to live in a universe where those traits were more general than she'd found them in the past.

Still, there was no point in giving the senator *all* the details of her reasoning. If the *Milton* were destroyed by a mine, the death of everyone aboard would be instantaneous. There was nothing to be gained by worrying about the possibility.

Daniel had shifted to the captain of the third cruiser, the damaged *Arcona*. It would have company before long.

"We can expect damage, certainly," Adele went on. "In the past I've been on ships that were badly hit but not, now that I think about it, one that took a direct hit by a solid projectile. We're—well, Admiral Leary is the one to discuss the likelihood of that, not me."

Forbes glanced toward the command console, where Daniel was going over his orders with a destroyer captain. The destroyers were to loose at the six Alliance cruisers. The two heavy cruisers each were to be the target of three destroyers, but the four light cruisers would also have incoming projectiles to prevent them from using their plasma cannon as offensive weapons.

"If I were to attempt to disturb Master Leary, whom I promoted to admiral," Forbes said with the least touch of asperity, "I fear that his man would shoot me. I'll hear your opinion instead, if you please."

Adele blurted a laugh. She didn't often do that, not even this brief gulp of sound that could have passed for a cough if she were willing to lie. The thought of Hogg firing a powerful impeller on the bridge was as ludicrous as the image of Tovera in a tutu.

"Hogg has that impeller as a security blanket, I think," Adele said. "It certainly isn't for use inside a steel box like this compartment. But you're right, trying to talk to Daniel wouldn't have a good result."

Tovera might have shot her. The light pellets of the miniature sub-machine gun in Tovera's case wouldn't exit from Forbes's skull. But that sort of speculation might not amuse the senator as much as it did Adele.

Aloud she said, "The *Milton* is the second most powerful ship in Force Anston, and we identified ourselves as the squadron's flagship when we first arrived. It's probable that we'll be the target of two or more cruisers and possibly even an Alliance battleship. *I* think. We may be destroyed, we may be damaged. The only circumstance I can imagine our not receiving *some* damage is if you're notably devout, Senator, and the Gods choose to spare you."

Forbes smiled, but the expression dripped like warm gelatin; there was no sincerity behind it. "I can't claim that, Mundy," she said. After a pause, she said, "Then we're probably going to die?"

Adele shrugged. Daniel was nearing the end of his list of captains, but there was still more than enough time for Forbes to get back to her seat in safety.

"It's very possible that we'll die," Adele said. "I don't know enough to say that it's probable, but you may be correct."

She looked directly at the older woman instead of keeping one eye on her display; the console would beep if her input was necessary.

"Mistress Forbes," she said, "the title of Senator of the Republic of Cinnabar is one of weight and honor everywhere, as surely in Pleasaunce as in Xenos. That's true because we of the RCN *demand* that your title be respected."

Adele smiled, but she knew that her sadness must show through it. "You're about to learn firsthand how we make them respect you."

Senator Forbes rose to her feet; she'd been keeping an eye on Daniel's proceedings also. She said, "I'm a fortunate woman, then, Mundy."

"If we both survive this day," said Adele, "*then* we can claim to be fortunate."

But in her heart she knew that dying in the company of her friends and family was better fortune than she'd dreamed of in the years before she met Daniel Leary.

CHAPTER 26

Above Cacique

Daniel only noticed the extraction—as opposed to the fact the *Milton*'s sensors were again feeding him information regarding the sidereal universe—some minutes after it was complete. For a shivering moment he'd felt as though his body had been sectioned on a microtome and the layers were being shuffled. Normally that would have been excruciatingly unpleasant, but he was concentrating on the battle. He just paused for an instant until his vision cleared.

Oh, yes; the battle.

Admiral Petersen was bringing his squadron up in a spiral around Inner, gaining height with each circuit as additional ships joined. The battleship *Oldenburg* led, followed by the heavy cruisers *Sedan* and *Elisabeth*. The *Heimdall*, his other battleship, was fourth in line, just ahead of the light cruisers.

Normally a squadron lifting in an emergency would put the heaviest ships in the lead. Alternatively the commander might decide to bring all his ships up together despite the risk of collision; starships were notably unwieldy while operating on plasma thrusters. Likely the *Heimdall* had been slow to get ready, so Petersen had sent the cruisers up out of the planned sequence rather than delay the process.

Daniel couldn't fault either decision, though he would probably have ordered his ships to lift as soon as each was able, hoping to organize them in orbit. They'd be badly disarranged if the enemy squadron returned while the process was going on, but at least he'd have all the possible missile tubes available for a salvo, however ragged.

Borries and Chazanoff were handling the missiles without interference from their commanding officer. Daniel might feel—and in his heart, he *did* feel—that neither of them had quite the touch with an attack board that he did, but he'd be the first to agree that they were very good.

And he was squadron commander, operating without a flag captain. He'd like to be controlling the plasma cannon *and* to be out on the hull helping Woetjans and the rigging watches get the antennas in, but Admiral Leary had to focus on the squadron and let others get on with their proper business.

Daniel grinned. At least he didn't believe that he was a better rigger than Woetjans.

The heavy ships of Force Anston, now the Green element, had extracted as planned on the opposite side of Cacique from the Alliance squadron. The dispersion was much greater than Daniel had intended, though. The *Treasurer Johann* in particular was 17,000 miles out of position, which was absurd in a one light-hour transit.

The *Arcona* had taken three minutes above calculation to arrive, but that was understandable given the unbalanced state of her rigging. She was echeloned neatly off the *Milton's* starboard quarter.

Daniel ran his time projection, superimposing missile tracks on the courses of the ships of the two squadrons. It would be tight, but it would work. If a few of the RCN ships were late, that would usefully add to Petersen's uncertainty. *At least I can tell myself that.*

"Anston, this is Anston Six," he said. Adele would see to it that the signal was encrypted and transmitted in whatever fashion would most reduce the chance of interception. "One hundred and five seconds after the time hack, all ships will launch one salvo at their assigned targets. Prepare—*now*, out."

The only way to certainly avoid interception was to maintain communications silence. That would mean giving up control of a squadron whose crews were unfamiliar with their ships and whose captains had never worked together. Daniel was too proud of his own tactical skills to do that, and anyway Admiral Petersen wouldn't gain anything from the signal that he couldn't deduce from the salvo itself.

The *Milton's* rig was coming down in a range of sounds from creaks to clangs with a general background of shudders. Everything loose on and in the hull rattled in sympathy. Occasionally Daniel heard the *bang-bang-bang* of an impact wrench, and once there was even the brief scream of a rotary saw's diamond teeth biting steel: Woetjans was cutting a stuck cable instead of taking the time to clear it.

There wasn't time. The greatest advantage Admiral Petersen had in a long-range engagement like this was that his ships already had their antennas and yards stowed.

That didn't affect the ease of launching missiles because the tubes ejected straight out from a few fixed locations, but the turrets rotated 360 degrees. The plasma cannon—nothing else appearing—swept the whole area upward from a plane balanced on the ship's hull. If the rigging was stowed it didn't get in the way, but any stick of antenna raised above the hull could block the angle from which a projectile was screaming down on the vessel.

In a short-range combat where plasma cannon were themselves offensive weapons, spread sails could protect the hull from charges of ions which could otherwise damage hulls; Daniel had used that technique himself. Against incoming missiles, though, the rigging was a blindfold rather than a shield.

Admiral Petersen would have been aware of the RCN squadron even before the ships extracted fully into the sidereal universe. A starship was a micro-universe while it was in the Matrix. Precursor effects as it began to penetrate normal space distorted the electromagnetic spectrum and were noticeable at several light-minutes distance by a warship's sensors.

Despite that, the Alliance squadron hadn't adjusted its course from the calculations Daniel had made using the time slices of Alliance patrols as Force Anston approached Cacique and from Captain Robinson's after-action visuals. Petersen apparently believed that the RCN ships were extracting too far out for an immediate attack to be worthwhile.

Daniel grinned. Petersen's record showed him to be more of a politician than a tactician. That had stood him in good stead at New Harmony, but now he had a space battle to fight and he didn't have the skills for it.

He had the weight of numbers, though.

"*Launching four*," announced Borries.

"*Launching*—" said Chazanoff, but his "four" was lost in the *bang!* of a missile launching from the first of Borries's B Level tube sets. Chazanoff's own rounds syncopated those of his Chief.

Daniel brought up the *Milton*'s dorsal and ventral visuals as horizontal bars to frame his screen. He caught sight of one missile lighting, a blue glitter against the background of stars. The missile's body was a shadow, unnoticed at the scale of the display.

Missiles continued to eject and light. The quick cycle made the cruiser's hull ring like a giant jackhammer. A jumpseat against the starboard bulkhead cocked sideways; one of the bolts holding it had cracked.

Daniel hadn't liked to launch while the riggers were out; loose atoms of antimatter could splotch a face-shield or possibly puncture a suit. There hadn't been any choice, though, because the rig wasn't coming down as quickly as it needed to.

There had been a dust cloud in the volume of space where Force Anston reformed after the initial attack; it was uncharted and ordinarily of no real concern. Joints and bearings of ships which swept through it were a little more likely to stick the next time they were used, however; and if those ships were plunging straight into a battle, the slight delay of clearing the jammed rigging could be serious.

The *Milton*'s missiles were all away, or anyway the launches had ceased. A stutter within a sequence would've been subliminally obvious, but Daniel might not have noticed if the first or last round of eight hadn't launched.

The other heavy RCN ships were improving their alignment on the PPI, though the *Johann* was hopelessly out of position. Daniel's plan had been to keep his battleship and cruisers as the Green element; in the event, they were a smaller element accompanied at a distance by a lone heavy cruiser.

Meanwhile the destroyers, the Blue element, had extracted on the other side of Inner, complicating Alliance maneuvers and forcing them to split their defensive fires. There was at least some chance that Petersen would detach cruisers to deal with Blue, since it outnumbered the remaining Alliance destroyers. Putting the Alliance squadron in a pincers more than made up for the disadvantage of Force Anston arriving fully rigged.

Petersen must finally have projected the tracks of the initial RCN salvo. At the time of launch, Green was on a reciprocal course with where the Alliance squadron would emerge from a further circuit of Inner when the projectiles would arrive.

The Alliance column broke apart, each ship dodging to avoid a concentration of massive projectiles. The Alliance vessels weren't taking time to calculate their individual courses, much less trying to keep their formation intact. Admiral Petersen had lost control of his squadron at the very start of the battle.

Alliance ships began launching. The process was ragged enough that Daniel wondered if Admiral Petersen had ordered a salvo or if the captain of the *Sedan* had acted on his own and other captains had followed suit. The light cruiser *Agadir* was even aiming at the Blue element.

The rumble of reloading ceased. There was a distant *cling* as the inner lock of an F Level launching tube closed over its missile. Borries and Chazanoff were recalculating courses, preparing for the moment Daniel would order a second salvo.

He took a deep breath. He'd thought that commanding a squadron in battle would be a larger version of a single-ship command. It wasn't. When he gave orders to separate ships, he might be sending their crews to their deaths and sparing himself.

Realistically, taking a corvette like the *Princess Cecile* into action meant that the captain and crew would live or die together. Though the *Milton's* risk today was the same as that of, say, the *Arcona*, its fate might not be. That would only matter if the *Milton* did in fact survive, of course.

"Green, this is Anston Six," he said. The Blue element was under the maneuvering control of Commander Potts in the *Z44*, though the destroyers were not to launch save on Daniel's orders. "On command, turn fifteen degrees starboard—"

Toward the enemy.

"—and increase thrust by point two, I repeat point two, g. Prepare, *execute!* Six out."

The added acceleration would strain antennas which hadn't yet been folded. There were two still up on the *Milton* and the Gods only knew how many on the recently captured ships. That couldn't be helped.

The 8-inch turrets rumbled, this time with the separate whine of elevating screws adjusting the guns to meet incoming projectiles. It was time.

Daniel thrust the EXECUTE button, sending the queued recall signal to the hull. Each semaphore would extend its six arms equidistant, then collapse them all to the post. The riggers should begin coming in within less than a minute. They would all be safe inside the hull before the plasma cannon began to fire.

If Woetjans or any of her crew disobeyed, the side-scatter from the big guns would very probably fry them despite their rigging suits. Daniel very much hoped the bosun would obey.

But it couldn't be helped. This was war.

Adele's equipment read bolts from Alliance plasma cannon as radio signals. She could have filtered them, of course, but instead she was recording the bursts with the intention of later synching them to the visual imagery to determine rates of fire for individual Alliance ships.

It didn't appear to her that the information had any practical utility, but one can never be sure of the future. Adele was of the opinion—she *believed*, as a religious fanatic believes in her God—that one couldn't have too much information.

The twin forward airlocks on the *Milton*'s spine were placed on the rotunda not far aft of the bridge. They opened almost together, the dogs ringing as they withdrew and sticky hisses as the valve seals broke. Riggers clashed into the rotunda, bringing with them the chill of a hostile environment.

"Clear the lock, you bloody fools!" snarled a bosun's mate in an urgent voice. "D'ye want to leave your buddies out there to fry?"

The inner valves sucked closed; the sound of the dogs sliding home was subtly different from that of the same bolts withdrawing. The remainder of the rigging watches would be able to get off the hull now.

Adele smiled faintly as she worked. "To get to safety," she'd thought momentarily, but there was no safety aboard the *Milton* today. The cruiser was second in line of a squadron which was closing with an enemy of twice its strength.

Cory handled normal communications while Adele attempted to read the enemy traffic. Under normal circumstances that would be impossible, even for her. All ships of the Alliance squadron were exercising proper communications security, running their messages through a generator which converted them to the squadron's own separate day code.

Cracking the day code in real-time became a theoretical possibility because the *Milton* had Alliance equipment and the captured ships of Squadron Varnell had been part of the same unit as the present enemy only a few weeks before. That provided Adele with a seven-month record of the squadron's code transformations as a base. The increasing number of messages from the present engagement were the goal of her calculations.

The information she had didn't allow Adele to predict the sequence of changes in Petersen's day code, but a computer capable of calculating courses within the Matrix could bring a great deal of brute force to the problem. Adele was simply running alternative solutions in hopes of finding one which turned the current Alliance messages from gibberish to—

The alphanumeric string at the top of her display became ENEMY IN SIGHT. ONE BB FOUR CA.

The airlocks opened again. Shoulders and boots clacked as the airlock emptied its human cargo into the hull. The preceding watch had remained in the rotunda; they might at any moment be ordered back out. Along with the new arrivals—and all wearing bulky rigging suits—even that large compartment became crowded.

Until the moment she succeeded, Adele hadn't had any thought beyond that potential success. When it happened, though, an opportunity flared like the sun burning through the fog over her mind. She couldn't hand the Alliance interceptions off to Cory and expect him to keep on top of Force Anston's traffic as well, though. The *Milton* was the squadron's flagship, and its signals had to have top priority.

Midshipman Cazelet stamped onto the bridge, still wearing his rigging suit. Condensate crusted the joints where metal bearing surfaces underlay the structural plastic skin.

He seated himself at the rear display of the communications console and opened the couch wider. Naval workstations were designed to accommodate personnel in any sort of dress an emergency might require. That included a crew working in suits because the ship's hull was no longer airtight.

"Rene, I'm glad you're back," Adele said, verbally keying a two-way link. She'd trained Cazelet in her duties even before he'd been allowed to join the RCN, and she'd modified her software to reflect that reality. "I want you to take over these Alliance interceptions. Send Daniel and Blantyre what's useful, converted to text. Can you do that, over?"

"*Yes, certainly,*" Cazelet said. "*You broke their day code? Adele, that's . . . even for you, I mean, ah . . . Over.*"

He'd brought up his display, but the suit's stiff arms made him clumsy. His expression became briefly savage, then settled again as he regained control of both the equipment and his temper.

"Ah," Cazelet added as his fingers caught the rhythm of the keyboard, "*Captain Leary put all of us midshipmen on the hull to make sure the riggers, ah, obeyed the recall signal. He didn't say quite that, but that's what he meant. Over.*"

Adele remembered that Daniel had once sent Hogg out onto the hull to shoot Woetjans if she didn't bring her riggers in when he ordered her to. But what could Rene—who'd never fired a gun and didn't carry one—have done if the bosun ignored him?

That was the point, though. The bosun might ignore the semaphore, even knowing that Six himself was on the other end of the hydromechanical linkage. She wouldn't ignore an officer standing in front of her and making peremptory gestures.

Woetjans was a disciplined spacer. She would take orders from a midshipman half her age and strength, because it was her duty to do so.

Woetjans didn't react to Daniel as she would to a superior officer, however; the relationship of this captain and this bosun was much more complex than RCN regulations could deal with. On Woetjans' side, it was something between a mother protecting her son and a worshipper ready to sacrifice everything to her God.

Adele adjusted a tight-beam microwave cone; she thought she had the answer. Neither the Signals Officer nor the lieutenant in charge of communications aboard the *Heimdall*, the Alliance flagship, was a woman, but Admiral Petersen's aide-de-camp was his niece. It might not work, but it was certainly worth a try.

"*Oldenburg*, this is Command Three for Squadron

Command!" Adele said in what she hoped was a
tone of furious denunciation. "Cease fire, cease fire!
You're launching at friendly vessels. The admiral says,
I quote, 'Hallahan, you're an idiot and I'll relieve you
if you launch again,' unquote. Command Three over."

Adele wasn't very good at denouncing. When she
became very angry, she spoke even more slowly and
precisely than usual. That was a problem, because
people tended not to listen to her words even when
she was warning that she would kill them if they
persisted in their course of action.

"Command Three, this is Oldenburg," said a male
voice. Adele felt a smile twitch the corners of her
mouth upward. *"Hold one, please, over."*

If the *Oldenburg's* signals officer responded to the
Heimdall, there would be a degree of confusion on
the bridges of both battleships. That would useful to
the RCN certainly, but not earthshaking.

Instead the fellow responded to the message without checking to see which ship had transmitted the
microwave. A transceiver aboard the *Oldenburg* automatically turned to a reciprocal of the incoming signal.
This was *much* better than random confusion.

"Command Three, this is Oldenburg Command!"
said an angry voice. Captain Edmond Hallahan was
probably shouting, but Adele's console smoothed the
volume to where she'd set it. *"What's this bloody
nonsense about shooting at friendlies? We're shooting
at the bloody Cinnabar battleship, over!"*

"Oldenburg, my uncle says, 'You bloody fool, Hal-
lahan, the *Direktor Friedrich* is friendly,'" Adele said.
She was smiling about as broadly as she ever did.
"Cease fire, cease fire, over."

The *Milton*'s dorsal turret, then the ventral, fired in quick succession. Adele was used to the 4-inch guns on the *Princess Cecile* hammering at a round every two seconds, but the bores and chambers of the cruiser's big guns took far longer to cool between discharges. During the lull between the first four shots, the continuing snarl of the High Drive seemed muted by contrast.

"Command Three, this is Oldenburg Command," Captain Hallahan said. *"I'm ceasing fire, but why are they bloody shooting at us, over?"*

The RF spectrum was hash now: the ships of the RCN Green element were firing plasma cannon as quickly as they could. Alliance missiles were on their way toward the heavy RCN vessels, whose guns were straining to nudge the dangerous ones to one side or another.

"Oldenburg, Admiral Petersen is working on that," Adele said sharply. "Your orders are to stop making it worse. Do not fire without direct orders from Squadron Command. Out."

The *Milton*'s plasma cannon slammed stunningly again. The 8-inch guns were causing strains. An audible hiss of outgoing air and a stutter in the environmental system followed each quadruple discharge: plates were starting as the ship twisted.

The *Milton* might take a direct hit at any moment, and everybody aboard her might die. Adele didn't care about that or anything else which was out of her hands. If it happened, however, she had the satisfaction of knowing that her last act on behalf of Cinnabar and her shipmates had been carried through very skillfully.

She smiled even wider. *If I do say so myself.*

CHAPTER 27

Above Cacique

"Green element," ordered Daniel, "launch at maximum rate. Squadron out."

He hadn't spoken the last words before Borries and Chazanoff had stabbed their EXECUTE buttons. The *Milton's* hull began to twist to the rhythm of her missile launches while the sharper, heavier slamming of the four plasma cannon punctuated the tubes.

Daniel had launched the first salvo at long range to break up Petersen's formation, but continuing to fling missiles while the targets scattered wildly would have been wasteful. Now that the Alliance ships had settled—onto individual courses, not into a formation— it was possible to launch with some purpose.

Space battles involved a great deal of nothingness. A missileer who thought random launches would have a good result was either a cretin or in a blind panic. The Alliance missileers who'd been launching at Force Anston while their own ships gyrated had probably been panicked.

"*Six . . . ,*" said Vesey on the command channel, her voice showing the strain of heavy acceleration. "*Unless we begin braking within forty seconds, we risk being in the pattern of either the* Heimdall *or the* Elisabeth, *over.*"

Daniel placed her calculations in the lower right-hand quadrant of his display and opened them. She'd coded the missile tracks red for the battleship and green for the heavy cruiser. It was the seventh salvo for each and the first to even approximate accuracy. The *Heimdall*'s spread was aimed to cross the *Milton*'s current course a little ahead of the *Elisabeth*'s.

But Vesey was being overly cautious—well, very cautious, which in a battle was the same thing. You couldn't predict courses precisely until the missiles had burned out and split, since the process of separation induced variables. It was just possible that the projectiles would spread as widely as Vesey feared, but even if they did there was little chance of them hitting anything but vacuum.

"Green element," said Daniel. "On command, turn two points toward enemy and boost thrust by point-two gees. In thirty seconds, over."

"*Sir!*" said Vesey on a two-way link. The strain in her voice wasn't entirely due to their present acceleration of 2.1 g. "*We'll lose rig if we do that and tumbling yards could damage the hull, over!*"

"Needs must when the devils drive, Vesey," Daniel said. "Break, Squadron, execute!"

Not even Daniel could feel the incremental acceleration, though a change in the buzz of the High Drive was barely perceptible. The added stress was real, however: just as Vesey had warned, the Port E antenna, jammed with only the topmast telescoped, carried away. The shriek of twisted steel shearing was followed by the nervous jangle of broken cables lashing the ship as they flailed past.

There was only one further *WHANG!* though, when one or the other end of the antenna spun back against the hull. Daniel hoped it hadn't penetrated the plating, but he knew very well that they'd be lucky if they got out of this affair with nothing worse than a bad dent.

The Alliance commanders weren't just wasting the contents of their magazines when they made maximum-effort launches at extreme range. The first missiles of an engagement had been pampered: loaded at leisure and checked whenever the missile crew had a moment's leisure.

After that—and inevitably even then, to some degree—things began to go wrong. The locks of launching tubes jammed or—worse—sprang open. Reloads jumped the rollerways and sometimes slammed the breech of a tube, putting it out of action until the machinists could turn it smooth. Electrical contacts might fail, feed lines might kink or clog, and a missile which had been on the lowest tier for years might have been hammered enough out of round that it wouldn't seat.

For that matter, a hydraulic ram could malfunction instead of sliding its missile the proper distance into the tube. Ordinarily "malfunction" meant that several inches of missile stuck out into the compartment and the tube couldn't be closed, but Daniel remembered once on the *Defiance* when the ram overtravelled and thrust itself a hand's breadth deep through the missile casing. That had been a *bitch* of a job to clear, and nobody was shooting at the old training cruiser at the time it happened.

A half-salvo from the *Heimdall* was forty-eight missiles if everything operated to specification; the spread she launched at the *Milton* was thirty-one. Miserable as the battleship's performance was, it was still a better percentage than the seventeen out of twenty-eight missiles that the *Elisabeth* managed.

Mind, one missile was enough to put paid to a ship, even a battleship. Neither vessel appeared very accurate, but a spacer never discounted luck. Particularly not bad luck.

The remaining ships of Green element were conforming to the *Milton's* course, though the seriously underpowered *Arcona* had been forced to light her plasma thrusters in addition to her High Drive, and the *Treasurer Johann* was so far out of position that only by plotting her course could you tell that Captain Rowland really had obeyed Daniel's orders. If the engagement continued any length of time, the *Arcona* might have to borrow reaction mass from another ship before she could risk landing. The trick, of course, would be to survive long enough for that to be necessary, let alone possible.

By turning toward the enemy and accelerating, Daniel reduced the length of time Admiral Petersen's squadron had to react to incoming missiles. It reduced the RCN's reaction time also, but thus far at least the Alliance ships were shooting very poorly. They hadn't recovered from the disruption of realizing Daniel's initial salvo was coming straight down their collective throat, and most of the navigating officers appeared to be maneuvering without informing the missileers.

As Daniel had directed, Blue element, the RCN destroyers, was shadowing the Alliance squadron but not closing the considerable distance separating them. Every two minutes or so, the Blue vessels individually loosed a pair or two pairs of missiles toward the Alliance battleships.

The range was well beyond the possibility of accurate shooting, but Daniel expected a number of projectiles to come close enough to their targets to be noticed. That would prevent the Alliance captains from concentrating wholly on the threat from Green element.

And who knew? Maybe some Alliance vessel would have bad luck.

The enemy destroyers were keeping close to their heavy ships, acting as a screen but not actively trying to engage Blue element. If asked, the Alliance captains would probably claim that the RCN destroyers were too far out to be dangerous, and that the greater risk was that RCN assets which had been concealed to that point would mousetrap them if they attacked Blue.

Daniel wouldn't have done that even if he *had* hidden assets. He knew to keep his eye on the main target, and that was the pair of battleships.

Speaking of which, the *Oldenburg* had stopped launching. Had something gone wrong with her missile control apparatus? Battleships had several-times-redundant systems, but combat stresses were beyond what the most careful captain could test for. Sometimes that caused a catastrophic failure.

There was nothing wrong with the *Oldenburg*'s defensive armament, though. Her six turrets mounted twin 20-centimeter plasma cannon. At present her gunner was mostly working the turrets in pairs. Four high-intensity bolts hitting in quick succession were enough to convert a projectile into a gas cloud which caromed off at a slant from its dangerous original course.

Once, however, five turrets fired together at a projectile from the *Milton*, catching it before burnout. Even at extreme range, that was enough energy to rupture the tanks of reaction mass and leave the melted remains to tumble harmlessly in the void. Somebody on the *Oldenburg*'s bridge had recognized a threat even before it developed and had removed it with a skill beyond anything Daniel had seen before.

His sudden smile was harsher than usual. It was an article of faith with Daniel Leary that the RCN was the finest naval organization in the human universe. The RCN did not, however, have a monopoly on skilled personnel.

The four Alliance light cruisers were at the end of their formation. Three—one continued to launch at the Blue element—were concentrating on the *Eckernferde*, the rearmost vessel of Green element.

Lighting her plasma thrusters, the *Eckernferde* made a desperate attempt to avoid a well aimed spread of eighteen missiles from the *Ratisbon*. The acceleration would flatten any personnel who weren't already in couches as well as shaking loose all manner of things. When the multiple frequencies hit harmonics, they could shatter metal.

A missile from the *Emden* struck the *Eckernferde* squarely amidships. Bits flew away: antennas and yards broken by the impact, and hull plates blasted off when the solid remainder of the projectile exited the hull. The *Eckernferde*'s plasma cannon hadn't engaged that missile because it hadn't been a danger until the target accelerated into its path.

When Daniel ordered his Green element to resume missile attacks, the *Treasurer Johann* had launched a salvo of twenty-five, followed by a second of— remarkably—twenty-six missiles from her twenty-eight tubes. The entire spread was aimed at the *Heimdall* because the leading Alliance battleship masked her consort from the *Johann's* angle.

None of the Alliance ships were engaging the *Johann*, so her crew wasn't distracted. Also, her Chief Missileer was very good. Daniel didn't know that officer's name, but he would after the battle—if there was an after for him.

The *Heimdall's* bridge crew had been concentrating on the half-salvos from the *Direktor Friedrich* and to a lesser degree on missiles from the *Milton* and the two cruisers accompanying her. The dead-accurate spreads from the *Johann* went unnoticed until they were too close to maneuver away from. They fell on the battleship like the Wrath of the Gods.

The *Heimdall's* 20-centimeter plasma cannon were in their element. Ordinarily the faster rate of fire of lighter guns made up at least to a degree for the enormous wallop from a heavy bolt. Now there wasn't time for multiple shots, but each twenty-centimeter round destroyed the integrity of an incoming projectile. No solid missile got through the battleship's defensive fire.

But four clouds of recently vaporized metal swept over the *Heimdall*. They scoured off rigging, sensors, and everything less sturdy than the hull itself. The steel fog didn't penetrate the gun turrets, but they and the cannon themselves were welded in place.

The *Oldenburg* resumed launching. This time the full salvo, sixty-three missiles, was aimed at the *Milton*.

Daniel brought up the High Drive control panel. There probably wasn't going to be a happy ending; but still, you did what you could.

If the *Oldenburg's* spread had been better aimed, he would have found it easier to choose a response. The central clump of about half the salvo was just that, a random distribution which grouped around the center.

Whether the *Milton* braked or tried to increase what was already high acceleration, there was a likelihood that one or more projectiles would hit her. The remaining missiles were scattered around that lethal core.

Daniel gimballed the motors to slew the *Milton* sideways at maximum output. The new course would be a shallow tangent to the previous one, the sum of the new thrust acting on the original momentum. It didn't mean safety, but if the cruiser held together she had a chance of survival.

If. A cadet who proposed that solution in a ship-handling class would be flunked for the exercise, with the notation that the High Drive mounts wouldn't take the unsupported strain.

On the other hand, the Academy instructors would be doing the same bloody thing if they had this many incoming missiles to deal with. They would if they thought quickly enough, at any rate.

One of the motors in the cruiser's stern section broke the welds on one side, then banged against the outrigger because the other side still held and the attachment plate folded under the strain. The other motors stay put for now.

The *Oldenburg's* captain, unlike her gunner, was

uninspired and leisurely in his responses. The *Direktor Friedrich* and the *Milton* directed full salvos at the remaining Alliance battleship now that the *Heimdall* was out of action.

The *Oldenburg* braked with both High Drive and thrusters, the first evidence Daniel had seen that her captain understood the gravity of his situation. The strain would make even a battleship squirm like a snake, but it did drop her out of the spread from the *Friedrich.*

That put the *Oldenburg* squarely in the path of Borries's fifteen missiles. The Chief Missileer had allowed for maximum braking, while his mate had aimed the remaining fourteen missiles of the *Milton's* salvo ahead, reasonably assuming that the *Friedrich* would fill the center of the box.

As the *Direktor Friedrich's* salvo neared the target, a missile struck her amidships. It was high, slamming into A Level, though the fireball would scoop away all internal subdivisions in that section down to the armored deck between E and F Levels.

The battleship began to roll away from the impact. A second missile struck well forward, engulfing her bow including the bridge. She was out of the fight and probably beyond economic repair.

The *Oldenburg's* cannon were swatting away incoming projectiles with contemptuous ease. *How the bloody hell are they keeping up that rate of fire? It's too fast even for 6-inch—*

As Daniel formed the thought, a change cued his console. It threw up a visual of the *Oldenburg*. A turret lifted from the battleship's spine, shedding bits as it tumbled outward. Two of the fragments were the barrels of plasma cannon, the portions that were outside the armor when a round vented through the breech. The blast plucked the turret from the barbette on which it rotated.

If you fired a plasma cannon faster than its tube could be purged of vapor sublimed from the bore, the charge reflected back instead of stabbing toward the intended target. Bad things happened, then.

Worse things happened to the *Oldenburg* some nine seconds later: a projectile hit her starboard outrigger at a quartering angle and raked sternward. By the time it slanted out through the port outrigger it was a cloud of superheated steel, more a shock wave than an object. The battleship's hull wasn't seriously damaged, but the thin plating of the outriggers vanished like chaff in a flame.

The High Drive motors went with the outriggers, and in all likelihood most of the plasma thrusters—set into the lower curve of the hull—were burned away also. The *Oldenburg* had become a drifting hulk. A considerable portion of its armament remained, but it was unusable.

Three projectiles were driving toward the *Milton*. Their grouping was accidental: they weren't segments of the same missile.

Sun fired his dorsal turret, bouncing the ship seriously despite the other violent inputs. One of the incoming trio diverged from its previous course, driven by the thrust of the half its mass which sublimed when struck by the heavy ion charges.

The ventral turret didn't engage the remaining projectiles. Because of the angle of approach, the *Milton*'s lower pair of guns didn't bear.

Daniel touched his port thruster controls, giving them a blip to rotate the *Milton* slightly on her long axis. That would bring the ventral turret into action. The dorsal guns alone couldn't cycle quickly enough to take out both projectiles.

The PPI showed the *Arcona* holding station, though she must have taken damage: her two most recent salvos were of only six missiles each. The *Eckernferde* drifted without power; the missile had cut her almost in two.

Meanwhile the *Treasurer Johann* continued to fight her own private war, ignored by the enemy. She had just launched a second salvo at the Alliance light cruisers, a choice of target so wrongheaded that for a moment Daniel found it perverse. Then he took in the whole tactical situation.

The enemy battleships were out of action. The *Oldenburg* was in freefall and spinning around her long axis, driven by the missile which had ripped away her outriggers. Even veteran spacers in her crew would be finding it difficult to keep their breakfasts down. The *Heimdall* was even more hopelessly crippled: her shutters and hatches were welded shut. Launching at either of them would merely kill fellow spacers to no military purpose.

The heavy cruisers *Sedan* and *Elisabeth* were the next most important Alliance assets, but from the *Johann*'s angle they were largely screened by the *Heimdall*. The light cruisers, however, had reformed in a line ahead after their initial panicked scattering. They provided the *Johann* with a zero-deflection shot. The *Emden*, leading the formation, blocked the view of the following ships unless they were communicating better than they'd seemed to be in the past.

When the *Emden* realized the danger, she broke

onto starboard tangent from her original course. As she turned, she slewed so that two of her three twin 15-centimeter turrets could bear on the incoming missiles without causing blast damage by overfiring her own hull.

The next in line, her sister ship *Ratisbon*, reacted only moments later. Her captain was obviously on his game.

The older *Thetis* slewed and turned also, but to port. She carried six 10-centimeter twin turrets. Five bore on the incoming, but the stern dorsal and ventral turrets didn't fire.

Last in line, the *Agadir* launched another spread of twelve missiles in the direction of the RCN destroyers. Her captain seemed oblivious of everything that was going on around him.

The *Milton* started to rotate, but three more High Drive motors on the port side broke their mountings. Unbalanced thrust made the ship yaw violently.

Her dorsal guns slammed. Sun was trying to bunt one projectile into the path of the other. Remarkably, he came close to succeeding.

The last things Daniel remembered from his display were—

A projectile spiking the *Ratisbon* just aft of center and slanting out near the stern. The impact carried with it the contents of half the target's internal volume.

A second projectile striking the prow of the *Agadir* on a reciprocal. The cruiser became an expanding cloud of debris which followed the course she had been on when she was destroyed.

An Alliance missile hit the *Milton*'s stern. Everything went white for Daniel, then black.

❖   ❖   ❖

The crash was so loud that Adele perceived it as a flash of light. Her data unit was tethered to her equipment belt. It flopped around, of course, but the display corrected for movement.

Adele's wands twitched also, but she automatically clutched for one or the other of her mechanical aids in a crisis. Reflex didn't send her left hand for her pistol when a missile hit; instead she kept her data unit controls in a grip which would have required surgical shears to break.

The unit was bulkier than most of its capacity, because it had internal cushioning and an outer case that would stop a pistol shot. It wouldn't have been harmed if it had gone flying across the compartment, but it would have injured anybody who got in its way.

A jumpseat leaped from the aft bulkhead and cracked Daniel in the head, splitting his commo helmet. The seat caromed off the ceiling, then fell to the deck. One of its broken attachment bolts skittered around the compartment, sounding peevish but not able to do real harm.

Hogg stepped toward his master. He rode the careening deck as he would a small boat in a storm off the coast of Bantry.

"Tovera!" Adele said, jerking her head toward Daniel because her hands were busy with the control wands. Her console had blinked when the missile hit, but after running its self-check it was back in service.

Tovera had been taught field medicine during her training with the Fifth Bureau. This certainly wasn't the first head injury Hogg had seen either, but Tovera probably knew more about painkilling drugs—besides alcohol—than he did.

Adele wanted Daniel to make a full recovery more

than she wanted anything else in life. The only thing she could do to aid the process was to carry out her own duties, which was what she would have done anyway.

She smiled coldly. Other people seemed to make life more complicated than she found it to be. For example—

"Sir! Sir!" Vesey cried. She'd turned to stare at Daniel and was fumbling for the catches of her seat restraints.

"Lieutenant Vesey!" Adele said. If her most recent transmission—and Adele couldn't remember—had been on the command channel, then this rebuke was going to all the *Milton's* surviving officers instead of remaining between her and Vesey on a two-way link. That didn't matter. "Take control of this ship *now!*"

"Sir!" said Vesey, but this time it wasn't her earlier whimpering. She straightened, bringing up the High Drive and thruster controls on the lower half of her display.

On the upper portion, Vesey had been trying to view the damage through the *Milton's* external sensors. That was an obvious waste of time, at least obvious to Adele. Her wands flickered.

The High Drive shut down momentarily. Things—including Daniel's head on the couch—lifted. Before weightlessness was more than a lurch in Adele's stomach, the motors resumed their snarl, though at a lower level: they were developing no more than the standard 1g acceleration. The cruiser's wild gyrations gradually slowed.

While Vesey did her proper job, Adele imported visuals of the *Milton* from the sensors of the *Arcona* and the *Direktor Friedrich*. The battleship was operating in emergency mode, limited to passive data collection. Adele switched the command console back to normal, then directed it to amplify the image and transmit it through the laser link.

After her own computer had sharpened both sets of imagery, Adele forwarded them to Vesey at the astrogation console. As expected, they were ugly sights.

The missile had taken off fifty feet of the *Milton's* stern. The outriggers, though tattered at their stern ends, remained to provide scale; otherwise Adele would have had to superimpose a before-action schematic of the cruiser over its present image.

The Battle Direction Center was gone, along with everyone in it. The missile's trajectory must have been nearly perpendicular, striking on the spine and blasting everything beneath down through the keel.

Armored bulkheads divided the ship vertically. It was lucky that the one ahead of the impact hadn't ruptured—or again, perhaps it had. The riggers acted as the damage control party on a warship, since they were normally inside the hull during action. Woetjans was chivying sternward the personnel waiting in the forward rotunda.

Adele glanced around the bridge. Chazanoff looked groggy, but he was trying to plot a missile attack.

"Officer Chazanoff!" Adele said. "Take command of all the missile sets. Officer Borries is dead, over."

The only reason she gave the order was that it would waste time to pass the information to someone who had command authority, which Signals Officer Mundy assuredly did not. That was a good reason, though, and in a crisis like this it might well be the best reason.

"*Aye aye, sir,*" said the new Chief Missileer phlegmatically. He adjusted his display. As Adele had expected, an order delivered in a tone of command was sufficient. Chazanoff was operating on trained reflex rather than intellect as chaos rained down on him.

Did the *Milton* have any functional missile tubes? Well, that wasn't Adele's problem.

"Mundy!" Senator Forbes shouted over the racket. She wasn't linked to the cruiser's commo net, but she'd managed to cross the bucking deck. She clung to the supports of the signals console. "Take command of the fleet! Somebody needs to, and that puppy Vesey certainly can't!"

"Sit down, Senator," Adele said. "I don't have the authority or the skill either one."

"*Launching four!*" said Chazanoff. Only two missiles banged out in response. Still, that was two more than there might have been.

"You know which ship is which," Forbes said. "And you know how to fight someplace besides on the Senate floor."

"I can't—"

"May the demons eat your tits, you bloody fool!" Forbes shouted. "I'll make you an admiral, does that satisfy you? I'm brevetting you! You're a bloody admiral!"

Adele opened her mouth, then closed it. Forbes was an unpleasant woman, but she wasn't stupid; and in this case, she wasn't wrong.

Commander Potts in *Z44* was probably competent to handle the task or Daniel wouldn't have given him command of the Blue element, but Adele wouldn't trust a destroyer's communications suite to coordinate a fleet action. The *Arcona* was damaged, and Adele didn't know how badly. The *Treasurer Johann* was untouched, but Daniel would rise from his stupor and strangle her if she passed the command off to an officer who couldn't astrogate better than Commander Rowland had.

And Forbes was right about Vesey too. The lieutenant wasn't a puppy, but this was a job for someone who was ready to kill without hesitating an eyeblink.

"All right," said Adele, bringing up a PPI screen. She'd done so in the past, but only for curiosity. "Now get out of here, I'm busy."

"*Mistress?*" said Rene Cazelet urgently. "*The squadron on Cacique is coming up, over.*"

And so they were. Five, no, six icons; one was crosshatched because it was in the planet's shadow relative to the *Milton*'s sensors. Each had a six-digit alphanumeric designator which Daniel would have identified immediately. Adele could have looked them up, of course, but that would have taken time which she could better spend on other matters.

"Cory, how long before those ships from Cacique are able to maneuver, over?" Adele said.

Cory's image stared from her display like a death mask. Adele recalled that he and Midshipman Else, who'd been stationed in the BDC, had become friends.

"*Mistress,*" he said and swallowed. "*The* Jervis, *seven minutes. The* Lupine, *eight minutes. The* Dido, *nine minutes, and the other three cruisers spaced behind her at a minute each. Over.*"

"Very good," said Adele. "Break. Anston elements, this is Mundy of Chatsworth speaking for Anston Six. Engage the enemy more closely. Mundy out."

The force from Cacique guaranteed victory, but if the remaining Alliance forces began launching into the gravity well, they could destroy the reinforcements before they came into action. Therefore the remnants of Admiral Petersen's squadron had to be fully occupied for the next ten minutes or so to ensure an RCN victory.

There wasn't any doubt what Daniel would have done if he were alert. Adele couldn't execute the details of the plan, but the decision itself hadn't been difficult.

She wondered if the other RCN captains would refuse or ignore the order. She smiled faintly. If so they wouldn't have to worry about court-martials if she survived. Adele tried to take a more relaxed attitude than came naturally to her, but Mundy of Chatsworth had given the order. Lady Mundy was quite meticulous about the family honor.

A single gun fired from the *Milton*'s ventral turret. Adele frowned at the visuals. The dorsal turret was intact but unmoving; the plasma cannon were cocked upward at a high angle. Perhaps there was an electrical fault that would be quickly remedied. More likely the turret had jumped its ring and couldn't be repaired short of a dockyard.

It wasn't likely that the *Milton* would survive long enough to reach a dockyard, of course. The mission was to drive the Alliance out of the Cacique system. If that required throwing cripples against undamaged enemy ships to buy time, so be it.

Adele looked at the PPI again. She'd basically exhausted her expertise when she ordered the squadron to attack.

None of the slowly moving dots on the display were

missiles. She knew that it was possible to track the missiles on the PPI—Daniel did it all the time—but she had no idea of how. There was a great deal of what was necessary in a naval battle which she had no idea of. Ordinarily that wasn't a problem.

Chazanoff continued to launch in sequences of one to three at a time, if a single item could be called a sequence. Adele had no way of telling how many of the launches were reloads; perhaps fewer than a dozen of the *Milton*'s thirty-two tubes were functional.

Sun's single plasma cannon continued to fire slowly. How much immediate danger was the *Milton* in? Adele hoped that the way they'd spun after the missile blasted off the stern had taken them out of the zone the Alliance ships had been targeting. The enemy had had time to revise its course predictions by now, but the distances involved meant the projectiles might be some time arriving even if they meant certain death when they did.

Adele wasn't an admiral save by fiat of Senator Forbes, but she *was* a signals officer. "Cacique Squadron," she said, broadcasting in clear. "This is Mundy of Chatsworth, speaking for Admiral Daniel Leary."

The ships rising from the surface might well have lifted with partial crews. If the missing personnel included the signals officer and code clerks, Adele wanted to be sure that her orders were nonetheless understood. They might be her last words, after all.

"You will carry the attack to the enemy with all available means," Adele said. "Under no circumstances will you break off the engagement until the enemy base and all Alliance vessels in the system have surrendered or been destroyed. Do you copy, over?"

"Chatsworth, this is Commodore Battenberg," replied a harsh female voice. She was transmitting from the first ship to lift. *"We copy you. I think I speak for the entire New Harmony Squadron when I say that I've never received an order which will give me greater pleasure to execute. Cacique Six out."*

Several additional ships were laboring up from Cacique now. Judging from the example of the first six, Adele estimated that it would be at least half an hour before the newcomers could possibly join the action.

"Sir!" said Lieutenant Cory on the command channel. *"Two transports are lifting from the moon base! I suggest we send destroyers to capture the prizes, over."*

Adele thought of what Daniel would say, then quirked a smile. She didn't need Daniel's advice on the matter: their instincts were the same.

"No, Cory," she said. "Nothing else matters until we've eliminated all the enemy warships. Out."

During their conversation, Forbes had clung to the communications console and shouted into Adele's ear to be heard. No one else on the *Milton's* bridge had the faintest notion that the Plenipotentiary had raised Signals Officer Mundy to the brevet rank of admiral.

Nonetheless, the *Milton's* officers accepted her orders as though she had the right to issue them. Adele suspected that was because they viewed her as Daniel's friend rather than anything she'd earned in her own right...though earning Daniel's friendship wasn't a small matter, when she came to think of it.

Adele's smile was minuscule, but it had more warmth in it than she usually displayed. She would

much rather be Daniel's friend than be an admiral
in her own right.

The beads on the PPI which indicated the four
Alliance cruisers began to fade. The enemy destroyers blurred also as Commander Potts led the Blue
element down on them.

Adele frowned and switched from the console to the
much less capable internal display of her personal data
unit. There could be a delayed fault in the console
from the missile impact....

The Alliance ships had vanished. Only wreckage
and the two disabled battleships remained in the
Cacique system.

"*Mistress!*" Rene Cazelet said. "*They're running!
All of them that can get under way are running into
the Matrix!*"

"We've won!" shouted Cory. "By the Gods, we've
won!"

Neither youth remembered to sign off properly.
Perhaps they'd been infected by a signals officer who
tended to be cavalier about such things herself.

*What do I do now? Hand the whole business over
to Vesey, I suppose.*

"*Mistress,* Heimdall *is signalling to you, over,*" said
Cory. Communication from the enemy flagship seemed
to have brought back his professional demeanor.

Cory had been handling the ordinary signals traffic,
but it continued to run as a text sidebar on Adele's
display. Adele found the thread easily: PETERSEN
CALLING CHATSWORTH, OVER. PETERSEN CALLING
CHATSWORTH, OVER....

"All Anston elements, cease fire," Adele said,
taking care of the main priority first. She couldn't

be certain that the Alliance commander wanted to surrender, but if he didn't nothing would be lost by delaying the final salvos by a minute or two. "Break, Officer Chazanoff, cease fire. Break. All Cinnabar elements—"

Cory would be directing the transmission to the destroyers and the ships rising from Cacique, though Adele's real concern was for the cruisers which had been attacking the heavy Alliance vessels.

"—cease fire by order of Admiral Leary."

The Alliance didn't provide proper missile targets any more, but Adele knew human beings too well to be sure no one would launch at the crippled battleships. Missileers on most warships had few opportunities to practice their craft. A battleship in freefall and without defensive armament would tempt even what passed in the RCN for a saint.

"Break," Adele continued. "Petersen, this is Chatsworth. Go ahead, over."

The *Heimdall* was sending by tight-beam microwave, but the transmission was badly broken. Damage to the battleship must be more extensive than Adele had assumed from the visuals.

The vaporized projectiles had wiped everything less refractory than the gun turrets off the *Heimdall's* port and under sides, but the remainder of the hull appeared normal at a distance. Apparently redeposited steel had plated equipment on that side also and seriously degraded its performance.

That also explained why the *Heimdall* was limping along on the power of seven thrusters, inadequate to impart more than a modicum of acceleration to 80,000 tonnes. A thruster nozzle was wide, and even a partial blockage would merely reduce power. If the minuscule throat of a High Drive were plated shut, the explosion which destroyed the motor would be only the start of the problem.

"*Lady Mundy*," said Admiral Petersen, his voice breaking despite his painstaking formality. "*Fortune has not favored the Alliance of Free Stars today. I ask that you accept the surrender of the forces under my command, over.*"

"Admiral . . . ," said Adele. As she spoke, her wands expanded real-time imagery of the Alliance base and both battleships. "When you say 'the forces' do you include your base and any ships there, over?"

"*Yes of course, Lady Mundy,*" Petersen said. With a flash of miserable anger he went on, "*Do you think I don't see they'd be bloody slaughtered if they tried to run? We surrender, over!*"

The transports that had been trying to escape were back on the ground, their thrusters cooling. When the Alliance warships fled, the unarmed vessels must have realized that their situation was hopeless. The base personnel were shooting up flares, white star clusters which burned out almost before they started drifting down in the low gravity.

"Admiral, I have no authority to do so in my own right," Adele said. "However, my commanding officer, Admiral Daniel Leary, accepts your surrender on behalf of the Republic of Cinnabar. My colleague Commander Potts will coordinate salvage and rescue operations. Chatsworth out."

She took a deep breath and sank back onto her couch. Hogg and Tovera were carrying Daniel out of the compartment on a cocooned stretcher; there was a Medicomp only fifty feet down the corridor. They hadn't been able to move him until Vesey reduced acceleration and brought the ship under control.

Adele supposed she needed to give Potts a direct order, though he would have heard the entire exchange already. She would get to that in a moment.

Adele closed her eyes. *Be well, Daniel. The Republic needs you almost as much as I do.*

"He's coming around," said Daniel in a cold female voice.

"I dunno," Daniel objected in a gruffly male voice. "He still looks pretty bad. I think it's going to be a while."

"The readouts say he's awakening," Daniel said, her enunciation clipped and precise. "Therefore he's awakening. We don't know whether or not there's been brain damage, but he *will* awaken."

Daniel opened his eyes and blinked. Adele and Hogg were watching down at him. *They were talking, not me.* Cory and an older, angry-looking woman— *Senator Forbes, of course*—were looking at him also, and Tovera was looking both ways down the corridor.

Cory looked worried. *Why is he wearing lieutenant's pips?* But then Daniel remembered he'd promoted the boy himself...*and when was that, a long time ago?*

"What happened to me?" Daniel said. He tried to lift his torso. Everything around him blurred to gray shadows against a lighter gray background.

He relaxed. He was hooked to a Medicomp, as he should have guessed; and he would *not* be trying to get up again for a moment or two.

"We were hit by a missile," said Adele. "A seat

broke loose and the metal frame gave you a nasty crack on the head."

She paused, then said in the same flat tone, "If you hadn't recovered, I would have invented a more heroic story. Much as I dislike to lie."

By the time Daniel managed to stop laughing, it didn't hurt much at all—which was a welcome change from the agony with which he'd started. He sobered, though he was careful to leave a smile on his lips.

Adele lied expertly when carrying out her duties to the RCN and to her other master. Daniel didn't recall her ever lying about a personal matter, however. Her offer was a monument more impressive than the statue on the Pentacrest which a grieving Republic might well erect to his memory.

Aloud he said, "What damage did the missile do, besides breaking the seat?"

"Cory?" said Adele with a curt nod. She was holding her data unit, but she hadn't taken the control wands out of their conformal restraints.

"Sir!" said Cory. "We've lost everything aft of Frame 260, but the bulkhead there held. Other than that, surprisingly little damage."

He coughed. "Leaks everywhere from the whipping," he added. "Of course."

"Of course," Daniel said. He closed his eyes, but that didn't help so he reopened them.

"Even so the *Millie*'s tighter than a lot of ships that never saw action, sir!" Cory said earnestly. "Ah, there's thirty-three casualties beyond bruises and such. Mostly they were in the aft section—"

And therefore vaporized.

"—but there were half a dozen broken bones and—"

He actually smiled as he nodded.

"—head injuries. Woetjans says she'll have the out-riggers watertight in six hours so we can land. We'll ride low, but there's enough buoyancy. I estimate seventy percent of the rig is serviceable. We've got over half our High Drive motors now, and Pasternak figures he can raise that to eighty percent in a day or two when he's replaced feed lines. And the plasma thrusters, all but the aft eight, they're fine."

"You haven't asked about the battle, Leary," said Senator Forbes in a rusty voice. "Don't you care?"

Daniel looked up at her. It wasn't a silly question to a civilian, he supposed.

"Your Excellency," he said aloud. "At the point I left duty—"

Hogg guffawed. Adele and Cory smiled; hers cold, his startled. The senator didn't react.

"—I already knew that we'd won. The fact that I'm alive and the *Milton* is functional if not healthy means that we've won at lower cost than I'd feared. I'll get to other matters in good time, but first I had to learn *our* status."

He tensed to rise. That went well enough, so he began to lever himself up. Hogg put his broad hand beneath Daniel's shoulders to steady and carefully assist, though his frown showed that he didn't approve of the young master's decision.

"We're still above Cacique," Adele said. "You've only been unconscious for three hours. Captain Battenberg of the *Jervis* is in operational command. She, ah, was commodore of the ships that escaped from New Harmony, and she appeared to be fully competent."

"She is indeed," Daniel said. "She commanded

one of the destroyer flotillas under Admiral Ozawa, I believe."

He was puzzled to detect—he thought—a defensive note in Adele's voice, as though the command was something to do with her. Since Battenberg was the senior captain, she naturally took command after the—he grinned—admiral had been incapacitated.

"Can this ship get to Cinnabar, Leary?" Forbes said. "Or do we have to transfer to another one? I want to get back with this news immediately."

"Ah, Your Excellency...," Daniel said. He wondered if he were hallucinating. "We've effectively captured the Montserrat Stars. Organizing the cluster will be an enormous job."

"Yes, it bloody well will," snapped Forbes. "A job for a Senatorial Commission, whole shiploads of bureaucrats, and I shouldn't wonder if it required any number of people from Navy House and the Xenos Barracks as well. For now there's nothing here that Governor Flanagan on Cacique and Captain Battenberg can't handle as well as we could."

"As you say, Your Excellency," Daniel said. "But I would have expected that you'd want to take charge of the reorganization yourself?"

"What?" said the senator. "Bury myself here in the boondocks? I don't think so, Leary!"

She tented her hands and grinned over them. "No, no," she said. "We'll go back to Xenos, where you will make a personal report to the Senate in open session."

Forbes chuckled. Her expression was almost a parody of delight. "Let's see them keep me out of the cabinet now, when I've recovered the Montserrat Stars," she said. "At the side of the Navy's greatest hero!"

I will *be buggered*, Daniel thought. He didn't speak.

Adele turned to Forbes. There actually was humor in her smile, which made it all the more horrifying.

"If we're to be the supporting players in your little drama, Senator," she said, "you should learn that the correct terminology is 'the RCN,' not 'the Navy.' But regardless, you can expect us to honorably accomplish the tasks assigned by our political masters."

EPILOGUE

Xenos on Cinnabar

"The Senate has met here occasionally, you know," said Deirdre Leary, looking around the Main Lecture Hall of the Library of Celsus. "I've never been inside myself, though."

Daniel shrugged and smiled. "History wasn't one of my strong suits, Deirdre," he said. "It's a suitable room for this affair; that's all that matters."

Though thinking about it, he wasn't sure that Adele would have been in this hall before. She said she'd spent her youth largely in the Library, but to her that meant carrels in the stacks and the offices of individual librarians whom she respected.

The dais was three steps up from the mosaic floor and behind a knee-high screen of carven stone. Adele stood in the center, wearing Dress Whites with a non-regulation thigh pocket. Today that did not—somewhat to Daniel's surprise—hold her personal data unit.

Adele looked not so much uncomfortable as absent. She seemed to have shut down emotionally.

Behind her were the chief dignitaries. On the left end of the line was Admiral Anston; as a concession to his health, he sat on the only chair in the hall. The remaining officials were members of the Senate in full regalia, with Speaker Bailey opposite Anston and Senator Forbes immediately to his right. Her robes had the dark blue stripe of the Defense Ministry.

Daniel frowned in puzzlement. Unless he was badly mistaken, the remaining senators were leading members of four different—and mutually antagonistic—factions.

"I, ah, appreciate the way you've handled this for me, Deirdre," he said in his sister's ear. Onlookers who shuffled and chatted before the start of the proceedings raised a curtain of white noise, but he didn't want to be overheard in a chance silence. "When I'd put the request through RCN channels on our return from Diamondia, I didn't expect a problem."

He looked away, then back to Deirdre. "I wasn't willing to let it pass. Not . . . this."

"No," said Deirdre. "A Leary can't ignore an obligation to a retainer."

"I'm not sure," Daniel said, "that Adele would approve of being considered a member of the Leary household."

The smile remained on his lips, but his mind was on the night when he, Hogg, and the Bantry retainers waited around the manor, armed with anything from hay forks to stocked impellers. His mother and her maids were inside. She'd thought that Daniel should be with her, but Hogg had been firm: "The young master's a good shot. We might need him."

Daniel Leary had indeed been a good shot, for a seven-year-old. That was the night the Corder Leary crushed the Three Circles Conspiracy. Adele's parents had died then, and during the next few weeks hundreds of their friends and associates had died also during the Proscriptions.

Adele was on Blythe at the time, so she wouldn't have personal memories of that night. She preferred to get information at second hand, however, from books and records. The Proscriptions were well documented in all their bloody horror.

Deirdre sniffed. "When has a Leary ever cared about what somebody else thought was right?" she said.

Daniel chuckled, but that was the truth. He was a Leary and he would do what was right, regardless of what others thought about it.

The body of the lecture hall was almost entirely filled with RCN uniforms, though they alternated between officers in Whites and common spacers in liberty suits. Daniel and his sister were in front, and Woetjans was a little farther down the row.

Deirdre was the only person near the dais who wasn't one of the original Sissies...though that was stretching the point slightly for Tovera, standing primly at Deirdre's left with her hands folded on the handle of her attaché case. Rank today was determined by how close a person was to Adele Mundy, and no one was closer than the shipmates from Kostroma whose lives she'd saved and who had in turn saved hers.

"Father says it was a useful exercise," Deirdre said. "A show of unity now will help the conduct of the war, and this was a cause all factions could support without losing face. He described it to his colleagues as a necessary assertion of Senatorial authority over bureaucrats who were getting above themselves."

She gave the senatorial finery on the dais a professional appraisal. She wasn't a member of the Senate yet, but that would change whenever she and Corder Leary decided that it should. Daniel's elder sister was in all ways their father's proper heir.

The only important senator who didn't stand on the dais was Corder Leary: still Speaker Leary to his colleagues. His absence was more than mere courtesy. If Adele didn't have her data unit, then she probably hadn't brought her pistol either. She could have borrowed something from Tovera, though, and she would have.

The Mundys were just as careful of their honor as the Learys were. If Adele were forced to meet the man who had ordered the massacre of her family, she would act.

"This was worth doing for itself," Daniel said, his mind still back on that former time. "I'm glad it benefits the Republic, but that had no bearing on why I'm doing it."

He cleared his throat. "I, ah, wasn't sure how much difficulty I'd put you to, Deirdre," he said. "The lady in question is formidable, I believe?"

"She wouldn't be of much use to the Republic were she *not* formidable," Deirdre said with another sniff. "I talked with her myself, though, and found her quite willing to accept the judgment of a united Senate. To tell the truth—"

She looked around, though her modest height—neither child had gotten Corder Leary's craggy stature—prevented her from seeing beyond the second row. Mistress Sand wouldn't have been present anyway.

"—I don't believe she was too deeply disturbed. It seems that the problem you asked me to look into was caused by someone in her organization exceeding his authority and not reporting his action. I know how I react when something like that happens at the bank."

"Ah," said Daniel, for he *did* understand. He thought for a moment, then said, "I haven't been a notably obedient subordinate myself, but if I'd acted to embarrass my superiors, my career would have been shorter."

"Yes," said Deirdre. "I don't think the fellow will repeat his mistake. So that was no problem, but oddly enough Navy House made some difficulty."

"Ah, Vocaine," Daniel said. It wasn't a surprise that the Chief of the Navy Board disliked Daniel Leary enough to carry the enmity to Leary's friends, but it was a disappointment nonetheless.

"Not really," said Deirdre. "According to Senator Forbes, who handled the negotiations—"

Daniel raised an eyebrow.

Deirdre nodded. "Father thought she provided a suitable mixture of goodwill toward the RCN and a disinclination to be bullied by bureaucrats. And it was the bureaucracy generally which objected, on principle—a concept which Navy House seems to take more seriously than the Senate does."

She shrugged and smiled. "In the end, they decided that because Lady Mundy had been an acting admiral—"

"*What?*"

"Yes, that's right," Deirdre said in a tone of amused superiority. "I gather it happened during your absence."

Her expression changed. "You have a hard head, brother," she said. "I've never before been so pleased at the fact."

He looked away and nodded. "Yes, well," he muttered.

"In any case," said Deirdre, "the fact that Mundy had acted as a commissioned officer was significant. Mistress Forbes told them that she didn't care what excuse they found, but that she was glad they *had* found one or there would shortly be empty offices in Navy House."

"I'm glad it didn't come to that," said Daniel quietly.

A slim man in Dress Whites came from a side aisle and took the steps up to the dais. His face was set, and he held a small casket covered in red leather.

Daniel straightened to attention. He was smiling broadly.

The hall grew silent. Adele looked at the pale misery on Lieutenant Commander Huxford's face as he approached. *I wonder if he thinks I did this to him?*

She smiled at the thought. Her record should have told Huxford that she would either have ignored the matter as she ignored most such matters, or she would have dealt with it in a more direct fashion. But then, if Huxford had bothered to study her record to begin with, he wouldn't have chosen to be so superciliously insulting.

Adele's smile appeared to make the smooth young man even more wretched. Direct action—shooting him—might have been kinder at that.

Huxford transferred the casket to his left hand and saluted Admiral Anston. The admiral returned it, smartly but with a smile that Adele read as one of mocking triumph. Chiefs of the Navy Board had to accept the fact that sometimes intelligence personnel would wear RCN uniforms, but Adele couldn't imagine that they liked the fact.

She was, she hoped, a different animal: an RCN officer involved with intelligence. Not that she cared what Navy House thought, so long as her family accepted her.

She had first seen Anston in person at the funeral of Daniel's uncle, three years before. Then he'd been ruddy, plump, and vibrant; a lively man though one who gave little outward evidence that he was capable of managing the RCN with genius.

Anston was white, now, and the skin sagged from his cheekbones. There was still a spark, but its casing of flesh was tottering toward dissolution.

"Admiral Anston," said Huxford, his voice clear. Though unamplified, it easily filled the hall. The architects of the Celsus had created a temple to human knowledge. To them, knowledge was the greatest of Gods, and to Adele also. You don't skimp your duties to God.

"Senators and fellow citizens of the Republic," Huxford said.

Daniel, resplendent in his medals, flashed Adele a broad grin. She found herself grinning back, because it *was* funny.

At least Huxford has the decency not to address his audience as "fellow spacers." There were some present who might have tossed him out into the street without his trousers if he'd tried that. And Anston might have been leading them if he managed to get out of his chair. . . .

"I have been chosen to grant the Republic's highest award for bravery to Signals Officer Adele Mundy," Huxford said. "The commendation refers to her activities in bringing Dunbar's World into the Friendship of the Republic. Those of you who are familiar with Lady Mundy's career know that there have been many other exploits, any of which would have amply justified the award."

"Bloody well told!" muttered Hogg in the brief pause. He looked startled, obviously surprised at *how* good the acoustics were.

Huxford opened the casket and took from it the small red-enameled star on a gold ground. The ribbon's vertical red stripes framed the blue stripe in the center. An RCN Star would reverse the colors....

Adele's eyes blurred. She hoped she wasn't going to cry.

"Signals Officer Mundy...," said Huxford. "As agent for the Republic, I hereby award you the Cinnabar Star."

She felt the pressure of his fingers above her left breast. His face was out of focus, a blob of white.

Huxford stepped back. The cheers were immediate and stunning. The hall couldn't hold more than two hundred people, but they sounded as if there were thousands. And it went on....

Adele made a decision. She raised both hands, a gesture she didn't recall having made in the past. The noise didn't stop but its level reduced, and finally it stopped.

Adele swallowed. "Fellow spacers," she said. She'd been afraid that the words would choke her, but she got them out.

Turning enough to look back at the robes figures behind her, she said, "Senators of the Republic of Cinnabar."

If anybody had a problem with her priorities, that

was regrettable. She felt a smile of sorts lift the corners of her lips. *But not very regrettable.*

"I cannot accept this honor for Signals Officer Mundy," she said. "And certainly not as Mundy of Chatsworth."

There were puzzled expressions in the audience. Good.

"I *will* accept it, however," Adele said, feeling her voice grow firmer with each word, "as the representative of the many thousands of common spacers, and of—"

Huxford had stepped to the side. She turned to him, nodded, and faced the audience again.

"—of all the other unseen personnel who sacrifice and often die to maintain the Republic's freedom."

And me among them. Not me alone, but me also.

Adele couldn't see anything for the tears filling her eyes. "RCN forever!" she shouted.

The hall echoed her a thousandfold.

The following is an excerpt from:

WHAT DISTANT DEEPS

DAVID DRAKE

Available from Baen Books
September 2010
hardcover

CHAPTER 1

The Bantry Estate, Cinnabar

"Come and join, Squire Daniel!" called a dancer as she whirled past. "I'm not partnered!"

Daniel vaguely recalled the face, but he knew he must be thinking about an older sister. Ten years ago, he'd left Bantry to enter the Republic of Cinnabar Naval Academy. This girl was no more than sixteen, though she was undoubtedly well developed.

Mind, he didn't recall the sister's name either.

Steen—Old Steen since the death of his father, who'd been tenant-in-chief before him—elbowed Daniel in the ribs and said, "Haw! Not just a dance she's offering you, Squire! Going to take her up on it? You always did in the old days!"

Steen's wife was hovering nearby, though she hadn't presumed to enter the group of men centered on Daniel and the cask of beer on the seawall. Foiles, the commodore of the fishing fleet, and Higgenson, the manager of the estate's processing plant, were from Bantry, like Steen, but also present were the owners of three nearby estates who had come to the festivities. Waldmiller of Ponds was over seventy and Broma of Flattler's Creek wasn't much younger; but at twenty-five, Peterleigh of Boltway Manor was a year Daniel's junior.

Before Daniel could pass off the comment with a grin and a shake of his head, Mistress Steen clipped her husband over the ear with a hand well used to hoeing. Fortunately Steen hadn't gotten his earthenware mug to his lips, so he merely jerked the last of his ale over his bright purple shirt instead of losing his front teeth.

"Where's your manners, you drunken old fool?" Mistress Steen demanded in a voice that started loud and gained volume. "Can't you see Lady Miranda close enough to spit on? You embarrass yourself and you embarrass the Squire!"

Daniel caught Mistress Steen's hands in his own, partly to forestall the full-armed follow-up stroke she was on the verge of delivering. "Now, Roby!" he said. "My Miranda's a sensible woman who wouldn't take note of a joke at a celebration, or even—"

He bussed Mistress Steen on the cheek. It was like kissing a boot.

"—this!" he concluded, stepping away.

"Oh, Squire!" Mistress Steen gasped in a mixture of delight and embarrassment. She put her hand to her cheek as though to caress the memory.

"Oh, you do go on!" she said as she stumped off, seemingly half-dazed. Daniel thought he heard her titter when the piping paused.

The original piper, gay in a green vest with blue and gold tassels, was snoring in a drunken stupor behind the bench. His son—who couldn't have been more than twelve—was making a manful effort to replace him. All the will in the world couldn't increase the boy's lung capacity.

Daniel's eyes touched Miranda, who was with her mother Madeline a good twenty yards away—Roby Steen had been exaggerating. She waved with a merry smile, then went back to describing the stitching of her bodice to more women than Daniel could easily count.

The wives of the neighboring landowners were there, but Bantry tenants made up most of the not-quite-crush. The tenants observed protocol in who got to drink with Daniel, but their wives and daughters weren't going to give way to outsiders from other estates at their first chance to meet the Squire's lady.

"A pretty one, Leary," Peterleigh said. "Your fiancée, is she?"

Daniel cleared his throat. "Ah, Miranda and I have an understanding," he said, hoping that his embarrassment didn't show. "There's nothing formal at this moment, you'll understand, until, ah, some matters have been worked out."

Miranda herself never raised the question. She was an extremely smart woman, smart enough to know that others would prod Daniel regularly.

"For the gods' sakes, boy," Waldmiller said with a scowl at Peterleigh. "If you weren't raised to have manners, then at least you could show enough sense to avoid poking your nose in Speaker Leary's affairs, couldn't you?"

Peterleigh could probably buy and sell Waldmiller several times over, but seniority and the words themselves jerked the younger man into a brace. "Sorry, Leary, sorry!" he said. "Don't know what I was thinking, asking about a fellow's private affairs. Must've drunk too much! My apologies!"

Bringing up Daniel's strained relationship with his father was calling in heavier artillery than Peterleigh deserved, but the young man could have avoided the rebuke by being more polite. Corder Leary was one of the most powerful members of the Senate—and certainly the most feared member. He hadn't visited Bantry since Daniel's mother died, and Peterleigh—who was both young and parochial—had obviously forgotten who the estate's real owner was.

"Not at all, Peterleigh," Daniel said, smiling mildly. "But as for drinking, I think it's time for me to have another mug of our good Bantry ale. It's what I miss most about Cinnabar when the RCN sends me off to heaven knows where."

So speaking, he stepped to the stand beside them where a ceramic cask of ale and a double rank of earthenware mugs waited. He knew his neighbors—Bantry's neighbors—would be surprised at having to pump their own beer, but Daniel was providing a holiday for *all* the Leary retainers.

He'd thought of bringing in outside servants, but city folk would mean trouble. One of them would sneer at a barefoot tenant—and be thrown off the sea wall, into the Western Ocean thirty feet below.

Daniel was dressed more like a countryman than a country gentleman, but he *was* wearing shoes today. He generally wouldn't have been at this time of the year when he was a boy on Bantry.

A pair of aircars landed in quick succession, drawing the men's attention. "That's Hofmann in the blue one," Broma said. "I don't recognize the gray car though."

"I think that's...," Daniel said. "Yes, that's Tom Sand, the contractor who built the hall. I, ah, invited him to the dedication."

Broma squinted at the limousine which was landing a hundred yards away, on the field of rammed gravel laid for the purpose beside the Jerred Hogg Community Hall. "That's quite a nice car for...," he began.

He stopped and turned to Daniel in obvious surmise.

"You don't mean the Honorable Thomas Sand of Arch-stone Construction?" he said. "By the gods, Leary, you do! Why, they're one of the biggest contracting firms in the whole Capital Region!"

"They did a fine job on the Hall," Daniel said with a faint smile, turning to look at the new building itself. All four sides had been swung onto the roof as they were designed to be, turning the building into a marquee. The drinks—no wines or liquor, but ale without limit—and the food were inside, where Hogg was holding court.

Hogg had been the young master's minder when Daniel was a child and his servant in later years. He'd taught Daniel everything there was to know about the wildlife of Bantry which he and his ancestors back to the settlement had poached. He'd taught Daniel many other things as well, much of it information which would have horrified Daniel's mother, who was delicate and a perfect lady.

Hogg had a tankard of ale and a girl half his age ready with a pitcher to refill it. His arm was around a similar girl, and as many tenants as could squeeze close were listening to his stories of the wonders he and the young master had seen among the stars. Daniel was probably the only man present who knew that the wildest stories were absolutely true.

Hogg was royalty in Bantry today. Daniel smiled faintly. That was a small enough payment for the man who'd taught the young master how to be a man.

Tom Sand walked toward Daniel in the company of half a dozen children including at least one girl. They could claim to be guiding Sand, but they were more concerned with getting a good look at a stranger who was an obvious gentleman. Sand had weather-beaten fea-tures and more chest than paunch, but his suit—though gray—shimmered in a way that neither wool nor silk could match. Daniel suspected it had been woven from the tail plumes of Maurician ground doves.

"You'll be spending more time in Bantry now that we're at peace again, Leary?" Waldmiller asked, letting his eyes glance across their surroundings. His tone was neutral and his face impassive, signs that he was controlling an urge to sneer. This was a working estate, not a showplace.

They stood in the middle of the Bantry Commons, a broad semi-circle with the sea front forming the west side. The shops bounded its south end and the sprawling manor was to the north; tenant housing closed the arc. The dwellings facing directly on the common were older, smaller, and much more desirable than the relatively modern units in the second and third rows. Younger sons and their sons were relegated to the newer housing.

Instead of turning the manor into a modern palace to reflect the family's increased wealth and power, Daniel's grandfather had put his efforts into a luxurious townhouse in Xenos. Corder Leary had visited Bantry only as a duty—and not even that after the death of his children's mother. The house looked much as it had three centuries ago.

Birds screamed overhead. The fish processing plant was shut down for the celebration, and they were upset at missing their usual banquet of offal.

Daniel grinned. At that, the flock wasn't much less musical than the piper...and there'd been enough ale drunk already that the dancers could probably manage to continue even if the boy on the bagpipe gave up the struggle he was clearly unequal to.

"It's true that many ships have been laid up since the Truce of Rheims," Daniel said, "and that means a number of officers have gone on half pay."

In fact almost two-thirds of the Navy List had put on Reserve status. That meant real hardship for junior officers who had been living on hopes already. Those hopes had been dashed, but they were still expected to have a presentable dress uniform to attend the daily levees in Navy House which were their only chance of getting a ship.

"But I've been lucky so far," Daniel continued. "I'm still on the Active list, though I don't have an assignment as yet. And anyway, I wasn't really cut out to be a—"

He'd started to say "farmer," but caught himself. Thank the gods he'd drunk a great deal less today than he would have even a few years earlier. Daniel hadn't become an abstainer, but he'd always known when he shouldn't be drinking; and the higher he rose—in the RCN and in society generally—the more frequent those occasions were.

"—a country squire."

Sand joined them; the entourage of children dropped behind the way the first touch of an atmosphere strips loose articles from the hull of a descending starship. Miranda was leading Mistress Sand to the house, having shooed away a similar bevy of children.

Waldmiller opened his mouth to greet Sand. Peterleigh, his face toward the sea, hadn't noticed the newcomer's approach. He said, "Well, I think the truce is a bloody shame, Leary. You fellows in the navy had the Alliance on the ropes. Why the Senate should want to let Guarantor Porra off the hook is beyond me!"

"Well, Peterleigh . . . ," said Daniel. "You know what they say: never a good war or a bad peace."

"And maybe it was a good war for folks who live out here in the Western Region and don't leave their estates," boomed Thomas Sand, "but it bloody well wasn't for anybody trying to make a living in Xenos. Off-planet trade is down by nine parts in ten, so half the factories in the Capital Region have shut and the rest are on short hours."

Peterleigh jumped and would have spilled ale if he hadn't emptied his mug. Waldmiller and Broma masked their amusement—Broma more effectively than his colleague. The tenants, Foiles and Higgenson, maintained their frozen silence. They'd been quiet even before Maud Steen had torn a strip off her husband, and that had chilled them further.

"Didn't mean to break in unannounced," Sand said. "I'm Tom Sand and I built the hall there."

He nodded in the direction of it.

"And not a half-bad job, if I do say so myself."

"These are my neighbors," said Daniel. "Waldmiller, Broma, and you've already met Peterleigh, so to speak. Have some ale, Sand. We're setting a good example for the tenants so that none of them bring out the kelp liquor they brew in their sheds."

Sand laughed, drawing a mug of ale. "I understand, Leary," he said. "I have a capping party for the crew on each job, but it's beer there too. It doesn't hurt a man to get drunk every once in a while, but I'd as lief give them guns as hard liquor for the chances that they'd all survive the night."

He shook his head, then added, "No offense meant about trade being strangled. The RCN did a fine job. But any shipowner who lifted at all got a letter of marque and converted his hull into a privateer. In the neutral worlds, chances are he's got warrants from *both* us and the Alliance. That was better business than hauling a load of wheat from Ewer to Cinnabar—and likely being captured by some privateer besides."

"No offense taken, Sand," Daniel said. "Every word you say is true."

He swept his neighbors with his eyes. "You see, Peterleigh," he said, "our tenants work hard and they live bloody hard by city standards. But they never doubt there'll be food on the table in the evening, even if it's dried fish and potatoes. The folk in the housing blocks around Xenos don't know that, and I'm told there were riots already last year."

He flashed a broad grin and added, "I wasn't around to see them, of course."

"Right!" said Sand, turning from the keg with a full mug of ale. To the others in the circle he said, "Captain Leary was chasing the Alliance out of the Montserrat Stars with their tails between their legs. Splendid work, Leary! Makes me proud to be a citizen of Cinnabar."

"That's the Squire for you!" blurted Higgenson, pride freeing his tongue. "Burned them wogs a new one, *he* did!"

There was commotion and a loud rattle from the Hall. Hogg and a tenant of roughly his age were dancing with rams' horns strapped to their feet. The curved horns made an almighty clatter on the concrete floor, but the men with their arms akimbo were impressive as they banged through a measure to the sound of the bagpipe.

"That's Hogg himself, isn't it, Leary?" asked Broma. The hammering dance had drawn all eyes, though the tenants around the Hall limited what Daniel and his fellows could see from the seafront.

"Aye, and that's Des Cranbrook who's got a grain allotment in the northeast district and a prime orchard tract," said Foiles. Since Higgenson had spoken without being struck by lightning, the fisherman had decided it was safe for him to say something also.

"Plus the common pasturage, of course," Daniel said, speaking to Sand; his fellow landowners took that for granted. The dancers—both stout; neither of them young nor likely to have been handsome even in youth—hopped with the majesty of clock movements, slowly pirouetting as they circled one another.

"Haven't seen a real horn dance in law! twenty years if it's been one," said Higgenson. His social betters were intent on the dancing, which gave him a chance to speak from personal knowledge. "The young folk don't pick it up, seems like."

"That'll change now," said Foiles. "The young ones, the ones that didn't know Hogg before he went away with you, Squire—"

He dipped his head toward Daniel.

"—they all think the sun shines out of his asshole. And some of the women as did know him and so ought to know better, they're near as bad."

The dancers collapsed into one another's arms, then wobbled laughing back to their seats. Girls pushed each other to be the ones unstrapping the rams' horns. Cranbrook was getting his share of the attention. The lass hugging him and offering a mug of ale might have been his granddaughter, but Daniel was pretty sure that she wasn't. He grinned.

"Ah . . . ?" said Higgenson in sudden concern—though he hadn't been the one who'd actually commented on Hogg's former reputation. "Not that we meant anything, Squire. You know how folks used to say things, and no truth in them, like as not."

"I suspect there was a lot of truth in what was said about Hogg," Daniel said, thinking back on the past and feeling his smile slip. "And about me, I shouldn't wonder. It's probably to Bantry's benefit as well as the Republic's that the RCN has found the two of us occupation at a distance from the estate."

Georg Hofmann approached the group. He looked older and more stooped than Daniel had remembered him, but that was years since, of course. His estate, Brightness Landing, was well up the coast.

"I didn't recognize the woman who got out of the car with Hofmann," Daniel said in a low voice. She was in her early forties and had been poured into a dress considerably too small and too youthful for her.

"He remarried, a widow from Xenos," said Waldmiller with a snort. "Damned if I can see the attraction."

"And she brought a son besides," said Peterleigh. "Chuckie, I believe his name is; Platt, from the first husband. That one might better stay in Xenos, *I* think."

The youth was tall and well set up. He looked twenty from Daniel's distance, but his size may have given him a year or two more than time had. Accompanied by two servants in pink-and-buff livery—those weren't Hofmann's colors, so they may have been Platt's—he was sauntering toward a group of the younger tenants on the seawall not far from the manor house.

Daniel's eyes narrowed. Platt took a pull from a gallon jug as he walked, then handed it to a servant. His other servant held what looked very much like a case of dueling pistols.

Hofmann joined the group around Daniel. Up close, he looked even more tired than he had at a distance. He exchanged nods with his neighbors, then said, "It's been years, Leary. Good years for you, from what I hear."

"It's good to see the old place, Hofmann," Daniel said, "though I don't really fit here any more, I'm afraid. Hofmann, this is Tom Sand, who built the new hall."

"I heard you were doing that work, Sand," said Hofmann, extending his hand to shake. Hofmann was the other member of the local gentry who'd been active in national affairs; though not to the extent of Corder Leary, of course. "How did that come to happen, if I may ask. It's not—"

He gestured toward the new building.

"—on your usual scale, I should have said."

Daniel heard the low-frequency thrum of the big surface effect transport he'd been expecting and gave a sigh of relief. He'd set the arrival for mid-afternoon. He hadn't wanted his Sissies to party for the full day and night with the Bantry tenants, but he'd been so long in the company of spacers that the rural society in which he'd been raised had become strange to him.

"I asked for the job," said Sand, squaring his broad shoulders. "I wanted a chance to do something for a real hero of the Republic."

He gave Daniel a challenging grin and a nod that was almost a bow. "Hear hear!" said Peterleigh, and the others in the group echoed him.

"Much obliged," said Daniel in embarrassment. He drew a mug of ale for an excuse to turn away.

The bid for the Community Hall had seemed fair. Deirdre, Daniel's older sister, had handled the matter for him; she'd been handling all his business since prize money had made that more complex than finding a few florins to pay a bar tab. Deirdre had followed their father into finance with a ruthless intelligence that would doubtless serve her well in politics also when she chose to enter the Senate.

The building that appeared wasn't the simple barn that Daniel had envisaged, though. The wall mechanisms were extremely sophisticated—and solid: Daniel had gone over them with the attention he'd have given the lock mechanisms of a ship he commanded. Only then had he realized that this was more than a commercial proposition for the builder; as, of course, it was for Daniel Leary himself.

The transport rumbled in from the sea, a great aerofoil with a catamaran hull. It slid up the processing plant's ramp—which had been extended north to support the starboard outrigger—and settled to a halt.

The reel dance had broken up for the time being. All eyes were on the big vehicle.

"This something you were expecting, Leary?" said Waldmiller, frowning. To him such craft were strictly for trade, hauling his estate's produce to market in the cities of the east.

The hatches opened. Even before the ramps had fully deployed, spacers were hopping to the ground wearing their liberty suits. Their embroidered patches were bright, and ribbons fluttered from all the seams.

"Up the *Sissie*!" someone shouted. The group headed for the Hall and the promised ale with the same quick enthusiasm that they'd have shown in storming Hell if Captain Leary had ordered it.

"It is indeed, Waldmiller," Daniel said. "These are the spacers who've served with me since before I took command of the *Princess Cecile*. I invited them and some of my other shipmates to share the fun today."

Officers waited for the ramp, not that they couldn't have jumped if they'd thought the situation required speed rather than decorum. For the most part they wore their 2nd Class uniforms, their Grays, but Mon—a reserve lieutenant, though he'd for several years managed Bergen and Associates Shipyard in Daniel's name—had made a point of wearing his full-dress Whites.

The shipyard had been doing very well under Mon's leadership. That had allowed him to have the uniform let out professionally, since his girth had also expanded notably.

Two slightly built women were the last people out of the transport. Adele wore an unobtrusively good suit, since she was appearing as Lady Adele Mundy rather than as Signals Officer Mundy of the *Princess Cecile*. Tovera, her servant, was neat and nondescript, as easy to overlook as a viper in dried leaves.

"I say, Leary?" said Broma. "Who's the civilian women there? Your Miranda's meeting them, I see."

Miranda, accompanied by another flock of children—generally girls this time—waited at the bottom of the ramp. Mothers and older sisters were running to grab them when they noticed what was happening.

"That's my friend Adele and her aide," Daniel said with satisfaction. "And I'm *very* glad to see them again!"

—end excerpt—

from *What Distant Deeps*
available in hardcover,
September 2010, from Baen Books

DID YOU KNOW YOU CAN DO ALL THESE THINGS AT THE
BAEN BOOKS WEBSITE ?

✦ Read free sample chapters of books `SCHEDULE`

✦ See what new books are upcoming `SCHEDULE`

✦ Read entire Baen Books for free `FREE LIBRARY`

✦ Check out your favorite author's titles `CATALOG`

✦ Catch up on the latest Baen news & author events
`NEWS` or `EVENTS`

✦ Buy any Baen book `SCHEDULE` or `CATALOG`

✦ Read interviews with authors and artists `INTERVIEWS`

✦ Buy almost any Baen book as an e-book individually or an entire month at a time `WEBSCRIPTIONS`

✦ Find a list of titles suitable for young adults
`YOUNG ADULT LISTS`

✦ Communicate with some of the coolest fans in science fiction & some of the best minds on the planet
`BAEN'S BAR`

GO TO
WWW.BAEN.COM